THEY HANGED
MY SAINTLY BILLY

THEY HANGED MY SAINTLY BILLY

ROBERT GRAVES

INTRODUCTION BY
CATHERINE PELONERO

SEVEN STORIES PRESS
NEW YORK · OAKLAND · LONDON

Seven Stories Press
140 Watts Street
New York, NY 10013
www.sevenstories.com

Library of Congress Cataloging-in-Publication Data

Names: Graves, Robert, 1895-1985, author.
Title: They hanged my saintly Billy / Robert Graves.
Description: New York : Seven Stories Press, 2017.
Identifiers: LCCN 2017005687 | ISBN 9781609807641 (paperback)
Subjects: LCSH: Palmer, William, 1824-1856--Fiction. | Outlaws--Fiction. |
   BISAC: FICTION / Historical. | FICTION / Crime. | FICTION / Legal. |
   GSAFD: Biographical fiction. | Western stories.
Classification: LCC PR6013.R35 T5 2017 | DDC 823/.912--dc23
LC record available at https://lccn.loc.gov/2017005687

College professors and high school and middle school teachers may order free exam-ination copies of Seven Stories Press titles. To order, visit www.sevenstories.com, or fax on school letterhead to 212-226-1411.

Printed in the USA.

9 8 7 6 5 4 3 2 1

CONTENTS

Introduction by Catherine Pelonero   vii

Foreword   xi

I.   The Old Bailey: May 14th, 1856   3

II.   The Wiles of Jane Widnall   11

III.   Mr Duffy's Sample Box   25

IV.   Colonel Brookes's Resolution   39

V.   Stafford Infirmary   55

VI.   At Bart's   65

VII.   The Courtship of Annie Brookes   83

VIII.   The Nursery   99

IX.   An Unfortunate Series of Deaths   115

X.   English Cholera   129

XI.   'A Good Life'   141

XII.   A Gentleman of Property   155

XIII.   'Two Narrow Shaves'   173

XIV.   Financial Straits   185

XV.   Death at The Talbot Arms   197

XVI.   Step-father to the Deceased   213

XVII.   The Inquest on John Parsons Cook   227

XVIII.   Stafford Gaol   241

XIX.   Unreliable Witnesses   257

XX.   Absent Witnesses   279

XXI.   If Doctors Disagree   293

XXII.   The Verdict   303

XXIII.   A Change in Public Opinion   327

XXIV.   The Execution   343

INTRODUCTION TO THE 2019 EDITION

If William Palmer had committed his crimes in the twenty-first century instead of the nineteenth, odds are that a cable network mini-series would've been in production before his trial even got underway. Palmer's salacious life, deceptive veneer of upper-class respectability, and Machiavellian misdeeds provide all the kindling to ignite the sparks of a media firestorm—which his case did, Victorian-style.

The 1856 murder trial of Dr. William Palmer provided daily fodder for tabloids and respectable publications alike. The case was written about, discussed, and debated throughout England and beyond, with onlookers holding strong opinions one way or the other on Palmer's guilt or innocence. Charles Dickens even weighed in, publishing a lengthy front-page piece titled "The Demeanour of Murderers" in which, in addition to referring to William Palmer as "the greatest villain that ever stood in the Old Bailey dock," he vehemently argued that the seeming incongruity of Palmer's manner in court, namely the defendant's "complete self-possession," "profound composure," and "perfect equanimity," were strong indicators of his guilt and lack of conscience rather than an inner knowledge of innocence and misplaced hope of acquittal.

Coverage of Palmer's arrest and investigation by police had been so relentless that the trial was moved from Staffordshire to London in an effort to assure an impartial jury. Not that the change of venue actually made a whit of difference, since by that time the buzz had spread across Europe and other continents, basically to any place equipped with printing presses and a populace with the time and inclination to read about other people's problems. In a move that feels downright postmodern, the media even gave him nicknames: Palmer the Poisoner; the Rugeley Poisoner; or sometimes just the Poisoner. Nothing says criminal celebrity status quite like multiple monikers.

The method of murder was not the big draw here. Poisoning as a means to a homicidal end was as relatively common in Victorian England as horse dung and usually went just as unnoticed, except by locals who found themselves in the middle of the mess. Dr. Palmer's case had that extra something, or somethings, that raised it from the routine depths of provincial incident to the ignominious heights of international spectacle. From illicit love affairs to treacherous greed to the string of unfortunate family members, friends, and foes who seemed to conveniently die and, in so doing, enrich William Palmer's bank account, the case had all the key elements to make it a sensation. Palmer was tried for the murder of his well-to-do friend John Parsons Cook, but those who believed in Dr. Palmer's guilt pointed to all the other gruesome deaths (and near-deaths) in his orbit along with his pattern of underhanded thieving from his rich mother, who nevertheless came to his defense but whose own sexual escapades nixed her as a potential character witness for her son.

Sex, wealth, betrayal, and murder. Dominick Dunne would've been all over this one.

The icing on this irresistible criminal cake was the controversy. Complaints of judicial misconduct and clashing opinions of expert medical witnesses were thrown into a mix already thick with tantalizing bits. After all the sordid details of Palmer's life had been exposed and discussed ad nauseam, the mystery and debate remained, culminating in the million-dollar question: Did he or didn't he?

Robert Graves wrote *They Hanged My Saintly Billy* on the centenary of William Palmer's conviction and execution. (Capital murder cases wrapped up much faster then, "death row" typically being a residence of very short duration for the condemned.) Published in 1957, it was his last historical novel. Calling this book a novel doesn't seem to do it justice, however, considering the remarkable amount of research and adherence to fact. Graves tells us where he stands in the first paragraph of the foreword. He doesn't believe William Palmer was a murderer. This is by no means a spoiler, nor even an indication of bias in the telling of the tale, as one might suspect. To his great credit, Graves manages what only the very best writers can: he lays out the narrative with scrupulous balance and never lets his own conclusions intrude. He doesn't suppress details that are unflattering to his subject (and there's no shortage of them, Palmer being as prolific a scoundrel as Graves was a writer), nor does he paint Palmer's persecutors as dolts or incompetent fiends. It's as if Robert Graves felt a duty as a journalist to relay the events and facts in full without attempting to sway anyone to his way of seeing things. Instead he informs us, allowing readers to reach their own conclusions without the taint of agenda or spin.

What a brilliant concept!

Yet another reason why *They Hanged My Saintly Billy* is one of the best and most absorbing nonfiction accounts I've ever read.

Graves not only builds the life and circumstances of William Palmer to its dramatic end, he also chronicles the public reaction—and it's all too eerily familiar. Spectators fighting for seats at the courthouse. Reporters hunting down anyone who ever knew Palmer, hounding them for quotes that appeared on front pages within hours. Newspapers rushing to get day-to-day accounts of the trial into print ahead of their rivals, accuracy often taking a backseat to speed. The sale of "Rugeley Poisoner" souvenirs before the body was even dissolved in a convict's quicklime grave.

You can almost picture Nancy Grace alighting from a carriage to hold after-court analysis with crime fanatics at the local pub.

Robert Graves is in the minority in his belief that William Palmer was wrongfully convicted of murder. Frequently labeled as a serial killer, Dr. Palmer ranks only a couple steps below Jack the Ripper as one of the iconic figures of Victorian-era true crime. While Graves's conclusion might be surprising to some, the fact that he advances it is not. Robert Graves never shied from taking a controversial or unpopular stand on history, even when it meant laying himself open to criticism or ridicule. Graves never made things easy for his detractors, however, at least not when it came to attacking the level of thought and knowledge that pours forth from his work, nor with his absolute mastery of the written word. His independence and vision are part of what made Graves a literary powerhouse, as readable today as ever. As an author, poet, and journalist, the constants in his work were his ability to capture human authenticity and his incredible talent for engaging his audience, no matter the topic. Agree with him or not, we can't help turning the pages to see what happens next. Graves is just that extraordinary. And so is this story.

That powerful combination is what makes this book such a mesmerizing read. *They Hanged My Saintly Billy* is one of those stranger-than-fiction true stories, told by one of the greatest storytellers of all time. Knowing the grisly fate of William Palmer is no more a spoiler than knowing upfront where the author comes down on the big question. There's really no spoiling such a macabre mystery so well told, with more twists and turns and dark corners than the fog-enshrouded streets of Victorian England.

The only letdown is that Graves is not around to write more.

CATHERINE PELONERO
Los Angeles, California, June 2018

FOREWORD

Today is the centenary of Dr Wm Palmer's public execution for the alleged poisoning of his friend John Parsons Cook; and all opponents of capital punishment should be wearing black. 'I am a murdered man,' Dr Palmer told the prison Governor after his twelve-day trial, one of the best attended, and most scandalous, ever staged at the Old Bailey; which was the truth. The medical evidence against him had broken down completely and the circumstantial evidence conflicted, but the Lord Chief Justice and the Attorney-General were both out to secure a verdict of guilty from the hand-picked jury.

Dr Palmer was, I grant, a scoundrel and spendthrift—though hardly in the class of John James, Q.C., one of the Crown Counsel who helped to hang him and got disbarred five years later for frauds amounting to over sixty thousand pounds—but he was also well known for his generosity to the unfortunate and his remarkable stoicism when things went wrong. James, then a member of Parliament, got safely away to New York, owing one hundred thousand pounds and there not only resumed his legal practice but became a successful actor at the Winter Garden Theatre. Palmer had no such luck. His wax effigy appears in the Chamber of Horrors at Madame Tussaud's Exhibition, among England's most notorious poisoners: doubtless as a warning to all who dare challenge the combined might of the Police, the insurance companies and the Jockey Club.

Mr James Hodge, editor of *The Trial of Wm Palmer*, in the *Notable British Trials* series, is pleased to rank Dr Palmer among the 'mass-executioners'. To me, however, he recalls 'Hanging Johnny' in the sea-chanty:

> *They say I hanged my mother,*
> Away, boys, away!
> *They say I hanged my brother,*
> Then hang, boys, hang!
> *They say I hanged my Annie,*
> Away, boys, away!
> *I hanged her up so canny,*
> Then hang, boys, hang!
> *They say I hanged my daddy,*
> Away, boys, away!
> *But I never hanged nobody,*
> Then hang, boys, hang!

Palmer was similarly accused of murdering fourteen people: in particular his wife Annie, the last survivor of a suicidal family. That she poisoned herself to get him out of debt by her life insurance is the only theory that covers all the facts; but his deep grief has been unkindly dismissed as hypocritical. The case did not come up for trial. My conclusion is that 'he never killed nobody.'

My uncle, Dr Clifford Pritchard, M.D., to whom I dedicate this book in grateful acknowledgement of advice, and the loan of books, is my sole personal link with the Palmer case. He took over a medical practice at Highgate from his friend, the late Dr George Fletcher, J.P., Palmer's leading biographer, who as a boy met many of the characters in this story, including old Mrs Palmer, and once even carried John Parsons Cook's cricket-bag.

In reconstructing Palmer's story, I have invented little, and in no case distorted hard fact. But the case is so complex that to argue it out in historical detail would have made a very bulky and quite unreadable book. I worked from the following main sources:

THE TIMES *Report of the Trial of Wm Palmer, Illustrated,* London, Ward & Lock, 1856. *The Queen v. Palmer: Verbatim Report of the Trial, in two parts,* London, J. Allen, 1856. *The Queen v. Wm Palmer: Official Report of the Minutes of Evidence,* London, George Hebert, 1856. *Illustrated Life and Career of Wm Palmer of Rugeley* (Anon.), London, Ward & Lock, 1856. *Last Hours and Execution of William Palmer the Poisoner* (Anon.), London, Taylor & Green, 1856. *The Cries of the Condemned: Proofs of the Unfair Trial of Wm Palmer:* by Thomas Wakley, Esq., Coroner, London, C. Elliot, 1856. *A Letter to the Lord Chief Justice Campbell:* by the Rev. Thomas Palmer [*mainly written, it seems, by Edward Kenealey, Palmer's junior Counsel*], London, T. Taylor, 1856. *In Favorem Vitae: A Letter to Mr Serjeant Shee on the Trial of Wm Palmer* by Henry Conington, London, John Russell Smith, 1856. *W. Palmer Exhumed: A Few Words on the Trial* by L. B. (M.A. Cantab.), London, Palmer & Son, 1856. *The Principles and Practice of Medical Jurisprudence* by Professor Alfred Swaine Taylor, London, John Churchill, 1865 edition. *Sixty Years on the Turf* by George Hodgman, London, Grant Richards, 1901. *The Life and Career of Dr Wm Palmer of Rugeley* by Dr George Fletcher, London, Fisher Unwin, 1925. *The Trial of Wm Palmer:* edited by E. R. Watson (*Notable British Trials Series*), London, Wm Hodge, 1952.

Unfortunately, the thirty-four 'lascivious' letters written by Dr Palmer to Jane Bergen have disappeared since 1933, when Dr Fletcher's collection of Palmeriana was dispersed at his death.

As usual, I have to thank Kenneth Gay for his constant help with this book at every stage.

ROBERT GRAVES
Deyá, Mallorca, Spain, June 14th, 1956.

THEY HANGED
MY SAINTLY BILLY

CHAPTER I

THE OLD BAILEY:
MAY 14TH, 1856

The trial of William Palmer, aged thirty-one, surgeon and race-horse owner, began yesterday at the Old Bailey after a delay of nearly five months. He had been arrested on Friday, December 15th, 1855, by the police superintendent at Rugeley, Stafford-shire—a town of which he is both a native and a resident—on a charge of having, three weeks before, feloniously, wilfully, and with malice aforethought, committed murder on the person of his friend and brother-sportsman John Parsons Cook. The arrest followed upon a verdict of wilful murder returned by a coroner's court at Rugeley. Palmer was thereupon committed to Stafford Gaol, of which he has since been an inmate.

Popular excitement rose to such a pitch, when he was further accused of several other poisonings, that in the view of the county authorities he could not expect to meet with a fair trial at Staffordshire Assizes. An application for a trial in London having been granted, a special Act (19 Vict. cap. 16) was needed to regularize the procedure; and this having been hurried through Parliament, the Crown resolved that the prosecution should be conducted by Attorney-General Cockburn himself, rather than by any private person.

3

Yesterday, May 14th, the case was at last called at the Central Criminal Court, Old Bailey, before Lord Chief Justice Campbell, Mr Justice Cresswell and Mr Baron Alderson; the other Commissioners present being the Right Hon. the Lord Mayor of London, two Sheriffs, two Under-Sheriffs and seven aldermen—including Mr Alderman Sidney, late M.P. for Stafford, who happens also to be a native of Rugeley and, we understand, formerly well acquainted with the prisoner's family.

Supporting Mr Attorney-General for the Prosecution, were Mr Edwin James, Q.C., Mr Bodkin, Mr Welsby and Mr Huddleston.

Mr Serjeant Shee had been appointed to conduct the Defence, with the assistance of Mr Grove, Q.C., Mr Gray, and Mr Kenealey.

To judge by the very numerous applications for admission to the Court, which were made so soon as ever the trial was appointed, and by the vain endeavours of large crowds to force their way into the building yesterday, despite an unseasonable chilliness of the weather, the keen interest which this case excited when first called to public attention has in no degree abated. Every entrance was besieged at a very early hour, and even the fortunate holders of admission cards had to pass the scrutiny of many stern janitors before they could be accommodated in the body of the Court. Among the distinguished visitors were the Earl of Derby, Earl Grey, the Marquis of Anglesey, Lord Lucan, Lord Denbigh, Prince Edward of Saxe-Weimar, with other peers of lesser rank. The Lord Advocate of Scotland sat beside the Attorney-General during the trial.

Punctually, at five minutes to ten o'clock, the learned judges entered, accompanied by the Lord Mayor, the aldermen, and the Sheriffs, and took their seats on the bench. A jury consisting largely of respectable City tradesmen was empanelled, after which the Lord Chief Justice ordered all witnesses, with the exception of medical men, out of Court.

The prisoner, on being called upon, pleaded 'Not Guilty' in a firm voice.

As a final earnest of the Crown's intention to give the prisoner a scrupulously fair trial, it was demanded by Mr Serjeant Shee for the Defence, and granted by Mr Attorney-General for the Prosecution, that any juryman who might be either a proprietor or shareholder in any insurance company should be asked to withdraw. Frequent allusions to insurance companies, with which the prisoner had dealings, would be made in the course of the trial: particularly to The Prince of Wales, The Solicitors' and General, and The Midland Counties.

No juryman, however, withdrew, and the Attorney-General thereupon began his speech for the prosecution.

Outside the Court, crowds still gathered thick, and included many Rugeley folk who had come up by train on the previous day in the full expectation of being admitted to witness the trial, and now expressed their disappointment most forcibly.

'By what right have the Under-Sheriffs admitted those d—d nobs to satisfy their idle curiosity? There ain't a Staffordshire man in the whole bunch, and I'll wager not a one of them so much as knows Dr Palmer by sight!'

'Did you see Lord Lucan? Him whom the Commander-in-Chief sent home from the Crimea? Perhaps his admission card should be regarded as a consolation prize for his military failures.'

'Some pretty murders were done in the Crimea by these self-same nobs, but it's hardly likely that they'll ever be brought to justice. Murder by neglect is more difficult to prove than murder by strychnine or prussic acid; and if charged, they would plead to be tried by their peers.'

'A right denied, however, to house-breakers, pick-pockets and other criminals in a small way.'

'A very shrewd hit, Sir!'

'I am obliged for your agreement, Sir.' 'Did you know Dr Palmer?'

'Did I, indeed? I'm a near neighbour of his. James is my name: a book-seller of Rugeley.

And you, Sir?'

'I'm from Uttoxeter—a betting man, as you'll have gathered from the cut of my jib. I wonder whether your impressions of Dr Palmer tally with mine? I cannot claim to have known him well, but I should say that he's a good-principled man. Of course, he couldn't pay when he didn't have the money, and he had the ill-luck to be barred from the Ring at Tattersall's, because of a failure in that respect. But, my dear Sir, he was a devil when it came to "punting", as we call speculation on the Turf. And he knew as much about making a book as yourself—if I may be so bold! For though book-makers and book-sellers come close to each other in a dictionary, so also do card-makers and card-sharpers, ha, ha! and are equally ignorant of the other's trade . . . They talk of his clever-ness; I wouldn't call him clever. Why, I've heard my fellow-Turfites wonder how he ever managed to win a penny . . . But what is your experience of him?'

'Well, Sir, I should agree that he's not a clever man. I should also add that neither is he a deep man. But he's a very cool man. Though speculative, as you say, he never seemed to be either elated or depressed by the results of his speculation, as so many gen-tlemen of your profession unfortunately become at times. And from the cut of his jib, as you put it, nobody would ever guess him to be anything but a country surgeon . . . 'He doesn't drink, I understand?'

'He drinks but little, and was only once seen the worse for liquor . . . At The Talbot Arms Hotel in Rugeley he would sit still and bite his nails, listening to the conversation of others; a habit which must have been of considerable profit to him, because "in wine is truth"; and I have seen betting men come reeling out of the Talbot, one after the other, when he was paying the score. In short, he's a perfectly sober, cool man; kind and generous to all around. And here with me, Sir, is our Rugeley sexton to confirm what I have said.'

The old sexton removed his cloth cap in greeting, and sang out eagerly: 'Yes, Sir, I've known Dr Palmer, man and boy, these thirty years. He's the very last person in the town as I should have suspected of such an ungodly thing. He's a religious gentleman, and many's the time, when I've had a sup of ale too much, he's chastised me for it. He'd say: "Do keep yourself respectable, Jemmy, and don't go to them public inns. If you wants a drink of ale, come by my house." And there's Bill Hawton, used to be clerk in the saw-mill, which was Mr Palmer, Senior's business. Bill Hawton fell ill last year and couldn't come to The Yard for a long time. Well, Sir, the only member of the numerous Palmer family who sent him joints of meat and coal, and other things he might need, was the Doctor; and he lent him money into the bargain. He called it "lending", Sir, but bless you! that was but his kind way of giving without causing poor Bill to regard it as a charity. Above ten pound, he gave Bill Hawton in money, apart from the value of the goods. And anyone at Rugeley will tell you that the Doctor was affectionate to his family, to his widowed mother in particular, though 'tis said that he had good cause to be ashamed of her giddy ways. And many's the labouring man will regret what's happening here today! For even if they acquit Dr Palmer of the charge—and, for myself, I'm prepared to swear him innocent—he's ruined, and suspicion will always attach to him.'

The book-seller smacked the sexton on the back. 'I like a man who speaks up for a friend in trouble. And, if you ask me, the special Act of Parliament, which was passed to let the judges try him here, conveys a hundred times more prejudice than it removes. Dr Palmer may have enemies in Staffordshire, but he also has many friends—and the friends outnumber the enemies. If he had been committed to the county assizes, the trial would have been conducted in a perfectly quiet and Christian atmosphere. You have only to ask the servants at the various hotels he frequented, within thirty miles in all directions of Rugeley: they will invariably speak of him as "a nice, pleasant, decent sort of man"—unless the Police have got at them, like some I know. And it's the talk of good people of that sort that moulds public opinion far more than the newspapers, such as *The Illustrated Times*, which have already poisoned London against Dr Palmer.'

Inside, the Attorney-General had opened his speech for the prosecution. He set forth the complicated nature of the facts on which the Crown's case rested, and begged the jurors to lend their patient attention to them, while discarding from their minds all prejudiced opinions which they had acquired either from hearsay or reading. This might be difficult in a case already so widely discussed throughout the country, but he begged them to make the effort.

'Gentlemen,' he then proceeded, 'William Palmer, the prisoner at the bar, is by profession a surgeon. He practised as such at Rugeley in Staffordshire for some years, until he became addicted to Turf pursuits, and was gradually weaned away from his profession. During the last two or three years, I am informed, he had made over his practice to his assistant, by name Benjamin Thirlby, who was then and is now a chemist and druggist of Rugeley. He kept only one or two patients . . .'

Here the Attorney-General coughed, paused, and with an accent that seemed to some persons in Court unwarrantedly pointed, went on: '. . . patients in whose lives he had—shall I say?—a more immediate interest than in others.'

The Rev. Thomas Palmer, who loved his elder brother William with a sincere devotion, half-rose in his seat to protest; but their sister Sarah Palmer, a modest and beautiful young lady, who helps Thomas in his parochial duties, at Coton Elms in Derbyshire, tugged at his coat to restrain him. 'Be patient, Tom,' she whispered. 'Take an example from William, who sits there no less calm and conscious of his innocence than Bishop Cranmer at the stake.'

The Rev. Thomas thereupon subsided in his seat, and the little scene passed unobserved by the Court officers, for all eyes were fixed on the prisoner at the bar. William Palmer certainly looks at least ten years more than his thirty-one, with which he is credited on the indictment. He is solidly built, very broad-shouldered and bull-necked, though not above the average height. His complexion is florid, his forehead high, his features somewhat mean, yet respectable enough. He has thin, lightish-brown hair, brushed back over an almost bald head, and whiskers inclining to red. Nothing in his appearance suggests either ferocity or cunning; and his manner is exceedingly calm and collected, without a trace of bravado, guilt or remorse. Shrewd observers, however, will notice a remarkable discrepancy between the ruddy coarseness of his face and the extreme prettiness of his hands—which are white, small, plump and dimpled, almost womanly in their appearance, and which he spends a deal of time admiring as he sits in the box, sometimes picking at his nails for lack of a pen-knife to trim them neatly. He is no longer allowed to wear wash-leather gloves as a protection for these hands against the sun, but little sunlight penetrated into the County Gaol and House of Correction at Stafford this last winter, and their colour seems to afford him great satisfaction.

The Attorney-General's speech occupied the entire morning; and in it he gave a lucid and detailed account of what he intended should be established by the witnesses for the prosecution. The Rev. Thomas Palmer and Miss Sarah Palmer listened with set faces;

their tightly compressed lips and narrowed eyes evinced disgust at what Miss Palmer was overheard to call, *sotto voce*, during a momentary pause in the speech: 'A wicked bundle of hearsay, lies and scandal.' When the speaker began to discuss the prisoner's pecuniary difficulties which suggested a motive for the crime, and pronounced: 'A man may be guilty of fraud, he may be guilty of forgery; it does not follow that he should be guilty of murder,' a deep frown settled on both brows. Some offence was also felt by a gentleman in a back row, who exclaimed: 'Give a dog a bad name and hang him, Sir!'; whereupon the Rev. Mr Palmer turned round in a fury, and shouted: 'Who calls my brother a dog?'

The gentleman in the back row could not be discovered, but the Lord Chief Justice threatened to clear the Court if any further interruptions occurred. He would, indeed, have ordered the ushers to eject the Rev. Mr Palmer, but that Mr Alderman Sidney apprised him of the latter's identity. Nor could he greatly object to the warmth of his rejoinder which, though officious, had been uttered in reproof of the unknown voice. He therefore contented himself with the dry warning: 'Sir, if you respect my wig, I'll undertake to respect your cloth.' The Rev. gentleman duly apologized, and no further incident broke the dignity of the day's proceedings.

Certainly, the Rev. Thos Palmer did not forget what he has since called 'the one fatal instance on which my brother William infringed the commercial code of this country.' But that had been many years before, and he now persuaded himself that William, a regular church-goer, who took the sacrament every Sunday, and contributed generously to all church charities, repented with all his heart of that lapse, which had been attended by strongly extenuating circumstances.

CHAPTER II

THE WILES OF JANE WIDNALL

Dr Palmer's immediate family consists of his elder brother Joseph, a former timber-merchant and colliery owner, now retired from business, and living with his wealthy wife at Liverpool; his younger brothers George, a Rugeley attorney, who married a rich iron-master's daughter and Thomas, a clergyman of the Established Church; and Sarah, an unmarried sister, who devotes her life to good causes. There was another younger brother, fourth in the list, named Walter, a bankrupt and drunkard, recently deceased; also a sister who married a Mr Heywood of Haywood and, after a life of indecent scandal, drank herself into the grave.

Old Mrs Palmer, the mother, a hale woman in her late fifties or early sixties, is still living at The Yard, in Rugeley, the house where all her seven children were born. It takes its name from the tim-ber-yard which old Mr Palmer, the sawyer, used to manage. Joseph succeeded him for a while in the business, but presently abandoned it altogether. The Yard is a handsome, comfortable place, built of red brick. On one side, next St Augustine's Church, a splendid ivy-tree climbs to the very roof, its dark foliage making the blind of the staircase window shine snowy white by contrast. On the other side, a bulging two-storey bow window, built of stone and over-looking the canal, has been awkwardly patched on to the original structure. The windows are glazed with plate-glass, and their gay wire blinds and rich silk curtains are very much in the fancy style of a prosperous public house. Another bow window, behind, is as old as the house, and has small diamond-shaped panes set in lead, like the stern lights of ancient ships. The entrance door is pro-tected by a wide verandah, respectably painted in clean white but which, not being overgrown by clematis, honeysuckle, or other creeping plants, has a naked sort of aspect. Well-clipped box and privet enclose the front garden, so that anyone with half an eye can see that a gardener is kept here. The wharf, where the timber was formerly loaded on canal barges, and the yard where it was stacked, has of late been converted into a gently sloping lawn. A few shrubs line the gravelled carriage drive, but they are brown at the tips and look unhealthy. The great crane, which once creaked under the weight of heavy timber baulks, now rests idly at the water's edge, planked over against the weather. Occasionally, long and narrow barges pass, each draught-horse forced slantwise by the strain on the tow rope. At the farther end of the timber-yard a few blackened planks remain, piled together in the form of a pent-house, which serves as a convenient roosting place for Leghorn fowls and a bantam or two.

The back premises are so foul that they charge the front with hypocrisy. Here the garden has been allowed to go out of cultiva-tion—the flower beds trodden underfoot until they are as hard as the gravelled walks that surround them. A few dish-clouts hang up to dry. We noticed a water-butt with rusty hoops; and a coach-house and stable that even a London cabman would cough at. The black thatch of the stable is dripping away, and its woodwork seems too rotten even for kindling. Old Mrs Palmer, to be sure, no longer keeps a carriage.

'The nearer the church, the farther from God,' is a proverb of doubtful truth. But true it is that William Palmer, as a child, had two churches frowning down on him, and scores of graves around. He could take reading lessons from the inscriptions on the gravestones and vaults, such as the large one near the gate with its carved letters picked out in green moss:

> Praises on tombs are trifles vainly spent;
> A man's good name is his best monument!

The gardener, by name Littler, once top-sawyer at The Yard, knew the family well and is ready, for a pint of ale, and a half-ounce of tobacco, to talk about them. Here is his account.

ROBERT LITTLER

Old Mr Palmer was very strict with the children generally: made them play in the grounds, or in the graveyard, and kept them out of the village lest they should run into mischief. When he died, however, they were allowed to run wild. Mrs Palmer, you see, is of a very different character from her late husband; but, being in her employ, I cannot say more than that. You must inquire elsewhere, if you are still curious. The old master never flogged William so often as he did the others, Walter in especial, and not because he was a particular favourite, but because he was careful to avoid trouble. Walter was very racketty, and the people hereabouts used to agree on William as the best of the bunch; though perhaps fear of the birch made him a trifle sly. He was Mrs Palmer's darling, yet I never saw him fly into a pet, as Joseph was apt to do.

I often carried William through the fields in my arms and played at marbles with him—he was a capital aim at marbles, or ball, or tipcat. As a baby he was very fat and lusty, but so were all his brothers and sisters—not a one of them could walk before sixteen or eighteen months. When William reached the age of five he went as a day-scholar to the Free Grammar School, the next house along the road; that was in old Bonney's time. Mr Bonney was reckoned a man of great discrimination, he could tell a boy's character at a glance—a pity he's dead! We had as many as eighty-three scholars in his day, come in from all the towns and villages around. We have only twenty-four at present, the new master not being of the same quality. Yes, William received a sound education under Mr Bonney. And he went of his own accord to take singing lessons from Mr Sheritt, him who's now our Parish clerk and would take no boy unless he was of good character—he speaks highly of William still. Indeed, a better-tempered or more generous lad there never was; and a very nice young gentleman he became. In the case of a school row, he would always stand up for the weaker side, and use his fists to advantage. Perhaps that was why his school-fellows never took to him, as they did to his other brothers, but kept their distance. I have heard it said of late—since this wretched business started, I mean—that he would borrow money under false pretences from the men employed at The Yard, and not repay them; but he never tried such a trick on me, nor did I ever hear any complaint from my mates at the time. Well, William was just as generous when he grew up; he never forgot an old face. Why, whenever he met me or Mr Sheritt, he'd say: 'Will you have a glass of something to drink?' He gave a deal to the poor, and in a quiet way, too; as one who stores up treasures in Heaven, not with a sound of trumpets.

When he left school at the age of seventeen, his father apprenticed him to Messrs Evans & Sons, the wholesale chemists of Lord Street, Liverpool. There he behaved very well indeed for some months, and was attentive to his various duties, and caused every satisfaction; until, like Samson in the Good Book, he met his Delilah. William, you see, lodged a few streets away from the counting-house, with one Widnall. He could not be put up by his

brother Joseph, because at that time Joseph was working a colliery at Cannock Chase, not many miles from here—a business,
let me tell you, which lost him a few thousand pounds. William
had hitherto lived an innocent life, and was still what they call
a he-virgin when the landlord's red-headed daughter Jane, who
was William's senior by two years—decoyed him into her bed.
She thought William a pretty good catch, having heard that he
possessed seven thousand pounds of his own, and was determined
to lay her hands on it. After a few weeks had passed she pretended
to be with child and, coming to him with eyes red from weeping,
begged that he would marry her.

When he protested that this was out of the question, much as
he loved her and regretted her plight, she demanded fifty pounds
for the performance of an abortion. William replied that he had
not above five pounds in his pockets, and would not enjoy his
inheritance until the age of twenty-one.

'Very well,' said she, 'if I cannot turn away the brat you have
given me, then I must needs bear it; and my father will make you
either marry or support me.'

William stood at a loss. 'I am a respectable girl,' she went on,
'and you have seduced me.' 'But where am I to find the fifty
pounds?' asks William. 'That's a deal of money,' he says. 'You have
a rich brother,' answers the red-haired lass. 'Borrow from him.'

'Joseph is the last man in the world I can approach,' says William.
''Tis like this. My father, in the year of the Queen's Coronation,
comes home to dinner one day, eats and drinks with gusto, but
falls dead of heart-failure with his bread and cheese still clutched
in his hand. The will he left behind was unsigned; and Joseph,
as the eldest son, might by law have taken all the property in his
own right, bar the widow's thirds. However, he was kind enough
to execute a deed by which he should keep only seven thousand
pounds, and we others should have the same sum apiece; and my

mother, the remainder and the landed property, for her lifetime—
on condition that she would not re-marry. And there's a clause
in the deed, my dear, which debars any of us from enjoying our
inheritance if we marry before the age of twenty-one, or commit
any grave fault. Joseph is a good-hearted man, but he's also a severe
one, and I don't propose to vex him.'

'Why did you hide all this from me?' cries Jane Widnall in a
rage. 'I'd never have let you so much as kiss me, if I'd known how
matters stood!'

'You never asked me,' says William.

Presently the lass goes off to an abortionist, or pretends to; then
she comes back and takes to her bed for a few days. She tells William that all's well, but that he must find two hundred pounds
within six weeks, because she's stolen that sum from her father's
strong-box, and there'll be the Devil to pay if it's not put back
before he makes up his quarterly accounts. 'I shall accuse you of
the theft,' she threatens William.

'Why did you pay two hundred pounds, and not fifty?' he asks,
in surprise.

'I couldn't find the ready money,' she explains, and says: 'The
wretch has threatened to inform my father, and I'll be ruined.'

William is a greenhorn, and suspects nothing. He should have
known that no abortionist would perform an operation except for
cash on the nail, or afterwards run the risk of going to gaol for
the crime of abortion and the equally serious crime of extorting
money by threats. Then, on the advice of a fellow-apprentice, he
backs a certainty at the Liverpool Races. It loses him five pounds.
So he sells his gold watch, given him as a present by old Mrs Palmer
when he left home, and with the five pounds it fetches, backs a
certainty at the Shrewsbury Races. He loses again, and in despair
resorts to other means of money raising.

Messrs Evans & Sons are troubled. Various customers write to

say that they have paid their accounts owing to the firm, but have
received no acknowledgements. What, then, has happened to the
cash, which they are positive has been sent? It seems as if there are
thieves at the Liverpool Post Office. Now, as I've heard the story,
the merchants of Liverpool have their own letter-boxes into which
letters addressed to them are placed by the Postmaster, as soon as
the mails come in by coach or railway train. Confidential clerks go
to collect these letters, which arrive much earlier this way than if
they had been delivered by the penny-postman.

Well, complaints of lost money became more frequent, and
the Liverpool Post Office denied responsibility; so Messrs Evans
wrote to the General Post Office in London, and the authorities
there sent an inspector down to Liverpool to lay a trap for the
thief. But no thief was caught, and the missing letters remained
a mystery, and fresh complaints came pouring in that money had
been despatched by post, but had not been acknowledged. One
customer had remitted twenty pounds, and another forty-two
pounds, no less.

It occurred to Mr Evans, Junior, that, though the inspector had
done all he could in tracing letters from the various country Post
Offices to the one at Liverpool, it yet remained to trace them from
the Liverpool mail-box to the counting-house in Lord Street. It
happened to be the day when William went to fetch the letters—
for he shared this task with a respectable senior apprentice—and
Mr Evans, Junior, decided to watch him from a little distance so
soon as ever he emerged from the Post Office. William was seen
to finger and feel all the envelopes in turn, to make out if any of
them had enclosures. One happening to be more bulky than the
rest, he paused at the entrance to an alley-way, and opened it.
But it contained only a wad of advertisements by some manufac-
turer of patent medicines, so he crammed it into his pocket and,
finding the other letters lean and uninviting, took them to the

counting-house. Meanwhile, Mr Evans, Junior, had hurried past the alley-way and reached Lord Street ahead of William. There he stood at the counting-house, waiting to receive the letters.

'Why, Palmer,' he exclaims, 'these are not all that came today, surely?'

'Certainly, Sir,' answers William, lying with a good heart to save what he thought was the honour of the girl.

'Where, then, is the letter which I saw you open in the alley and thrust into your pocket?' Mr Evans asks him.

'Oh, that!' says William, readily. 'I forgot about it. The fact was, I recognized the handwriting. It is the advertisement for patent medicines that comes regularly once a quarter. I thought no harm to open it and see what new lines they are offering.'

But Mr Evans, Junior, ain't satisfied. He takes William before Mr Evans, Senior, and though William positively denies all guilt, he has been observed fingering and feeling all the letters. The Evanses don't risk taking proceedings against the lad, for want of evidence that would convince a jury, but they immediately discharge him, and write to Mrs Palmer at The Yard about the matter.

Mrs Palmer, she fell in a great pother when she heard the news, and went complaining to all and sundry, myself included, that her dear son was unjustly accused of a crime that he did not have it in his heart to commit. She should have remembered the proverb 'Least said, soonest mended.' For, as I heard later from Mr Duffy, the linen-draper—but I reckon I should keep my mouth shut on the subject of Mr Duffy—William confessed everything to his mother, who came at once from Rugeley, accompanied by his brother Joseph, who happened to be there on a visit, and implored Mr Evans, Senior, to be merciful. Mr Evans tells her: 'It don't rest with us, Ma'am, but with our customers, whose money has been stolen to the tune of two hundred pounds or so. You must deal with them.'

'Oh, that I'll gladly do,' says Mrs Palmer. 'Pray give me the names and addresses, and the amount owing in each case! The poor boy borrowed the money to save a girl's honour.'

They gave her the names and addresses and other particulars, and she made good the money stolen. William confessed his guilt to Mr Evans, saying that he was properly penitent, and begged that he might remain until his apprenticeship ran out.

Howsomever, they hardened their hearts, though it was a first offence; but to prevent the public scandal that would be caused if they cancelled the indentures, they consented to take on another young Palmer to finish William's apprenticeship. So they got Thomas, the same as is now a clergyman, in William's place; and Thomas, who had been a wild lad hitherto, conducted himself in a most exemplary way, because William begged him to restore the family reputation which he had tarnished.

That should have been a lesson to William to have no more dealings with his Jane, especially as the lass had been put up to the lark by her mother, a woman of very bad character. Though passing as Simon Widnall's wife, she was no wife at all, and Jane was her illegitimate daughter by another man. This woman didn't allow William to get out of Jane's clutches, as I shall tell you, though she always kept in the background and acted silly.

At the age of eighteen, William, who already had a good knowledge of drugs and their uses, was apprenticed for five years to Mr Edward Tylecote the surgeon of Haywood, not far from here. His house stands opposite to that of William's sister—the elder sister who, I'm sorry to say, was the black sheep of the family and whose goings-on I should be ashamed to relate, because of the pain they have given Mrs Palmer. She died of drink soon afterwards. Mr Tylecote is a capable surgeon, but, his practice being a poor and scattered one, he was glad to have William's assistance, especially as Mrs Palmer undertook to pay his bed and board and fifty guineas a year for instruction, if only Mr Tylecote, at the close of the apprenticeship, would get him admitted into the Staffordshire Infirmary as a walking pupil.

William was doing pretty well at Haywood when, one day, he was startled to hear banns read in the church between James Vickerstaff, the assistant-gardener at Shoughborough Park, near by, and Jane Widnall. Howsomever, the bride proved not to be the redheaded lass, but her mother of the same name; and the union was in every way satisfactory, since Vickerstaff had been the lass's father, d'ye see? They say the mother's decision was made for two reasons. As to the first, Simon Widnall had turned her out of the house for receiving stolen goods; as to the second, she knew that William was apprenticed to Mr Tylecote, and young Jane had not lost hope of getting her fingers into the seven thousand pounds that William would enjoy when he came of age, and wanted to keep an eye on him.

William was remarkably true to the girl; indeed, you may say that he was besotted by her. He didn't wish his family to know that he loved her still, and saw her daily; and therefore had to use deceit. I believe he felt remorse at having, as he thought, taken her maidenhead, and wanted to make her his wife, if she would but wait. Jane, who had pretended great surprise at finding him in the same village as herself, managed the affair pretty well: she kept him uncertain of her love, and admitted him to her favours rarely and in a grudging manner. When Mr Tylecote, tired with his morning's round and anxious for a short rest after dinner, was settling for a nap, William would enter the dining-room and announce that a patient of his, over at Ingestre (as it might be) had requested a visit; at the same time offering to go. 'By all means,' Mr Tylecote would say, 'take the strawberry roan and the usual black draught!' William would mix a black draught, harness the roan, ride up village towards Ingestre, then circle about by the 'Abbey' and through a croft belonging to The Clifford Arms Hotel. He would enter the inn-yard by the back way, put up his nag, go off to Jane Widnall (who lived next door) and in due time empty the black draught on the midden and return to the surgery.

At last William had a row with Peter Smirke, Mr Tylecote's other assistant. Smirke was a little sprig of a man, who dressed in a dandiacal fashion and was received in the village society. The story they tell at The Clifford Arms is that Smirke once saw William emerging from Jane's cottage at an hour he should have been elsewhere, and scolded him very severely. William put him off with a story of having dropped in to ask whether Mr. Vickerstaff, her step-father, could supply him with a few seedlings for the garden at The Yard—they always have seedlings of all sorts to spare at Shoughborough Park—and Smirke thought no more of the matter. William, however, told Jane the story, and she now began making eyes at Smirke, and even one day invited him into the cottage on some excuse and arranged for her mother to surprise him stealing a kiss. Jane pretended, for William's benefit, that this had been done to prevent Smirke from bringing any accusation against him at Mr Tylecote's; but her true object was to make William jealous.

In this she succeeded. William, being kept short of money, could not afford to dress so smartly as Smirke. But he went upstairs and poured acid over all Smirke's fine clothes and linen; finishing with a new pair of dress-boots that had just arrived from the bootmaker in time for a ball at The Clifford Arms, where Jane was to help the landlady with the service. William took a pen-knife and slashed those boots into ribbons. That was true lover's jealousy. All being fair in love and war, he never owned up to the deed; though it could only have been his.

I don't know the whole story of how William ran away with Jane to Walsall; but I'll tell as much as I do know. Mr Tylecote was not in the habit of going to church except at Christmas, Easter, and Harvest Thanksgiving, and for the funerals of his richer patients. William, on the contrary, always attended the early morning Communion Service, and again Matins. At Matins, he would arrange for a lad to come as if from Mr Tylecote, and call him out a few minutes before the sermon—the parson over at Haywood being a very powerful and long-winded preacher—and go off to see the lass.

One Sunday, half-way through a sermon on the Last Days, the new Mrs Vickerstaff nudged old Vickerstaff, who was a careful, plodding sort of fellow, saying that she felt faint and would he take her home? So Vickerstaff starts up from his doze and takes her home, where he finds William in bed with his step-daughter, as had been arranged. There is a great row, and Vickerstaff threatens William with a fowling-piece if he will not swear, in the hearing of them all, to marry Jane. William solemnly swears, and is talked into visiting Walsall, to plead with brother Joseph for his blessing on the match, the lass coming along too. So, early on the Monday, William asks Mr Tylecote's leave to go for a day's rabbit shooting; Mr Tylecote agrees, and William hires a nag from The Clifford Arms, meets Jane a mile out of town, pulls her up behind him, and trots off.

Nothing is heard of the pair for some days; but at last comes a letter to Mr Tylecote, apologizing heartily for having been called away to Walsall on sudden business, and asking him to forward a letter which he enclosed, to a Mr Lomax of Stafford. Mr Tylecote steps across the road and consults William's brother-in-law, Mr Heywood, who says: 'I don't like the look of this, and they say in the village that the scamp has gone off with Vickerstaff's step-daughter. I think, Mr Tylecote, you would be in your rights, as his employer, to open the enclosure.' So they unseal the envelope, which is to ask Mr Lomax as a great favour to redeem William from an inn at Walsall, where he is being held in pawn for a bill which he cannot pay, because Joseph will do naught for him. Now, this Mr Lomax was a wealthy young man, his school- fellow at Bonney's, whom William had once saved from a sad scrape.

The seal broken, Mr Tylecote could not in honesty send on the letter to Mr Lomax; nor did he feel inclined to redeem William himself. Mr Heywood therefore rode over to Rugeley to tell old Mrs Palmer what was afoot. She could not be found, having gone out visiting a friend, but not left word which friend it was; so Walter and George set off on their own to fetch William home from Walsall. They came upon him with the lass, at dinner in the inn, quietly cracking walnuts and sipping his port. George behaved in a hectoring manner, and rudely ordered him back to Rugeley. William replied that he would not stand for such insolence from a younger brother and, rising from his chair, offered to fight him; but Walter quoted the text: 'Be ye kindly and affectionate one to another in brotherly love,' and reconciled the two. Then George goes off to pay the bill, and William to collect his gear. But in the inn-yard he gives both brothers the slip, takes chaise to Stafford, where he leaves the lass, and makes his way alone to Rugeley.

The lass had money in her purse, no less than a hundred pounds of old Vickerstaff's savings, which she had stolen, in case William should have no luck with Joseph. She sees now that the game is up: if Mrs Palmer tells Joseph the truth about the thefts at Liverpool, which have hitherto been kept from him—for Joseph has heard no more of the lass than that William wants to make her his wife—William will lose his seven thousand pounds, and she may as well call the marriage off. But she can't go back to Haywood and face old Vickerstaff's wrath. So she writes secretly to Peter Smirke, saying that she has been deserted by William upon her confessing that she loves another, namely Smirke. Peter Smirke at once leaves Mr Tylecote, believe it or not, and marries her. They set off together for Australia, where Smirke sets up in practice at Sydney, and nothing is heard of either for many a year.

Ay, that is how it went. And Mrs Palmer forgave William, once more. Perhaps Tom Clewley, at The Shoulder of Mutton, will be able to fill in some of the gaps in the tale that I have left on purpose.

CHAPTER III

MR DUFFY'S SAMPLE BOX

Rugeley, a long, straggling, over-grown village which ranks, however, as a town, is kept very clean, and occupied by some persons extremely well-to-do in the world. It is about the size of Twickenham, but seems to have enlarged itself without any apparent design beyond the whim of the bricklayer and the varying price of building sites. Commercial travellers call it a good place for business, and declare that the accounts here are particularly safe. Lovers of bustle and crowded pathways might well find the quietude of Rugeley's cottages (with their large leaden lights and heavy shutters) not a little oppressive, but many visitors profess themselves charmed by its almost deserted streets. Housewives may be seen at the windows busily plying the needle behind rows of red geraniums, while their men-folk are away in the fields, or hard at work at Bladen's brass-foundry or Hatfield's manufactory.

The Town Hall occupies the centre of the Market Place; with its justice-room in the upper storey and, on the ground-floor, a literary institution next to a Savings Bank. Three or four London-looking shops are supported by plenty of countrified ones: butchers' with only a half-sheep as stock-in-trade; grocers' that sell bread; tailors' that keep stays and bonnets for sale.

Soon after you go out of the Railway Station, to cross the

bridge by a flour mill, leaving The Yard and Rugeley's two churches behind, you reach a bend of the road where stands the shop that has most benefited by what are alleged to have been William Palmer's crimes—Mr Keeyes, the undertaker's. You are now in Market Street and approaching The Talbot Arms Hotel, generally still called The Crown, as before it assumed its present lordly name. You must be careful to distinguish it from The Talbot Inn, a much smaller place, which you have already passed. The Talbot Arms Hotel, where John Parsons Cook died, is a bold-faced house, not unlike a cotton mill from the outside, except that the windows are too large; and behind stretches an acre of back yard, surrounded by stables and coach-houses, which are well filled during the celebrated six-day Horse Fair held in June, and during the lesser fairs in April, October and December; but quite empty for the rest of the year. Here you may well catch sight of Mr Thomas Masters, a trim old gentleman in drab breeches and a cut-away coat, standing at the door of his hotel, propped on a knotted blackthorn stick. He has lived here for seventy-four years, and what he does not know about Rugeley and its people is hardly worth knowing. He rides a brown mare thirty years of age: 'The two of us make a good bit over a hundred together,' he will tell you.

Opposite, and set back a little from the road, behind a fore-lawn no bigger than a billiard table and a few evergreens enclosed by iron railings, stands the two-storied building with broad modern windows and a grey 'rough cast' façade, which Dr Palmer occupied at the time of his arrest. Its neighbours are the humble Bell Inn on the left side, and the house of Mr John Bennett, shoemaker, on the right.

As you pass on, the shops become bigger and you even come across a book-seller's, Mr James's, with a fashionable mahogany front of plate-glass. The first turning to the left is an ugly lane, like a back street in Manchester, leading to the foundries. If you detain and question an inhabitant who has strayed into the street, he will tell you: 'Down there stands the old Post Office, where Palmer's friend, Mr Cheshire, got into trouble on the Doctor's account. We have a new Post Office now. And here's Mr Ben Thirlby's chemist shop—he worked for Dr Palmer—and yonder's the crockery shop where the Doctor used to deal, and there's George Myatt, the saddler's, where he had his harness repaired, and yonder's the tailor who made his suits.'

Everything in Rugeley is 'Dr Palmer' now; no other topic of conversation will serve. By the way, if we give him his courtesy title of 'Doctor', which is a country custom when surgeons are concerned, we trust to be forgiven. The correct form of address is, of course, 'Mr Palmer', or William Palmer, Esq.

So on to the Bank—open from ten to three. Here Dr Palmer kept his flickering account, sometimes reduced to a few shillings, but then again swollen to thousands of pounds, only to shrink again from his losses on the race-course or the demands of greedy moneylenders. Now you are in Brook Street, the tree-lined scene of the annual Horse Fair: as broad as Smithfield, and as long as Regent Street, with plenty of room to inspect the horses, even should they stampede and charge down towards the Market Square like a cavalry regiment. The tall Maypole facing you could serve for a three-decker's mast. Boys sometimes swarm to the top—the young Palmer brothers were well known for their climbing feats—but they must surely hurt their legs on the iron hooping half-way up. The houses on both sides of Brook Street are large and commodious, and to the south-west, in the far background, the dark hills of Cannock Chase frame a pleasantly rural view of sheep, cows and immense wagons standing before the miller's door.

The miller's wife proves to be both comely and loquacious. She says: 'The landscape around us is most beautiful for miles: nothing else but noblemen's mansions and grounds. Do you think the aristocracy would come and settle here, so far from London, if it wasn't so sweet a spot? There's Shoughborough Park, the Marquess of Anglesey's place, within four miles—"Beau Desert" they call it—with the most lovely country you can imagine all along the Shoughborough road. In the other direction there's Lord Hatherton's park and timber, from which half the Royal Navy's dockyards are supplied. Oaks, Sir, with trunks as big around as cart wheels! Then there's my Lord Bagot's—the finest woods in Europe, Lord Bagot's got. And Earl Talbot's magnificent estate, which has named both our oldest inn and our principal hotel; and Weston Hall; and a hundred such. Bless you, Sir, compared with Rugeley, Nottinghamshire's a fool to it. Then there's Hagley Hall within a hop, skip, stride and jump of us—a short mile in fact—the finest shrubberies man ever saw, and the Honourable Mr Curzon is so kind as to allow us all to walk in them. It's only this plaguey Dr Palmer has set people against Rugeley; or else the whole world would be singing its praises.'

Retrace your steps at this point, and go back by way of Market Square to the other end of the town, where The Shoulder of Mutton Inn stands, an inn no larger than a cottage. Thomas Clewley, a fine-looking man with white hair and a cherry-red face which puts one in mind of trifle at some evening party, has been landlord here for more years, he says, then he would care to reckon. The inn has a tall roof from which dormer windows peep out across the street and over its entrance door hangs a crude painting of an immense shoulder of mutton, dwarfing the very respectably sized dried hams seen suspended from the kitchen hooks as one glances in through the passage window. The front parlour is lined with shelves containing what seem to be medicine bottles but are, in reality, traveller's samples of various wines, cordials and spirits.

There is also on view the plaster image of a cow, such as grace dairymen's shops, or Hindoo temples, with the following Gothic inscription sunk in its base: 'No Milk like Bristol Milk!'

The tap-room is built out from the side of the cottage, with a slate roof of its own; the windows have heavy white sashes and small panes, twelve to the square yard; broadsheet ballads and hand-coloured prints of pugilists, murderers and race-horses paper the walls. On a shelf over the door stands a bottle containing a two-headed piglet preserved in spirits of wine; and scrawled across the face of a broken American hanging clock, above a coloured view of Sharon Church, Connecticut, you may read the jocose warning: 'No tick here!'

Mr Clewley is even less reluctant to discuss the 'Palmer affair' than old Littler, and equally positive about the Doctor's innocence. We have taken down the following from his lips, in shorthand:

THOMAS CLEWLEY

Palmer never had it in him to hurt a fly. The way they now talk of him in the London papers, and in towns where he was barely known, nigh makes me vomit! I reckon Littler has given you the particulars of his two false starts in life—at Liverpool and at Haywood—and how he was twice deceived by that foxy-maned harlot, Jane Widnall. But he never tells the whole story, on account of loyalty to his employer, Mrs Palmer, Senior.

The fact is, that when the poor lady had buried Mr Joseph Palmer, Senior, under a fine stone vault in the graveyard, she began to feel lonely and cold at nights. She would have married again, being a lively, handsome enough woman—as 'tis said coarsely in this town: 'Many's the good tune played on an old fiddle'—but that the deed drawn up by her eldest son Joseph forbade this. It's my suspicion that Mr Joseph, Junior, knew of a certain attachment she had formed on the very day of the funeral, and did not relish her beau as a step-father; the man, Moody by name, had once been a collier, and was now managing the pit at Brereton for him. That danger passed, since Moody soon after got knocked over by a railway train when his horse bolted across the lines; But I'm sure that, a few years later, if Mrs Palmer had been free to follow her inclinations, she would have married Cornelius Duffy, the linen-draper. I don't suppose Littler said much about that business, did he? Very well, Sir: I'll tell you the story just as it happened.

Duffy was a strapping fellow of forty or so, a linen-draper from Belfast. Though a man of good looks, we reckoned him a pretty dull chap in the house; he'd sit still and drink, spirits mainly, and read the newspapers from back to front and from side to side, spelling out every word with his lips. He came to lodge here twice: the first time, when young Mr William—now Dr Palmer—had just been dismissed from his apprenticeship at Messrs Evans & Sons of Liverpool, but not yet gone to Dr Tylecote's at Haywood; the second time, just before Mr William broke his apprenticeship with Dr Tylecote. I remember that, on the first occasion, Mr William paid the score Duffy had run up—it wasn't a large one, but Duffy had been lodging with me the better part of a month, and I had not yet seen the colour of his money. I wasn't sorry to see his back. I wondered why Mr William, who was only seventeen years old, and did not appear particularly friendly disposed towards Duffy, should do this for him. Mr William seemed to guess what was in my mind, for he said: 'Mr Duffy once rescued my father from an overturned coach on the Wednesbury road; and we Palmers like to show our gratitude.' Yet there was little warmth in Mr William's good-bye when Duffy went off, nor any gratitude in Duffy's. To tell the truth, it was a most disagreeable leave-taking.

Then Duffy comes here for the second time, drinking and reading the newspapers slowly through as before, and still seems to shun company. I try to get him to talk about the coach accident, but he shuts up like an oyster. In the evenings, when this parlour and the tap-room attract the most custom—and we draw it from miles around because of our home-brewed, which is unequalled in this county, though I have not travelled widely enough to make any grander claim—Duffy always slips out for a country walk, well muffled up, and don't come home until close on midnight.

Where he might go was none of my business, nor what he did when he went wherever he might go. On the day that Mr William's brothers George and Walter ride to Walsall for the fetching back of Mr William, Duffy goes off after supper for his usual stroll and this time don't return at all. He owes the house some three or four guineas, and when I question Mr William, who comes in for a drink, he seems surprised to hear that Duffy's been along again. He don't offer to pay the bill, though I mention it; and says no word either for Duffy or against Duffy. 'No doubt, he's been called away suddenly,' he says, 'and will soon be back. I understand that he has big interests in Liverpool.'

'Well, we still have his traps,' say I, 'including his sample box.'

'Then you may depend on it that he'll be back soon,' says Mr William.

I do no more in the matter, but wait; and time goes by, and no Duffy. Mr William, he says no word to me on the subject either, and I don't care to pump him. Presently, Duffy's boxes begin to smell very bad, and at the last my missus opens them. It was no murdered child, as we feared, but a quarter of Stilton cheese which had grown over-ripe, among a few dirty shirts and stockings, a rusty razor, two or three tradesmen's bills, old letters and suchlike. In the sample box we found some small pieces of linen, which I held as a pledge for the debt owed the house, though not worth above five shillings in all. I never set eyes on Duffy again, and he went away with no clothing but what he wore on his back.

I often puzzled on his sudden disappearance, and feared foul play—no, Sir, don't mistake my meaning! He went away the day before Mr William's return from Stafford, and Mr William knew nothing of the matter at all. But the contents of the sample box gave me a clue to what happened. In among the papers, not put by with care as though they were of particular value, but just lying anyhow, my missus found a number of love letters which made her cry out: 'Well, I never did!' and nearly split her sides with laughing.

The first of the letters in date ran as follows—for which you may take my word. It's a long time indeed since I read that letter, but like the celebrated Scottish historian Mr Macaulay, I am gifted—or, as you may say, cursed—with a memory like a photographic camera. What I have once read I can recall at will years later without effort. I have won many a wager thereby. This, as I say, was how the letter ran:

The Yard: Dec. 3rd, 1841.

I trust you will pardon the liberty I take in writing to you, and the still greater liberty of begging you the favour of calling here tomorrow at 3 o'clock, with the same cambric linen samples that you offered me yesterday. I know you will have some scruples as to my request, knowing that linen is unlikely to form the sole topic of our conversation, if you will be so kind as to accede to my request. You will find me alone at that hour. May I beg of you the kindness to forgive me this note in anticipation of the cause which I shall explain to you? What I have written is strictly confidential, and having been informed of your high and noble sense of honour and your absolute discretion, I need say no more. Although we exchanged only a formal few words, and those in the presence of my son George, yet believe me, I am one of your warmest, most sincere friends,

SARAH PALMER

—To Cornelius Duffy, Esq.,
The Shoulder of Mutton Inn.

It seems that Esquire Duffy took his box of samples around to

The Yard next day at the hour named, and was satisfied with the promised explanation, for the second letter read even warmer and more sincere. Now, how did that one begin? Ah, I have it:

The Yard: Dec. 5th, 1841. My Dearest and Best Friend,

This morning I received a note from a lady neighbour, whom I am to go visiting, that she would prefer my taking tea with her on Monday instead of Tuesday. Now, can't you come Tuesday, at five o'clock? The boys won't be here, and I have given the servant leave to sit with her sick sister; but pray come by the back premises which are reached least obtrusively by the canal tow-path. You will come, won't you? I had anticipated so much delight in seeing you Monday. The postponement of one day seems very long to me, but I have to exercise discretion, because it would never do if unkind and malicious gossip about our love were to reach the ears of my son Joseph. All Monday I shall be thinking of the pleasure of seeing you, and I hope the time may pass quickly until our meeting. I am a lonely woman, and you have been very generous to me, more generous perhaps than you guess. Don't laugh at this note, for I have written it fresh from my heart. And pray, if not too late, accept Mr Sheritt's invitation which you declined before, to sing the tenor parts in the choir tomorrow. It will make you well thought of in the town, and also give me the opportunity to rest my eyes for an hour or more on your dear face; since my pew is so fortunately placed that I shall be able to do this without turning my head.

If you cannot come Tuesday, I will excuse myself to the lady on some pretext, for on no account on earth would I miss another meeting so happy as the last proved to be.

Most affectionately yours,

SARAH PALMER

The remainder of the letters were written in a more abandoned style, and always finished with loving kisses. The lovers made appointments to meet in many places, among them the graveyard and the coach-house, and were never, it seems, discovered until Mr William returned from Liverpool. I was in no way interested in their loves, nor did I censure them. It was but natural that a high-spirited woman like Mrs Palmer, forbidden to re-marry, though still young in heart and sturdy in body—having, moreover, reached an age when she need not fear the disgrace of bearing an illegitimate child—should solace herself with the embraces of a fine, upstanding, tenor-voiced Irishman, such as Cornelius Duffy, her junior by several years. And Duffy, to judge from the tradesmen's bills we found in his traps, and the poverty of his possessions, would have been glad to oblige so wealthy a protectress as Mrs Palmer, to the full extent of his powers.

At all events, I should have burned the letters, if I had had the sense, but my missus and her sister grabbed them and used them for the purposes of business. It's been said that I charged sixpence a head for the peep-show; but that's a lie. The way in which they came to be seen was that my missus got speaking of them, and one or two young chaps at the bar gammoned her to let them take a squint. 'Not until you've spent a shilling or two in grog, that you don't,' says my missus. They held her to that—I was out at the time, trying the ale at Bilston, for a man gets plaguey tired of his own brew, be it never so good—and she showed the letters. Then in comes another young chap, and another, and all take a look, those of them as can read; until at last I stagger home. Seeing what's afoot, I get properly vexed, and snatch the letters from the missus, but the harm's done; and though I hide them in the family Bible, which is the last place I'd expect her to look, and swear I've burned them in the grate, she don't believe me. A day or two later, I consult the *Song of Solomon*, where I'd put them and 'behold, they are vanished away, like unto a dream remembered on waking,' as Parson Inge would say sorrowfully when the choir-boys prigged his poultry or rabbits. I didn't know what my missus had done with the letters, and if I had asked, she'd only have said: 'What letters?—them as you burned in the grate, Mr C.?' There's no keeping women quiet in these matters, but I'm sorry that The Shoulder of Mutton earned a bad name in consequence of my carelessness. I've told you the whole tale to show you how it all came about.

The construction that I put on Mr William's case, since you ask me, is that he had a certain hold on his mother on account of being at first the only person who knew of her goings-on with Duffy. I believe that he was greatly distressed and shocked at the revelation. A lad can laugh at a matter of that sort if it happens in a stranger's house, and shrug shoulders if it happens at a neighbour's—but his own mother! I daresay you remember how Shakespeare's Prince Hamlet felt—not that I'm accusing old Mrs Palmer of being in any way concerned with her husband's death, though there are cruel tongues in this town have hinted even at that. Well, as I should guess—but, mind, it's no more than a guess!—Mr William reads his mother a lecture on her sins, and threatens to tell Mr Joseph about them if she doesn't send Duffy packing. She gives in at once. Mr William asks her for money to settle Duffy's score with me, and she gives it to him. Be sure, Duffy already had screwed a deal of money out of her, but Mr William surmises that he'll pretend to be waiting for a remittance from Belfast to settle the score—with the object of making more money yet. Which, I reckon, is exactly what Duffy has in mind; but when Mr William surprises him by paying the score, and then (as I suppose) threatens him with the thrashing of his life if he ever returns to Rugeley, Duffy takes the hint. Mr William was very handy with his dukes, as we say here.

Months later, Mrs Palmer writes to Duffy at Liverpool to say that the coast is clear, because her son William has gone to Haywood and nobody else is in the know. She invites him back to The Shoulder of Mutton. He comes for three weeks or so, and those letters prove that she continued on the same course as before, only with greater heat. It seems she had lost all her modesty, and there are phrases in the last letters which would cause a pedlar to drop his pack with surprise. Then came news that Mr William had broken his apprenticeship, and that George and Walter had ridden off to Walsall to fetch him back. That must have put Mrs Palmer in great fear. She sends Littler with a sealed letter to Mr Duffy, containing money and warning him (as I reckon) to clear out at once for both their sakes, and leave no vestige behind— not even sending his boxes by carrier to any place, where they might be traced. All I can say for sure, is: she tells Littler that the letter contains money for Mr Duffy, who has undertaken to send her some fine linen sheets from Belfast. I reckon she'll have sent a fifty-pound note to make it worth Duffy's while to humour her. My missus remembers Littler coming in with the letter, and Duffy going upstairs to fetch something from his box—maybe a watch and chain she's given him.

Well, Mr William returns and hears about Duffy from me; the news is a great surprise to him and though, as I say, pretending to be unconcerned, he seems to have used it to his good advantage. His mother could not now reproach him for having continued in his youthful attachment to Jane Widnall (whom he wished one day to marry), when she had been making a fool of herself with a chap like Duffy—a married man, by the bye—after her promise to William to have done with such frolics for ever.

I don't mean to say that Mr William would have threatened his mother: 'If you will not plead my case with Joseph, I will expose you to him!' That he would not have done, for he loved his mother, with all her faults. But he may well have said: 'Mother, I forgive you, as I trust that you will also forgive me.' At all events, she did plead with Mr Joseph and, I am told—but this is only hearsay—offered to tell his wealthy wife certain things very discreditable to him unless he forgave Mr William. For it was known that Mr Joseph still paid five shillings a week for a bastard daughter of his, whom he fathered on a nailer's daughter, by name Alice Plummery, over at Darlaston; and other tales are told of him, besides.

So Mr William is forgiven, and Mrs Palmer is forgiven, and Mr Joseph relents, which goes to show what a Christian spirit the knowledge that we are all sinners together in the eyes of God can awaken! However, Dr Tylecote would not take William back as his apprentice, because of the scandal that he caused in Haywood, and the deceptions he practised. This resolve greatly incommoded Mr William, who wished to renew his studies and make his way in life by industry. He was now so disgusted by the news of Jane's elopement with Peter Smirke that he swore never to trust a female again, and once cried out in my hearing that if they had gone away to any nearer place of refuge from his wrath than Botany Bay, he'd have followed them with a gelding-knife. And I think that this talk of a gelding-knife, and his offer to fight his brothers, and Duffy, shows well enough that Mr William was the violent sort when aroused, not the cold, crafty poisoner, which he is now falsely represented as being. To be sure, he poured acid on Smirke's clothes, but Smirke was such a little wisp of a man, and so unhealthy- looking, that William could hardly in honour have gone to fisticuffs with him.

Well, as the saying goes, there's always a way out while there's brass in the purse.

Dr Tylecote had no desire to hinder Mr William's advancement in life; but he made a great deal of trouble before finally consenting to get him admitted as a walking pupil into the Stafford Infirmary at the end of his term, and write him a certificate of good conduct.

It may well be, I can't say, that money changed hands; for pretty soon Dr Tylecote was seen driving on his rounds in a very handsome new gig, which until then he could not afford. He's a good surgeon, is Dr Tylecote, and a kindly man into the bargain.

The problem of Mrs Palmer's loneliness was not yet resolved, of course, but resolved it was later. I daresay before this trial is over, something will be said about Mr Jeremiah Smith to the learned judges. Captain Hatton of the Stafford Constabulary came down here around Christmas, with his colleague, Mr Bergen, and asked a great many pointed questions on a great many subjects. In the end, they seized those courting letters written by Mrs Palmer to Duffy. My missus pretended at first she knew nothing of them, but they threatened to take away the licence if she would not give them up; so my sister-in-law brought them in—which she had kept for a lark, she said, without my missus's knowledge, when ordered to burn them in the bread-oven.

But why should the letters be taken off? The reason, Sir, is plain enough. If old Mrs Palmer were called by the Defence lawyers to give evidence on behalf of her son, which she'd do with a good heart, then the Prosecution would out with those letters and get leave from the Court to put them in as 'evidence of character'. She couldn't deny 'em as her own, and even if she told the truth about Dr Palmer, proving his *alibi* (as it's called) on the particular hour when he is supposed to have poisoned Cook with strychnine pills, who would believe her? Those letters are plain evidence of schemings, lyings, and adultery. No, Sir, old Mrs Palmer won't appear in the witness box at the Old Bailey, of that you may be sure! If she did, not only would she do her son no particle of good, but the secrets of her heart would be published by the newspapers throughout the length and breadth of England.

CHAPTER IV

COLONEL BROOKES'S RESOLUTION

Abbot's Bromley, the country house belonging to Charles Dawson, Esq., a wealthy wholesale chemist from Stafford, is one of the handsomest and most comfortably furnished in the entire county, besides being wonderfully placed for scenery. It lies some seven miles from Stafford. Close by, rise the famous oaks of Bagot's Park, said to be the largest in England and perhaps in the world. Within walking distance you come upon Cannock Chase with its grassy slopes and great wealth of wild flowers, and Shoughborough Park with its banks of tall ferns. Abbot's Bromley also commands a view of Colnwich Nunnery, and of the swans reflected in the Trent's placid waters.

Charles Dawson, a robust and mellow-voiced widower in his sixties, has a fine eye for horseflesh, an epicure's taste in port, a connoisseur's knowledge of pictures, statuary, medals, *et alia*—and much to tell about the next stage in William Palmer's chequered career. The rest of this chapter will be related in his own words.

CHARLES DAWSON, ESQ., J.P.

Poor little Annie, how sadly we all miss her here! I did my best to cure her infatuation for that smooth-tongued young scamp—as much, I swear, as any loving guardian could have done—but she would not listen to me. She had set her heart on becoming Mrs Wm Palmer. I also quarrelled mortally on her account with my old friend Mr Thomas Weaver, the solicitor; nor have I since had reason to repent my attitude, the way things turned out. Far otherwise, indeed!

Let me begin at the beginning—though, I warn you, it's by no means a savoury story. One day, while I was still actively conducting my druggist's business at Stafford, a gentleman with trembling hands and a face as yellow as a guinea pushed open the shop door. I summed him up at once as an officer, attached to the East India Company's forces, who had ruined his constitution by persistent bouts of fever, over-exertion in the sweltering heat of the Bengalee Plains, and constant indulgence in the curree and chutney used by the native cooks to disguise the unpalatable taste of their goat's flesh and chicken. He asked whether we could furnish him with a certain foreign drug which one of the retail druggists of the town, to whom he had applied, ignorantly asserted did not exist. I attended to this customer personally, and produced a sample of the drug named; though counselling him in a friendly manner against its indiscriminate use. He then explained that it was recommended to him by an English physician in Bombay as strongly assisting the action of the liver. I told him, with what I hope was becoming modesty, that some druggists often know more about the action of drugs than do some physicians; and suggested another course of treatment as both less costly and more efficacious. A few days later the gentleman returned to thank me for my advice and, introducing himself as Colonel Brookes, late of the East India Company's service, asked me to do him the kindness of dining at his newly-purchased house in Front Street.

Colonel Brookes proved to be a reserved and gentle man, the veteran of many hard-fought campaigns against the Pindaries and Mahrattas. He was considerate, generous and wealthy, but unmar-

ried and, though a Staffordshire man, had been so long absent from
our shores as to have very few friends or acquaintances left in the
county. I took a liking to the Colonel and presently introduced him
to Dr Edward Knight, the most competent physician in Stafford,
and old Mr Wright, the brewer; and we were very glad of him to
make a fourth at short whist in our twice-weekly sessions, and thus
fill the place vacated by the late Captain Browne, R.N., recently
dead of an apoplexy. We found the Colonel to be a keen and
skilful player, with a fine sense of sportsmanship, and though he
never became our intimate in the rollicking style of poor Captain
Browne, we congratulated ourselves on our acquisition. He opened
his heart most fully to Dr Knight, with whom he discovered that he
had been a fellow-scholar at the Grammar School some fifty years
before, and who was married to a cousin of his. When Dr Knight
inquired privately one day: 'Colonel, may I be permitted to ask a
perhaps indiscreet question—why is it that you have never married?' he heaved a deep sigh and took fully a minute to answer.

Then he explained that he had been one of five brothers, of
whom he was now the sole survivor. 'They each and all died by
pistol shot,' he added.

'They were inveterate duellists, I suppose?' Dr Knight suggested. The Colonel shook his head mournfully.

'Ah, so they fell in battle?' pursued Dr Knight.

Again a shake of the head. 'We Brookes are a melancholy
breed, Sir,' the Colonel at last forced himself to say, 'and each of
my brothers in turn, when the unhappiness of living this life out
proved too great for him, blew out his own brains. That is the
reason why I have never married; I cannot wish either to perpet-
uate the family taint of suicide by begetting children, or to bring
disgrace on their mother. For though I have fought successfully
against the temptation of self-murder all my life, and though its
recurrence has become both less frequent and less violent with

advancing age, I can never be sure that it will not one day leap upon me like a lurking tiger. Indeed, only the other evening . . .

Emotion prevented the Colonel from completing the sentence, but Dr Knight made him promise that if he ever felt a return of the evil, he would promise on his honour to call without delay at the surgery, whatever the hour, for consolation and friendly support. Colonel Brookes pledged him his word as a soldier, and appeared to be much heartened by the old Doctor's evident sympathy.

I had, by the way, also introduced Colonel Brookes to the Mr Thomas Weaver of whom I spoke just now: a competent solicitor, then entrusted with my own business affairs, who seemed willing enough to undertake the Colonel's. Mr Weaver advised him to buy a property in the town consisting of seventeen acres of land, valued at three to four hundred pounds the acre; also of nine fine dwelling houses at the back of St Mary's Church, the leases of which brought in a handsome income, or at least handsome in comparison with the purchase price. The largest of these had lately become unoccupied at the expiration of its lease.

Now, though Colonel Brookes was a model citizen in all other respects, chronic ill-health had blunted neither his sexual appetite nor his virility; and when he engaged a widow and her daughter to be, respectively, his cook and parlourmaid, trouble soon ensued. Disdaining the widow, a buxom woman of forty who had already set her cap at him, he made surreptitious love to the seventeen-year-old daughter who (let me be frank) failed to repel his advances with the firmness that might have been expected of a decent girl. The mother, returning from the market one day, caught the pair together in the parlour: the Colonel seated on the sofa, the girl mounted astride his bony knees, while his aged hands greedily explored her young bosom. Rage and jealousy did their work: the widow not only gave immediate notice, but demanded fifty guineas from him as the price of silence.

Their precipitate departure from the house, and the blushes of the daughter when questioned on it, gave rise to so much talk among neighbours and trades-people that the Colonel was hard pressed to find domestic service; for Stafford is not a large town. He therefore privately consulted Mr Weaver, making a clean breast of the affair and begging for his help. Mr Weaver hummed and hawed for a while before he ventured: 'Well, Colonel Brookes, I understand that you are not a marrying man, but that neither are you a monk, and I daresay during your stay in India you found little difficulty in assuaging . . .'

'No difficulty at all,' agreed the Colonel. 'Among the heathen Hindoos these matters are easily and cheaply arranged. And I have always liked young bed-fellows; the younger the better, let me confess.'

Mr Weaver hummed and hawed again. Then he came out with: 'Well, Sir, I am not a pander by profession, but now that you consult me as a friend in trouble . . . well, there's pretty Mary Ann Thornton, who was in great distress last year. Captain John Browne, of the Royal Navy, her employer . . . in short, he died suddenly, leaving her in the family way. However, since the child did not long survive its birth, no claim for maintenance was made on his estate, and Miss Thornton is at present unemployed. She has the reputation of being a hard worker, and appears to prefer mature men to her own contemporaries. She can't be a day above eighteen years old, with fair hair, blue eyes, and a good figure. May I send her along to your residence?'

The affair was thus arranged, and Mary Ann Thornton came to the Front Street house, bringing with her as cook an elderly aunt, whom the Colonel agreed to pay pretty high wages. Miss Thornton herself doubled the parts of housekeeper and concubine. The Colonel became passionately addicted to her company.

Well, Sir, men are men, and we of the Whist Club turned a blind eye to these domesticities, as being none of our business;

especially after Dr Knight dropped a broad hint of why the Colonel shrank from marriage. 'And I am sure it is far better,' he said, 'that the Colonel should keep a healthy young mistress, than to be obliged to seek the doubtful solace of a bawdyhouse—his visits there would be not only dangerous, as exposing him to venereal infection, but also scandalous. We do not, I take it, wish to be known as persons who regularly associate with an old rake.'

We assented, though not without presentiment of some unhappy sequel. Miss Thornton soon came to realize the Colonel's increasing dependence on her services. She grew worldly and ambitious, and nothing would satisfy her save that 'he should make an honest woman of me,' as she put it, paradoxically enough. Yet he continued obdurate in his resolve to stay a bachelor, even when she announced her pregnancy. It has, by the bye, been said that a younger lover fathered the child; this is market gossip, though, and the Colonel at least believed himself responsible for her condition. I took the view that he could do worse than marry the girl, despite her gross ignorance and low birth. The former fault might have been remedied by private tuition; the latter would have been cancelled by the adoption of his name. He felt very tenderly towards her, that is certain, and made a solemn undertaking, in Mr Weaver's presence, not only to keep her in the style which she might have expected as a wife, but to remember her handsomely in his will. All her tears and pleadings, however, failed to shake his resolution not to marry. When he offered to arrange an abortion, if she so desired, she professed to be outraged, saying that this was crime both against the laws of England and against Nature. Until the very end of her confinement she cherished hopes for a change of heart in him, but all that he would do by way of placating her was to move from their somewhat cramped and public quarters in Front Street to the more commodious vacant house behind St Mary's Church, and furnish it regardless of expense. She suffered a difficult pregnancy, which made her behave in a very strange manner, casting the wildest threats at the Colonel. On one occasion (so he confided to Dr Knight) she snatched up a kitchen knife and chased him around the table. On another, when he went to his bedroom, shortly before dinner, he found her lying drunk on the floor, with an empty quartern bottle of gin tumbled beside her.

Nevertheless, the child, a girl, was born safe and sound. The Colonel felt lasting chagrin, since it had been to avoid the begetting of children that he had registered his vow; and Mary Ann Thornton, unappeasable resentment. Even if he now made her Mrs Brookes, that honour would come too late: the child was born illegitimate. She continued to drink heavily and, since the Colonel had guilty feelings in regard to her, tyrannized over him with impunity. The affair reached such a pitch that neither old Mr Wright, Dr Knight, nor myself dared call at his house for fear of witnessing disgraceful scenes. The blue-eyed belle was fast losing her looks, becoming thin and angular, with that blueish pallor which betrays a constant recourse to gin; and made no attempt to rule her excessively foul and vulgar tongue. She never ceased to blame him for 'whoring' her and, by his cruelty and neglect, driving her to the bottle.

The chief bone of contention between them now was the child, whom Miss (now Mrs) Thornton regarded with possessive greed, and on whom Colonel Brookes doted, for he loved the company of children. In better moods she encouraged his affection for little Annie, but when the gin was working in her, would roughly order him out of the nursery. 'This is my b—child,' she would scream. 'It could also have been yours, you toad, you turd, you Turk, if you had been the gentleman I first mistook you for! But you have cast a blight on the poor innocent's life by your refusal to lend her your name, and neither she nor I will ever forgive you. Now, go, go—out with you—before I tear your eyes from their sockets! And one word of protest—you b—you—and I'll dame you with these shears!'

She would then pick up the shears, or it might be a knife, or a cleaver, and my unhappy old friend would run for shelter to The Lamb and Flag. He even, on one occasion, took sanctuary in the vestry of St Mary's Church. Thus the scandal which Mr Weaver had hoped to avert, by his discreet pandering to the Colonel's weaknesses, grew a thousand times worse than if the unfortunate man had merely been known as a frequenter of bawdy-houses. He could, of course, have posted out of the county for his weekly pleasures; to Liverpool, for example, and little harm done. But now, when one of her ungovernable rages overcame her, she would follow him all the way to The Lamb and Flag—not fully clad neither, her hair in curling pins—where with her ramping, stamping, tearing and swearing, for all the world like a drunken Lifeguardsman, she would create a most horrible scene, finally catching him by the collar and hauling him off home. 'Poor gentleman,' some of the rough fellows who frequented The Lamb used to say naïvely, 'he might as well have been married!'

After long deliberation, we of the Whist Club decided not to exclude him from the twice- weekly sessions at my house, and thus add a last, and perhaps fatal, drop to his cup of bitterness; nor did the woman ever venture to pursue him there. I have since heard it said that these two evenings were sacred to amatory revenge; she had a lover, a bricklayer's labourer, whom she entertained in style during her protector's absence.

So it went on for some years, until the reign of the late King William—the year 1834, to be precise—when one morning Colonel Brookes was found dead in the parlour of his house, clad in dressing-gown, slippers and cap, with a bullet through his heart and a still smoking pistol lying on the carpet beside him. The old cook made the discovery. She had heard her niece's voice raised in a shriek of anger, which was followed by a cry of despair from the Colonel, and then a pistol shot. A moment later Mrs Thornton quitted the parlour in hysterics and, rushing upstairs, slammed and locked the bedroom door behind her. The cook at once hastened to summon Mr Weaver, who in turn sent post haste for Dr Knight; and the two of them—so soon as Dr Knight had satisfied himself that life was extinct—mounted the stairs to the bedroom and demanded that Mrs Thornton should come out and give them an account of this melancholy event. When she made no reply, Mr Weaver entered the room by way of the window—a ladder left by the painters affording him convenient and easy access to it. He snatched the gin bottle from Mrs Thornton's hands, and unlocked the door to admit Dr Knight.

Fortified by the spirits, Mrs Thornton agreed that she had had words with the Colonel, whom she reproached for his constant and unnatural demands on her services between the sheets; but swore, by all that she held most holy, that the cry overheard by her aunt was one of indignation, when he drew a pistol from beneath a sofa squab, pointed it at his heart, and warned her very coolly: 'If you utter one more word, I shall kill myself.' Then, inadvertently (they were told), she had uttered another word, or words, namely: 'For God's sake, don't! Think of the child!'—whereupon the Colonel pressed the trigger.

Dr Knight and Mr Weaver went pensively downstairs again. Unable to decide on the truth of the story, they came to ask my advice as a Justice of the Peace. In the absence of any witnesses other than the aunt, who was hard of hearing, and Mrs Thornton herself, the truth could never be exactly known; but Dr Knight pleaded that the child's future must, at any rate, be safeguarded. Little Annie was already proverbial in the neighbourhood for her simplicity, goodness of heart and gentle manners, and had become a leading scholar at St Mary's Sunday School. 'It is bad enough to be born out of wedlock,' said Dr Knight, 'it is worse to be the daughter of a suicide. And what girl in Christendom, however saintly, could face the world in the knowledge that her mother had committed murder?'

'How does the will run, my dear Sir,' I asked Mr Weaver, whom I still esteemed highly at that time.

'Well,' said he, 'all I know is that you two gentlemen are named as his executors. The Colonel drew the will himself last July—against my advice, because it's no easy matter for a layman to draw a sound will unassisted by a solicitor—and would not show me the document, but deposited it, sealed, in my safe.'

'Can you explain the hugger-mugger?' I asked.

'Well, Sir,' he answered, 'it may be that Mary Ann Thornton figures in the will, which made him ashamed to discuss her case with me. She has occasioned him much unhappiness of late years, and because I recommended her to him as his servant . . .'

'As his concubine, Sir,' I reminded him.

'For Heaven's sake, let me be! You'll be saying next that I charged a stud-groom's fee for the transaction.'

'You have earned it, at all events,' said I bitterly.

Mr Weaver then accompanied us to his office and unsealed the will in our presence. The Colonel had divided his property into two parts: the nine houses were to go to Mary Ann Thornton absolutely; a capital of some twenty thousand pounds, mainly in Sicca rupees, and the rents of the farm land (which might not be sold in her lifetime), were to be divided between Mary Ann Thornton and his daughter Ann Brookes, in the proportion of three parts to two. Dr Knight and I were also appointed guardians of the child, and charged to pay her only the interests of her fortune until she came of age or married, when she might receive the whole of it. The Colonel, however, insisted that the child must be taken from her mother, a confirmed drunkard, and brought up genteely.

We professed ourselves happy enough to comply with the testator's wishes, but Mr Weaver sighed as he said: 'This will is flawed. I fear it will be disputed.'

Disputed it was, by Mrs Thornton, who went to another solicitor for advice. While not objecting to the legacies, she was outraged by the Colonel's animadversions on her character and his attempt to rob her of Annie, whom he claimed as his own daughter; and vowed that she would fight the case in every court, low or high.

Meanwhile, she was in danger of the rope; for all Stafford knew her character and openly accused her of murder. A coroner's inquest could not be avoided. Dr Knight managed the business very well; he somehow contrived to bring Mrs Thornton to the inquest cold sober and decently garbed in widow's weeds. He also coached her into telling the same story she had told before, though omitting the scandalous part and altering the account of her quarrel with the Colonel. When she had done, Dr Knight himself gave evidence of the Colonel's confidences made him some years previously, as to why he would never marry, and mentioned the Colonel's promise to call upon him at the surgery if ever he felt the suicidal mania threatening him again.

The Coroner then asked: 'Dr Knight—pray remember that you are on your oath—did the Colonel in effect call upon you at the surgery, and did he warn you of the recurrence of his mania?'

Dr Knight replied: 'The answer, Mr Coroner, is both yes and no. He came, as I now believe, ready to make such a statement, and if he had done so, I should have taken immediate steps to place him under restraint, But he contented himself with hints, which I was too obtuse to grasp. He came calling at about five o'clock, and talked somewhat disjointedly; a condition characteristic of the malarial fever from which he suffered at regular intervals. I at once urged him to take the usual stiff dose of quinine. He promised that he would do so upon his return home; but before rising to go, he asked me: "Dr Knight, are you a Freemason?" I smiled as I answered: "If you were yourself a Mason, and if I were also a Mason, you would have already known me as your fellow by my manner of shaking hands on our first acquaintance; but if you are not a Mason, as I suppose must be the case, how can you expect me to reveal myself as one, if indeed I am? You must surely be aware that membership of the Order is a close secret." '

Colonel Brookes let that comment pass, and launched into a story. "I have just had very sad news from Liverpool," he said. "It concerns a friend of mine, the Captain of a fine East India-man, which makes a regular run between Liverpool and Bombay. I dined at his table every day, both when I returned to India in 1817, as a major, after a six months' convalescence; and again on my last voyage, when I sold out and came home to die among my own people. This Captain was a Freemason, and as conscientious in his loyalty, Dr Knight, as you seem to be. Well, one day he was aggrieved to find that his first mate had confided to a lady passenger some disquieting news about the soundness of the ship's rigging, and added: 'God knows, Madam, what our fate will be if we chance to run into foul weather off the Cape!' The lady's husband, a Madras merchant, ran in alarm to the Captain's cabin and demanded to know the facts of the matter. My friend reassured him that the rigging was sound—though, in truth, he had been forced by the owners to sail, on penalty of losing his command, despite his protests that 'the yards were rotten as damp straw.' The merchant having gone, my friend charged the first mate with spreading dangerous alarm and betraying nautical secrets. To which the mate replied, rudely laughing in his face: 'And I suppose, Captain, that you yourself have never betrayed any secret which you solemnly swore "to heal, conceal and never reveal"?'

"'At this reference to the Masonic oath, my friend looked up sharply, whereupon the first mate quoted to him certain prime Masonic secrets entrusted only to adepts of a high degree."'

The Coroner somewhat testily asked, at this point, whether the evidence was relevant.

'Pray have patience,' answered Dr Knight, 'and you will see that it is not only relevant, but crucial.' He proceeded: 'The Colonel then told me that his friend the Captain, knowing the first mate not to be a Mason, was both amazed and alarmed; but it came out that he had himself betrayed these secrets one night in a feverish delirium, when the first mate came to him for orders. He had the impudent officer put in irons, then returned to his cabin, and was found soon afterwards shot through the heart-clad in dressing-gown, slippers, and cap . . . This, Sir, was the end of the Colonel's story. He took his leave of me, and from the circumstance that his corpse was found the next morning similarly clad and similarly shot, my opinion is that you may, without the least compunction, bring in a verdict of suicide. If anyone is to blame it must be myself, for not insisting that he should take the quinine then and there in my surgery.'

The Coroner thanked Dr Knight for his frankness, confessed himself satisfied with the evidence, and 'suicide while under the delusive influence of a malarial fever' was the verdict returned by the jury. When I afterwards complimented Dr Knight on the fertility of his invention, he made no reply.

Mrs Thornton, as I have said, disputed the will in so far as it denied her a mother's natural rights. It was also disputed by a Mr Shallcross, who represented himself as Colonel Brookes's heir-at-law; he pleaded that the Colonel had not been of sound mind for the past three years, as large bequests to the drunken and sordid woman who made his existence a living hell sufficiently proved. The Court found that the Colonel had been of sound mind, save during his occasional bouts of malaria, and therefore had the right to bestow his property at pleasure. He had, however, wrongly described the child as 'Ann Brookes', and wrongly assumed the right to appoint guardians for her. Nevertheless, Mr Shallcross's evidence, and the testator's own considered opinion, made it apparent that the child stood in want of suitable protectors. The Court also ruled that the testamentary language was not sufficiently forcible to convey the estate to mother and child absolutely, but gave them only a life interest in it. At their decease, it must become the property of Mr Shallcross, or whoever else might then be the late Colonel's heir-at-law. The estate was therefore thrown into Chancery, the costs of the trial deducted from its value, and Ann Thornton made a ward in Chancery. The Court appointed Dr Knight and me her guardians, at the charge of the estate; and the Colonel's wishes were, in effect, respected—except that the value of the estate, after the lawyers had been satisfied, was whittled to less than a half, and that Annie's fortune now consisted solely of a two-hundred-pound life-annuity, purchased for her by us.

Well, as little Annie Thornton's guardian, and a married man, it was only natural that I should take her to live in my house, where I put her under the same governess as my own children. And let me tell you, Sir, that I never had a moment's cause to regret my action. That child was a paragon of virtue, and had not an enemy in the whole world. Though painfully sensible of her false position as an illegitimate child—even if one of independent means—and as being banished for her own good from the society of an ill-bred and dissipated mother, yet she trusted in the kindness of God; showing in all her looks and actions the profoundest gratitude to Dr Knight and myself for the care bestowed on her. We had no scruple in referring to her as 'Annie Brookes', and thus keeping alive in her mind the nobler part of her natural inheritance.

Soon after Annie's arrival in our house, my wife had the misfortune to be struck down by an incurable disease. Though still only a little girl, Annie insisted on acting as sick-nurse, and her intrinsic kindness of heart and constant vigilance by night as well as by day were something more than surprising. My poor wife's sufferings terminated six weeks later. Annie wept bitterly; and after a decent interval I married again, for the sake of my children. What I had done to deserve further chastening by Heaven, Heaven alone can say; but as the result of a fall on a slippery road, my new wife miscarried in the first year of our marriage; and the complications of this accident were also mortal in their effect. Once again Annie played the ministering angel, and was constantly at the sufferer's sick-bed; not only to administer medicine and perform the often distasteful duties of a nurse, but to give her spiritual consolation in the dark hours of the night when sleep was far, and pain unabating. Indeed, Annie combined three noble professions in those sad months: those of doctor, nurse and clergyman. She was reduced to a mere shadow, when my wife's death at last released her from these self-imposed tasks.

I did my best to restore Annie's spirits, as soon as the period of mourning ended, by arranging treats and excursions for the family; and little by little her natural gaiety returned. But Dr Knight and I agreed that the time had come when she must go to a finishing school; and we unluckily decided upon one recommended by his cousin, Dr Tylecote of Haywood—the medical man whose then assistant was none other than William Palmer.

Miss Bond's school enjoyed, and still enjoys, a high reputation for good schooling in all ladylike accomplishments—Annie learned to play the pianoforte there in a quite masterly way—and the girls were, it need hardly be added, under continuous surveillance. It happened once or twice, however, that Palmer, as Dr Tylecote's assistant, was sent to visit the school, when a girl had been overcome by a colic, or cut her finger, or suffered some other slight accident which lay within Palmer's limited powers to alleviate. On one occasion, the sufferer was Annie, and it appears that he treated a strained ligament in her ankle with such gentleness that she fell head over heels in love with him—though he had no suspicion of her feelings, being busily engaged at the time in an intrigue with a red-headed girl from Liverpool, the step-daughter of a local gardener. Moreover, Annie happened to be very advantageously seated in church, for her pew commanded Palmer's profile at a short distance, straight across the aisle.

My quarrel with Mr Weaver grew out of this unfortunate affair. His elder daughter had also been sent to Miss Bond's finishing school, and one day, in the course of general conversation, she chanced to reveal Annie's secret attachment to Palmer, for which the girls were teasing her unmercifully. Weaver mentally noted the fact and, when Palmer was about to inherit his seven thousand pounds, and asked him to arrange for their conveyance, brought it out. 'Do you want a wife, Mr Palmer?' asks he. 'For if you do, I can introduce you to a very pretty young girl with a snug little fortune. She's a ward in Chancery. Colonel Brookes, her father, left her eight thousand pounds, which gives her a secure income of two hundred pounds a year.'

'There is nothing I should like better,' says Palmer, 'but can you be sure that this beauty would look twice at me?'

'Indeed, I can,' Mr Weaver answers. 'She has fallen deep in love with you already. Annie Brookes is eighteen years old, and highly accomplished.'

Yet Mr Weaver was fully acquainted with the circumstances of Palmer's leaving his appointment in Liverpool, and of his ill-behaviour at Dr Tylecote's; and doubtless also of his profligate life while walking the wards in Stafford Infirmary. To encourage such a depraved young man to marry my Annie for her money was nothing short of criminal; and so I told him to his face.

CHAPTER V

STAFFORD INFIRMARY

Stafford, an ancient borough and market-town celebrated for its red bricks, its shoes, and its salt works, contains no less than thirteen thousand inhabitants; of whom at least three thousand (or so we were assured by the landlord of The Junction Hotel) are usually sober—reckoning children among that number. As seen from the railway, the town appears, at this season, like an island lying in a yellowish lake. The farmers here flood their meadows to manure them, and the aptly named River Sow is therefore divided into a dozen or more streams, which career crazily along with their discoloured waters, in haste to hurl themselves into the swollen Trent below.

All the new houses are built in brick so red that it hurts the eyes—as though one were staring at the fire—and capped by ugly slate roofs. Yet cross the long wooden bridge with its white railings, near the Railway Station, turn around by a flour mill and follow the lane until you reach Greengate Street; and there you will find a charming row of old half-timbered houses on either side of the street, some large, some small, but all with heavy carved gables, and warm-coloured plaster set between the dark-brown timbers.

One house close to the Market Place is well worth a visit. Its great forehead hangs half-way over the pavement, with large bay windows like four-poster bedsteads let into the wall. The pale oaken beams standing out from the plaster work are arranged in a variety of graceful lines that recall the tattooing on the body of a South Sea Islander. Messrs Jenkinson & Co., linen- drapers, occupy the premises, and their shopwindow is decked out with every article 'that fashion can require or beauty desire'—as an advertisement informs us. Festoons of pink and blue ribbon elegantly droop from side to side, and bright yellow driving gloves are arranged in straight lines across the panes. At the entrance door, a bundle of coloured silk parasols and another of sober black umbrellas are stacked like so many halberds in an armoury; and through the bay windows above you can see piles of blue hat boxes, tall slabs of linen cloth, and portly canvas blocks of unpacked goods, bound around with bands of iron, as if to keep their figures in. Mr Jenkinson, the proprietor, will be introduced to our readers presently.

Meanwhile, here is the Town Hall, towering up from the Market Place, with a clock stuck against it like a target. It can hardly be called a pretty building, having no more ornament than a blank sheet of writing paper, and the windows are mere holes in the wall; but at least it is built of Portland stone, not red brick. On either side of it stand half-timbered houses, with cock-hat roofs and their fronts slashed like a soldier's uniform, which lend its pallid stucco walls a certain aristocratic dignity, as it might be an austere and gloomy Tsar surrounded by his merry Muscovite bodyguard. Then, for Tsarina, you have the tall, white, square tower of St Mary's, a church founded by King John, and famous for its memorial to Stafford's most celebrated son—Izaak Walton, the Angler. Passing the Grammar School, an ancient foundation enlarged by King Edward VI, you will observe a dozen or more inns; an elegant bowling green; and the Stafford Infirmary, about whose architecture the less said the better, but which has now acquired a certain historic lustre from the circumstance of William Palmer's having, for a period, walked its wards.

There are many better—and we fear, many even worse—hospitals for the indigent sick than dais Infirmary. Money for its support being grudgingly voted, because the expense falls on the rates, the accommodation is wholly inadequate, and amenities are very few. Most patients regard their transference here as tantamount to a sentence of death, though the medical staff, we understand, show a praiseworthy devotion to their duties, and though one or two at least of the younger surgeons are aware not only of the anaesthetic use of ether in operations, but also of the principle of antisepsis as recently discovered by Mr Joseph Lister, house-surgeon at University College Hospital. For in practice, ether, as an unnecessary expense, is never administered; and antisepsis is difficult to achieve in an out-of-date building where hospital gangrene and pyaemia must remain a constant scourge, and where the shortage of nurses, except the drunken and incapable, rules out even elementary cleanliness in the wards.

Hospital reform, however, is not the subject of our study; let it suffice to say that a walking pupil in Stafford Infirmary, or any other similar institution—if he is not to become the victim of a nervous disorder—must habituate himself to distressing sights, noisome smells, and such a scene of human misery, despair, and degradation, that his susceptibilities will soon become blunted. To relieve his mind of these horrors he may well be tempted to abandon shame in the wildest larks and most outrageous debaucheries.

William Palmer went to the Infirmary about Midsummer, 1845; but did not remain there for more than a few weeks.

Mr Edward Jenkinson, linen-draper, a small, stout, irascible man with a huge strawberry mark spread across his face and very disagreeable features, was holding forth about William Palmer in The Dolphin Inn the other day, shortly before the trial at the Old Bailey began. Mr Jenkinson drinks neat brandy only, and can afford this luxury; for he is well-to-do and has no family to support, his physical disadvantages having decided all the women to whom he ever offered marriage that they would be far better off in any other circumstances whatsoever. The contempt with which some of them accompanied their refusal has turned him into a misogynist, though one unable to conceal the jealousy he feels for men to whom women freely yield their favours, even uninvited.

MR EDWARD JENKINSON

It would never have come to this, I swear, had my fellow-jurymen listened to me eleven years ago, when the first of Palmer's vile crimes came to light. He was then a walking pupil at the Infirmary, and had not yet inherited his fortune. But he talked freely about how he proposed to spend the money, and the number of foolish girls whom he persuaded that they had been born expressly for the purpose of assisting him to do so must have run into double figures. Palmer had the power of deceiving himself as a means of deceiving his victims: he proposed marriage to each in turn, and convinced himself that she was the most desirable woman alive. If the girl anticipated marriage by granting him what he asked, Palmer at once cooled towards her, as too giddy to be his wife; if, on the other hand, she refused, he thought her cold, and abandoned the chase. It is said that he got two girls in the family way during his apprenticeship with Dr Tylecote at Haywood, and three more in Stafford; but that is mere gossip from the public houses.

One day I was summoned to attend a coroner's inquest on the death of a shoemaker named Abley, and my fellow-jurymen elected me their foreman as perhaps the most talented . . . well, for whatever reason it may have been, they elected me. The evidence was provided by Mrs Bates, the landlady. It appears that Palmer invited Abley to take a drink at The Lamb and Flag—it was a cold, raw day—and asked him what he fancied.

'A pint of ale, if you don't mind,' says Abley.

'Come, come,' says Palmer, 'don't stint yourself! A pint of ale falls chill on the stomach in weather like this. I'll treat you to something better. What about a sip of brandy?'

Abley says that he's no great shakes at brandy drinking, but at this a young Rugeley fellow named Timmis, who had been at Bonney's school with Palmer, pipes up: 'Abley's damnably modest. He's one of the grandest brandy-drinkers in the county. Why, I've seen him toss down three tumblers full, one after 'tother, and not turn a hair.'

'I'll lay you three to one in half-sovereigns,' says Palmer, 'that he can't down more than one.'

Timmis then takes Abley aside and says: 'Did you hear that? Palmer's word is his bond, and if you drink a couple of tumblers it will be worth thirty shillings to yours truly.'

'What you win is of no interest at all to me,' says Abley. 'Nor am I any sort of a drinking man. All I want is my pint of ale, and if Mr Palmer grudges me that, I'll pay it myself.'

'Come, don't be unreasonable,' says Timmis. 'What are two tumblers to a bold fellow like you? Drink them down quick, as if they were medicine, which indeed they are, and I'll give you one half-sovereign of my three.'

'Agreed for fifteen shillings,' says Abley, 'which must be handed in cash to Mrs Bates, who'll pay me when I've sobered up.'

'Very good,' says Timmis, and entrusts the money to Mrs Bates.

Abley then accepts his first tumblerful of brandy—right French brandy from Cognac—and drains it, like a soldier of the Line. While all eyes watch him do so, Palmer waits at the bar, with his hand on the second tumbler, which he presently takes over to Abley. 'You conquered that manfully,' he said, 'but I wager this will make you choke.'

Abley downed his second dose, without heel-taps, neither. The men in the tap-room laughed and joked a bit at Palmer's expense.

'Never mind,' Abley says, 'I'd do the same again for fifteen shillings, these hard times.'

Presently he turns greenish and, says he: 'I'll go into the stable. I'll be cleared out just now and ready for my pint at last.'

'Good luck to you,' says Palmer. He pays his debt to Timmis, and then launches into a long, tantalizing story, a cruelly funny one too, so the fellows said, about the straits to which a ship's crew were reduced for lack of women on a long voyage of exploration in the Arctic Seas. Never you mind the details, but it kept the house in a roar, being very comically told. Timmis capped it, and then another customer chimed in—the landlady meanwhile hiding her blushes behind a row of bottles. Everyone had forgotten Abley, and it was nigh an hour later that Palmer paid his score and sauntered off. Then someone remarks: 'Abley's not come back for his pint, has he? I wonder how he's faring?'

A search was made, and they found Abley stretched on a heap of sacks in the stable, groaning, with both hands pressed against his stomach. Two men carried him home and put him to bed between warmed sheets; but he died the same night.

At the inquest we jurymen viewed the body, and some of us were satisfied that since Abley had been a thin, pale man in indifferent health, to drink two full tumblers of brandy on an empty stomach and then lie in the cold stable for an hour or longer was a fatal act—even though the intention cannot have been suicidal.

But I smelt a fishy smell to the business, and when the other parties wished to bring in a verdict of death from natural causes, I said: 'Gentlemen, that don't satisfy me, and I'll tell you why. Stafford is a small town, and a good deal of talk goes on in one tavern and another, some of it false, some of it true, some of it half and half. Well, I was at The Junction last night, and heard talk there about this Palmer, who laid with his old school-fellow that Abley couldn't down more than a single tumblerful. It seems that

Mrs Abley, a buxom young wench, has been an out-patient at the Infirmary—she goes to be dressed for a severe scald on her thigh, caused by a jet of boiling water from a kettle. Palmer was directed to dress the wound in this intimate part of her frame, and from the confidences which she made to a neighbour's wife it seems that a mutual attraction ensued. However, Mrs Abley is not entirely lost to shame. She is reported to have said: "Mr Palmer, though I admit to a sincere affection for you, I am not forgetful of my marriage vows, and while Abley lives I shall be faithful to him."

"'Why, that is a pity,' says Palmer, "for you are the very woman I should otherwise have asked to be my wife and help me spend my inheritance wisely and well. But there's no help to it, I see. If you take marriage that seriously, we must both pine apart."

"'I have no complaints against Abley,' says she. "He's a good husband in his way, industrious and thrifty, though not everything I could wish as a lover—no, not by any means. And his stomach never having been good, I have to cosset him with baby-food, a diet which does nothing to whet his desire for me. If only I could give him shell-fish, and great bloody beef-steaks, and roasted love-apples! Yet I have never seen him drunk in my life, nor even the worse for liquor, and there are all too few married women in Stafford who can say that of their husbands.'"

A juryman asked me: 'You think, then, Mr Jenkinson, that the business at The Lamb and Flag had been rigged—that it was Palmer's intention, with the connivance of Timmis, to discredit Abley in the eyes of his wife by sending him home reeling drunk? Or was it perhaps so to stupefy him with drink that he wouldn't come back at all that night, but leave room in his bed for another?'

'No,' I answered, 'my suspicion is an even graver one. I think that he planned to murder the poor shoemaker!'

'You are suggesting, Mr Jenkinson,' says the juryman, 'that, having diagnosed a weak heart, he counted on the action of the brandy to kill him, and deliberately embarked on that smutty story of the sailors and the polar bear to distract attention from Abley's fate?'

'It is my decided opinion that he did not count on the action of the brandy alone,' I said. 'I keep my ears open, and one of my carters happens also to be an out-patient at the Infirmary. Yesterday I asked him: "Bowles, what do they say up yonder about young Palmer, the student?" And Bowles told me that Palmer is said to be the devil of a rake with flighty young women; and that a new order posted on the notice-board is aimed at him. "What order?" I asked Bowles. "Why, Master," he answers, "I mean the order which forbids the Infirmary pupils to have anything further to do with the dispensing of medicines. There's a shortage of hands at the Infirmary, you see, Master; and no paid officer employed at the dispensary; in consequence, any pupil can go there and mix what drugs he pleases, pretending that he's been ordered to do so by a medical officer. Well, it's buzzed about that Palmer has been in the habit of conducting experiments of his own in the dispensary—'for a lark,' he says. He's been putting drugs in fellow-pupils' drinks to make them vomit, or piss green, or fall into drowsy fits from which they awaken only with hardship and aching heads."'

I continued: 'This is all hearsay evidence, gentlemen, I admit. But there's no smoke without a fire, and I therefore propose we demand an autopsy, and thus satisfy ourselves that no "lark" was perpetrated on the unfortunate man by Palmer. On the evidence, he had the opportunity to slip something into the second tumbler of brandy, while all eyes were watching Abley's consumption of the first.'

My fellow-jurors objected to this as an unproved surmise, and argued that on my own showing Palmer did not love Mrs Abley with sufficient passion to plan her husband's death; and that if he had perhaps dosed the brandy, this was not done with intent to kill. The verdict would, at the worst, be 'manslaughter'. 'He's well loved at the Infirmary,' one of them said, 'and I should not, myself, care to set so black a mark upon a young fellow's name.'

'The law's the law,' I insisted, 'and we have been charged to decide upon the cause of Abley's death without fear or favour.'

In the end, I persuaded them to demand an autopsy, despite the inconvenience that the delay must cause us all; and Dr Masfen from the Infirmary duly performed his disagreeable and thankless task. But the vomit in the stable had meanwhile been swabbed up, and Abley's stomach was empty, except for some cordial draught which he had been given by his wife when at the point of death; thus it was too late to secure a sample of the fatal draught for analysis. Moreover, the stomach showed signs of chronic inflammation; and Dr Masfen pronounced that death seemed due to natural causes. This was accordingly our verdict, though I didn't like it, by no means.

A fortnight later—not so soon as to make it seem that the warning had any connexion with the inquest, but soon enough—Palmer was privately advised to leave the Infirmary. In my opinion, the medical officers feared that if they took disciplinary action, Palmer would charge them with defamation of character; and their own negligence in the matter of allowing pupils to dispense dangerous drugs might come to light. It may even be that if some medical gentleman unconnected with the Infirmary had performed the autopsy, he would have found more than Dr Masfen troubled to find. For if the state of Abley's stomach had betrayed the action of poison, would the Infirmary staff have escaped censure? Tell me that!

Idle talk, I say, idle talk! All I know for sure is that Palmer let his acquaintance with Mrs Abley lapse. He suspected, I have no doubt, that its renewal would be dangerous.

CHAPTER VI

AT BART'S

The following account was furnished by a young surgeon, late of St Bartholomew's Hospital, now settled in Harley Street, and a decided luminary of his profession. He does not, however, wish his name to be mentioned in connexion with the Palmer case—not, at least, until his friend's character (as he hopes and trusts) shall have been vindicated in all respects. Disclosure would embarrass him professionally.

"A SURGEON"

One can judge a man only as one knows him. History has made the name of Nero odious, yet it is admitted by the historian Suetonius that, after his suicide, loyal friends still laid flowers on the imperial tomb, and continued to play certain musical pieces which he had composed, though no longer forcibly obliged to applaud them—indeed, quite the reverse! Tears of sincere sorrow were likewise, we read elsewhere, shed at the tombs of such monsters as Genghis Khan, William Rufus of England, and Lucrezia Borgia the Italian poisoner. Not that I should have shed any myself; but allow me to depose—and I would sign my name to this but for the delicacy of my present situation as a consulting surgeon to Royalty—that I found William Palmer a thundering good fellow and a deuced good friend.

He came to London in the latter part of the year 1845 and, like myself, engaged the knowledgeable Dr Stegall as his 'grinder' to help him pass the medical examination and secure his diploma. He offered Dr Stegall a fee of fifty guineas should he succeed, to which, I understand, his widowed mother promised to add the sum of ten guineas; and his friend, Mr Jeremiah Smith, a solicitor of Rugeley, a further ten.

For some days after his arrival in London, Will Palmer lodged at Dr Stegall's house; but the course of behaviour expected of him there did not suit his book at all. It was 'early to bed, early to rise', constant study and no distractive pleasures—unless he counted it a pleasure, of an evening, to participate in a family game of cards at a half-penny a hundred points, or in a dramatic reading of Mr Dickens's *Barnaby Rudge*, each person representing one character in the novel, while Dr Stegall undertook the narrative. Will Palmer had just come into a fortune—some seven thousand pounds, I believe—and greatly enjoyed the sense of liberty that being flush gave him.

Once Dr Stegall gently rebuked Will for having bought, in the space of four days, a gold-headed malacca cane, a jewelled snuffbox, and a French watch of exquisite workmanship. 'Money, Dr Stegall,' replied Will, 'is meant to be spent. It's the mean habit of hoarding that dries up trade, cripples industry, and bloats the funds of the rogueish assurance societies. What's more, these trinkets, as you call them, are solid investments which will add to my consequence when I put up a brass plate as a qualified surgeon.'

But that same afternoon he honoured me with a confidence during our walk in the Hospital grounds. 'Charley,' he said, 'if you knew how my inheritance has been earned, you would hardly blame me for the small value I give it.'

'I'm ready to listen,' I replied.

'Then here goes,' he said. 'My father ground the faces of his

workmen in a shameful manner. Moreover, the principal with
which he started his sawyer's business was got together by very
dubious means. If I now give you the story, it's only to show you
how wholeheartedly I detest my origins, and how determined I
am to start afresh.'

'You want to be your own ancestor?' I suggested. 'As one of the
ancient Romans, a man of vulgar birth, very happily put it.'

'That's the nail hit on the head, Charley,' he agreed. 'Well,
to tell of my maternal grandfather: he began as a gunner in the
Royal Navy and, pray spare me your blushes if I confess that he
acted as bully to one Peggy Taff who kept a brothel in a back street
at Derby. Peggy drove a pretty good trade, and was continually
sending my grandfather to the bank with her earnings. The old
scoundrel took the precaution to enter them all in his own name,
not hers, and at last, when she reproached him with showing too
much fondness for one of the women of the house, a certain Mrs
Sharrod, he knocked her about severely and drew the whole of her
fortune from the bank, some five hundred and sixty pounds. My
grandfather and Mrs Sharrod, who later became my grandmother,
migrated to Litchfield, where they rented a small farm and lived
like respectable people. My mother, their daughter, used to visit
Litchfield Market, twice a week, selling poultry, butter and eggs.
They did well enough, and presently settled in King's Bromley,
near Stafford, where Field-Marshal the Marquess of Anglesey has
his seat: that glorious old soldier who fought at Corunna, lost a leg
at Waterloo, and afterwards became Lord Lieutenant of Ireland.'

'I saw him in Queen Victoria's Coronation Procession,' said I,
'and how the crowd cheered!'

Will sighed and went on: 'My mother had two strings to her
bow: the Marquess of Anglesey's steward, and my father, a young
sawyer of low origin. The steward was named Hodson, and would
have married my mother, but that he already had a wife; so my

father saved him the trouble, by marrying her himself. Mr Hodson continued to be romantically attached to my mother; indeed, I've been told that my eldest brother Joseph may thank him as the author of his being. My own parentage was never, I understand, in doubt; because soon after Joseph's birth the family quitted King's Bromley and came to Rugeley. By this time, my father was in a fair way to make his fortune, for he and Hodson had not only gone snags in my mother's favours but done the same with the profits of the Marquess's timber, then being felled to supply the Royal Navy. The Marquess was away in Ireland, and his eldest son, the present Marquess, showed such negligence that Hodson had a clear run. Now, it seems that while Hodson courted my mother, my father was quietly marking the fallen logs 1,1; 2,2; 3,3—so that he got six for the price of three. Or even more; an old fellow by the name of Littler who worked for him in those days has told me that he had seen no less than ten No. 10's carted out of Shoughborough Park during a single day. My father prided himself on a little rhyme which he had composed himself; and taught us at his knee:

> It is a sin to steal a pin,
> But guineas are fair game.
> The hound who hounds a million pounds Writes
>   "Lord" before his name.

This inheritance of mine, Charley, is ill come by, and the sooner it's spent, the better I'll be pleased.'

I felt dismayed by the bitter tones in which Will Palmer branded his father as a cuckold, his mother as an adulteress, and both of them as thieves. His story reminded me forcibly of the Biblical text: 'The fathers have eaten sour grapes and the children's teeth are set on edge.'

'Nay, but Will,' I objected, 'I heard you tell Dr Stegall the other day that you were directly descended from Sir James Palmer, Chancellor of the Order of the Garter, in the reign of the martyred Charles I; and from his son Roger, the Earl of Castlemaine, a boon companion of the Merry Monarch, Charles II!'

'So I did,' he said carelessly, 'but Stegall is no friend of mine; and I reserve the truth for my friends only, if I may count on you as such. To do so relieves my heart of a heavy burden. Though it may be unscientific to believe that dishonesty, infidelity, or cruelty is inheritable—as one may well inherit a gouty tendency, or short sight, or a syphilitic taint, or melancholia—I can't choke back the resentment I feel towards my father. Now, look'ee, Charley, I don't relish Stegall's household or the regimen he forces on me. I shall clear out, bag and baggage, at the end of this week. What do you say to rooming with me? I hear you well spoken of as a thoroughbred entire, sound in wind and limb, without vices and a good stayer. In short, I'd be proud to have you as my stable mate.'

'If it puts me to no greater expense than I am incurring at present,' I answered, 'I should be most happy to join you. I won't say that I'm enchanted with the company I'm keeping; but my purse is light, and the rooms are cheap.'

'Tell me more,' he says, handing me an uncommonly good cigar and igniting it for me. 'Well,' I said, 'it's this way. My "chums", as they call themselves, are sad dogs; very sad dogs indeed—though what the significance of "sad" in this phrase may be, I'm sure I don't know. They are, in point of fact, confoundedly gay, so gay as to be perfect bores. The *summum bonum* of their happiness seems to consist in strolling along the Haymarket or Regent Street of an evening, clad in ruffianly overcoats, smoking foul black cigars, and peering under the bonnet of every poor little dressmaker or milliner making her solitary way home, wearied after a day's toil, and weighed down by a heavy oilskin-covered wicker basket. They call it a lark to ogle the unfortunate girls and put them out of countenance—I call it blackguardly. Then, when the shops are closed, and they have refreshed themselves at some public-house bar with copious draughts of half-and-half, they call it a lark again to march arm-in-arm, four or five of them, down quiet streets and shouting "*Lullaliety!*" at the tops of their voices.'

'Myself, I could never abear boisterousness,' says he.

'And I draw the line sharply,' I continued, 'at the sport of wrenching knockers off street doors, and proudly displaying them to one's fellow-chums, very much as a Sioux or Ojibway "brave" exhibits his scalps.'

'What are their peculiar habits at table?' Will asks with mock gravity, as one might inquire about some strange variety of jungle animal.

I told him: 'They make beer their morning beverage—"drunk from the native pewter," as the cant phrase is—and chaff me when I suggest that tea or coffee, both of which quicken rather than dull the intellect, may be the more civilized brew. "Charley the slop-drinker" one of them waggishly called me, until I flung a pint of half-and-half in his face, and followed it with the native pewter. There came no more waggishness from that quarter for a while, I warrant you. They breakfast from whatever happens to be in the cupboard—bread, cold meat, a stale pasty, or a petrified cheese-rind—and if the beer is expended, gin and water must serve. Generally half a dozen chums from the lodgings opposite thrust their way in, to join the merry meal and talk over last night's lark—how Johnny bonneted the policeman, or how old Tom stole the garter off a young lady's leg as she was mounting into a hansom cab. Savages, Will, ignoble savages! Nor do these visiting chums remember to bring the necessary breakfast tools with them; but the meat and cheese is sliced with a rusty pocket-knife, or the very scalpel with which one of my party has been operating on a mouldering human femur, now carelessly tossed into the cupboard next to the loaf of bread. Gin and water is drunk from pickle-jars or gallipots, or the ornamental vases on the chimney-piece.'

Will chuckled at my recital, and I went on to tell of my chums' dinner taken at a 'slap- bang', or cheap eating-house, where they ate cow-heel or hot alamode, and offered familiarities to blowsy women waiters, who returned them in kind; I also described their disorderly supper. 'You'll live a very different life when you room with me, Charley,' he said. 'You'll eat and drink of the best, and never have a chum in the world to plague you.'

Will now rented a fine set of rooms in Bartholomew Close, belonging to a fellow by the name of Ayres, and fitted them up in approved medical style, covering the walls with anatomical charts and models, and laying out two or three hundred guineas on professional works. This was a great convenience to me during my home-studies, and Will did not deceive me by demanding any larger contribution than I had paid at the hole-in-the-wall from which he rescued me. I drank tea for breakfast out of a handsome china cup, and ate bacon and eggs, or grilled kidneys, or kedgeree and fish (a capital food) off a well-heated plate with excellent table silver. Our rooms were never in disorder, and Will himself showed a particular niceness about his morning dress, which was neat rather than showy; and though somewhat provincial in his manners at the start, he soon learned London etiquette and became quite the gentleman.

So far as I know, he always paid his debts, even to tailors, which many a peer of the realm disdains to acknowledge—as though tailors were not also God's creatures, and entitled to payment for their tedious labours! When not walking the hospital, I stayed at home and studied; but for the first few months Will Palmer did not join me and proved very remiss in his attendance at the Lecture Theatre. I thought this none of my business; for if he chose to make the rounds of the betting-houses and mix with the racing fraternity—already his thoughts were turning to the Turf—at least he did not bring any doubtful characters back with him to Bartholomew Close. He respected my quiet, and showed me the most thoughtful consideration.

One evening, I remember, he said to me: 'Charley, you look fagged. Much study is a weariness to the flesh. Come out with me to supper! I'll stand you treat, and shan't expect any return but the pleasure of your company.'

I could hardly refuse, though I pointed out that if he took me to a more than ordinarily genteel place, I had no suitable togs for the occasion.

'Oh, damn the togs!' he answered. 'Borrow some of mine, if you like—we're much of a height, and your shoulders are as broad as mine.'

So presently we walked down the Strand, where he led me to an oyster shop, described as a 'night house', where scarlet lobsters and crabs like giant tea-roses jostled one another in appetizing profusion on the stone counters; where pickled salmon lurked in shady groves of fennel; where Finnan haddocks, truly Scotch in their hardness and crispness were ranged in thick layers; where oyster tubs crowded the walls; and where a gilt placard hanging from the flaring gas jet invited us to partake of chops, kidneys, or steaks. At the counter stood a row of swells, cooling their parched throats with Colchester natives, and swearing unrestrainedly at the flannel-aproned attendants. Through the doorway of an inner room I caught sight of many ladies of the Town, in silks, satins, feathers, and plenty of 'slab', that is to say, red ochre and bismuth, staining their cheeks.

Will was leading the way in, when he turned sharply about and came out again. 'Let's away,' he muttered, 'there's a fellow here whom I'd as lief meet as the Devil himself.'

'Who can that be?' I inquired, disappointed of my oysters and crab-meat.

'A fellow named Dawson,' he replied, 'who owns a big house near Stafford, and has done me an ill turn. I'm determined to marry his ward, the sweetest and most engaging little girl in the world. But he stuffs her ears with ill-natured tales against me. It's my opinion he wants to make her his third wife.'

We retraced our steps and presently walked across St Martin's Lane, where he led me to a public house, and said: 'Charley, I shall now show you England's greatest living hero, next to the Iron Duke, of course.' He nodded at the publican behind his bar, a white-haired, battered giant who stood ringed about by prize fighters with broken noses, cauliflower ears, and bleary eyes, and by a mixed assembly of dog-fanciers, book-makers, ratting-match concocters, and the very scum of sporting life generally. Ah, those cutaway coats, the nankeen trousers fitting tightly to the leg, the bell-shaped hats, the blue and white neckties, the queer jargon and outrageous oaths!

'Who's your friend?' I asked.

'Who's he, indeed, Charley? Are you really so green? You should be ashamed to ask the question! Why, that's the great Tom Cribb, formerly pugilistic champion of England; who sparred in the presence of the Russian Tsar and the King of Prussia in the year before Waterloo; and who guarded the entrance to Westminster Hall at the disorderly Coronation of his late Majesty, King George IV. Though now attained to the age of seventy, he could still, if he pleased, dash all the teeth from your jaw, with a mere back-hander.'

Then we turned up Little New Street, even at that late hour blocked by the carts opposite a cheesemonger's; along King Street and the illumined windows of the Garrick Club; then down a steep flight of steps, and into Evans's Supper Room.

'Here you'll find a scene rather more to your liking, I hope,' said Will Palmer. And, in effect, Evans's of Covent Garden is an estab-

lishment that has ever since delighted me when I could afford to
sup there. You don't know it? Why, it's the finest place of its kind in
the metropolis—I rate it far above Rhodes's, or the Cyder Cellars
in Maiden Lane, or the Coal Hole in the Strand. It's divided into
two parts, do you see? First, the café, furnished in truly Parisian
fashion—except that it doesn't spill over into the street—and hung
around with portraits of the most famous theatrical personages
in ancient and modern times. The café is where men of importance from every walk of life gather to exchange gossip. In fact,
so much gossip is exchanged that a 'syndicate', or combination,
of newspaper reporters has been formed to spread out among the
tables, each secretly cocking an ear to the disclosures of the group
sitting nearest him. Afterwards they pool their takings, perhaps
less honestly than the members of a thieves' kitchen, but honestly
enough to keep the syndicate in being. The newspaper proprietors
pay them a fixed sum for their suppers so long as they continue to
collect, or at least fabricate, printable news.

Then there's the Singing Room, a hall with a platform at the
upper end on which a grand piano is stationed, and to which the
singers climb when called upon by the chairman who sits beneath.
The important business of eating is solemnly and industriously
undertaken here by six or seven hundred men. Ladies are, of
course, debarred, owing to the freedom of language which is permitted the performers; and women of the Town equally so, owing
to the respectability of the audience. It happened that some most
distinguished guests were present on this occasion, including several Members of Parliament, and two tided race-horse owners
whom Will pointed out to me; and (a thing that interested me
far more) seated at the next table to us were two men whom I
recognized as the famous novelists William Makepeace Thackeray
and Charles Dickens! Mr Thackeray, a member of the adjoining
Garrick's Club, still makes Evans's, as he has put it 'my nightly

chapel of ease'. He was then engaged in writing his immortal *Vanity Fair*, though under the misfortune of being married to an insane wife. Mr Dickens, already the author of *Pickwick Papers* and *Oliver Twist*, had just been offered, and accepted, the editorship of the recently founded *Daily News;* and Mr Thackeray had been invited to celebrate this success. Mr Dickens lay under the almost equal misfortune of being unhappily married to a woman who had borne him a number of children, while he loved her younger sister to desperation. Will told me all this, *sotto voce*, observing that domestic unhappiness often positively assisted men of genius to pen immortal works. 'Not that I would ever have read a word written by either of them,' he added, 'had it not been for Dr Stegall and his merry evenings. I find *Ruff's Guide to the Turf* engrossing enough.'

He ordered 'Black Velvet', (which proved to be champagne mixed with stout), a couple of dozen oysters, and thin slices of buttered whole-meal bread as a commencer; to be followed by rump-steak and a good claret. On the other side of our table sat a party of provincials, Wolverhampton tradesmen by their accent and garb, who gazed at Will with veneration and astonishment, until presently one of them recognized him. Will bowed gravely but paid no further attention, though it appeared that this was an old school-fellow; and the chap's 'Dang me, if it isn't Billy Palmer of the Rugeley Yard!' got drowned by a growl from his mates: 'Howd thy rattle, Tinny!' For now the Chairman had rapped on the table with his hammer and was crying: 'Attention, pray, my lords and gentlemen, to the music from *Macbeth*, No. 63 in the books, *if* you please!'

Up came the singers, half a dozen of them being boys with well-controlled trebles, and their rendering of Locke's beautiful melodies entranced us all. A decorous silence reigned, the audience abstaining from any clatter of hardware; but at the end broke into tumultuous applause, clapping their hands and beating on the table with fists and knife-handles.

I kept my ears open for some sublime or witty remark from the famous novelists, but apart from 'May I trouble you, Sir, to pass the mustard?' or 'These are indeed capital chops,' I heard nothing of interest except Mr Dickens's discourse on the beneficial effect of Sunday Schools in increasing the number of children who can read and write, thus yearly swelling the literate public. 'I rely upon these former Sunday School pupils to keep my young brood in beef, mutton and potatoes, my dear Thackeray,' said he, 'not upon the University men and their families.'

'So I judge by your style and your subjects,' Mr Thackeray replied with a sigh that doubtless referred to his own childless state; though it would have sounded deuced crushing to any writer who had a lower opinion of his talents than Charles Dickens.

The Chairman then rapped for a comic singer, whose name escapes me, but I remember that he sang 'The Derby Ram' in a very arch manner, persuading the audience to expect obscene words because of the rhymes that led up to them, yet shutting his mouth fast like a fresh-water mussel when he came to the point, and treating us to a most prodigious wink, as who would say: 'If you know the missing words, laugh by all means, gentlemen, but do not blame me for indecency—for I did not teach you them myself.'

Will kept replenishing my glass, only occasionally sipping at his own, and derived considerable amusement from the calf-eyes which a great, bearded, bald-headed Fellow of the Royal Academy was making at a handsome boy-soloist, as he sang:

> 'Mother would have wed me with a Tailor
> And not gi'en me my heart's delight;
> But give me the lad with the tarry trowsers That
> shine to me like diamonds bright!'

He remarked: 'Although Cupid is said to have been a beautiful boy, I think it both foolish and unnatural to worship at any shrine save that of his mother Venus.'

The next song happened to be 'Here's a health to the King and a Lasting Peace,' bawled by a tremendous *basso*; and Will nudged me delightedly with his oyster-knife at the lines:

> 'And may misfortune still pursue
> The senseless woman-hating crew . . .

Soon after eleven o'clock we slipped out. Will called a cab and we drove to Moss's, a first-class hell in the aristocratic neighbourhood of St James's Street. Moss's had a bright fan-light over the door, and a police constable stood guard on either side of the entrance. They had orders to take account of all visitors, their style of dress and apparent station in life; and hoped to be rewarded for their quiet 'good-night' with a half-crown, or a good cigar. 'Many little perquisites like these solace the arduous duties of the West-End peeler,' Will told me confidentially, as he pulled at an ivory bell-knob.

At once, as in the children's story of the White Cat, the portals flew open. In we went, and they closed behind us as if by magic. We found ourselves faced by a second door, iron-panelled and covered with green baize, from the centre of which a gleaming eye viewed us through a small square aperture. When Will nodded affably, an iron bar swung back, two bolts were shot, we mounted a flight of softly-carpeted stairs, and I was at last introduced to the mysteries of a London gambling house. Splendid rooms they were: brilliantly lighted, warmly curtained, much-mirrored; and in one of them stood a table spread with cold fowl, ham, tongue, beef and salads. 'These are provided gratis,' said Will, 'and so are the wines, spirits and cigars. Help yourself at Rabbi Moss's expense!'

Seeing me somewhat embarrassed by my situation, he muttered jovially: 'Cheer up, my hearty! Though you may not be one of Swan & Edgar's young men, nobody will mistake you for anything but the gentleman you are. Step over to the gaming table!'

This was an ordinary billiard table, furnished with cushions, pockets, and a rack of cues to disguise its illegal employ. Police raids had been frequent lately, and no sooner did the alarm go, than a billiard game began. As an added precaution, the lame croupier, a sharp-looking, wiry manikin, dispensed with the rake in vogue at Baden-Baden and Aix—using instead a hooked stick which was also his crutch. He called the odds, never making the slightest miscalculation; and a tall, blond-moustached, handsome man shook the dice box. Will told me afterwards that the latter was of noble family, held a commission in the Blues, and did not come here in the hope of pecuniary gain. It was merely to pass the time on his way home from the club, for he had a horror of going to bed. Two years later I saw this same swell leaning against the orchestra at the Opera, and examining the house through an enormous tortoise-shell lorgnette. He is now dead: killed at Balaclava with the Heavy Brigade, I understand.

'Seven's the main!' the blond moustache shouted.

'Seven's the main!' echoed the croupier. 'Make your game, please. The castor's backing it at seven, gentlemen!'

Down came the box, out rolled the dice. 'Eleven's the nick,' said the croupier. Stakes were raked in with the crutch, winners paid, and a fresh main called a quarter of a minute later.

Will ventured a five-pound note, and lost. Presently a bright thought occurred to him. 'Confess, lad,' said he, 'have you ever played?'

'Never,' I answered, 'and don't intend to.'

'Ah, but for me you surely will? I'll lay heavily on your virgin luck.' 'I haven't a shilling in my pocket,' I protested.

'Then here's a couple of sovereigns,' he said. 'I'll stake you.
Lose, and it costs you nought.

Win, and we go snags.'

Very reluctantly I placed the two coins on the nearest number.
The main was again called, the dice shaken, and before I knew
what had happened, six sovereigns were in my hand. 'I have kept
my half-share,' he told me. 'Now stake your winnings.'

'No, no!' I cried. 'Let it be my perpetual boast that I never lost
at dice, and never won less than six times my stake.'

He laughed at that and clapped me on the shoulder, saying:
'Ah, my lad, if only I had your firmness of character, what a noble
life mine would be—and how infernally dull into the bargain!'

Then he placed his winnings on the number I had favoured,
lost, and scratched his head. 'I believe old Moss rigs it somehow,'
he mused. 'I wonder what the trick is. The dice aren't cogged.' He
selected a splendid cigar from a box stamped 'Benson', offered it
to me, took a couple for himself, and when I had been regaled
with a glass or two of excellent hock, out we went.

To one policeman at the door he handed half-a-crown, to his
companion the third cigar. We hailed another cab. Our next port
of call was a Dance Hall in the vicinity of Leicester Square. We paid
a shilling each to the money-takers at the entrance, with another
sixpence for a reserved seat, and watched the noisy, ragged polka
in progress. I have not been able to find this establishment since;
but I remember thinking it strange that the gentlemen would
dance, tall hat on head, and umbrella, or knobbed walking-stick,
clasped in the same hand which guided a partner's delicate fingers. The buffet here was not a free one: indeed, I considered the
prices exorbitant. However, Will settled me in a plush chair and
supplied me with liver- sandwiches and more hock, while he went
in search of a dancing partner. I felt most disinclined to follow
his example, especially with one of the ladies of the Town who

frequented this place—I recognized two or three among them as our out-patients—and therefore sat still, drinking and dozing, until Will appeared at about one o'clock and loudly condemned my lack of enterprise. I begged to be taken home and, though protesting that the night was yet young, he steered me from the hall into a cab. Back at Bartholomew Close, he helped me remove my togs—or, rather, his own. I have never before or since seen double: but Will now had two heads and, true to form, I took a deep clinical interest in the phenomenon.

Afterwards he made coffee, a large cup of which soon improved my condition. Then he sat on my bed and divulged yet more family secrets—including some horrible tales about his father's callous treatment of the workmen. But of his mother he said gently: 'True, she's a vulgar and lecherous woman, but she's helped me out of many a scrape—a kindness for which I've rewarded her most filially. I've always taken her side against my four brothers— the first, Joseph, a drunkard; the second, Walter, also a drunkard; the third, George, a close-fisted and ambitious lawyer; the fourth, John, a narrow-minded saint of the sort they call "prigs". All she needed, when my father died, was a capable bed-fellow; and when she lost her first fancyman, a collier, and her second, a Belfast linen-draper whom she wished to marry—but my brothers would not allow it—I induced Jerry Smith to take the Irishman's place and keep her sweet- tempered. Jerry's an obliging fellow, and quite enjoys his commission; besides, he's always short of money, and she's no niggard.'

From any other man's mouth this would have been a disgusting admission; but he had never yet, he said, confided in a fellow-student as he now did in me; which I found flattering. And Will spoke in such a humorous, affectionate way that I made no protest; being indebted to him for the many kindnesses he had done me, as well as for the night's entertainment. This much is certain: he showed great tenderness towards the poor patients at Bart's, supplying them with such dainties and nourishing foods as they had neither enjoyed before in our wards nor, some of them, ever in their lives; and he would often get up subscriptions for them when they were due to leave, and head the list with a couple of guineas.

As the summer advanced, Will realized that not many weeks remained for him to take the College examination, and that he was sadly in arrears of study. All at once he abandoned his usual free and easy course of life, and joined me in my grind, working eight or nine hours a day, Sunday included; and only last week did the reason for this sudden furious industry appear. I found a letter of his hidden in the leaves of an anatomical treatise which I had then possessed; he must have put it there to mark a page, and later forgotten its whereabouts. The letter was addressed to Mr Dawson's ward, the very lady whom he afterwards married, and I have given it to Mr Serjeant Shee, Will's Defence Counsel, to prove what manner of man he was in those days. It ran something like this:

My dearest Annie,

I snatch a moment from my studies to write to your dear, dear, little self. I need hardly say that the principal inducement I have to work is the desire of getting my studies finished so as to be able to press your dear little form to my breast.

With best, best love, believe me, Dearest Annie, your own
WILLIAM

Will would often sit up until midnight, dissecting, and beg me to keep him company. He used to say: 'I don't feel quite comfortable over such work when I'm alone. It's very stupid, I know, but one can't always control one's thoughts.' And when I happened to fall ill for a few days, he would pay a porter to occupy my chair of nights. Will Palmer, if he set himself to accomplish a task, always brought it to a successful conclusion. He had a remarkable memory, a delicate hand with the lancet, and a surprising power of correct diagnosis. Though none of my former chums—many of whom were ignominiously plucked—expected him to win his diploma, and some even swore that he must have hired another student to impersonate him, he passed very creditably. It was also said that he defrauded Dr Stegall of his grinder's fee; but that I cannot believe, because he was most conscientious about paying his debts and Dr Stegall, who was equally conscientious about his grinding, would not have failed to dun Will if he had not paid up. The origin of the story was, I surmise, Mr Jeremiah Smith's failure to pay the promised ten guineas, and the conversion to his own use of the further ten guineas offered by Mrs. Palmer. Dr Stegall issued a writ against Smith, but the case was settled out of Court, Mrs Palmer paying.

That I myself satisfied the examiners, and even earned their praise, I attribute largely to Will's generosity, which enabled me to work undisturbed. And if it is true that he spent the better part of two thousand pounds while at Bart's, what business of mine was that?

No, I have only met him once or twice since, our ways having parted. He presently devoted himself wholly to the service of the God Apollo, Patron of Racing, and I to that of Apollo's son, Aesculapius, the God of Healing.

CHAPTER VII

THE COURTSHIP OF ANNIE BROOKES

'William Palmer, Esq., Surgeon', as he could now style himself, returned to Rugeley from London with the intention of abandoning all his former irregular ways and settling down decently. The principal reason was, it appears, a serious attachment which he had formed.

One day in the August of 1845, just before William went to work at the Infirmary, Mr Thos Weaver, the solicitor, had invited him to dine, and arranged that he should meet with Annie Brookes as if by accident. Although her annuity was the bait offered him, Annie possessed remarkable beauty, and the joy and surprise of meeting the man whom she had so long idolized made her eyes shine and her cheeks flush very engagingly. The young couple exchanged no more than a few words, but William expressed hopes of their further acquaintance; and Annie stammered that this would make her happy, and that her guardian, Mr Charles Dawson, was kindness itself, as Mr Weaver could testify. 'Perhaps you would care to call upon him?' she artlessly pleaded.

A day or two later, at dinner, Annie mentioned the meeting to Mr Dawson, in Dr Knight's presence. Mr Dawson saw at once that she had warm feelings for William Palmer, but said nothing until dinner ended, and the ladies left the table. Then he asked Dr Knight who, being very deaf, had missed the conversation: 'Do you know anything of this William Palmer whom Annie says she met briefly at Tom Weaver's?'

'If he's the fellow whom I take him to be,' Dr Knight answered, 'Annie would do well not to renew her acquaintance. He studied with my cousin, Dr Tylecote, over at Haywood. Come, fill my glass, and you shall hear what Tylecote told me about him only last Wednesday . . .

'"I've just ridden to Rugeley," he said, "to dun old Mrs Palmer for a debt that the young rake her son has long owed one of my neighbours, Farmer Parker. A labourer's widow, do you see, was tossed by Farmer Parker's bull at Gayton, breaking one leg and a couple of ribs. I'm her club doctor, but I happened to be in bed with a colic and couldn't attend her; so I sent young Palmer to summon Dr Masfen from the Stafford Infirmary, undertaking to pay his fee on the widow's behalf; and Palmer was to make up any medicines Masfen might prescribe. Masfen duly attended the widow, set the leg, saw that she was comfortable, and rode off, after giving Palmer instructions for certain medicines. Farmer Parker stood at the bedside, very solicitous, as to some extent responsible for the widow's injuries, his bull having attacked her on a public foot-path. He asks Palmer: 'What's the amount of Masfen's fee?' Palmer says: 'Two guineas,' and Farmer Parker takes up a weighty canvas bag, puts his great paw in, scoops out a handful of gold and silver, and throws two guineas on the coverlet. Palmer eyes the bag thoughtfully and inquires: 'By the bye, can you change me a five-pound note?' 'Certainly,' answers Parker, who had not expected to get off so lightly as with two guineas. He hands Palmer five sovereigns new from the Mint. Palmer searches his pockets for the five-pound note, and looks alarmed; but suddenly his face clears and he says: 'Ah, now I remember! I was in such a hurry to ride over for Dr Masfen that, when changing my trowsers for these breeches, I left the note in a pocket. Well, it's of no consequence—I can send it along tonight by the boy who brings the medicine.' But he fails to do so.

'"A couple of months later," Dr Tylecote continued, "Farmer Parker demanded the money from me, threatening me with the law, and saying that he had three times written to Palmer for it, but got no reply. Knowing nothing about the matter, I summoned Palmer, who struck his forehead and exclaimed that the debt had clean escaped his memory, and that Farmer Parker had not reminded him of it, neither. 'But at the moment,' he said, 'my purse happens to be empty—I've just paid my tailor.' So I advised him to ride home before breakfast and borrow the money from his mother. I'll do that,' he said cheerfully. He rode to Rugeley right enough, but he never paid Farmer Parker those five pounds; for yesterday I accidentally met with Parker, who accused me, very rudely, of encouraging my assistant to cheat him. By then, however, Palmer had run away to Walsall with that red-headed girl, and I refused to take him back. So I went myself to call on Mrs Palmer at The Yard, and she settled the debt."'

Mr Dawson looked grave and said: 'I shall not mention this matter to Annie until I have had a word with Tom Masters of The Talbot Arms Hotel at Rugeley; he'll know, if anyone, what character young Palmer bears in the neighbourhood. Old Tom can be counted upon for an honest report: he rides straight and never baulked at a gate. It may well be that negligence, rather than crooked dealing, accounts for that unpaid debt.'

'Get a second opinion, by all means,' Dr Knight hastened to say. 'I'm not one to blacken any man's character on hearsay evidence alone.'

Masters's revelations seem to have been highly unfavourable.

When Mr Weaver one day proposed to take William Palmer with him on a visit to Abbot's Bromley, Mr Dawson discouraged him. He said: 'My dear fellow, you, your wife, your family, and your kin to the seventh degree are most welcome in our domain and, I hope, always will be, even when I am gone; but pray do not bring along that young reprobate—for I have daughters.'

Mr Weaver flushed, and wanted to know what he meant. Mr Dawson explained: 'From Tom Masters's account, your protégé has seduced no fewer than four girls in the course of this last year. Even if the number has been exaggerated one hundred per centum, it yet remains considerable. Nor do I care to be asked, as was Fanner Parker of Gayton: "Can you change a five-pound note?" for I should then be forced either to lie and pretend that I have no such sum in the house, or else oblige and never see my money again.'

Mr Weaver flushed still more deeply. 'Sir,' he said, 'I am deeply sensible of your kindness in giving me, and extending to my family in perpetuity, the freedom of Abbot's Bromley. Were it not for that, and for our long friendship, I should at once report this conversation to young Palmer and advise him to bring an action for slander; because an action certainly lies. As things are, I shall simply desire you to retract your words.'

Mr Dawson replied very quietly: 'Sir, you must forgive me if, while retracting my accusations against your protégé, which I admit are based only on hearsay (however credible the source), I do not make amends by inviting you to introduce him into this household. I have daughters; and I also have a pretty ward for whose well-being I am responsible to the Court of Chancery.'

The two friends parted coolly. How Mr Weaver excused or explained this failure to young Palmer is not exactly known, but he must have conveyed a broad hint of Mr Dawson's aversion to him.

At this period of his life, William Palmer had nothing in particular to occupy his attentions. He had quitted Dr Tylecote's employ, but not yet proceeded to Stafford Infirmary; Jane Widnall had betrayed him; he lacked the funds demanded by betting or other diversions, and must rely for food, shelter, and pocket-money on his mother at The Yard. As was very natural, he decided to challenge fortune by secretly renewing his acquaintance with Annie Brookes. On the pretence of botanical study, he would lurk in the woods and fields near Abbot's Bromley, especially among the great oaks of Lord Bagot's park, keeping one eye open and one ear cocked for Annie's approach on her afternoon walk; but unless she came alone he would not disclose himself. These tactics succeeded pretty well. On the first occasion, Annie passed by the spot in Bagot's Park where he leant against an oak examining some ferns under a magnifying glass. She happened to be walking, arm-in-arm, with Miss Salt, daughter of Dr Salt, the Rugeley surgeon; and, though she evidently recognized young Palmer, did not call Miss Salt's attention to him, being averse to betraying her feelings. He therefore resumed his station in the park at the same hour on the following day and presently, to his joy, saw Annie approaching alone, with careful glances in all directions, as if satisfying herself that she had not been observed. Now, Annie Brookes was an honest girl and therefore offered no pretence of surprise when she saw him waiting for her on a log; but stood still in the lane with a look of love and appeal that affected him strangely. He slipped his glass back into its case, flung down the ferns which he had been examining, and boldly advanced to take both her hands in his own.

They remained thus for perhaps a quarter of a minute; then he laughed, and so did she. Almost at once they began to talk merrily and naturally, though with lowered voices, like children hiding together in a hayloft or woodland cavern. Annie recalled his gentle sympathy when she had sprained her ankle at Miss Bond's school; he declared that he had already fallen in love with her then. Yet he attempted no vulgar familiarities, and even held her in a sort of awe, this being the first well-bred young lady for whom he had ever felt any tenderness. They agreed to meet at the same spot, at the same hour, two days later; and this second meeting was so successful that she even invited him to kiss her, and nearly swooned with pleasure when he saluted her, very chastely, on the brow.

But the course of true love—for it certainly was true love on Annie's part, and almost certainly on his—never runs smooth. One of the Dawson girls soon suspected from Annie's manner that she was hugging a secret, and decided to spy on her from a safe distance when next she took an afternoon walk. Being an ill-natured creature, Miss Dawson ran home at full tilt, as soon as she had satisfied her curiosity, to fetch her father. She found him in the green- house, inspecting his tomatoes, which were a new and superior strain, with a strawberry flavour. (In Stafford, by the way, the appearance of tomatoes at table is still the subject for humorous comment, owing to their supposedly aphrodisiac qualities, and Mr Dawson's gardener always threw him arch glances when he inquired after the plants.) Learning that Annie lay at that moment locked in a passionate embrace with a young stranger, Mr Dawson hurried behind his daughter to the glade where this indecent event had been reported, but arrived too late to surprise them in any compromising posture. Quite the reverse: Annie and William sat at some distance from each other, he with his legs crossed, smoking a cigar; she, with no evident disarray of either dress or hair, intently poring at the structure of an unusual fern, through the magnifying glass that he had lent her. On Mr Dawson's appearance, Annie sprang to her feet with a little cry of joy: 'Oh, Papa,' she said, 'do come and look at this lovely sight—who ever would have thought that Nature would hide her marvels so closely as to demand a magnifying glass for their discovery!'

William also rose, but slowly, removed the cigar from his mouth and swept off his hat in gentlemanly style.

Mr Dawson ordered his tell-tale daughter home, and as soon as she was out of earshot, turned to Annie and said: 'Mother Nature is not, I think, the only female hereabouts that hides her secrets. Who is this young gentleman? I don't think I have the honour of his acquaintance.' 'Why, Papa, it's Mr William Palmer,' she answered. 'He is training to be a surgeon. I met him first at Miss Bond's, when he dressed my sprained ankle, and more recently in Mr Weaver's office—Mr Weaver has only good to tell of him— and three weeks ago last Monday we met by accident in these woods. Mr Palmer is a keen botanist, and so am I, as you must know from my collection of pressed flowers and ferns. We meet on our rambles, now and again, and sometimes he kindly lends me his glass.'

Mr Dawson was silent for a while, and then, choosing his words with great precision, 'Mr Palmer,' he said, 'Bagot's Park is not my property, and clearly you have as much right to enjoy its natural beauties as I have. But these beauties do not include my ward, Miss Brookes.'

By no means disconcerted, William bowed to Annie, and then answered, smiling: 'Well, Mr Dawson, she comes here often enough to be mistaken for a native. And it seems only right to count her among the natural beauties of Bagot's Park; that is to say, I should hesitate, myself, to call her either ugly or artificial.'

'Have done with compliments, young Palmer,' cried Mr Dawson angrily. 'How dare you force your noxious company on this innocent girl without a word to me?'

Will appealed to Annie. 'Miss Brookes,' he asked, 'did I force my noxious company on you?'

'Oh, no, Mr Palmer, no!' she exclaimed in confusion. 'Indeed, quite the reverse. I saw you first, and came to thank you for your kindness at Miss Bond's; and then I became interested in the sights revealed by your magnifying glass and suggested that we should meet again to continue botanizing together.'

'That exculpates you, Annie,' said Mr Dawson as kindly as he could, 'but it does not exculpate Mr Palmer. He should have called at my house on the very morning after that first accidental meeting (if accidental it was) and asked my permission to bota- nize with you,'—here all at once Mr Dawson grew portentously stern—'and, if there be such a word in the dictionary, to *amourize*! What answer have you to this, Mr Palmer?'

'I should certainly have called at your residence, Sir, had our mutual friend, Mr Weaver, not informed me that you discouraged such a visit.'

'Worse and worse! You knew my ill opinion of your manner of life, yet you made love to my ward?'

'With the greatest respect, Sir, this love was not a one-sided ardour, as I think Miss Brookes will have the truthfulness to confess.'

Mr Dawson cut short Annie's gasping assent. 'You take advan- tage of Miss Brookes' innocency,' he exclaimed, 'to force deceit upon her! I repeat, Mr Palmer, that she is my ward. The Court of Chancery holds me responsible for her moral welfare.'

'Her moral welfare cannot be nearer to your heart, Sir, than it is to my own.'

'Mr Palmer, I will not venture to call you a liar or a hypocrite, because my opinion of your morals is formed from hearsay alone; but there's a great deal of talk current which is most unfavourable to you. I took the precaution, when Annie mentioned a Mr Palmer some weeks ago, to consult her fellow-guardian, Dr Knight, as to your antecedents. He gave me Dr Tylecote's report upon you . . .'

'Dr Tylecote, Sir, is prejudiced. He took no trouble to teach me his trade, and not only used me as an errand-boy, but also set his assistant Smirke to spy on my actions. I finally quarrelled with Dr Tylecote about a loan of five pounds, for which a rascally farmer demanded payment twice over . . .'

'Pray be silent! Dr Knight then recommended me to consult Tom Masters of The Talbot Arms Hotel.'

'Ha, ha! That's very good! I warrant old Tom had nothing to say in my favour? He hates each and every Palmer, dead or alive, ever since my father won a suit against him for trespass on our property.'

'That may be as you say,' Mr Dawson continued unperturbed. 'Nevertheless, I have heard enough discreditable talk to warrant my forbidding you the house, and to restrain Miss Brookes from seeking you out again, either in this park or elsewhere.'

William exchanged a quick loving glance with Annie, who appeared much distressed and ready to faint. Then he said: 'You, Sir, are Annie's guardian, but not her father; and there must come a time when you will be unable to oppose your ward's marrying the man of her choice. I would gladly take a wager that I can count on Annie singling me out, and holding by this choice. Therefore, unless you are prepared to lose her altogether when your guardianship expires, you would be wise to show me greater consideration. Annie, will you marry me some happy day?'

Annie looked miserably from one to the other of the two men whom she loved best in the world. 'Dear Will,' she said, turning very pale, 'I cannot give you that promise while Mr Dawson entertains such a bad opinion of you, however mistaken he may be. It would make life wretched both for him and me. I don't know what these ugly stories about you are, and I don't want to know. Perhaps you have been foolish. But if you love me truly, you won't be offended by Mr Dawson's anxiety on my behalf. You can see how much store he sets by my virtue and discretion; and I do blame myself a little for having hidden my true feelings from him. So now, you had best apply yourself seriously to the medical profession and secure the necessary diploma. Then you'll be a full-fledged surgeon; you'll soon earn the respect of the world as well as Mr Dawson's, and give the lie to all those disagreeable stories. I won't forget you; pray count on that.'

'You may say good-bye now, my girl,' said Mr Dawson. 'Papa, may I kiss my friend?' she pleaded.

'No, you may not!' came Mr Dawson's gruff reply.

William, looking very sulky, said to Annie: 'Very well, then; let's leave it at that, my dear! I had thought better of you. Good-bye!'

He did not deign to take his leave of Mr Dawson; but turned his back and strode away towards the park gates.

The above account was given by Mrs Remington of Rugeley, at whose cottage William Palmer lodged on his return from London, to avoid a clash with his brothers George and Walter, then staying at The Yard. Mrs Remington is a frail old body with a pink, unlined face and the whitest of hair, who dresses in a fashion that had been no longer new in the year of Trafalgar. She heard the tale from William Palmer's own lips, and declares that love for Annie Brookes was the greatest thing in his life and that, though he may have been a wild young scamp before, he now decided to reform for her sake.

We then questioned Mrs Remington about his bad behaviour at Stafford Infirmary.

MRS REMINGTON

Ah, that was just it! Annie's refusal to offer him any sure hope of marriage so cast him down, and conditions in the wards were so shocking, that he does seem to have behaved pretty ill. However, he and she continued to correspond secretly, and he pressed his suit with such fervour, representing himself as a lost soul who would go straight to the Devil unless she held out a hand to rescue him, that Annie at last gave in. But this was conditional on his working hard, gaining his diploma, and loving no other woman beside herself—as she would love no other man. And they both kept their word, you may be sure! Whilst at my cottage, which was nearly a twelvemonth, Dr Palmer was as good a young fellow as ever walked. 'I'll marry that girl,' he used to say to me, 'or know the reason why!'

Only the other day I came across some of his letters, left behind in a drawer when he went off, and here they are. The first is from her to him, immediately after that sad scene in Bagot's Park:

Tuesday.

My own dear William:

Why did you sulk when you bade me good-bye in the park this morning? Mr Dawson is always very kind to me, and I should ill requite his goodness by acting directly contrary to his wishes. Come, put on one of your best smiles and write me a real sunshiny note, for you have made me very unhappy. I shall expect a letter on Thursday.

Ever yours, Dearest,

ANNIE BROOKES

He always wrote to her, at this time, in care of Mr Dawson's gardener; and made it very much worth the man's while. This next letter was sent him in London, about a month before he gained his diploma:

Abbot's Bromley, Sept. 13, 1846
9 A.M.

Dearest William,

I think it was your turn to write, and I fancy that if you

will only try and recollect you will think so too. But, never mind, although I have not written, you know quite well that I am *always* thinking of you.

Mr Dawson went to London on Monday last and yesterday Miss Salt came over to see us. We gathered ferns together. I hope you will continue your botanical studies, and allow me the opportunity of puzzling you. I have two secrets to tell you, but these I must reserve for Saturday. I don't mind telling you that I think it is your friend Masters who is trying to prejudice Dr Knight. Miss Salt says she knows it is that very crabbed gentleman—whom, of course, you will now love dearer than ever.

I have got a present for you, but as it is intended as a surprise, I must not spoil it by telling you what it is. Suppose, instead, that I tell you something you will not care to hear half so well, namely that I am ever, my very dearest William,
        Your affectionate

ANNIE

The present she gave him was a pair of bed-socks knitted in scarlet wool, because he had complained of the coldness of his bed. What the other two secrets were, I'm sure I don't know. Then here's a letter which he wrote, but never sent. Perhaps it's what he called a 'trial gallop'. He used to write his letters at night, then sleep on them, and polish them up in the morning. This one is dated 'Rugeley, May 16th', of the next year, which was the very day he had hopefully fixed for their marriage. He asked me once when my own wedding-day had been. 'May 16th,' I answered. 'Well, then, Mamma,' he said—he always called me 'Mamma'—'it shall be mine, too.' But though Annie Brookes had given him her solemn promise, and informed Mr Dawson that she was satisfied as to the young man's reformation, both Mr Dawson and Dr

Knight still strongly opposed the union. It was only because of Mr Weaver's writing to the Court of Chancery on her behalf, and vouching for Dr Palmer's respectability, as being now a qualified surgeon and a man of substance, that the Lord Chancellor made out an order permitting the marriage. It was to take place in the September of that year, when Annie turned eighteen; or sooner, if her guardians would let her. Here, read this:

Rugeley,
May 16, 1847

My Dear Little Annie,
   It was not the rain that prevented me from joining you at Stafford, as you wished. I sprained my foot and it was so painful that I could not keep it on the ground. I slid off the pathway as I was turning the corner of The Yard, past Bonney's. Now you know the reason, I am sure you will forgive me.
   Oh, Annie! You cannot tell how dull I have found the last few days; I sit and think over my miserable bachelor life, and feel so dull and lonesome, I really cannot explain. I resolved, yesterday, to write again to Mr Dawson, but you forbid me doing this, so I must wait the other four months. My dear Annie, I cannot tell you how much I love you, and how I long to call you mine for ever.
   P.S. Did Dr Knight get the game I sent? Did he mention anything about it?
   Yours most affectionately,

W.P.

There's no more letters, Sir, but when he left this cottage on the occasion of his marriage—the wedding dinner was provided for

forty at Abbot's Bromley, and he invited my husband and me—Dr
Palmer declared that he had spent the happiest days of his life in
my cottage. I felt rather hurt when I found my rooms let by him
to a friend of his without my consent; but he says: 'Never mind,
Mamma, I have let them to a very respectable man, and have got
you two shillings a week more rent. I'm sure you deserve it, you're
so very kind.'

He had leased a nice house from Lord Litchfield. You'll find it
immediately opposite The Talbot Arms Hotel—he chose the situation, I think, to spite Mr Tom Masters, the landlord; and there,
at the entrance, he set up his brass plate. I should have mentioned
that, while lodging with me, he worked regularly at his profession, helping old Dr Bamford, the Palmers' family physician, with
patients who lived in remote farms and hamlets. That gave him
good experience for, as he used to say: 'A diploma's not everything.
Dr Bamford may have no diploma nor medical degree, but experience he has, and that's what counts in doctoring.' I think that
Dr Bamford, who had always liked Master William, came to feel
great gratitude for him, especially as he demanded no fee for his
assistance, but only out-of-pocket expenses.

No, there's little more to tell you, except that one night he came
home intoxicated from a party. 'Mamma,' he said, 'I'm very ill. But
it's not that I drank a deal of wine: as you know, I'm very abstemious. Someone seems to have played a trick on me, by drugging
my drink. Serves me right for doing the same, as a lark, once or
twice last year when I was at Stafford.' He began telling me of
his love for Annie Brookes, right poetical he was, too. Then suddenly he stops and says: 'I'll tell you the truth, Mamma, because
you're so good and truthful yourself. One of the reasons I love
Annie is that she's like a sweet, pure lily-of-the-valley sprung from
black, stinking mud. Her father was a poor coward, the laugh-
ing-stock of Stafford, and a suicide; her mother a greedy, spiteful,

foul-mouthed strumpet, from whom she had to be rescued by the Court of Chancery. If Annie can be virtuous and hold up her head despite all the misfortunes of her birth—for you know, Mamma, that she's illegitimate into the bargain—why, then so can I! Need I drag out my own family history, Mamma? Surely you'll know it, including the dirty new scandals which my mother's behaviour has caused in the town. You'll have heard of them, no doubt?'

I nodded sadly, for everyone said that, to begin with, Dr Palmer's real father, like the elder brother's, was Hodson, the Marquess of Anglesey's steward, to whom his mother had been leased in return for a few loads of stolen timber.

'Well,' he goes on, 'Mr Weaver did very wisely when he sponsored the match. Annie and I are birds of a feather, and neither of us can cast faults of parentage in the other's teeth. Together, we'll make a clean new home, and raise healthy children, and live in love and truth until death do us part.'

His words were so beautiful that I hugged him to me, and called him my poor lamb.

CHAPTER VIII

THE NURSERY

When Dr Palmer married Annie Brookes on October 7th, 1847, he could count himself tolerably well off. His house, rented at only twenty-five pounds a year, was furnished with elegance; he had a handsome carriage for going his rounds, and although three or four surgeons were already practising in Rugeley, the town boasts four thousand five hundred inhabitants, and the outlying villages another couple of thousand. Consequently Dr Palmer did not lack for patients; indeed, he made quite a reputation, during the December Fair that year, from his skilful setting of broken bones, and soon had more work in hand than pleased him. Benjamin Thirlby was employed at this time by Dr Salt, Rugeley's leading surgeon, to make up medicines and dress wounds; and two years before this had opened the chemist's shop already mentioned in our sketch of the town. One day, according to the account most usually heard, Thirlby felt aggrieved because Dr Salt had reprimanded him sharply for an oversight in the matter of some prescription, and poured out his woes to Dr Palmer when he next visited the shop.

'Nay, Ben,' said Dr Palmer, 'this trouble is soon remedied: why don't you cut your stick and come to me? I'll pay you better than Salt.'

'I'll come with all my heart,' cried Thirlby, still very angry. 'The nineteen years I worked for that ill-mannered old skinflint have been nineteen too many!'

Dr Palmer stretched out his hand for Thirlby's, to shake on the bargain; and Thirlby grasped it firmly.

Dr Salt, though often grumbling about his assistant's pig-headedness, never expected him to break his engagement, however harshly he might be scolded. But Mrs Thirlby now informed him—for Thirlby himself hid his shame under a mask of surliness, and turned to walk in the opposite direction whenever he saw Dr Salt approaching—that Dr Palmer had offered her husband twenty pounds a year more than his former wage. The news made Dr Salt very angry indeed. That a surgeon should entice away another's assistant is considered as grave a breach of professional etiquette as when a gentleman steals his neighbour's French cook, or a minister of religion poaches for souls in a fellow-minister's congregation. Dr Salt, who was much respected locally, did not scruple to complain in public of Thirlby's ingratitude and Dr Palmer's ill-manners, and earned a deal of sympathy; Rugeley being a town where sharp practice has never been condoned as a good joke, as it so often is in Liverpool and London.

Miss Salt, Dr Salt's daughter and Annie Palmer's closest friend, when she called the next day as usual, explained how difficult her situation had become as a result of Thirlby's sudden change of employment.

'Oh, but my dear child,' cried Annie, 'I'm afraid you have been given quite the wrong notion. William told me all about Thirlby as soon as he came home. It appears that your father scolded Thirlby because he had forgotten to prepare some pills, and when he pleaded that the prescription was written so illegibly that it would have been dangerous to guess at its meaning, your father called him a bleary-eyed clod-hopper and dismissed him on the spot. William, happening to pass by, found Mrs Thirlby in a flood of tears, and kindly told her not to despair—Thirlby should first make sure that the dismissal was final, and if so, come to work with himself. She sent Thirlby off to try at the surgery whether your father might perhaps relent, but he soon returned, saying: "Dr Salt swears that he never goes back on a dismissal. I'll come to you, Will, if I may." As you see, Will is not in the least to blame.'

Miss Salt naturally concluded that Thirlby had been lying to Dr Palmer. She told her father so, but he merely remarked 'Humph!' and never troubled to inquire into the matter; though when Dr Palmer offered him neither an apology nor an explanation, he cut him dead one morning in the Market Square.

Dr Salt did not forbid his family to continue their friendly relations with the Palmers. He knew that Miss Salt had been Annie Palmer's bridesmaid at the wedding and loved her dearly; and that his son Edwin thought highly of Dr Palmer. 'It takes all sorts to make a world,' he would say in sour tones that showed his ill opinion of a world so made; but he was kind enough not to involve his children in the quarrel.

Annie Palmer grieved to think that Dr Salt had taken an aversion to her beloved husband. She had inherited a tendency to melancholia from her father and, though hitherto the fits had been slight and short-lasting, some drunken talk she now overheard from the tap-room of The Talbot Arms Hotel across the street, about her husband's escapades at Stafford Infirmary, plunged her into a black misery. Yet Dr Palmer was tenderness itself, and did all in his power to cheer Annie up, attributing these moods to her condition; for she had found herself pregnant after three months of marriage. He bought her a chaise and a beautiful pair of ponies to drive about the country with, and she used to tell Miss Salt: 'I really can't explain these black fits, unless Will is right in saying that they're due to my baby, for you know I'm very happy indeed.

I have all that heart could desire, or that money can buy. And to be a mother is a glorious thing!'

When at last he begged to be taken into Annie's confidence, it came out that guilt was gnawing at her conscience. By order of the Court of Chancery she had been separated from her mother, whom the Bible required that she should honour, and had never asked leave to be re-united with her. 'Mr Dawson and Dr Knight,' Annie told him, 'both spoke unkindly of my mother, and I dared not oppose them. Neither have I dared to mention the matter to you. But I should think very ill of myself if I didn't long whole-heartedly to see her again. I can't pretend that I have pleasant memories of her, but perhaps I was a difficult and disagreeable child. If so, I should like to do better now and make her love me again; as she must have done once. All mothers dote on their children until some little thing turns up to disappoint them. What if I died in childbirth? Would that not be God's punishment on me for not having insisted on visiting her while I yet could?'

It speaks exceedingly well for Dr Palmer that though he had heard the whole story of Colonel Brookes and Mary Ann Thornton from Mr Weaver, if from nobody else, he decided to humour his wife. Mrs Thornton, by this time a haggard and prematurely aged eccentric, still occupied the house behind St Mary's Church, Stafford, where Colonel Brookes had died and Annie had been born. She kept no servants, seldom appeared in the street except on her brief visits to shops, and lived among a swarm of cats with which she held prolonged and one-sided conversations about subjects certainly well above their heads.

Mrs Thornton would not at first open the front door to the elegant young couple who came calling in their chaise-and-pair; but when Annie had made herself known, through the key-hole, she unlocked the door hastily and, with tears coursing down her dirty cheeks, sobbed out: 'My little love . . . My own lost darling!'

Annie timidly asked her mother not to squeeze her quite so hard because she hoped, within a few months' time, to become a mother herself.

'At last I have something to live for!' Mrs Thornton exclaimed, raining alcoholic kisses on Annie's face. She promised to put the house in better order for a next visit which, she hoped, would take place as soon as possible. Dr Palmer showed great attention to the poor creature, even bringing himself to address her as 'Mamma'; and Annie returned home deeply grateful for his kindness and understanding.

She was very religious, and persuaded her husband to be the same. They regularly attended the new church of St Augustine's, near The Yard, which is kept up in style, with gravelled walks and turf well-swept and trimmed. (The old Parish church, on the other hand, is a mere Gothic ruin. Its square tower has empty holes for windows, like the eye-sockets of a skull, and is swathed with tattered ivy. Its chancel, roofed in with boards and tarpaulin, has been turned into a Sunday School.) Enter the new church by the great oaken door, and the swinging inner doors faced with red baize, as new and bright as a postman's coat in May, and you will find the Palmers' pew well to the fore. Black-bound prayer books and Bibles with gilt edges rest on its ledge, and the fly-leaf of a Book of Common Prayer is inscribed: *William Palmer, Rugeley, Aug. 28, 1837; the gift of his mother, Mrs Sarah Palmer, Rugeley.* A Bible contains some pencil notes in Dr Palmer's handwriting: '*He was a teacher come from God—Means, Prayer—God's word all the means of grace—Particular means, faith in Christ—Faith has a heavenly influence.*' The interior of the church is newly white-washed, and flooded with light streaming in cleanly through diamond-paned windows; but a huge red curtain casts a warm glow upon the sides of a polished, goblet-shaped pulpit. Dr Palmer is said to have been exceedingly attentive to the sermons, and the only member of the congregation who took notes; he would also read the responses louder than anyone else and give generously to all charities.

A rumour, almost certainly unfounded, had of late coupled his name with that of Mrs Salt, Dr Salt's daughter-in-law, whom he was treating for some female ailment; and this, added to Dr Salt's ill opinion of him, caused a decided shrinkage in the flow of patients. But he did not care, being already tired of medical work. The following letter to his wife, which has come into our hands, must have been written from Rugeley about this time, when she had gone for a change of air to stay with Mr Edwin Salt and his wife some fourteen miles away.

Sunday Evening.

My ever adored Annie:

I feel certain that you will forgive me for not writing to you last night, when I tell you that since I last saw you I have not had two hours' sleep. I do assure you, I never felt so tired in my life—I am almost sick of my profession. Sorry I am to say, my Mother has had another attack and one of my late sister's children I think will be dead before morning. It is now half past ten, and I have just come home from Haywood to write you: for I do assure you, my dearest, I should have been very unhappy had I not done so.

My dearest Annie, I propose, all being well, to be with you tomorrow about three, and depend upon it, nothing but ill health will ever keep me away from you—forgive me, my duck, for not sending you the paper last night, I really could not help it. I will explain fully tomorrow. My dear, remember I must say something about needlework— you will be amused. My sweetest and loveliest Annie, I never was more pleased with you in my life than on Friday afternoon last—it was a combination of things. God bless you! I hope we may live together and love each other for sixty years to come.

Excuse me now, for I must go. Till tomorrow at 3. Accept my ever-lasting love and believe me,

Ever your most affectionate

WM PALMER

On the advice of a sporting friend, George Myatt the Rugeley saddler, Dr Palmer now resolved to supplement his earnings by an altogether different means: namely, the breeding of race-horses. In Rugeley, where horses are almost the sole subject of serious conversation among the mass of the people, there was nothing surprising or improper in such a resolve. On the contrary, should he succeed in his new trade, a great number of men would offer themselves as patients who judged a physician or surgeon by his ability to judge a horse. He must be able to pronounce on its good and bad points; accurately diagnose its diseases, if any; reckon its speed and staying-power; and, at the finish, by an abstruse but rapid calculation, tell to within a couple of guineas what it should fetch in the ring. If by virtue of his critical faculty, Dr Palmer could buy cheap and sell dear; and if he could lay his hands on three or four useful mares, engage famous stallions to cover them, and so breed foals which sporting men would come many miles to look at—why, his fortune was made! So Dr Palmer laid out most of his remaining capital on horseflesh, and leased from Lord Litchfield a large paddock at the back of the house, with stabling for twelve horses and several fields adjacent—altogether some twenty-one acres enclosed by hawthorn hedges. He had the property in order shortly before the birth of his first child, whom he christened William after himself, and who is today a healthy seven-year-old, showing promise of great intelligence.

'Harry Hockey', the withered old groom, until recently employed by Dr Palmer at Rugeley—his real name seems to be Henry Cockayne—talked to us, straw in mouth. Since Dr Palmer's arrest, the fields have reverted to Lord Litchfield, and Harry keeps an eye on the hunters and carriage horses put out to grass there.

HARRY HOCKEY

No, Sir, I could never complain that Dr Palmer treated me badly, nor could any of the boys employed. But ours was a rum concern. What I mean is that the Doctor's chief passion was racing, yet he never bred any colts to run, barring Rip van Winkle, whom Nat Flaxman coaxed into second place at the Brighton T.Y.O. Sweepstakes last year. He bought a good many for that purpose, that's certain, at very large prices, too, and sent them to train at Saunders', in Hednesford. I reckon he began his racing career four years ago— the Spring of 1852—and his colours were registered as all-yellow.

This place was a nursery only; with no training done, except for the ringing we gave the colts. He kept, on an average, three or four brood-mares at a time, and there always used to be a good many young things about. He was proud of his stables, and often brought parties of friends to view them, and talked big about the mares. However, he seldom kept up an interest in any particular animal for more than a week or two after he bought it. They say, Sir, that he was the same with his fancy women. For a short while they entranced him, but because of some slight fault, real or fancied, he would suddenly wish himself rid of them. He used to sell them—the mares, I mean—for most curious prices. Once, I remember, he priced a couple at ten pounds. Perhaps he needed the money, but I'd have offered three times that sum for either of them, had I known he was selling, and pledged my cottage to raise it. He bred some good horses, I can assure you, but all to what purpose? The money he made can't have paid the expenses, not one quarter! He always seemed to buy at the highest price, and sell at the lowest; all Rugeley called him a mug. Yet even Tom Masters allowed he had a wonderful eye for a horse, and most people were glad to get his free opinion on their own purchases. It's my view that he had a great contempt of money, which was matched only by his need of it. He paid me well, not regular, but well enough: a guinea a week, sometimes two.

The races were meat and drink to him. There's many racing gentlemen I know who find time for shooting and fishing, or else they hunt foxes. The Doctor wasn't one of them. He had a good, clumsy seat on a horse, and used to ride beside Saunders to watch colts of his being tried out; but I never saw him going over the sticks, or jogging off to a meet, though there's three packs of hounds that meet regularly hereabouts.

No, bless you, Sir, a good eye for a horse and a close attention to the stud-book don't suffice to win a man money at racing, which is a dirty business, and best kept out of by honest folk, among whom I hope to reckon myself. Come, Sir, sit down on this bench with me. I understand that you're green to the game. What's that you want to know? About the ringing?

Well, now, a colt begins with a dumb-jockey, which is a log we strap on his back when he's old enough to take the weight, and which he flings off again and again until he gets tired of the sport, and doesn't kick and plunge quite so often. Presently we start the ringing: which is to bridle him, and then I stand with a whip in my hand and keep him a-going around me in a circle, the dumb-jockey on his back; and I don't care whether he runs, trots, plunges, gallops, or dances, so long as he keeps a-moving. When he's got the notion, we put up a lad instead of the log, and carry the game on. Before long he's ready for the trainer's, and we're done with him here.

It's like sending a young lord up from dame's school to Eton

College. He takes his groom with him, as a footman, and the fees asked ain't any too low, I assure you! But there's this difference between Saunders' training establishment and Eton College: that the colt don't lead so irregular a life. There's no drinking rather too much claret on the sly, nor smoking more cigars than is good for the growing creature. At Saunders', they calculate his feed to the very grain of corn and thread of hay that will hold him in the pink of condition. And his drink is just as sharply watched, being calculated to the go-down—or gulp, if you please. When he's been in training for some weeks, Mr Will Saunders, he puts his own groom up for a trial run, and the colt is placed with several others in what's called a 'string'. Then he's taken off at a gentle gallop, known as 'the pipe o'peace', and Saunders rides on one side, about the middle, and watches the action of each and every beast.

After the pipe o'peace, Saunders gives them all a clever going-over, to look out for injured legs or hoofs. Then they are bathed in warm water and bandaged, and perhaps they get gruel to drink, and bran mash instead of corn. I've heard Dr Palmer say: 'I'd a thousand times rather be a colt at Saunders' than a pauper in Stafford Infirmary!' Often the horses gain too much flesh—which never, by the way, happens to an Infirmary pauper, unless he suffers from the dropsy—and have to be sweated, which is done with extra cloths and cutting down of their feed . . . Believe me, it's a severe training, as much for the lads as for the horses.

Now, even at Rugeley, which is famed for its Horse Fair, and has its own race-course yonder, there's still many folk as green as you, Sir, who think that all the trouble and expense which an owner incurs in getting a beast into prime condition will invariably make him wish it to win races. They are also innocent enough to suppose that the best horse always wins, barring natural accidents. But let me put you right, Sir. You should bear in mind that, large though the Derby Stakes are, and many others, such as the St

Leger and the Oaks, an owner's interest may not always require that his horse passes the post first; I mean, that it may frequently pay him better to lose . . .

Then why should one go to such trouble with the training, you ask? Why, to make the horse look as much like a winner as possible, don't you see?—and persuade those who think he's running on the square to back him heavily. Such bets are taken up by the owner's friends—though they're mighty careful not to show themselves as such, you may be bound—to a far greater amount than the value of the stakes.

Many's the time I've been given a last-minute stable tip-off, as we say, that such-and-such a horse ain't going to win a race, though the favourite; and to bet against him, however short the odds. And I've been present at the starting-post, and seen the admiring glance the owner casts at the beast. If I hadn't heard it muttered from the corner of the jockey's own mouth, I wouldn't in my heart but have believed that the owner was running the horse to win, and had staked his entire fortune on him. Yet the jockey has been ordered to 'rope him in', and so make him fall back out of the running while in full career. There's a double advantage to that little game: at the next meeting the odds will be longer, and at the one after that, if the horse is roped again, longer still. When it's profitable for the owner to run the horse on the square, then he'll do so.

Another trick used to be played to prevent the best horse from winning, called the 'false start'. An owner entered two horses for the same race. One was meant to win, and the other to make the pace. When all the runners were stationed at the starting point, and the word 'Go!' rang out, the horse meant to win stood stock still, the other rushing off at a good gallop. That was a false start, the whole line not having started at the same time. So they were called back, and then sent off again, and after a couple of such false starts the horses were fatigued and irritated by these constant pullings-up; all except the horse kept back. He was fresh as paint, and at the third 'Go!' started boldly forward with every advantage in his favour; and very often won at long odds. But they've put a stop to that game now.

There's still the 'painted bit' game, however. The horse which the owner's laid against comes on the course in full vigour, and the jockey rides him to win. But there's poison smeared on the bit. Half-way along the course, the poor animal foams at the mouth, staggers, turns sick, and falls behind.

Now, to the best of my knowledge, Dr Palmer never played tricks of that sort on his own horses: he always gave his jockeys orders to win. But he certainly was accused of 'nobbling', if you understand my meaning. Nobbling is to dose a rival horse, to prevent him from winning. Scarcely a race is run at which some case or other don't occur, despite the vigilance of the stablemen. The fact is that stable-boys are not highly paid and, for fifty pounds, will sometimes agree to 'make a horse safe' by giving him a drug. Strychnia is a favourite these days, and easy for a surgeon to obtain—as Dr Palmer was. Half a grain will stiffen the muscles, but won't kill. It may interest you to know, Sir, that a valuable horse was destroyed here at Rugeley, during the October meeting of 1853, a favourite for the Marquess of Anglesey's Stakes. I can't recall his name, which was one of them tongue-twisters; howsomever I know that the noble owner had stabled him at The Crown. Very early in the morning of the race, someone scoops a hole in the stable wall and pushes through it a carrot hollowed out and filled with arsenic. The poor beast must have died at once; the offender was never caught. Dr Palmer's Doubt won that race at useful odds. Mind, I'm saying nothing, not having been in Rugeley at the time; but those are the facts, I believe.

Dr Palmer plunged in his betting, and I thought it very rum that he never changed countenance whatever happened. He wasn't the man to thrust a walking-stick through a pier glass in celebration of a victory, as I have seen done. We all used to notice him when he came back from the races and looked in at the stables. None of us could tell whether he had won or lost. Only once did I see him out of temper, and that was nearly at the end of his run. A fellow named George Bate, formerly a fanner, was put in charge of us then, and took a sudden dislike to the Doctor. Maybe he had his reasons. Maybe also they'll appear at the trial, for he's been summoned to London as a witness, and so has yours obediently . . .

At any rate, one day George Bate comes to me, and says: 'Harry, what's passed in the eight-acre field?'

'How should I know?' I asks.

'Come and take a morris down there!' says he. So we stroll through the home-paddock, and into the eight-acre, and he says to me: 'The turf's mighty cut about. It's as if the mares have been galloping about in the night. Did you hear aught?'

I says: 'No, I didn't.' Then I pointed and said: 'Look'ee, Mr Bate, here's the mark of a hound's paw on this mole heap, and it's made fresh! However did a hound happen in?'

So I went to see whether the mares had come to harm, and we found that the Duchess of Kent had slipped her foal, as Goldfinder had one night a week before; nor did we discover any signs of it nowhere. The hounds must have ate it. Mr Bate, he tried to tie the blame on me, but I told him that I wouldn't be made a scapegoat. It was none of my business to see that the gaps were stopped. He argued a bit, but I held my ground, and presently we heard the sound of wheels, and along came Dr Palmer in a fly. He asks me after the Duchess.

I says: 'Sorry to tell you, Sir, she's had an accident—slipped her foal.' He turned a trifle pale and says: 'You rascal, how did that occur?' 'Ask Mr Bate,' I said, 'it's his affair, not mine.'

'George,' cries Dr Palmer, 'what in the Lord's name happened to the poor creature?'

George looks steadily at him and says: 'She was run by hounds, last night. It will be some enemy of yours, Sir, popped them in through the hedge.'

'You'll pay for this, George, as I live!' shouts the Doctor.

Then George answers quietly: 'You should have taken an insurance policy for a few thousand pounds on the foal's life; the same as you tried to do with mine.'

At once the Doctor's manner changes. He put a hand on George's shoulder. 'Why, George,' he says sorrowfully. 'You didn't owe me that smack in the face. Surely you knew we were gammoning?'

But George didn't change his tone, not he. He says: 'You and your precious friends Cook and Jerry Smith—I owed you something for that trick you played on me. And now I think we're quits.'

He turns his back and walks away.

Dr Palmer looks at me, and an unhappier face I seldom saw. But then he shrugs and twiddles a forefinger at his temples: 'George's daft,' says he to me, 'don't pay any attention to him! It was all on account of a practical joke concocted by Mr Cook and Mr Smith, and others of my friends, which he took in earnest. But it's a bore about that foal. I had great hopes from it. Maybe Tom Masters set those hounds at the mares. If so, I'll be even with him, you'll see. I'll poison the lot of them!' I made no answer, thinking silence to be the safer course.

The Doctor goes away, and an hour later comes back with a gun, which he shows me how to load and fire, and gives me cartridges. 'Keep this by you in the corn-store, Harry,' says he. 'And if you see anyone around here behaving in a suspicious manner, don't hesitate to shoot. I won't have my valuable foals murdered. That's the second in ten days.'

'Very good, Sir,' I says, but I resolved never to touch the weapon, whatever might come to pass.

I told George Bate about the gun, and he gave me a wise look. 'You had better lose them cartridges, Harry,' says he, 'because now that the insurance company have refused to insure my life for Palmer, he won't benefit nothing by my accidental death, the same as he's benefited from others. That Inspector Field who came down the other day told me the whole story; but I was to keep my mouth shut, which I do.'

'Here are the cartridges, Master Bate,' says I, and he takes and puts them in his pocket and goes away, whistling. That happened not long before Dr Palmer's arrest—the first week in November, it must have been.

CHAPTER IX

AN UNFORTUNATE SERIES OF DEATHS

At his wife's entreaty, Dr Palmer invited her mother, Mrs Thornton, to come and live with them. Copious draughts of gin, scarcely supported by any food, had now reduced her to a pitiable state. The swarm of cats that surrounded her must starve or fend for themselves, and her fine residence had deteriorated sadly: in another couple of years it would be almost valueless. Dr Palmer therefore persuaded Mrs Thornton to write him three cheques, in the amount of twenty or thirty pounds each, which would enable him to pay for the necessary repairs on her behalf. But he found it hard to wean the poor woman away from the house, even under colour of making it more comfortable for her, because, as she told a neighbour: 'I'll not live long, once I'm away.'

On January 6th, 1849, Mrs Thornton was found stretched dead-drunk on the dining-room floor, a victim of acute *delirium tremens*; and that evening Dr Palmer brought her, under restraint, to his own house, where Annie, though still weak from childbirth, prepared to tend her with loving care.

Soon, however, Annie wished that accommodation might have been found elsewhere for her mother, who used to shriek and scream in the night, arousing the whole household, and swear terribly, especially at 'that awful devil Palmer,' who was accused of robbing her and murdering the faithful cats. The swarm of cats had, indeed, been mercifully destroyed by him, being so thin and mangy that no neighbour would offer them a home. She demanded gin all day long, but Dr Palmer refused to allow her a drop, which made the case worse. When she began to complain of violent headaches and sickness, and desired to see 'a real doctor, not a robber and murderer', he obligingly called in old Dr Bamford. Dr Bamford shook his head dolefully as he remarked: 'Gin is her poison, but it's also her sole medicine; I'd let her take a little now and then, if I were you, Billy, my boy. But make it a condition that she eats at the same time. And an effervescent mixture might be helpful.'

Dr Palmer therefore conceded her a little gin, but still she would not eat, and raised such a hubbub when he pressed thinly sliced bread and butter on her, that for his wife's sake he added an opiate to the next noggin. Since Annie no longer ventured into the sickroom, lest the distress it occasioned might dry up or sour her milk, and hazard the life of their infant son, Dr Palmer took charge of the nursing himself, with the help of Mrs Bradshaw, the handywoman. Annie suggested that Dr Knight should be called, for a second opinion; but he was suffering from a severe cold and could not come until January 14th—when he briefly examined the patient, shook his head, as Dr Bamford had done, and went off without demanding a fee. Four days later, Mrs Thornton died in a wandering delirium, and Dr Bamford duly signed the death certificate, ascribing her death to apoplexy. 'It would not be seemly to put "died of gin and prolonged self-neglect",' he remarked.

The nine houses in which Mrs Thornton had a life-interest, now reverted to Mr Shallcross as the heir-at-law—but not before Dr Palmer had paid a further sum out of his own pocket towards their repair. Mrs Thornton, it appears, had been responsible, as landlady, for mending the fissures in the walls and the leaks in the roof but, since she had failed to do so, the tenants had revenged themselves by not paying rent. That Dr Palmer thus acted against his own interest in repairing these houses is an effectual proof that, so far from poisoning Mrs Thornton, as has since been unkindly alleged, he had hoped, by bringing the sick creature home, at great inconvenience, to increase her span of life. She was not yet fifty years old and, her expenses being small, the longer she lived, the better for the Palmers as her guardians.

Mr Shallcross, when informed of Mrs Thornton's death, claimed the property, and not only refused to allow Dr Palmer anything for the repairs, but when these were presently completed, and the tenants therefore paid their arrears, demanded the entire sum, amounting to nearly five hundred pounds. Dr Palmer brought an action against him, but Shallcross won the case.

An even more unfortunate event happened two or three months later. Old Mrs Palmer's brother, one Joseph Bentley, was living at Dodsley near Uttoxeter in Derbyshire. Since Dr Palmer had business near by, she asked him to call on his uncle and convey her affectionate remembrances; but forgot to warn him what sort of a customer to expect.

Joseph Bentley went by the nickname of 'Beau Bentley'. He always dressed in the height of fashion, and could well afford to do so, his first wife having left him a great deal of money. The people of Dodsley suspected him of murdering his second wife, who fell downstairs one morning and broke her neck; and he had since lived, for eighteen years, with a servant girl on whom he fathered an illegitimate daughter. Beau Bentley was now not only married a third time, but had also seduced his illegitimate daughter.

On Dr Palmer's arrival, Beau Bentley showed him a little female toddler, and said proudly: 'She's both my daughter begotten in adultery, and my grand-daughter, begotten in incest. If God grants me long life and continued strength in my loins, I hope to breed yet another daughter by her. Pray, young fellow, what do you think of that?'

Dr Palmer answered: 'I reckon you're the blackest sheep of a tolerably vile family, Uncle Joseph; and I don't hold with inbreeding, even in sheep.'

'Ah, but you don't know the half of it!' chuckled Beau Bentley, who had been drinking heavily. 'I surprise myself sometimes by my scarlet sins.'

'What crimes have you committed beyond incest?' Dr Palmer asked.

'Why, there's murder,' said Bentley, 'in the first degree, and also in the second; besides robbery, arson, and rape. But Jack Ketch will never get old Joe Bentley! He may drown; he'll never hang.'

'I almost fear to drink with you, Uncle!' cried Palmer.

'I almost fear to drink with myself,' he rejoined, 'lest I entertain too strong a dislike for the wretch whose face I see reflected in the brandy. Nevertheless, here goes!'

With that he downed a large tumbler of neat brandy, and toppled from his chair insensible. Dr Palmer quitted Dodsley in disgust, and heard next day that Beau Bentley had never recovered from his stupor.

No Coroner was called, but Dr Palmer made a sworn statement before the magistrate, exactly recounting the conversation, and Beau Bentley's body went to the graveyard without more ado. The magistrate commented: 'Well, Sir, he cheated us and took his own way out: for certainly he drowned in that tumbler of brandy!' As might have been expected in a town like Stafford, the case of Abley, who had died after drinking with Dr Palmer, was brought up in this connexion; and tongues also began to wag about Mrs Thornton's death. The Doctor was rumoured to have gained twelve thousand pounds from it; and an equal amount from Beau Bentley's—though, in effect, he gained nothing but trouble from either event. The bulk of Bentley's money had been willed to his illegitimate daughters, and not a penny-piece came to any Palmer.

Yet another fatality ensued soon afterwards. By this time, Dr Palmer had more or less abandoned the medical practice which his brass plate still announced. He spent most of his week away at race-meetings, betting and studying form. In May, 1850, a gentleman named Leonard Bladon, living in London and employed as collector for Charrington's Brewery, attended Chester Races with him. Bladon, it seems, backed two winners and made a pile of money, mostly by bets laid and paid on the race-course; it also seems that Dr Palmer owed him a great deal more. Bladon wrote to his wife in London that he would not be home for two or three days: '. . . but with what I have in "ready", and what Palmer will pay me, I shall come with a thousand pounds. Being a good loser, the Doctor has invited me to Rugeley, and promised me some sport with a gun.'

Bladon duly came to Rugeley, where the Palmers entertained him, and that evening inquired whether anyone would be driving over to Ashby de la Zouch, his native town. He had debts to collect there, he said, and would like to see his brother Henry again. Jeremiah Smith, the solicitor (Dr Palmer's crony, and old Mrs Palmer's present bed-fellow), volunteered to drive Bladon to Ashby and back the same day. It is acknowledged that Bladon carried one hundred pounds in his money-belt when he arrived at Rugeley. But we find a conflict of testimony about his subsequent wealth. Some say that Dr Palmer owed him six hundred pounds, and that a further sum of three hundred pounds was owing him at Ashby de la Zouch (which would account for the thousand pounds he hoped to take home); others, that he arrived at Ashby with five hundred pounds, and that he collected no money there, but spent plenty; and, further, that Dr Palmer owed him no more than four hundred pounds—from which it would appear that Dr Palmer had paid in full and on the nail. At all events, Bladon visited his old friend Mr Bostock, an Ashby printer; he also ordered a fine pair of riding boots from his brother Henry, a shoemaker, who undertook to bring them over to Rugeley when completed; and Jeremiah Smith drove him back to Rugeley that same night.

Now, though reckoned to be in tolerably good health, Bladon had not yet recovered from a recent accident at the Brewery, where a shaft of the manager's gig had caught him in the stomach. The London surgeon employed by Charrington's to protect them against frivolous claims for compensation, examined him and pronounced that the slight internal injury sustained would soon heal, if he consented to spend the next few days quietly; but for this Bladon had no patience. On his return to Rugeley he fell ill again, and Dr Palmer treated him, with Ben Thirlby's help. After they had exhausted their skill, and Bladon still complained of severe pains in the stomach, Dr Bamford was asked to prescribe a mixture; which he did. Bladon begged Dr Palmer not to let his wife know that he was ill; because she had strongly opposed his going to Chester in the first place. No letter was therefore sent her. However, a friend of Bladon's, by name Merritt, who had attended Chester Races and knew his present whereabouts, came over to Rugeley with a hot tip for the Oaks. Shocked by Bladon's dismal appearance, Merritt hurried back to the Railway Station and caught the London Express train; he told Dr Palmer in forcible language that Mrs Bladon should be at once acquainted with her husband's condition.

When Mrs Bladon arrived on the following day, she found him in the greatest pain, and no longer able to recognize her. Annie Palmer took the dismayed lady down into the parlour, made tea, and showed her the greatest sympathy. Bladon died soon afterwards. It has been said that Dr Palmer refused to let Mrs Bladon see the corpse, pretending that it was fast decomposing and not a pleasant sight; but, in fact, Annie charitably kept her from the room. Dr Bamford again signed the certificate, declaring that death had been due to internal injuries, received some weeks previously and aggravated by the journey along rough country roads to Ashby de la Zouch and back.

Mrs Bladon expressed surprise that a mere fifteen pounds had been found on her husband's person. He had made a large sum of money at Chester Races, she said. Jeremiah Smith agreed that he did indeed take a deal of money to Ashby de la Zouch, but suggested that it was spent there. William Merritt came down for the funeral with Mr Henry Bladon, the dead man's brother; both of them were convinced that Leonard Bladon had been robbed and poisoned, for his pockets had been ransacked, his private papers turned over, and some of them abstracted, including the betting-book. Merritt informed the Rugeley Police of the matter, hinting at foul play and demanding an inquiry; but on being approached by the Inspector, Mrs Bladon declared herself unready to make any charge against Jeremiah Smith, whom she strongly suspected of theft, or against Dr Palmer as an accomplice. She feared that they might bring an action for slander.

Here is a letter which she wrote to Mr Bostock, the Ashby printer, on this occasion:

June 14, 1850.

Dear Sir,
    I am exceedingly obliged to you and Mrs Bostock for the kind interest you take in my affairs, and have no doubt, from the respect you bore my late husband, you would have done what you say. But if you take into con-

sideration the afflicting circumstances I was placed in, with no one of my own friends round me to offer advice or counsel, ignorant of the distance from Rugeley to Ashby (which I considered much farther), and bowed down by grief, you will understand that I did not act with the coolness of reflection.

In the midst of my trouble Mr Palmer insisted on my signing a paper for £59–£50 of which he said Mr Bladon had borrowed of him, and £9 which he said had been paid to Mr Bladon for twenty gallons of gin not received. The gratitude I felt for the kind treatment my husband had, as I thought, received from them would have induced me to sign it on the spot, could I have done so without self-injury. But knowing the embarrassed state of my affairs I candidly informed them of it; still, Mr Palmer insisted on my signing the paper, though urging me that if it was not in my power to pay, he could not compel me to do so by law. And I think I should have signed the paper, but for his saying that he had never borrowed a farthing of Mr Bladon in his life. I knew that this was a falsehood, as I had seen a paper in my husband's desk in which he acknowledged £100, and I told him so.

From that moment he ceased to insist on my signing, and said he would make me a present of the debt; and on Mrs Palmer coming into the room, from which she had been absent a short time, he told her to throw the paper, which was lying on the table, into the fire.

Now as regards the suspicions that Henry and you seem to entertain of his brother's death, I did not share them. I felt, and still feel, extremely obliged to Mrs Palmer for her tenderness to me which could not have been greater if I had been a relative of her own. Consider how shocking it would appear, without some proof more than mere surmises, to accuse anyone of a foul crime which your letter more than hints at. If your mind is not easy, go over yourself and make inquiries; but pause before you do anything to render Mrs Palmer so uneasy as such a dreadful charge must make her. Think what in such a case your own wife's feelings would be, and consider mine. That Mr Palmer has acted unjustly in money matters I have good reason to believe. His letters I have placed in the hands of the Brewery firm and, if they think proper, and there are sufficient grounds, they will no doubt investigate the matter.

Thanking you and Mrs Bostock for your kind invitation, of which I shall be happy to avail myself, allow me to subscribe myself your sincere friend,

E. J. BLADON

No investigation was, in fact, made. We believe that an autopsy would have sustained Dr Bamford's diagnosis; also, that the lost money would have been traced to the possession of another than Dr Palmer.

Annie Palmer's position was by no means to be envied. She had, it is true, the affection of a husband who did not stint his generosity towards her, and loved her with passion; but he was now often away, attending race-meetings in different parts of the country, and could be expected home, for certain, only on Sundays. He never failed to attend divine service at St Augustine's, though he might have to travel fifty miles by railway train and fly, in order to reach Rugeley on Saturday night. Miss Salt had not cooled towards her in affection, and neither had Mrs Edwin Salt; she had, however, no other close friends, Mr Dawson having expunged her from the list of his intimates since the marriage.

Worse, she was pregnant every year, and with unfailing regularity every child of hers died within a month or two of birth. An unfortunate remark of Dr Palmer's now went the rounds: that a growing family would be too great a charge on his slender purse, and that he could not altogether blame Providence for having cut short the lives of little Elizabeth, Henry and Frank. They all, it appears, died in convulsions.

After the death of John, the fourth child, who died on January 30th, 1854, Mrs Bradshaw, the help, rushed into The Bell next door and shocked the customers who were nodding over their ale and talking sagely about women and horses—their two main subjects of conversation

—'I'll never go back to that house no more. That wretch has done away another of his children!'

Pressed to explain what method of infanticide Dr Palmer used, she declared: 'Why, he smears poison on his little finger and then dips it in honey and gives it to the poor innocent to suck.'

'Have you seen the Doctor doing so?' asked the landlord.

'No, but I know it in my heart,' said Mrs Bradshaw, reaching for her gin and water.

In our opinion, Mrs Bradshaw's imagination must have been morbidly stirred by the loose talk going the rounds in Rugeley. We find it difficult to reconcile Dr Palmer's love for his wife and his boy Willie with any such cold-blooded murder. Moreover, it is a common tragedy in families which are well-to-do, careful in their hygiene, and quite above suspicion, for the first child to be born safe and sound and the second, third, fourth and fifth to be either miscarried or born so sickly that they never survive infancy. Doctors cannot explain this phenomenon, except perhaps as indicating some failure of the mother's blood to agree with the father's; though why the first child should survive they do not venture to suggest.

Dr Palmer now sent his wife for a holiday to the little coastal village of Ramsgate, accompanied by her friend Miss Salt. A letter has come into our hands, undated but doubtless posted in 1854 on that occasion. It is written beneath a copperplate engraving of the Crystal Palace, with the inscription: '*Palace of Glass for the Industrial Exhibition, Hyde Park, 1850, designed by Joseph Paxton, Esq., F.L.S. This magnificent structure is 1848 ft. long, 408 ft. wide, and 66 ft. high, and is built entirely of glass and iron.*'
The letter runs:

> *My dearest Willie,*
>   I hope you are very happy and also very good. Mamma has been to purchase this little picture for you: I was sorry not to get a coloured one. I shall hear from Papa all about you, so let him have to tell me that you are a DEAR GOOD BOY. I shall not forget, all being well, some pretty toy for you. Give Papa twenty kisses for Mamma, and twenty for yourself, and with love ever—
>   *Your affectionate mother,*
>
>   A. PALMER
>
> *London, Thursday,*
>   Tell Papa I will write to him tomorrow from Ramsgate.

She was away at Ramsgate a fortnight, enjoying the sea breezes and collecting shells on the shore. While there, she unbosomed herself to Miss Salt, saying: 'My poor mother died on a visit to our house, soon after dear Willie was born; and then Mr Leonard Bladon died; and afterwards there was Mr Joseph Bentley, whom my husband had been to visit; and since then, four little innocents of our own. Whatever will people say?'
But she could guess what the Rugeley gossip would be; and

when the two ladies were packing their trunks for the journey back, she remarked to Miss Salt: 'My darling Willie—I hope he's safe!' Then, catching a look of surmise in her friend's eye, she changed her words: 'I mean, I hope he's *well!*'

And well he was, having a merry time playing at 'lions and tigers' with his father in the parlour, and listening to fairy stories from a book. But on Annie's return, melancholia settled more firmly than ever on her. She once remarked: 'If it wasn't so wicked, and if it wasn't for wanting to look after Willie, I'd think no more about taking my life than turning off a faucet. I've been a cruel disappointment to my husband, though he's as patient as a saint, and never addresses me harshly, or blames me for bearing sickly infants. He always says: "Your new treasure is just a bit nicer and prettier than the last." When I'm gone, he'll soon find another wife, with all that I lack in looks and accomplishments; but he gets cross whenever I tell him that.'

Since Dr Palmer's arrest, a great many new stories have come into circulation which represent him as having killed scores of people in these years; but they prove without exception to be clumsy fabrications designed to assist the sale of the newspapers that publish them. For example, *The Norfolk Chronicle* prints the following story, but gives no exact date, nor even a certain location for the poisoning. It seems to have been concocted on the model of Bladon's murder, which the Rugeley Police, after making due inquiries, decided to be no murder at all.

It seems that a few years ago a young man named Bly, residing near Beccles, had formed an unfortunate connexion with the Turf, and chanced to be professionally attended by William Palmer, either at Rugeley, or at some town adjacent to a race-course, by many said to be Leicester. Bly had, singularly enough, won largely of Palmer, when he was thus taken dangerously ill. His wife, having heard from him, immediately hurried to his bedside. On her arrival, Palmer tried to persuade her not to see her husband. She succeeded however in having an interview with him, and he told her he believed he was dying and, after expressing contrition for his ill-spent life, stated that in the event of his death she was to apply to Palmer for £800 which he owed him. He died shortly afterwards, and at his funeral Mrs Bly related to Palmer the conversation. Palmer replied that it was only a proof of the state of mind in which the deceased had died, for instead of owing him £800, it was just the reverse, the money being due from the deceased to him. He added that he should never have applied to Mrs Bly for it, if she had not mentioned the subject to him.

From what we have learned at Rugeley, Dr Palmer made game of the talk that went on about him. He would greet old friends in The Bell or The Shoulder of Mutton with a rollicking: 'Here comes the poisoner!' and then, turning to Jack, or Harry, or Bill, would ask: 'And what's your poison, lad? Prussic acid or arsenic?'

'What's your poison?' has since become a proverbial greeting in the inns of Staffordshire on Dr Palmer's account.

CHAPTER X

ENGLISH CHOLERA

The following account of the most tragic event in Dr Palmer's life has been kindly supplied by Dr Salt's daughter, Annie Palmer's closest friend.

MISS SALT

One afternoon, in the September of 1854, I found Annie Palmer in one of her blackest moods. When I tried to hearten her, she said: 'I'm afraid, dear child, all is over now. I have failed my husband both as a companion and as a wife. It would be unbecoming for me to entrust an unmarried girl like yourself with our marital secrets; but I daresay you have guessed how it can be with a young and vigorous husband . . . He wants to make love constantly, and if his wife has a headache or happens to be feeling dull, she can't respond as she should to his caresses. I try to hide my distaste for such encounters, but I can't deceive him always. It's only natural that he should get restive in consequence and, though he professes to love me as much as ever, his appetite remains unsatisfied.'

Here Annie paused, before making what seemed to be a very painful admission. 'That he has bedded with other women while away at distant race-meetings, I have no doubt; and while much disliking the notion, how can I blame him? Now, I fear, he has fallen in love with my own maid—yes, Eliza Tharm—who's eighteen years old and, as you know, full of life. Eliza's an honest girl. Yesterday she came to me and complained that "the Doctor, he's been acting very strange of late, Missus, pulling me about in the pantry and pretending to make love to me." "I hope you resisted him, Eliza," I asked, "like a good girl?" "Oh, yes, Missus," she answered ingenuously, "else I wouldn't have told you. And I hope as I always shall resist him, because it's not right, is it?—not under the same roof as a wife who's always treated me kind!'"

I suggested that Eliza should be dismissed at once, but Annie would not agree. 'Why make needless talk?' she said. 'I believe I can trust Eliza.'

'Did you charge Dr Palmer with the act?' I asked, most indignant on my friend's behalf.

'I did, though not very directly,' she answered. 'He laughed and said he had just given the wench a good-humoured tweak and a slap or two, as she passed; but wouldn't ever do such a thing again, if I objected. He hadn't thought that the girl would take on so; it was only his way, he explained, of cheering her up and showing he wasn't as stiff as most medical men.'

'Did you believe him?' I inquired.

'Why, of course, my dear,' Annie replied, opening her eyes very wide. 'Will never deceives me.'

'But you have just told me that he's in love with the girl,' I insisted.

'Oh, I don't say the poor fellow doesn't deceive himself,' she answered with a sigh. 'The sooner I'm out of his way, the better!'

I reproached her for this shocking remark, and she begged that I would never mention the matter to anyone. And I haven't until today, when I no longer feel bound to silence.

But I told her: 'Annie, my dear, I hear in a roundabout way that he has insured your life for a considerable sum. What is the meaning of this?'

Annie smiled mysteriously, as she answered: 'It was I who suggested that he should take out a policy.'

Observing my look of wonder, she went on: 'You know that I
greatly desire to leave this world. Perhaps I should add that with
the desire goes a clear presentiment that I shall not live long; and
therefore I told Will that he mustn't fail to insure himself against
my sudden death. You see, I have an annuity, from my father, of
two hundred pounds a year, which lasts only while I do, and it
would be a great blow to Will were it cut off without warning. He
listened most unwillingly, saying that mine was an unlucky notion,
and that the premium would carve a deep hole in the value of the
annuity. However, I won him to my view; and last January, Dr
Knight and Dr Bamford, and Dr Monckton all examined me and
pronounced me a "good life". Now I am fully insured and need
not worry on that score . . .'

Here I gave a slight cough and interrupted: 'But Annie, they tell
me that you are over-insured—the premium paid would cover the
risk of losing an annuity three or four times as valuable!'

Again she smiled mysteriously: 'I begged Will to set as great a
value on my life as possible; and I'm glad he rates me so high. He's
promised that if I die, he'll take Willie to your sister- in-law. She
treasures him, and Willie's always happy as a lark at their house, far
happier than at home, though he would never hurt my feelings by
telling me so, he's such a dear, kind boy.'

'But Annie,' I continued, 'if three doctors testify to your being
a good life, who are you to contradict them by an idle presentiment of death?'

She answered: 'I daresay they'd have testified the same for my
poor mother when she was twenty-three years old, as I am now;
yet she died of natural causes while in her early fifties. Besides, my
annuity isn't the only inheritance that Father bequeathed me.'

I said no more, knowing that the Colonel and all his brothers, and his father before him, had suffered from suicidal melancholia. I guessed that what preyed on her mind was a new pregnancy, which she could not face with her former courage. The oftentimes disappointed hope for a healthy little sister, to be Willie's play-mate and her darling, had worn quite thin by this time.

Next day, Annie was invited to accompany Dr Palmer's noble-hearted and sweetly charming sister Sarah on a visit to Liverpool. She appeared to be torn between desire for a holiday and fear lest her husband might press his siege of Miss Eliza. In the end she consented to go, but took the precaution of asking Mrs Bradshaw, their char-woman, to sleep in the house, on the ground that Dr Palmer would probably be away at the races, and Eliza feared to stay alone at night.

The sequel is now public knowledge. On Monday, September 18th, 1854, Annie went by train to Liverpool with Sarah, having bought tickets for a concert at St George's Hall, which she was anxious to hear. But she reposed too much trust in the weather; and on the following day attended the concert wearing a light summer dress. When the two friends emerged from the suffocat-ingly hot hall, they had to wait some time for a cab in a street swept by a bitter east wind. Annie caught a chill, but when they got back to the friends with whom they were lodging—none other than Mr Evans, Senior, Dr Palmer's former employer—would not take Sarah's advice by retiring to bed. Instead, she stayed up and entertained the company by playing sentimental pieces on the pianoforte; she played very well, too. Whist and conversation then continued until a late hour. The next day, Wednesday, September 20th, her chill had worsened, yet after a parting luncheon of cold roast beef, pickles, and a glass of wine, Sarah and she took the train home. On her arrival at Rugeley, Annie was suffering from a vio-lent looseness. She went to bed at once, without taking any food. The following morning, Dr Palmer fetched her a cup of sweet, milkless tea, which she vomited up.

Thereafter, Mrs Bradshaw prepared all her mistress's food: tea, toast, gruel, and once a little arrowroot, always first tasting it, but either Dr Palmer or Eliza Tharm brought it to the bedside. Dr Palmer diagnosed English cholera. Growing anxious when she was no better by Saturday, and still could not keep any food down, he sent for Dr Bamford. Since by now diarrhoea had given place to the opposite condition, and Dr Bamford prescribed some pills containing calomel and colocynth, and an opening draught. On the Sunday, Sarah called, and Annie admitted that she felt very ill indeed. She added: 'You must not come here. Stay with your sick mother—she has you alone to rely on. Your brother George is worse than useless in the circumstances. I'm in safe hands.'

All this time I was away in London on a holiday, and had no inkling of what was afoot.

Dr Bamford called again on the Monday. Observing that only one of his pills had been taken, he engaged Annie in conversation. Yet she felt too reduced to answer his questions audibly and, besides, he is very deaf. Dr Bamford suggested that Dr Knight, Annie's former guardian, should be sent for from Stafford. Dr Palmer, now much distressed by her illness—especially since his mother was also seriously indisposed, and being nursed night and day by Sarah—at once summoned him by a telegraphic message. Dr Knight drove over, and saw Annie the same afternoon. He is even older and deafer than Dr Bamford, and had to rely on Dr Palmer for an account of her symptoms. Having listened carefully, he· pronounced her to be dangerously sick, and gave orders that she must not take anything fluid or solid for three hours. Then he went out, called on Dr Bamford and a few friends, and finding his patient seemingly better when he called back, prescribed a small dose of diluted prussic acid to relieve the retching. In the evening he returned to Stafford.

According to Eliza Tharm (and I believe her), Dr Palmer was

very attentive to Annie, constantly kissing her hands or brow, stroking her cheeks and appealing to her: 'Pray get well, darling! Make a strong endeavour, for my sake and little Willie's.' She smiled faintly up at him, and murmured: 'It's best this way.' He gave her effervescing mixtures, and she intimated that they were most refreshing and made her feel better. Meanwhile, Mrs Ann Rowley had taken Eliza's place as a day-nurse; but Eliza remained on night duty.

On the Thursday, Sarah came to visit Annie again, found her asleep and, not wishing to disturb her, stole away.

On the Friday, Ben Thirlby, called in as a last hope, prescribed brandy and arrowroot, but this was never given Annie; for she died about dinner time. It was September 29th; well I remember hearing the news at Rugeley Railway Station on my return that afternoon.

I immediately made it my business to question Eliza Tharm, Mrs Rowley, and Mrs Bradshaw. Mrs Bradshaw told me that she had tasted, as well as cooked, every item of food or drink that went up to the poor lady, except for the medicine, which wasn't her affair. This Mrs Bradshaw is a good, honest woman as ever lived; but I could see that she suspected Dr Palmer of poisoning her beloved mistress—for she threw him hateful looks. Mrs Rowley, on the other hand, trusted him completely, and testified to the sincere and beautiful love between the two. Annie had whispered to her once: 'I'd do anything in the world for him, Mrs Rowley, indeed I would; and he for me, I believe, don't you?'

When Annie was at her last, Mrs Rowley rang the bell for Dr Palmer. He tiptoed into the bedroom and stood hesitating, aghast at the change in Annie's face. Mrs Rowley said: 'I fear your wife's dying.' He appeared stunned and hurt. He didn't come quite round the bed, Mrs Rowley says, but remained at the foot, staring down at Annie with a dazed look. Then he walked away into the next room, Mrs Rowley doesn't know why, and though he was back only half a minute later, she had died in the meanwhile.

'She's gone,' sobbed Mrs Rowley, and the news sent him stumbling out again. Mrs Rowley sat by the bed for the best part of half an hour, hoping that she had been mistaken, and that Annie was only in a deep coma. When she at last rose to fetch Dr Palmer, he was found in the next room, straddling a chair, with his arms folded on the rail and staring stupidly before him. She took him by the shoulder, and whispered: 'Come, Doctor, be a man!' He seemed not to hear, so she poured a little brandy into a tumbler and set it to his lips. At this he came to himself, muttered: 'I think I must have been asleep,' rubbed his cold hands together, and returned to the death-bed, where Mrs Rowley left him to indulge his grief.

As soon as I could find the time, I sought out Eliza. A wild look in her eye informed me that she was frightened. I drew her into the small room used for sewing, and said: 'My girl, you need have no fear. Dr Bamford, Dr Knight, and Mr Thirlby have all signed the death certificate to say that your mistress died of English cholera. There'll be no coroner's inquest, you may be sure. But I want the truth! Now, I suspect poison, though I cannot suspect Mrs Bradshaw, or Mrs Rowley, or Dr Palmer, or yourself, of wilfully murdering my beloved friend. If it were not manifestly impossible for her to poison herself without detection—except perhaps at Liverpool—I should think that she had taken her own life. Come, speak up, or I'll call the Police!'

The strange story that Eliza told completely satisfied me of its truth. Annie had asked her to slip certain powders into the gruel or tea while nobody was watching: she pretended that they were a charm procured from a wise woman over at Abbot's Bromley, and designed to restore her husband's love. Eliza believed Annie, and did as she was bidden. On the Thursday night, Annie whispered: 'Let him know quietly, when it's all over, that I have done it because I love him so. Suicide is the second crime I've committed for love of him, Eliza; but I trust God will pardon me, as Our Lord Jesus pardoned the woman in the Gospel "because she loved much."' So Eliza guessed that the powders must have caused her mistress's death.

I have lately learned that the poison was antimony, which she probably read about in her husband's medical books, and of which he kept a supply in the surgery. Yet even if I had known of this at the time, I should still have concealed my knowledge. Annie was dead, dead by her own hand, though using Eliza as a cat's paw, and nobody came under the suspicion of administering poison. Eliza had acted not only innocently, but nobly; for I could see that she was deep in love with the Doctor herself. An ill-natured girl would never have put the love-philtres in a rival's gruel to make her more attractive. Why, then, should I stir up trouble by speaking the truth? And why should I officiously make Annie's self-sacrifice a useless one? Dr Palmer was, she had hinted, in a terrible state of indebtedness, and would be ruined but for the insurance which she had urged him to take on her life.

When I told Eliza: 'For your sake, I'll remain silent. You have been a good girl, I believe!' she fell on her knees and kissed my hands. She must have delivered Annie's message to the Doctor; as I judged from his behaviour at the funeral, where he stood in the pew, with tears coursing visibly down his face, and sobbing loudly throughout the service. When the sad moment came for the coffin to be lowered into the Palmer vault, he cried aloud: 'I want to die, O God! I want to go to Heaven, with my darling treasure!'

Afterwards he said to me: 'I shall never forget your love and loyalty to my poor wife! But oh, how desolate my life will be henceforth.' He laid a peculiar emphasis on the words 'love' and 'loyalty' which was, I suppose, his way of hinting that Eliza had reported our conversation, and that he thanked me for my promise to keep silent.

When the funeral had ended, he drove little Willie to my brother's house, with all his clothes and toys, where my sister-in-law hugged him affectionately, saying: 'I'm your new mamma now, and hope you'll love me as I do you.' Dr Palmer promised to visit the child often and, what is more, kept his promise. He doted on Willie. But foul-minded people said that this was a sham, to conceal a guilty passion for my sister-in-law. How I detest this gossipridden town!

I puzzled for a long time about the other crime, besides suicide, to which Annie had confessed; but it is only lately that the truth has come out. Dr Palmer, I'm told, was in extreme difficulties for money, having borrowed from moneylenders at a ruinous rate of interest, and the sole security he could offer—except the race-horses, which he counted upon to restore his credit—was the fortune of his mother, old Mrs Palmer, reputedly worth seventy thousand pounds. She is a shrewd lady, however, and though doubtless he asked her help, must have been convinced that his one sure way out of trouble would be to declare himself bankrupt. Mrs Palmer loved him dearly and would afterwards, I feel certain, have relieved his distress—on condition that he promised to abandon the Turf and resume his medical career.

The Doctor is no hunting man, yet I can say, metaphorically, of his business career, that he has never been able to rein in his mount, nor does he baulk at any fence or five-barred gate. He rides straight ahead to his destruction. He decided to raise loans from the moneylenders on the security of old Mrs Palmer's estate, though without her knowledge; and this meant that he must forge her signature to every acceptance of indebtedness. But to imitate a female hand was beyond his power; so he persuaded Annie to commit the forgery. How he overcame her scruples I can only guess: perhaps he assured her that this was no more than a temporary expedient, to satisfy a pressing creditor, and that money would come from another source within a few days, enabling him to regain and destroy the forged acceptance. At all events, for love of him she became guilty of a crime which, if detected, would have earned her a long prison sentence.

I believe myself that Annie's dawning realization of his inability to redeem these forged acceptances prompted her suicide. She hoped that the insurance money would straighten out his affairs, and trusted that her self-sacrifice would be a harsh enough lesson to make him abandon his spendthrift ways for ever.

My brother tells me that Dr Palmer profited to the extent of thirteen thousand pounds. At Annie's insistence, he had applied for insurance to the value of over thirty thousand pounds at various first-rate offices, including (I believe) The Gresham, The Prince of Wales, The Scottish Equitable, The Atlas, The Norwich Union, and The Sun—of which Jeremiah Smith was the agent. After much correspondence and quibbling about terms, he had settled with The Prince of Wales for thirteen thousand pounds; and The Prince of Wales subcontracted with The Scottish Equitable and The Sun for three thousand pounds apiece. He nearly succeeded in getting twelve thousand pounds more from The Solicitors' and General, but that insurance fell through because, as it happened, they also tried to subcontract with The Sun; and The Sun replied that they were already engaged to assist The Prince of Wales in insuring the very same person for thirteen thousand pounds. The Solicitors' and General smelt a rat. They knew that to insure the life of a woman who had an annuity of two hundred pounds, and no expectations, for a sum of twenty-five thousand pounds would be absurd: the premium must enormously exceed the value of the annuity.

The first and only premium paid to The Prince of Wales was

seven hundred and sixty pounds; but though, my brother tells me, the official at The Sun who had been in treaty with The Solicitors' and General urged The Prince of Wales to refuse payment until a rigid inquiry had been made into the circumstances of Annie's death, the policy could not be invalidated. Three doctors had signed the certificate, pronouncing English cholera to have been the cause, and The Sun's own agent, Mr Jeremiah Smith, signed a sworn statement that nothing was amiss. The Prince of Wales therefore sent Dr Palmer a thirteen-thousand-pound cheque. Yet even that immense sum proved insufficient to wipe out his indebtedness. He still owed two thousand pounds to Mr Padwick, the commission agent: a loan covered by another forged acceptance in old Mrs Palmer's name.

The Doctor's reputation as a poisoner had recently increased; and when news of the insurance payment spread—for he deposited the cheque in the Market Square Bank at Rugeley—he found himself looked upon as a sort of leper. Old friends would cross the street when they saw him approaching. The only female who comforted him—besides his sister Sarah and old Mrs Palmer, both of whom continued affectionate as ever—was Eliza Tharm. He hated to sleep alone, and now that Eliza's moral obligations to Annie were at an end, she became his mistress and cared for him pretty well, I must say; though the affair disgusted me, as taking place so soon after Annie's death.

CHAPTER XI

'A GOOD LIFE'

It would not be amiss at this point to give a short description of Walter Palmer who, like his brother William, suffered from a fatal taste for racing and betting. Walter, a large, heavy, simple-hearted, drunken man, had been placed as a youth with Messrs Procter & Company, Corn Merchants, of Brunswick Street, Liverpool, to learn the business. He remained in their employment until, coming of age and inheriting the same sum as his four brothers, namely seven thousand pounds, he set up as a corn factor at Stafford. Familiarly known as 'Watty', he was a great favourite among members of the trade, both in Liverpool, where he continued to pay a weekly visit to the Corn Exchange, and in his new home. He courted a lady-like and elegant wife, by name Agnes Milcrest, who enjoyed an income of four hundred and fifty pounds a year, and was a sister-in-law of his elder brother Joseph. Joseph's wife, having by this time taken the measure of the family she had married into, and found that it fell considerably short of the ideal, warned Agnes against making the same mistake as herself; but to no avail. Walter already drank far more spirits than suited his health, and devoted considerably closer attention to his betting-book than his ledger; if Agnes hoped to redeem him, she came too late. His bankruptcy, in 1849, had the unfortunate effect of limiting his interests. He took no pleasure in reading, or in music, and since the corn trade could no longer afford to support him, nor could he afford to visit the race-course, there was little left for him to do but drink hard liquor, and he counted on it to stave off boredom. Agnes Palmer still possessed her annuity, of which she could not be deprived by Walter's creditors, and continued to love him. During the bankruptcy proceedings they went together to the Isle of Man, and rented a house in the picturesque old town of Douglas; but the quietude excited rather than soothed his nerves and, after an attack of *delirium tremens*, he unsuccessfully attempted suicide by cutting his throat with a kitchen knife.

A second attack, at Stafford, made Agnes Palmer decide, most reluctantly, to separate from Walter. She retired to Liverpool and there lived with her sister, who needed company, having just got rid of Joseph in much the same circumstances. Walter, now thirty-two years of age, settled down in Earl Street, Stafford. Agnes paid him one hundred pounds of her annuity, to which old Mrs Palmer added a further fifty pounds a year. For want of other amusement, he spent his mornings and afternoons at the Bowling Green, where he would bet in half-pennies on the matches. He always sent his wife an affectionate weekly letter; and she had promised to rejoin him so soon as he was himself again, though not before. Like the generality of drunkards, he had become reserved in his habits, and would walk up and down for hours in silence; but could not wean himself from the bottle, try as he might.

Dr Palmer's moral decline had, we believe, been precipitated by his wife's death. Far from taking to heart the lesson which she tried to teach him by her fond self-sacrifice—that he must abandon his gambling ways and seriously resume the practice of medicine— he had merely learned from her an exceedingly simple method of making money: which was to insure the lives of those who stood only a few steps from the grave. We may acquit him of knowing or suspecting that Annie had died of anything but English cholera; and he could hardly have been expected, when Eliza Tharm told him the truth, to let the Police know about the poisonous powders which she had administered in all innocence. With his brother Walter, however, he certainly took one step farther in the direction of crime: not by poisoning him, as was afterwards charged, but by encouraging him to a speedier end than he might otherwise have had.

'Inspectors Field and Simpson of the Detective Force', as they are called—though 'Inspector' is their self-assumed rank, and the 'Detective Force' consists only of themselves—are frequently employed by the larger insurance companies to inquire into dubious or suspicious claims. Both men had belonged to the regular Police Force; and Inspector Field especially, a burly, jovial officer with a face like a sporting farmer's, fists like hams, and a red velveteen waistcoat much stained with snuff, must be worth a fortune to his employers. We wonder that he does not demand a thousand pounds a year retaining fee from them, instead of the miserable three guineas a week and travelling expenses which is all they pay him. This account, as it happens, was given us by his colleague, Inspector Simpson, a lean, pale, clerkly man, who dresses in black as if in continuous mourning for the sins of the world. Inspector Field says of him: 'Simpson's not got so keen a nose as yours truly, but he has a far better head for dates and figures. You can rely on him for those.'

INSPECTOR SIMPSON

Inspector Field and I have been employed by the insurance companies to clear up a good many dirty businesses in our day, but this present affair proved to be among the dirtiest. Yes, Sir, we also undertake investigations for private persons, in our scant leisure time—always at your service!

Let me give you the sequence of events as we have reconstructed them by inquiry; though the ship's log (so to speak) will doubtless be produced at the trial, we know, by and large, how she sailed. Dr Palmer kept a stable for brood-mares at Rugeley, his home town, and had several race-horses in training at Hednesford and elsewhere. He hoped that these animals would earn vast sums of money for him but, as you know, Sir, race-horses are expensive to support and run; he achieved some successes, he met with even more failures.

The first horse he had in training was Goldfinder; she ran five times in 1852: once unplaced, twice second, twice third. In 1853, carrying nearly top-weight (7 stone 6 pounds), she won the Tradesmen's Plate at Chester May Meeting, Aldcroft up, which was worth £2770. Though Dr Palmer might have netted a deal of money on that occasion had he been able to lay heavily on the horse, at thirty to one, it seems he could only afford a five-pound note—hence the long odds. He backed her at the Shrewsbury May Meeting for the Queen's Plate, but again not heavily, because all the money she won at Chester had gone towards paying his creditors, and the odds were short; we estimate that he cleared three hundred pounds. He ran Goldfinder three more times in 1853, backing her generously. On each occasion he forfeited his stakes, for she never won a place and went out of training in November.

He also ran Morning Star that year—at considerable loss. It is true that Morning Star won the Cleveland Cup at Wolverhampton, with the celebrated jockey Charley Marlow in the saddle, and then the Optional Selling Plate at Rugeley, but he was unplaced in eleven other races. In 1854, he came second three times, and twice third, and often nowhere.

Then there was Lurley, who ran several times unplaced in 1853 and 1854, and obtained only three seconds. Doubt, who won the Wolverhampton August Handicap and the Marquess of Anglesey's

Stakes at Rugeley, proved more trouble than he was worth, because of a weakness in his feet, and went out of training the same year.

Dr Palmer now decided to secure a couple of first-class animals, though it were altogether above his means, and bought The Chicken and Nettle, both much fancied, paying two thousand guineas apiece for them, I believe. The Chicken earned his oats in 1854, by winning the Hopeful T.Y.O. Stakes and the New Stakes at Durham August Meeting, together with £150, and the £345 Eglinton Stakes at York in the same month, Wells up. Also the Mostyn Plate at the Chester Autumn Meeting, and the Handicap Plate at the Newmarket Houghton Meeting—I did not inquire their value. But Dr Palmer could not afford to run Nettle himself that year; so he leased her to Mr Wilkinson, under whose colours she won the Tyro Stakes at Newmarket, and the famous Gimcrack Stakes at York. I believe he had bargained for a percentage of the stakes. However, he had raised the money at such a high rate of interest, on acceptances forged in the name of his wealthy mother, that even these substantial gains by no means justified his original investment in the horses; and it seemed he must soon be pulled up short by his creditors—whereupon the forgeries would be discovered and make him liable to imprisonment for life.

In the autumn of 1854, his immediate wants were relieved by the thirteen-thousand-pound cheque which The Prince of Wales Insurance Company paid him for the loss of his wife; but he soon came knocking at the moneylenders' doors again. One of these was a London solicitor named Pratt, a tall, stout man, rather fashionable in his style of dress, with an enormous pair of brown whiskers, the eyes of a London street-boy, and the low voice of a retiring spinster. He practises in Queen Street, Mayfair, being, I understand, a good family man with three young children and a prominent supporter of the Church Missionary Society; yet never hesitated to charge Dr Palmer sixty per cent for his accommodation, despite the Biblical injunction against usury. He must have been well aware that the acceptances were forged, since the death of his wife had reduced Dr Palmer to copying the old lady's signature himself.

It was this same Pratt whom Dr Palmer used as his agent when insuring Walter Palmer's life. From what Inspector Field and I learned subsequently, the Doctor's approach to Walter was something of this nature: 'How about selling your life, Watty? You know it can't be a long one, not above ten years at the rate you're going; but you can at least make it a little merrier. I'll tell you what: I'm ready to insure it for a thousand pounds, paying the office their five-per-cent rate every year, and of that thousand pounds I'll advance you four hundred at once, free and for nothing, to spend as you please. If you last beyond eight years, I'll be the loser, yet I don't mind taking the risk, if you promise to play fair. What say you, Watty, old chum? It's easy money, like pledging your skeleton to a hospital: as paupers do for a tobacco allowance.'

Walter eagerly agreed, because four hundred pounds extra drinking money seemed manna from Heaven; whereupon Dr Palmer warned him that, to secure the usual five-per-cent rate, a couple of examining doctors must first pass him as a sound investment. For a month, at least, he would have to forswear hard liquor and pack good food into his belly. Walter protested that such self-denial would exceed his moral strength; but Dr Palmer undertook to keep him sober during that period. 'I'll engage Tom Walkenden as your trainer,' he said. 'Afterwards, if you please, you may drink again.'

Proposals were now made by Pratt, Dr Palmer's name not appearing in the application, to no less than four offices—The Prince of Wales, The Solicitors' and General, The Universal, and The Indisputable—for about thirteen thousand pounds apiece. Other agents of Dr Palmer's sounded two more offices (The Athenaeum and The Gresham) suggesting policies of fourteen thousand and fifteen thousand pounds respectively. The total sum sought was eighty-two thousand pounds, which called for initial premiums in the amount of some four thousand five hundred pounds.

On January 31st, The Prince of Wales, unaware that Walter was related to Annie Palmer, by whose insurance they had gone down so heavily, issued a policy of fourteen thousand pounds on the recommendation of Drs Hughes and Harland, both of Stafford. Dr Harland, an elderly physician newly arrived in the town, had passed Walter as a good life without making any close inquiries into his medical history. Dr Hughes also passed him but added the following qualification: 'The applicant is now temperate and healthy; previous habits, however, reduce his chance of longevity to less than the average. He owns to an attack of *delirium tremens* five years ago.'

One of the medical men consulted by The Universal was Dr Monckton of Rugeley. After first passing Walter, he soon changed his opinion as the result of a talk with Dr Campbell of Stoke-on-Trent, Walter's former physician. He appended to his report:

MOST CONFIDENTIAL!
Walter Palmer's life has been rejected by two Assurance Offices. He drinks hard and has had *delirium tremens*. His brother, Dr William Palmer, insured his own wife not long ago for £13,000. She died after a single premium had been paid.

Beneath this postscript Dr Monckton wrote in capital letters: '*BE CAUTIOUS!*'

Dr Waddell of Stafford, now Walter's private physician, was also consulted by The Universal, and likewise refused to recommend him. He counter-signed Dr Monckton's confidential report with: 'I believe that the above facts are true.'

Though not shown this paper, Walter knew at least that he had been turned down as a 'bad risk', and meeting Dr Waddell one day on Castle Knoll, reproached him with a lack of consideration. 'My habits are entirely altered,' Doctor,' Walter said. 'I drink no more than three glasses of bitter beer in a day, and eat like a thresher. Why didn't you pass me?'

Dr Waddell answered drily: 'Continue so for six months, and I'll begin to believe in your reform; continue for five years, and I'll do so with a good heart. But your last attack of *delirium tremens* caused me great trouble and anxiety, and I can't guarantee that there won't be others—not without stronger evidence than your own hopes of a cure.'

The Gresham, which appointed Drs Harland and Waddell to examine Walter, accepted the policy, while making it a condition that 'no insurance will be paid if this person dies before five years have elapsed.' On receipt of this reply, I am informed, Dr Palmer wrote to his agent, a Mr Webb: 'That would not suit my book at all. We had better drop the matter.'

In order to pay The Prince of Wales their initial premium of seven hundred pounds odd, Dr Palmer borrowed one thousand five hundred pounds from Pratt, at the usual sixty-per-cent rate, against one more forged acceptance from his mother; and, having done so, set about restoring Walter's former intemperance, and even enhancing it. He hired the same Tom Walkenden, who had hitherto prevented him from drinking, to be Walter's 'bottle holder'. Walkenden is a powerful man, with a broad, flat face and coarse features; he has been a potman, and once served a prison sentence in London for larceny. The assignment of the insurance policy to Dr Palmer was then drawn out, and witnessed by Jeremiah Smith, who took five guineas as his fee. Yet Walter did not get the promised four hundred pounds, but only sixty in cash, and unlimited credit with Mr John Burgess, the innkeeper and spirit merchant of Dudley Port.

Walter kept a cask of gin in the house and never drank less than a quart a day, besides the three-pint bottle which Walkenden placed every night at his bedside, and which he had always emptied by the early morning. He would toss off half a tumbler at a gulp. In the early morning, Walkenden had orders to bring him a cup of hot coffee and some buttered toast. This he would swallow but throw up again; afterwards he steadied himself with three or four glasses of gin and water, before starting the day's serious drinking. He constantly complained of pains all over his body, particularly below one shoulder-blade. He also coughed and spat a great deal.

Dr Waddell, meeting him one day at the Bowling Green, asked: 'Well, Walter, and how do you do?'

'Why, lad, I'm very bad indeed,' Walter replied. 'I fear I shall never recover. Pity me for a most wretched man.'

'Nonsense, nonsense!' cried Dr Waddell. 'I'll guarantee your cure, if you'll only obey my instructions.'

'Well, I think not,' said Walter, 'but my brother William is bringing me some pills tomorrow.'

'If you won't come back to me—if you put yourself under anyone else, even your own brother—I give you up!' Dr Waddell declared. 'But tell me, why have you relapsed, Walter, after being so much improved not many weeks ago?'

Walter replied simply: 'The fact is, lad, that I owe my brother William four hundred pounds, and it weighs on my conscience; he's pretty short of money these days. I feel like a pauper defrauding the hospital of its skeleton.'

Dr Waddell's being a near neighbour of Walter's may have been the reason why William Palmer now removed the latter to Castle Terrace, beyond the Railway Station. To make everything look aboveboard, he had invited Dr Waddell and Dr Day, The Prince of Wales's regular insurance doctor, who also lived in Earl Street, to keep an eye on his brother; but encouraged neither of them to see too much of him. In the middle of July he visited Walter, and pretended to be greatly distressed by his drinking. 'You must make an endeavour, Watty,' he said, 'to sober up. Come, what do you say to visiting Agnes for a week and showing yourself in your true colours? Tom Walkenden, here, will help you to train for the meeting, and I'll have a word with Dr Waddell first.'

Inspector Field and I have since questioned Walkenden about this episode. This is what he told us: 'Poor Watty was in a pretty bad way last July. He often begged me, if I ever saw that another attack of the horrors was on the way, not to take his gin from him, as I'd done in December before he went in front of the insurance doctors. "That sober stretch did me plenty of harm," said he. "If I'd only been allowed my gin then, when I wanted it, I shouldn't have been half so bad when I got it back again." Well, while he was under Dr Waddell's care, sobering up for the visit to his wife, I had orders to allow him only two or three small glasses a day, as when he'd had the horrors. But when I witnessed the poor fellow's despair, and he threatened to do himself an injury, I sometimes gave him a glass or two more than Dr Waddell permitted, if there was real necessity. What could I do? The wretched cove used to beg and cry for liquor as if that were his life. He used to do all he could to get gin, and be very cunning about it, too. One morning, after I'd been sitting up with him all night, I reckoned he was so ill he couldn't leave his bed. Downstairs I went, to the kitchen for my coffee and my plate of bacon and eggs; and was well engaged with the victuals when I heard a noise overhead. "Why," I says to myself, "that sounds as if he were out of bed, but it's hardly possible." Upstairs I went again, and found him on his hands and knees, searching beneath the dressing table, which was where he used to hide his gin from me.

'"Holloa, Sir," says I, "what are you doing there?" "'I can't find it," he whimpers.

"'No,' I answers. "Nor never will!" I lifted him up, though he was no light weight, and put him back to bed, where I charitably gave him a tot. He used to hide his gin bottle in all sorts of places—under his mattress, in his boots, anywhere. Well, after a hard week of it, we restored him to a condition where he'd eat again; and, once he got an-eating, the rest wasn't hard. Dr Palmer, he arranged for Watty's wife to meet him at Liverpool Railway Station; and we sat Watty in a train. The guard had orders that he mustn't alight at any station to buy drink.'

Walter Palmer spent five days at Liverpool and, it seems, stayed perfectly sober all the time, to please his wife, who did not let him out of her sight. On August 9th, he returned, and spent the next day at Rugeley with his mother, his sister Sarah, and Dr Palmer. That night he wrote his wife a letter which has since been printed in a newspaper. I have the cutting here in my pocketbook.

Castle Terrace, Stafford.
August 10th, 1855.

My dearest Agnes:
   I left you last evening and did feel I possessed a light heart; but on my arrival at Warrington I found the South Express was three-quarters of an hour late, owing to the flood washing away arches, etc. I was lonely—only myself in the carriage. The rain on my arrival was incessant. Thanks to God, I had not far to go. I have been home today; I am truly sorry to say Mother has been very unwell, but is better. I told Sarah you was going to the concert on the 27th, and she wishes to go too. Please write to her, and she can come with me. If I should bring little Miss Barber, you won't be jealous, will you? But I don't know whether we shall meet or not. I should like you to know one steady and

sensible creature upon earth, but not a teetotaller on principle. She says: 'I never drink one glass of wine in twelve
months and have, therefore, no occasion to be a teetotaller.'
I will write to you tomorrow and explain a few little secrets. Good night, God bless you, and ever believe in the
affection of

WALTER PALMER

P.S. Remaining sober with you was easy enough, because
you are a dear good creature and keep no spirits in your
house. Here drink is always at myelbow.

On Sunday, August 12th, Dr Day called at Castle Terrace and
found Walter and William Palmer together. Walter was so intoxicated that Dr Day deferred his visit until the afternoon, hoping
that he would by then be in a quieter state. Dr Palmer undertook
to do his best in the matter, but that afternoon, when Dr Day
called, he opened the door himself and said: 'Pray leave this to me.
Walter's no better and so very noisy and unmanageable it's no use
your seeing him, I'm afraid.'

On Monday, Dr Palmer attended the Wolverhampton Races;
meanwhile Dr Day saw Walter and prescribed some pills. When
he called on the Tuesday, Walter said, grinning: 'Doctor, those pills
of yours were twisters! But I threw them up, and now I'm off to
Wolverhampton. You needn't look in for another day or two. I'm
well again.'

He set out for Wolverhampton with Walkenden, stopping at
The Fountain Inn on his arrival. Here he felt so weak that he had
to lie down and never reached the race-course. Walter drank all
that day, and continued all night after his return to Castle Terrace. When Dr Day called on the Wednesday, August 14th, he was
told by Walkenden: 'Your patient is at the Wolverhampton Races,

Doctor.' Walkenden has since confessed that this was untrue; but swears Walter himself sent the message. At any rate, Walter lay upstairs drinking, and did not leave the house.

Dr Palmer was to have attended the Ludlow Races that Thursday; but changed his mind and instead went to Stafford where he spent the day with Walter, having asked Jeremiah Smith to keep in touch with him. At 1:32 P.M., Mr Smith despatched a telegraphic message: 'Lurley has a good chance for the Ludlow Stakes.' It arrived just as Walter was dying, after an apoplectic stroke. Ten minutes later Dr Palmer summoned the Boots at the Grand Junction Hotel, and offered him sixpence if he would take a telegraphic message to Stafford Railway Station, for delivery in London. This was addressed to his friend, Mr Webb, and ran: 'Lay £50 on Lurley for the Ludlow Stakes, whatever the price.' If Lurley won, Dr Palmer stood to make five hundred pounds. At a quarter past four, he sent another telegraphic message by the same Boots to the Clerk of the Course, at Ludlow: 'Pray, Mr Frail, inform me who won the Ludlow Stakes.'

In the event, Lurley did not catch the judge's eye, nor did Morning Star's winning of the Welter Cup by twenty lengths at that meeting compensate for the disappointment. Dr Palmer received word of Lurley's failure as stoically as usual. On the Thursday, he went by train to Liverpool and broke the news of Walter's death to Agnes Palmer, Overcome by grief, she asked why nobody had written or telegraphed to say that he was ill. Dr Palmer at once answered that, on asking Walter's leave to write, he had been told: 'No, Billy, I'm not so bad as all that. I'll write myself tomorrow from Wolverhampton; I don't want Agnes worried unnecessarily. You shan't say a word.'

Agnes Palmer then proposed to return with Dr Palmer for a last look at her husband; but he said, very truly, that this was no longer advisable. The body had begun to decompose very rapidly in the hot August weather, and was now closed tightly in a leaden shell. She therefore nursed her grief until the Monday, when the funeral took place at Rugeley; there, with her brothers-in-law William, George and Thomas, and her sister-in-law Sarah, she followed Walter to his grave in St Augustine's churchyard.

That evening, Dr Waddell met Walkenden, very drunk, emerging from the refreshment room on Stafford Railway Station. 'Holloa, old cock!' cried Walkenden. 'How's the hens?'

Dr Waddell, noticing the mourning band around Walkenden's hat, answered civilly: 'Good evening, Tom! May I ask in return whom you have had the pleasure of putting underground?'

'Poor Watty!' says Walkenden. 'Poor *whom*?' asks Dr Waddell.

'Poor Walter Palmer; died of an apoplexy. A fine funeral it was, too. His brother William didn't stint us of drink.'

Dr Waddell, terribly shocked, exclaimed in the hearing of the stationmaster and porters: 'I'll let the assurance office know of this affair.'

The Doctor must have suspected foul play. It was his letter to The Prince of Wales that first prompted them to contest the claim, although Dr Day had obligingly certified apoplexy as the cause of Walter's death.

CHAPTER XII

A GENTLEMAN OF PROPERTY

Inspector Simpson continued to unfold the story. He described how Dr Palmer sent Pratt, his London agent, the death certificate and other documents which would enable him to claim the fourteen thousand pounds insurance money; but also how Dr Waddell's letter, informing The Prince of Wales's managers that Walter was a brother of William Palmer—whom they had recently paid a similar sum upon the death of his wife—and that Walter's death might well have been brought about by wilful negligence, alarmed them into withholding payment. They referred Pratt to their solicitors.

Dr Palmer, dreadfully pressed for money, did not know which way to turn. In May, he had entered Nettle, his Sweetmeat filly, for the Oaks and engaged Charley Marlow as her jockey. Marlow, as I mentioned just now, had won a victory for the all-yellow colours at Wolverhampton on Morning Star, coaxing a fine performance out of that lazy beast, which had never won a race before, nor was ever likely to win one again. Palmer laid so heavily on Nettle for the Oaks that she started as a raging favourite, at odds of two to one.

It happened that on the previous night an old Yorkshire trainer had told Marlow: 'Hoi's noa going to win Oaks, and whoi? 'Cause hoi poison'd woife!'

Charley Marlow, very angry, appealed to Will Saunders the trainer, who was present. 'This is a pretty serious slander, Mr Saunders,' he said. 'You come from that part of the country, and you train for Dr Palmer; what do you know of the matter?'

'It's none of my business,' Saunders replied sourly, 'if the little boys of Rugeley say that Billy Palmer poisoned his wife. *I* don't.'

Whether or not the suspicion thus implanted in Marlow's mind affected his horsemanship, who can tell? At all events, Nettle was lying second and Marlow had not yet called on her for the final effort, of which he believed her well capable, when suddenly she swerved, fell over the chains near the New Mile post, threw him heavily, and galloped away into the furze bushes. Marlow's thigh was broken and, while being carried off the course, he exclaimed between groans: 'It served me right! What business had I to ride a damned poisoner's horse?'

Condoled with by George Myatt on his loss of the race, Dr Palmer said no more than: 'It *is* rather a bore, though, isn't it?' His losses must have been very serious, since he had stood to win no less than ten thousand pounds.

The Prince of Wales's refusal to pay the insurance money came as a thunderbolt. He considered himself cheated by Walter, on whom he had spent a considerable sum—not only the seven-hundred-pound premium, but sixty pounds in cash, and bills owing to the innkeeper for nineteen gallons of gin and a quantity of other liquor consumed at Castle Terrace. He therefore applied to Agnes Palmer, who was staying with friends at Great Malvern, for the payment of certain debts which her husband (he said) had left unsettled.

The following exchange of letters between Dr Palmer and his sister-in-law has since been published:

Rugeley,
Sept. 27th, 1855

Dear Agnes,

I hope the change of air and scenery has, by this time, done you good, and that you are more quiet and reconciled than when I communicated to you the painful, the sorrowful, news of dear Walter's death. Ah, poor fellow, I often think of him and only wish I could now do for him what I did while he was alive; and, I assure you, I did a very great deal for him—perhaps a great deal more than you are aware of.

I know not whether Walter told you that I had advanced him £85 on the drawing-room furniture—of course, I was well aware that some of it belonged to you, but he, poor fellow, told me that you would repay me the money—which I feel sure you will do, now that I have told you. There was also another item that you must, if you please, assist me to: *viz.*: £40 for a bill, which you knew well of the circumstance, and I must be excused going into particulars. This amount I should not ask you for, but Walter said that if I would only take up the bill you would pay me, and I feel sure you will, after all the money I have paid on his account. I have also received bills amounting to £200 which, I suppose, must be paid by someone. What say you to this? You cannot, for one single moment, but think that I ought to have assistance from someone, and I crave yours, because I feel certain that Walter must have told you how very, very often, and on very many occasions, I had stood his friend; and I believe that I and his dear mother were, except yourself, the only friends he had on earth. I only wish his career on earth had been a different one. He might then have still

been alive; but, poor fellow, he is dead and buried and I
hope and trust he is gone to Heaven.
With kind regards, Yours very truly,

WM PALMER

It seems that in breaking the news to his sister-in-law, Dr
Palmer had blamed her for not having come back with Walter
to Stafford and there resumed conjugal relations. Walter, he said,
had visited her in Liverpool, sober and hopeful, yet she disdained
this sincere reformation; therefore his death, which was a sort of
suicide due to despair, must be for ever after on her conscience.
The argument profoundly affected Agnes for a while; but at the
funeral she heard talk which persuaded her that Dr Palmer, not
she, stood in need of reproach. She answered his demands with
some asperity:

Edith Lodge, Great Malvern,
Sept. 28th, 1855

Dear William,
    I have just received your note, and must say that I am
much surprised at its contents. What right had you to lend
your money, supposing that I would repay it, without consulting me on the subject? Poor Walter's explanation to me,
over and over again, was that you had insured his life for,
I think he said, £1000; and that you had promised to advance him £500 of this sum, but that you had put him off
from time to time and were just giving him a few pounds
now and then to go on with, until you could find means to
pay him the whole. Now, if that is true, and I am much
disposed to believe it, you are the proper person to pay all
he owes; but if you make that out to be incorrect (and I have

no way, I am very sorry to say, of proving it) I still do not consider that I am the person to be looked to for paying his debts, never having received a farthing from him, or been kept by him, in the whole course of our married life.

I should not think your mother can be aware that you are applying to me for payment of her son's debts, and I will not have it for a moment supposed that I am the person responsible. In conclusion, I beg of you to remember, and beware how you belie the dead.

I am, truly yours,

A. PALMER

This letter goes to prove that neither Agnes, nor Walter himself, knew of Dr Palmer's insuring the latter's life for fourteen thousand pounds, and proposing to insure it with other offices for a further sixty-eight thousand pounds. He must now practise extreme caution, because Pratt, when he visited The Prince of Wales's solicitors, had admitted that though the insurance supposedly covered money advanced by Walter to old Mrs Palmer, the actual beneficiary from the death would be Dr Palmer, to whom total payment had been assigned by Walter in consideration of a four-hundred-pound loan. This confirmed The Prince of Wales in their determination not to pay; whereupon Pratt laid the case before an eminent counsel, Sir Fitzroy Kelly, who gave his opinion that:

> Want of consideration is not the ground on which William Palmer has failed to recover; but it is my advice that some other member of the family should take out administration to the estate of the deceased.

The first person legally entitled to do so was Agnes who had, however, already told Dr Palmer that she washed her hands of

Walter's debts. Dr Palmer consequently foresaw no difficulty in making her sign a formal surrender of the right to administer the estate—so long as she did not guess how much insurance money was at stake. The next natural administratrix was old Mrs Palmer, whom Jeremiah Smith, her lover, could easily persuade to sign away her rights. Pratt therefore produced two copies of a 'Renunciation' form from Doctors' Commons, and Dr Palmer instructed Jeremiah Smith to secure Agnes's signature on one, and the old lady's on the other. These two documents would be offered to The Prince of Wales as evidence that all was fair and aboveboard.

Smith first travelled to Great Malvern, where he asked Agnes Palmer to sign the 'Renunciation', as Walter's widow, and with it a surrender of her interest in the insurance policy. This she almost did but, on second thoughts, said: 'I should prefer my own solicitor to look over this document before I sign, Mr Smith. According to poor Walter, no less a sum than one thousand pounds is in question!'

He pricked up his ears at this remark, not having hitherto heard of Dr Palmer's pretence to Walter that the insurance was for a mere thousand pounds; and smelt danger. Saying merely: 'Very well, Ma'am, I shall acquaint your brother-in-law with your decision,' he took the papers away again. On the return journey to Rugeley he must have come to suspect that he was being used as an instrument of fraud, if not worse. Dr Palmer had privately told him that, because The Prince of Wales, which had paid him thirteen thousand pounds for Annie's death, might not otherwise have accepted the risk, the policy was taken out in old Mrs Palmer's name, not his own, and by the agency of Pratt. He further, no doubt, explained that Walter's drunkenness was incurable; and that he would take long odds against his lasting more than another couple of years.

Thinking the matter over carefully and piecing together scraps of conversation, Smith convinced himself that Palmer had hastened Walter's death; and that to raise the money for the premium he had probably forged old Mrs Palmer's signature. The situation appalled him; yet he shrank from confiding his suspicions to the old lady, who adored her scapegrace Billy, and from whose financial innocence—in return for certain favours—he made so substantial a profit himself. He therefore resolved on a roundabout way of freeing himself from embarrassment.

At this point, Inspector Field took up the tale:

INSPECTOR FIELD

My colleague, Inspector Simpson, has marshalled the facts very clearly, though he should perhaps have emphasized that Mr Smith's motives are presumed, rather than certainly known.

At all events, Mr Smith wrote to The Midland—a company which had not been approached when Dr Palmer wished to insure first his wife's and then his brother's life—and told them that he could, he believed, find them good business in Rugeley. They accordingly appointed him their agent, and being asked to suggest the names of referees, he sent in those of Dr Palmer's close friends: Samuel Cheshire, the Postmaster, and John Parsons Cook, a solicitor. Yes, Sir, the very man for whose murder Dr Palmer is now standing trial! What is more, when asked to suggest medical referees, Mr Smith proposed the name of Dr Palmer himself, and of Thirlby, his assistant!

I knew nothing of the case until The Midland officials called me to their office one day last September. 'Inspector Field,' the General Manager said, 'we wish to engage you on a somewhat delicate mission.'

'At your service, gentlemen,' I answered, 'if your terms are commensurate with the delicacy you mention.'

They smiled at my downrightness, and undertook to pay me an extra two guineas a week if I brought back information that proved useful. I stood out for the extra guineas, whatever the value of the information; and to this they agreed likewise.

'Here's the case, Inspector,' said the General Manager. 'Mr Jeremiah Smith, a Rugeley solicitor, has proposed the life insurance of a neighbour, one George Bate, Esq., for ten thousand pounds, and has named Dr William Palmer, also of the same town, as one of two medical referees. Now, despite the hot rivalry between insurance companies—often, I regret to say, evinced by something close on sharp practice—a certain solidarity may none the less be discovered among them. We now assist one another to compile a confidential black-list of suspicious customers, which is issued monthly for our mutual protection. The latest list contains the name of Dr Palmer, in respect of two dubious life insurances: the first on his wife Annie, which was settled at her death, though grudgingly, by The Prince of Wales; the second on his brother Walter, with which The Prince of Wales are also concerned, but which has not been settled. Here fraud is suspected, and even foul play. We wish you to visit Rugeley and find out what you can about this "George Bate, Esq." At the same time, The Prince of Wales, who have joined us in this inquiry, empower you to investigate on their behalf the death of Walter Palmer. I should add that Mr Jeremiah Smith has recently approached The Indisputable for a further insurance on Mr Bate's life.'

'Very good, Sir,' said I, 'but seeing that, if I understand you aright, there's suspicion of murder here, I'm not putting my head into any noose unless I have a colleague to stand by me, with a knife to cut the rope if it tightens.'

'Yours is a very sensible attitude,' the General Manager answered. 'Take Inspector Simpson, by all means. We will pay him his usual fee.'

He handed us five guineas on account, and we boarded the Rugeley train. Inspector Simpson went on to Stafford, to take statements from Dr Waddell and Tom Walkenden, and pick up what talk might be current in the inns near Castle Terrace.

On reaching Rugeley, I called on Mr Samuel Cheshire, the Postmaster, one of the referees. It has since transpired that Dr Palmer had some hold over this former school-fellow of his, though the nature of Cheshire's obligation remains doubtful. Some ascribe it merely to the pony-chaise which, after Annie Palmer's death, Mrs Cheshire constantly borrowed for Sunday outings; others hint at a disreputable disease for which Dr Palmer treated Cheshire. Whatever the truth may have been, this hold gave him the freedom of the Post Office: that is to say, Cheshire would detain incoming and outgoing letters addressed to whatever person Dr Palmer named and, after steaming open the envelopes in his presence, would allow him to read the contents. Most of the letters were then re-sealed and dispatched to the addressees, but some Dr Palmer had permission to pocket, upon his undertaking to deliver them in person without fail. Among these, we now know, were demands made by Pratt on old Mrs Palmer, and by Padwick, another moneylender, to repay loans for which Dr Palmer had fraudulently made her responsible. I knew nothing of this arrangement when I presented my credentials to Cheshire that day. He is a frail, simple-looking man in his early thirties, with fair hair and a nervous habit of twiddling the seal-ring on his little finger. I asked him, first, where I might find Mr John Parsons Cook's office.

He answered: 'Mr Cook has no office in Rugeley. At present, he's staying around the corner at Dr Palmer's.'

'Then where does he practise?' I asked.

'He used to practise at Watling,' Cheshire informed me, 'but since he took to the Turf, he has more or less abandoned the Law.'

On learning that I came as agent for The Midland Insurance Company, he appeared puzzled. I said: 'Mr Cheshire, pray be plain with me. Mr Jeremiah Smith, the company's Rugeley agent, has named you as one of our referees, has he not? Mr Cook is the other; Dr Palmer and Mr Benjamin Thirlby are the medical referees. I have come to discuss a proposed policy on the life of George Bate, Esq.'

Cheshire swallowed once or twice, and fairly spun the seal-ring around his finger. 'I had quite forgotten the circumstance,' he muttered at last. 'What do you require of me?'

'This is a mere formality, Sir,' I replied. 'My employers wish to be satisfied that your Mr Bate is a man of property.'

Cheshire answered, without looking directly at me: 'Why, of course, Mr Bate is well regarded in the neighbourhood. He is a fine judge of horses, and was a substantial farmer before he retired.'

I asked: 'And what do you suppose his income to be?' 'I shouldn't care to guess,' he said.

'For a life insurance of ten thousand pounds, he must doubtless be possessed of at least three hundred to four hundred a year?' I suggested.

'Thereabouts, perhaps,' he agreed.

'Does he live in style? Does he entertain much?' I continued.

'Oh, he has a capital cellar,' says Cheshire with sudden inspiration, 'and you should see his thoroughbred brood-mares! Dr Palmer envies him those stables, I can tell you.'

'And debts?' I asked.

'No, no debts of any consequence,' he replied.

Returning to the matter of the cellar, I asked: 'Has he good port?' 'Why, his bins are celebrated in Rugeley,' Cheshire asserted.

'That's good news,' I exclaimed. 'I have a slight weakness for port, and this is the hour when I usually take a glass. Perhaps, though, I had better hasten back to the Railway Station with my report and catch the London train.' Then I thanked him for his courtesy, telling him that in the circumstances I would not trouble Mr Cook; and when two customers came in, bade him good-day.

Instead of returning to the Railway Station, however, I entered The Shoulder of Mutton Inn, took a tankard of ale, and inquired for Mr George Bate. Clewley, the landlord, after directing me to a farm-house across the fields, asked: 'Have you come to dun the poor fellow? I hope not. Though he pays only six shillings a week rent to the farmer's wife for a room, there's six months' owing.'

'No,' said I, 'you mustn't mistake me for a bailiff. I've come to give him some good news.'

I proceeded to the farm, and the farmer's wife showed me a field, where 'George be a-hoeing turmuts.' Presently I heard the sound of singing:

> 'For the fly, For the fly,
> For the fly be on the turmuts, And it's all my eye
> For me to try
> To keep fly off the turmuts . . .'

and the singer was George Bate, Esq. He proved to be a red-snouted, bleary-eyed, youngish fellow, with ragged trousers, a filthy shirt and no more education, it seemed, than he had managed to snatch in his brief visits to Sunday School—whenever he was not herding geese, scaring crows, or doing something else of equal importance.

I took off my hat, and said: 'Mr George Bate, I presume?' He leaned on his hoe and asked: 'Who may you be?'

'I'm a representative of The Midland Assurance Company,' I answered, 'come to ask about this policy of yours.'

When I saw that he did not understand the word 'policy' and, on further talk, found that he was totally ignorant of the nature of life assurances, and that 'premium', 'proposal', and 'assignment' meant nothing to him, I said: 'They tell me at the Post Office that you're a man of property, Mr Bate.'

'Oh, no, you must have heard wrong, Sir,' he replied. 'I'm not a man of property yet, but they've promised me two thousand gold sovereigns, and a vote for the county.'

'Who are these benefactors of yours, Mr Bate?' I inquired.

'Well, it was like this,' he said. 'One day, along comes Dr Palmer in the company of Jerry Smith and that swell Cook, who's always at the races with the Doctor. I took the opportunity to ask for my pay, because I was behind with my rent, and the Doctor hadn't paid me for a while. The Doctor regrets that he's short of change, and asks Mr Cook to pay me my two guineas, which he obliges with. Dr Palmer then says, says he: "I'm sorry, George, to be so forgetful. I'd like to do something for you, that I would, and better your position." At this, Jerry Smith grins and says: "Then why not insure his life for, say six thousand pounds, and give him an advance of a couple of thousand? That'll enable him to live in style, and drink himself to death if he pleases." Then he gives Dr Palmer a peculiar look and bursts into laughter. The Doctor seemed put out, but all the same he says: "Why, Jerry, what a capital idea! Let's set up George as a man of property. Your life is worth every penny of six thousand pounds, isn't it now, George?" I tells him: "No, Doctor, it's not worth sixty pence at the moment, apart from these two guineas you've just paid me, and much obliged for them I am, too." "Well, it's about time a hard-working fellow like you should go up in society," says Jerry, "don't you agree, gentlemen?" Mr Cook, he agreed with pleasure, and the Doctor nodded, but as if his mind were busy with other thoughts. Then Jerry says again: "Let's invite George to dinner some day next week—eh, Billy?—and talk it over?" "Very well," says the Doctor, but not too readily. "Bring him to my house."'

I asked George Bate: 'Are you on good terms with Dr Palmer?'

'Oh, yes, Sir!' he answered. 'He never did me no injury, and is always ready to do me a service; so if I'm behind-hand with the rent, it's not his fault. Nor he don't mind my doing a bit of work here, on the side, while the beasts are a-grazing. But I get dead drunk every Saturday and Sunday night and Lord, how the money flies!'

'So you dined at his house the next week?' I asked.

'Indeed, Sir, that I did!' George answered. 'I'll never forget it. Mr Cook was there, and Cheshire the Postmaster, and Will Saunders, the trainer from Hednesford. When Jerry Smith brought me into the dining-room, Dr Palmer seemed surprised, but Jerry, he says: "You invited this gentleman here, Billy—surely you've not forgotten? He's been looking forward to a good dinner all week." Well, the Doctor makes me welcome, and that was the first time I ever sat down at a gentleman's table, with silver spoons and forks and fancy china, and port poured from a decanter. Jerry Smith told Saunders, who didn't recognize me: "This is George Bate, Esq., a gentleman of property. His cellar is the best in Rugeley. You'll excuse his rough appearance, but he's something of an eccentric: can't be bothered to dress for dinner, nor even change his shirt. He's worth a mint of money, however." Saunders shook hands with me, and I was grateful to Jerry for putting me at my ease; but, not to make a fool of myself, I watched carefully how the other gentlemen handled their knives and forks. I kept mum, as you can guess, except when a discussion came up about Lord George Bentinck's victory with Elis in the 1836 St Leger. It happened that nobody present could remember the name of her companion whom Lord George brought along with him travelling from Goodwood to Doncaster in a six-horse van—the book-makers laid heavily against Elis, thinking him a non-runner, for it's a good two hundred and fifty miles from Goodwood to Doncaster. The horses got there in time, you know, after stopping over at Litchfield for a gallop to loosen them up, and Elis wasn't dead meat after all—not by half, he wasn't! So at last I opens my trap. "Drummer was the horse in

Lord George's van," I says—just that! And everyone admitted I was right.'

George Bate rambled on of the sporting talk heard at table on that occasion, but I brought him quietly back to the matter of his life insurance. 'Why, for sure,' he said, 'Jerry Smith reminded the Doctor about it after dinner; and the Doctor protested: "Can't we leave this in pickle for another day or two, lad?" "Oh, no," says Jerry, "you pledged your word that you'd do something for George. Now I've taken the trouble to get the papers from The Midland, and suggested Sam Cheshire and Mr Cook and you to vouch for him; so what do you say?" The Doctor answers: "Very well, Jerry, as you please. But I've promised Will Saunders a bit of sport, and we mustn't waste the afternoon." "True enough," said Jerry. "Then permit me to take Will out to the warren, while you and Cook show George how to sign the paper." At this, Jerry and Saunders take their guns and go out. The Doctor stays, and says to Mr Cook: "I'm not sure that the wording's in order. Let's leave it for a day or two." "I'm a qualified solicitor, Billy, you forget," says Mr Cook. "I think George had better sign that paper, here and now, and take his first step towards prosperity." They showed me where to sign, and when Dr Palmer had vouched for my being healthy and sober, Mr Cook witnessed the paper, and sanded it, and folded it away. I never asked what amount had been fixed for the value of my life, but Mr Cook, he looks steadily at Dr Palmer, and says: "We can fix the amount later, but let it be sufficient to pay George his advance of two thousand guineas." The Doctor answers in an offhand manner: "Yes, the amount's of no consequence for so long and valuable a life as George's. Any sum between five and twenty-five thousand pounds will do. Come, Johnny, stop fooling and let's be off! Where's your rabbiting piece?" Then he asked me: "Will you join us, George?" But I shook my head and went home.'

George Bate's account suggested to me that Mr Smith had been forcing this insurance on Dr Palmer for a joke, and that the Doctor was putting as good a face on it as possible, but not liking his situation by any means. Cook seemed to have played his part under Smith's direction; but I couldn't fathom what they were at. That night, however, when Inspector Simpson and I compared notes, he having meanwhile talked not only with Walkenden and Dr Waddell—the results of which he's already told you—but also with Mr Lloyd, the landlord of The Junction Hotel, I came to understand the case better.

Jeremiah Smith had involved Dr Palmer's close friends-Cheshire, Cook and Saunders—in the practical joke on George Bate, by way of warning them against the Doctor as one who had procured his own brother's death for the sake of insurance money and might do the same again with any other simple drunkard. He was at the same time warning Dr Palmer not to press The Prince of Wales for payment, because if he did, the truth about his misdeeds must come tumbling out. It may be that Mr Smith suspected Dr Palmer of hastening Walter Palmer's death with prussic acid; for Inspector Simpson has uncovered some odd circumstances which may point that way.

To be explicit: the Boots at The Junction Hotel, Stafford, was entrusted by the Doctor on Wednesday, August 14th, with two bottles wrapped in white paper. Boots guessed from the feel that they were medicine bottles. Dr Palmer asked him to keep them unexposed to the air until he passed by again; which he did an hour later, and fetched them away. He was absent for perhaps another hour, then left them in Boots' charge once more. The next morning, Thursday, he came for the bottles again, took a very small phial from his waistcoat pocket and, having poured a little of its contents drop by drop into one of the bottles, which Boots describes as having been some four inches long, returned the phial to his waistcoat pocket. Mr Lloyd, the landlord, happened to visit the stables while the Doctor was engaged in this mixing operation, and reports that he did not look in the least surprised or flurried by the interruption. Mr Lloyd said: 'Good morning, Doctor, and how is your brother today?' Dr Palmer answered: 'He's very ill, very low; I'm going to take him something stimulating. Day, who's attending him, isn't so well acquainted with his habits as I am. Taking his gin away and giving him gruel instead won't help a man who's accustomed to drink heavily; but I hope this medicine will improve matters. He went, very foolishly, to Wolverhampton the day before yesterday. It might have been the death of him, from the state he was in. What a sad thing it is that honest folk like my brother deliberately drink themselves to perdition!'

That was the Thursday of Walter's death. Mr Lloyd told Inspector Simpson that the little phial seemed to contain sal volatile; and that Dr Palmer had bought a bottle of the very best old brandy from him on the previous Saturday, saying: 'If my brother wants any more of this, let him have it, and I'll foot the bill.'

Inspector Simpson also visited Messrs Mander & Company, the wholesale chemists of Stafford, and there confirmed, by an interview with George Wyman the assistant, a story current at The Lamb and Flag: Dr Palmer, on the day before Walter's death, had purchased an ounce of prussic acid from Mander's, along with certain other drugs. Inspector Simpson gave this event more importance than I cared to concede. The Doctor, it appeared to me, must have seen clearly enough that Walter was dying of drink, as had been expected, and would hardly have hastened his end by use of a poison which two people had watched him mix. I refused, in fact, to connect the prussic acid with the case. He might well, however, have employed the poison to make rival race-horses 'safe'; and that, I decided, was the explanation. What sort of medicine Mr Lloyd saw him mixing, I cannot say; but why not sal volatile, a harmless stimulant which might persuade Dr Day of an improvement in Walter's health? My guess is that Jerry Smith had heard the gossip, which not only decided him to make a game of Dr Palmer by suggesting the insurance on George Bate's life: he also forwarded the signed proposal to The Midland Company—so that the jest became earnest. He counted, I mean, on The Midland to inquire into George Bate's health and financial stability. They would soon discover that the proposal was fraudulent, and all eyes would then be focussed on Walter's death. Smith himself hoped to keep in the background, leaving the insurance companies to carry out their investigations with help from the Police.

Well, I had no means of proving my conjectures, and because Dr Palmer, having long ceased to practise as a surgeon, could be called upon to account for this unusual purchase of prussic acid, I naturally reported the circumstance to The Prince of Wales managers. It also came into my mind that perhaps Cook's demand, during Smith's absence from the dinner table, that George Bate should sign the proposal paper, had decided the Doctor to be revenged on him later. For when Dr Palmer heard from Bate of my questioning him, he said: 'George, you should never have talked to the Inspector. It was cutting your own throat. Now we can't proceed with your insurance, and you'll never be rich. If he comes again, pray tell him that you've given up the idea, and are letting it drop.' But Bate, I now think, had concluded, with the prompting of his neighbours, that the Doctor's intention was to poison him; and presently revenged himself by setting hounds on the brood-mares in his charge, so that two of them slipped their colts. I believe, too, that Dr Palmer, whom the loss of these foals sent into a rage, suspected Cook of having blabbed to Bate; and that this suspicion rankled, because the scheme of insuring Bate's life had not been the Doctor's own, but was foisted on him by Smith. He could not afford to quarrel with Smith, who knew too much, and guessed more; yet he could still play a trick or two on Cook, as I believe he did.

This account, Sir, has a nice dramatic close. Inspector Simpson and I went to visit Dr Palmer, where he sat at dinner, and told him that, as agents of The Midland, we had made inquiries into the proposal for Bate's life, and found it based on falsehood. He laughed and said: 'I'm sorry, Inspector Field, that you have had this trouble. The proposal to insure my overseer's life was a practical joke played on the poor innocent by some of my friends. I can only think that Mr Smith's clerk must have forwarded the proposal to The Midland in error, not realizing its farcical nature. Mr Smith will doubtless be glad to reimburse the company for whatever expenses they have incurred.'

I replied solemnly: 'That may be as it may be, Dr Palmer. But I regret to inform you that my colleague and I are empowered by The Prince of Wales to investigate the circumstances of your brother Walter's death. Our report has already gone to the London office: that he seems to have been unfairly dealt with. We intend, moreover, to push our inquiries further.'

I never witnessed such impassivity in all my life! Both Inspector Simpson and I expected that Dr Palmer, who is a powerful man, would leap from his chair and attempt to knock us down. He did not even stir, but continued to eat his steak-and-kidney pie—which he politely invited us to share—with complete unconcern. At last he observed: 'Quite right. I have my own suspicions of that fellow Walkenden; I fear he didn't carry out either Dr Day's advice or my own.'

CHAPTER XIII

'TWO NARROW SHAVES'

John Parsons Cook was an aristocratic-looking young man in his late twenties: tall, slim, thin-faced, sallow-complexioned, with long hair, a slight whisker, and a slight moustache. At the races, he sported a well-cut, rust-coloured coat, blue waistcoat, dove-grey trowsers, a beaver hat and a loose, long-sleeved overcoat. A gold cable-guard dangled from his watch, and two or three valuable rings sparkled on his fingers. He resided at Lutterworth in Leicestershire and, when he came of age, had inherited some fifteen thousand pounds; thereupon abandoning his profession as solicitor and addicting himself to the Turf. Cook was much liked for his generosity, scrupulousness in money matters, and gentle ways; but he had got into bad company and, after five or six years of keeping race-horses, found himself financially embarrassed.

His chest being weak, he formed the habit of consulting a London physician who happened to be an old family friend. Early in June, 1855, he visited this Dr Savage, complaining of a sore throat and eruptions or sores in his mouth. Cook did not disclose that he had suffered from venereal disease, but admitted to taking mercury for the sores, as advised by Dr Palmer—who regarded them as marking a secondary stage of this dreadful scourge. Dr Savage examined Cook's throat, found nothing amiss except that certain of its organs were somewhat thickened, prescribed tonics and sounded his chest. At the close of the examination during which, however, he did not invite Cook to remove his nether garments, Dr Savage pronounced: 'With care and commonsense you will yet live to be a hundred, my dear boy. But, pray take my advice and break with that company of turfmen, legs and idlers with whom I saw you at Epsom Races last week—the very worst of whom is that dissolute Dr Palmer. I warrant he'll rob you again and again. Sell your string of horses—that's your best course—abandon the Turf, go to Switzerland for a couple of years, taking your law-books with you. There study them attentively, and return with a strong chest and a clear eye to adorn the profession which you have so long neglected.'

Cook sighed, and said: 'I'm afraid, Dr Savage, your advice comes a little too late. You don't know the worst, and I can't tell it to you.'

'But John,' Dr Savage expostulated, 'why act like a beast? You were always a good-hearted, sensible lad until you inherited that accursed money. I felt ashamed for your family's sake a week ago when I saw you riding back from the Derby! I happened to be close behind your dray, and watched the disgraceful proceedings from the very edge of the race-course onwards. You threw a pincushion at the head of a solemn-looking gentleman in his four-wheeler, and caused him severe pain. When he quite naturally resented the assault, your ruffians discharged a volley of musical pears, snuff-boxes, dolls, china ink-wells and coloured balls at him—the whole range of "knock-'em-down" prizes won at the Epsom side-shows. Next, you stormed a van of cheap crockery, and occasioned the wretched owner many shillings' worth of loss. Then out came the pea-shooters, and every carriage, cab, or omnibus that you over-took was assailed with chaff, obscene vituperation and peas. You bombarded the windows of Cheam and Sutton with further peas.

Your post-horns, which had been turned into goblets that day by the insertion of a cork in each mouthpiece, were now post-horns again, and blew defiant, sentimental or drunken notes.

'You pulled up at The Cock in Sutton High Street, and so much brandy went down during your short stay that even the driver lost his head. I halted, too, in my gig, determined to keep an eye on you in case of accidents. Off you drove once more, and close by Kennington Gate my presentiments were justified. You ran into a fly containing an elderly tallow-chandler and his wife, and "upset the whole biling", as I heard one of your elegant comrades exult. You drove away, half a minute later, as if nothing had happened; leaving me to take care of the tallow-chandler, whose scalp was cut open, and his badly bruised wife, who had fainted.'

Cook looked abashed. 'Yes, we were all intoxicated,' he confessed. 'It had been a good day for us. I hope you found nothing wrong with the old gentleman's head that vinegar and brown paper couldn't cure? Dr Palmer, at any rate, handed him his card and offered to pay the damage done to the fly.'

'Dr Palmer gave him a card, as you say,' continued Dr Savage, 'but not his own! It was the Marquess of Anglesey's card, and his lordship angrily rejected the imputation that he had been in any way responsible for the accident.'

'Palmer's always a fellow for larks,' said Cook sheepishly, 'but he's very good-hearted. I'm sure he proffered the wrong card by mistake.'

'Dr Palmer's a calculating rogue,' pronounced Dr Savage, 'to which I may add that it does you no credit to be known as the intimate of a reputed horse-poisoner; a man who defaulted in the payment of a bet five years ago, and was consequently refused admission to Tattersall's Ring; who defaulted again the following year, and was forbidden by the stewards of the Jockey Club to run his horse Goldfinder in any race they managed until he had paid up. None of the first-class betting-men, several of whom are my patients, will receive him.'

'All this I have heard, and more besides,' answered Cook, with a gloomy frown, 'but one judges of a man as one knows him, and he's been very kind to me.'

After this, Cook continued to visit Dr Savage every few weeks; the last occasion being a fortnight before his death. The tonics which the Doctor prescribed had by that time improved his health and dispersed the sores in his mouth.

The Attorney-General's opening speech for the Prosecution was fairly temperate, later he developed a marked prejudice against Dr Palmer, as a result, we believe, of what he heard casually on the second day of the trial, from Fred Swindell, his Turf agent.

Swindell is a man of humble origin; he began as a cleaner of engines in a Derby fire-arms factory, but by judicious betting gathered together enough money to buy himself a well-placed public house. Dissatisfied with a life of perpetually serving beer by day, and making books at night, he determined, since he could not be one of the 'nobs', that he would at least sun himself in their society, and become necessary to them. He has now amassed a sizeable fortune by book-making, and moved into a pleasant small house on the east side of Berkeley Square, between Hay Hill and Bruton Street. There his shrewd wit, his independence of mind, combined with politeness, and his honesty—as honesty is understood on the Turf, where no strictly honest man can ever prosper—have won him many friends. I daresay, being born a Swindell, he finds more call to guard his reputation than some of his less invidiously named competitors: such as Bob Playfair, Jack Goodfellow, Harry Trueman, and Sam Shillingsworth. He has a wonderful fund of humorous stories, and we hear that no Diocesan Conference could remain unmoved by laughter were he to deliver his monologue about wedding customs at Oldham, or describe his accidental visit to the British Museum which, on first coming to London, he mistook for another sort of establishment altogether. Swindell used to back horses on Dr Palmer's behalf, but never forgave him for one day repudiating a gambling debt made verbally and not supported by a signed commission.

On the second day of the trial, then, the Attorney-General called on Swindell to discuss chances for the approaching Derby over a bottle of claret. George Hodgman was there—a young bookmaker in good repute—and we have this account from him.

Swindell opened by telling the Attorney-General that, so far as he knew, a certain horse was safe enough: the owner, running him to win, had engaged detectives as watchers by day and night, lest any attempt were made to nobble him—as with Wild Dayrell in 1854. This reference was made in compliment to Hodgman who, that year, had received a letter from a 'dangerous party' suggesting an appointment 'to our mutual advantage'. When he kept this appointment, the leg said: 'Lay against Wild Dayrell; get all you can out of him, and think of me when you rake in the jimmy o'goblins.' cried: 'Hey, whoa! I don't understand. Can Wild Dayrell really be dead meat?' 'That's it,' the leg agreed, 'he's due to be settled.' Said Hodgman: 'I'm much obliged, but I'm afraid you've come to the wrong shop. I don't wish to be mixed up in this business.' The leg whined: 'Well, as you say you won't act, I suppose you can at least be trusted not to interfere?' Hodgman nodded; yet as soon as the leg had slipped away, he jumped into a cab and whipped off to Frank Robinson's house in Bishops-gate Street. Frank Robinson, who had been charged with the London backing by the stable, immediately took train to Hunger-ford where Wild Dayrell was in training, and warned old Rickaby that the nobblers were after his horse. Rickaby pounced on a stable-boy whom he suspected and, without a word of explanation, pitched him neck and crop out of the stable. Wild Dayrell was then even more carefully guarded than before; and when the day came, he won from Kingstown by two clear lengths—much to the satisfaction of Hodgman, who had backed him heavily.

Thus invited by Fred Swindell, Hodgman told the Attorney-General: 'And now, Sir, I'll reveal the name of the "dangerous party". He was that little dwarf of a Dyke, who's always to be seen at Billy Palmer's side on the course. It's my guess that the nobbling had been arranged by Billy, who's a cool hand and can buy poisons without suspicion, being a qualified surgeon.'

The Attorney-General asked Swindell: 'Do you know anything about the business, Fred?' 'No, Sir,' Swindell replied, 'nothing definite; but seeing that you're engaged in prosecuting Palmer, I'll tell you what happened to me three years ago. Hodgy, here, has a couple of bedrooms and a sitting-room reserved for him every year at The Swan Hotel, Wolverhampton, for the August meeting. As you know, the Handicap is a rare betting race, both before and on the day. In fact, there's more money won and lost over it than over almost any other handicap in the country. So we don't like to be away from Wolverhampton when the fun's on, Hodgy and I don't . . . Well, Hodgy couldn't go down that year, because of a death in his family, so I asked him for permission to use his lodgings. "Certainly, Fred," says Hodgy. "But tell me, whom are you going with?" "Billy Palmer of Rugeley," says I. Hodgy answers—now, didn't you, Hodgy?— "All right, Fred, but take my advice and be wary of your pal. He who sups with the Devil must use a long spoon!" "Well," I said, "I've heard tales about him and I think they're all flam. By the bye, Billy Palmer says he has a good thing in Doubt for the Handicap.

Though I've put him five hundred pounds at seven to one against, you'd better risk a 'pony' on the mare, lad. Don't be misled by her form in the Liverpool Spring Cup; she's come on a deal since then. I'm taking a chance on her myself.'"

'I remember that race,' the Attorney-General remarked ruefully. 'I laid on Pastrycook and lost four hundred guineas.'

Swindell laughed. 'And if Doubt had lost too, Sir, we shouldn't be drinking this bottle of claret together! Come, let me spin you the yarn of how I was doctored for death in case of her defeat. Nay, Sir, I assure you, Billy Palmer would think no more of poisoning a man to gain his ends than a chemist would of dosing a mangy cat or a decrepit dog. On the Saturday night, then, as we sat in our private room at The Swan, drinking brandy and water, I asked him: "Why do you always empty your glass at one gulp, Doctor, instead of sipping at it, and prolonging the pleasure?" Billy explained that, in the first place, he gained more flavour by so doing and, in the second, he found the practice less intoxicating. "Why not try it?" Billy asked. I did so, and certainly the flavour was fuller; but by Heaven! how sick the drink made me! I put my gripings down to the shell-fish we had eaten—one should never eat shell-fish in the Midlands, especially during August—and, still feeling pretty queer the next day, I told him: "Billy, I'm not seeing out the race tomorrow; I'm for home." "Nonsense," said he, "you can't miss all the fun. I'll give you some pills that will set you right." Remembering Hodgy's warning, I replied: "No, I'm off." However, he persuaded me to stay (for, indeed, I wasn't fit for a ride in the train) by saying: "If you like, I'll get a second opinion for you. There's another doctor in this hotel." He went out and fetched a person named Thirlby . . .'

'His own assistant, ha!' exclaimed the Attorney-General.

'So I understand now,' agreed Swindell, 'though I didn't know it at the time; and the man's not a qualified doctor, but a mere country chemist. Thirlby advised me against travelling, for my bowels were turned to water, as the Psalmist says, and it would have been an awkward journey. "Dr Palmer is treating you admirably," Thirlby assured me, when told what the pills contained. "You couldn't be in better hands."'

'I wonder how much Thirlby knows?' the Attorney-General ruminated.

'On Monday,' Swindell went on, 'I was no better, but weak, very weak, and my mind had clouded over, though I foolishly continued to swallow Billy's pills. That was Handicap Day. Of the nine starters, Musician and Pastrycook were the most fancied, but the odds had shortened on Doubt—she started at five to one. Neither Musician nor your own fancy, Sir, gained a place, although Montagu seemed like a winner until Sharpe, who was at his best that season, pulled Doubt ahead to finish in the lead by half a length. Well, The Swan Hotel stands close to the course and the crowd was roaring like a stormy sea off Dover; yet how could I bring myself to care what beast won or lost? It hadn't occurred to me, do you see, that if Doubt came in first, which (not to pun upon her name) was far from certain, Billy Palmer stood to make three thousand five hundred pounds, as well as securing the stakes; but that he was protecting himself against the danger of losing his five hundred pounds by doctoring me to death—for every fool knows that "death before settling day voids the wager." Thanks be to the Almighty, despite Billy's having jeopardized my existence by his damned poisons, all was well. Doubt ran for my life, and brought it off! If I were to die, Billy would lose the three thousand five hundred pounds I owed him, so he hared back from the course, not troubling to acknowledge the congratulations of his supporters, and burst like a whirlwind into my bedroom. In the twinkling of an eye he and Thirlby had me out of bed before a big fire, and began rubbing the calves of my legs. Then they poured some exceedingly hot soup into me, and within a couple of hours I felt somewhat recovered, but weak as a new-born pup. It was a narrow shave, a near thing, a deuced near thing!'

'Fred,' said the Attorney-General. 'I can't understand how you ever had the heart to do business with Palmer again! But I'm sure to hang him—sure!'

'Oh, go easy with him,' said Hodgman, grinning. 'He was only giving Fred a little purge to reduce his weight. Fred could well afford to lose a couple of stone.'

'Easy?' cried the Attorney-General, 'yes, I'll go easy, by God! You mark my words, I'll hang him for that! I don't think poor Cook is much loss to the world, but if my Fred had perished untimely, where should I be?'

Though not believing Swindell's story to be wholly fictitious, we cannot rule out his prejudice against Dr Palmer. In our opinion, tainted shell-fish are as likely as not to have caused Swindell's stomachic disorder; nor was Swindell ever above improving a story beyond all recognition. The symptoms reported by him were vague enough; the remedy said to have been prescribed is more dramatic than plausible—how came a large fire in his room at the very height of summer?—and if Dr Palmer drank a couple or more tumblers of brandy and water at a gulp, he was never seen to do so before or since. Moreover, his supposed gains at Wolverhampton do not correspond with what is known of his financial position a week later. Nor do we believe that he ever purposely dosed a man to death: the Abley case having been, in our opinion, a pure mischance.

Equally dubious is the story told by Tom, the Boots at The Junction Hotel, Stafford, whom we have been at pains to question. The hotel stable is in the courtyard, a low-roofed, white-washed building with stalls for five horses. On one side a ladder stands flat against the wall, up which one climbs to the hayloft. Here Tom sleeps: a ragged, ferret-faced young man, notable for a cast in one eye and a very strong bodily smell compounded of liquor, blacking, stable and foul linen. Tom is a proud man these days: a local celebrity, a victim of Dr Palmer's poisoning who has lived to tell the tale. He declares that, after his interview with Inspectors Field and Simpson, Dr Palmer met him on the road between The Junction and the Railway Station, and asked: 'Tom, what will you have?'

The rest of the story is best told in Tom's own words, and he must here be imagined rubbing his hair to shine up his thoughts, then picking his nails as though the dirt they concealed were the evidence he was seeking, and finally crouching on a stone mounting block, knees to chin, and hugging his ill-shaped boots—which, for a Boots' boots, are singularly devoid of polish.

TOM THE BOOTS

I says: 'I'll take a drop of brandy, if anything, Doctor. It's a chill evening.'

'Then let's go to The Junction,' says he. 'I don't want to offend old Lloyd by standing you treat elsewhere.'

So we came back to the bar and he mixed the brandy and water. 'Take it here?' asks the Doctor. To which I answered: 'Well, I'd rather take it outside.'

'No, here,' he says. 'What are you afraid of?' And I drank.

The queer thing was it didn't taste queer, but oh, my dear Lord! what happened after? It was just like common brandy and water, as is made hot with sugar, my favourite drink, and I shouldn't have drunk it if it had tasted bad—because I'm very particular with my drinks, always have been, but oh, my dear Lord!

I went out into the yard, and was I took bad? I was indeed! I felt drunk, like. I didn't know where I was, like. I certainly had some recollection of what was said, but my senses were gone, like. Directly I'd drunk it, I knew I'd been nobbled: the drink lay heavy on my stomach, like a crab. Then up it all came. I clapped my hand over my mouth, I ran out that way into the yard and there, just where you're standing, Sir, I threw it up, together with my supper—pig's liver, ale, soused herring, red cabbage and all. It was a fair mess, like. I never was took that way after drinking brandy, not in all my life before. I don't drink so much of it neither, now. Ten shillings a week is what Lloyd pays me; you can't drink brandy on that, but only ale. And I'd spewed out two good quarts there on the stable floor.

I generally drinks brandy when I can get it. At one time, while I was working for old Mr Venables up by Castle Knoll, who kept a good cellar and didn't mind my sampling it, I used to drink all day, like. I'd begin in the morning and carry it on till night, and I kept this game up for nearly eight year, until Mr Venables died and the cellar ran dry, at much the same time. Then I had to come here to The Junction. Needs must when the Devil drives. Lloyd's ale is good ale for sure, but it ain't brandy; nor don't go well with brandy. The two liquors quarrel, like, in the belly. But they tell me Dr Palmer's a poisoner, so of course he must have gave me arsenic, or something wicked of the same nature, mixed in the water.

I was never so sick in my life before, not after drinking. I went and laid me down in the kitchen; and the missus she comes in and sees me there, all of a tizzy. 'Good God,' says she, 'why, what's the matter, Tom? You look white as a sheet!'

'I've been drinking, Ma'am,' says I.

'What have you been drinking?' she asks me.

'Some brandy and water along with Dr Palmer,' I says.

'The more fool you,' she says. 'Never heard what happened to poor Abley, down at The Lamb and Flag, eleven years ago? You're poisoned, Tom, that's what you are. Who's your doctor?'

'Dr Palmer,' says I.

'Don't talk foolish, Tom,' says she; so I go and lay me down in one of the stalls, for I couldn't mount the ladder to the loft, nohow I couldn't. My legs wouldn't support me, like. Well, I lived, as you see, Sir, and that's more than poor Abley did, or poor Watty Palmer. But I felt mighty queer for three or four days after. I remember very little about when I woke up, or how long I lay there.

I'm told the ostler came and covered me with a horse rug. I was as black as soot in the face, he says, which it wasn't only the horse dung on which I'd laid—that I'll swear—and he couldn't hear me breathe, nohow, nor nothing. He thought I was dead, like, and left me there, saying nothing to Mr Lloyd, nor the missus, for fear he'd be blamed. A narrow shave it was, you may be bound, in all honesty!

No, Sir, I never named it to Dr Palmer afterwards. I couldn't positively swear that he nobbled me, you see? And he was always a generous gentleman when I ran him his errands.

It is, however, not impossible that these two stories may, after all, have been substantially true—if Dr Palmer's motive was not, in either case, to kill but merely to prostrate his victims and cloud their judgement by the use of 'knocking-out drops': as these are termed in the taverns and brothels of sea-port towns, where sailors are forcibly enlisted for long voyages. If Doubt had lost, the Doctor would have been able to tear a page or two from Swindell's betting-book, and empty his money-belt of whatever cash it contained. In Tom's case, he stood to gain nothing but a petty revenge; yet it will be noted that the drug supposedly used on Swindell was a laxative, whereas the one supposedly used on Boots was an emetic. The latter may have been tried experimentally, with more important victims in view.

We can find no confirmation of a rumour, now widely current, that Dr Palmer also attempted to drug Lord George Bentinck, the race-horse owner. This is said to have taken place while he was still a student at Bart's, three years before Lord George's death in 1848; but the exact circumstances are never given.

CHAPTER XIV

FINANCIAL STRAITS

The Attorney-General's speech on the opening day of the trial has given a very fair account of Dr Palmer's financial troubles; save that, in our opinion, he misrepresented Jeremiah Smith's humorous proposals for an insurance on George Bate's life as serious ones prompted by the Doctor and designed to improve his own situation. This situation was, indeed, desperate. Yet, after careful thought, we accept his plea of 'Not Guilty' to the charge of taking Cook's life, by strychnine poisoning, with the object of pecuniary gain. The gain would have been utterly inadequate to re-establish his credit; and imprisonment is always a better fate than the gallows. Nor do we believe that strychnia was the cause of Cook's death.

THE ATTORNEY-GENERAL

Gentlemen, it seems that as early as the year 1853, Palmer had got into pecuniary difficulties—he began to raise money on bills. In the year 1854, his circumstances became worse, and he was at that time indebted to different persons in a large sum of money. He then had recourse to an expedient which I shall have to bring before you, because it has an important bearing on this case. Gentlemen, let me make a preliminary observation. I must detail to you transactions involving fraud and, what is graver, forgery—circumstances and transactions reflecting the greatest discredit on those connected with them. Yet while I feel it absolutely necessary to bring these circumstances to your notice for the elucidation of the truth, I am anxious that they should not have more than their fair and legitimate effect. You must not allow them to prejudice your minds against the prisoner as regards the real matter of inquiry here today. A man may be guilty of fraud, he may be guilty of forgery; it does not follow that he should be guilty of murder.

Among the bills on which Palmer raised money, in the course of the year 1854, was one for two thousand pounds, which he discounted with Mr Padwick. That bill bore upon it the acceptance of Palmer's mother, Mrs Sarah Palmer. She is a woman of considerable wealth; and her acceptance, being believed to be genuine, was a security on which money would be readily advanced. Palmer forged that acceptance, and got money upon it; which was, if not the first, at least one of the earlier transactions of that nature—for there are a large series of them—in which money was obtained from bills discounted by Palmer, with his mother's acceptances forged upon them. I shall show you, presently, how this practice involved him in a state of such peril and emergency that—as we suggest, but it is for you to form your own conclusions—he had recourse to a desperate expedient in order to avoid the imminent consequences.

By the summer of 1854, he owed a very large sum of money. On the 29th of September his wife died; he had an insurance on her life to the amount of thirteen thousand pounds—and the proceeds of that insurance were realized. Palmer used the thirteen thousand pounds to pay off some of his most pressing liabilities. With regard to a part of these liabilities, he employed as his agent a gentleman named Pratt, a solicitor in London, who is in the habit of discounting bills, and whose name will be largely mixed up with the subsequent transactions I shall detail to you. Mr Pratt received for him a sum of eight thousand pounds, and disposed of it in the payment of various liabilities on bills which were in the hands of his own clients. Mr Wright, a solicitor of Birmingham, who had also advanced money to the prisoner, received five thousand more, and thus thirteen thousand of debt was disposed of; but that still left Palmer with considerable liabilities. Among others, the bill for two thousand pounds, discounted by Mr Padwick, remained unpaid.

This brings us to the close of 1854. Early in 1855, Palmer effected another insurance in his brother Walter's name, Mr Pratt acting as his agent; and that policy for thirteen thousand pounds was immediately assigned to Palmer. Mr Pratt paid the first premium for him, out of a bill which he discounted at the rate of sixty per cent, and afterwards proceeded to discount further bills, the insurance policy being held by him as a collateral security. The bills discounted in the course of 1855 reached a total of £12,500. I find that two, discounted as early as June, 1854, were kept alive by being held over from month to month. In March, 1855, two further bills of two thousand pounds each were discounted; and with the proceeds Palmer bought two race-horses, called Nettle and The Chicken. These bills were renewed in June; they became due on the 28th of September and 2nd of October; were then renewed and became due again on the 1st and 5th of January, 1856. On the 18th of April, 1855, a bill was discounted for two thousand pounds at three months, which became due on the 22nd of July, and was renewed so as to become due on the 27th of October. On the 23rd of July, a bill for two thousand pounds, at three months, was discounted, which became due on the 25th of October. On the 9th of July, a bill for two thousand pounds, at three months, was drawn; renewed on the 12th of October, it became due on the 12th of January, 1856. On the 27th of September, a bill for one thousand pounds was discounted, at three months, the proceeds of which went to pay the renewal on the two March bills of two thousand pounds, due at the close of September, and the bill of the 23rd of July, due on the 12th of October.

Thus, in the month of November, when the Shrewsbury Races took place, the account stood as follows. There were in Mr Pratt's hands a bill due on the 25th of October for two thousand pounds; another due on the 27th of October for two thousand pounds; two bills together making one thousand five hundred pounds, due on the 9th of November; a bill due on the 10th of December for one thousand pounds; one on the first of January for two thousand pounds; one on the 5th of January for two thousand pounds; one on the 18th of January for two thousand pounds: making in the whole £12,500. In July, it seems, Palmer contrived to pay one thousand pounds; thus in the month of November bills amounting to £11,500 remained due, and every one of them bore the forged acceptance of the prisoner's mother! You will therefore understand the pressure which necessarily arose upon him, the pressure of enormous liabilities which he had not a shilling in the world to meet, and a still greater pressure arising from the knowledge that, as soon as his mother should be resorted to for payment, the fact of his having committed these forgeries would at once become manifest and bring on him the penalty that the law exacts.

Now, the deceased Mr Cook had been only partially interested in these transactions. I should mention, before I go into the further history of the case, that Walter Palmer, the brother, died in the month of August, 1855. His life had been insured for thirteen thousand pounds, and the policy had been assigned to the prisoner—who, of course, expected that the proceeds would pay off those liabilities. However, the insurance office in question declined to pay; consequently there was no assistance to be derived from that source.

As I was saying, gentlemen, Mr Cook had been, to a certain extent—but only to a very limited extent—mixed up with the prisoner in these pecuniary transactions. It seems that in the month of May, 1855, Palmer was pressed—by a person named Serjeant, I believe—to pay a sum of five hundred pounds on a bill of transaction. At that time, Palmer had in the hands of Mr Pratt a credit balance of three hundred and ten pounds; and asked him for an advance of one hundred and ninety pounds to make up the five hundred. When Mr Pratt refused this advance, except on security, Palmer offered him the acceptance of Cook, representing Mr Cook to be a man of substance; accordingly, the acceptance of Mr Cook for two hundred pounds was sent up, and on it Mr Pratt advanced the money. This appears to have been the first transaction of the kind in which Mr Cook figured, and though not knowing whether it has any immediate bearing on the subject, I am anxious to lay before you all the circumstances which show the relation between Palmer and Cook. Palmer having failed to provide for that bill of two hundred pounds, when it became due, Mr Cook had to provide for it himself, which he did.

In the August of 1855, a transaction took place to which I must again call your particular attention: Palmer informed Mr Pratt that he must have one thousand pounds more by the next Saturday. Mr Pratt declined to advance the thousand pounds without security; whereupon Palmer offered the security of Mr Cook's acceptance for five hundred pounds, again representing him as a man of substance. But Mr Pratt still declined to advance the money without some more tangible security than Mr Cook's mere acceptance. Now, Palmer explained this as a transaction in which Mr Cook required the money, and since I have no means of ascertaining how the matter stood, I will give him the credit to suppose that it was so, and that he had Mr Cook's acquiescence for the proposals he was making to Mr Pratt. Mr Cook was engaged

upon the Turf, sometimes winning, sometimes losing; and pur-
chasing horses. It may perfectly well be that he then required this
loan of five hundred pounds, as Palmer declared.

Since, as I said before, Mr Pratt declined to advance the money
except upon more available security, Palmer proposed an assignment by Mr Cook of two race-horses—the one called Polestar,
the horse that afterwards won at Shrewsbury Races, and the other
called Sirius—and, as Mr Pratt agreed, this assignment was executed by Mr Cook, in Mr Pratt's favour, as a collateral security
for the loan of five hundred pounds. Now Mr Cook was entitled
to as much money as could be realized upon this security; the
arrangement being that Mr Pratt should give him a sum of £375
in money and a wine-warrant for £65 which, with discount for
three months at £50, and expenses at £10, made up the total sum
of five hundred. But Palmer contrived that the £375 cheque and
the wine-warrant should be sent to him, and not to Mr Cook;
for he wrote, desiring that Mr Pratt should forward them to him
at the Post Office, Doncaster, where he would see Mr Cook. He
could not, in fact, see Mr Cook there, because Mr Cook did not
visit Doncaster; but by these means Palmer got the cheque and
the wine-warrant into his own hands. He affixed to the face of
the cheque a receipt stamp, and availed himself of the opportunity, now afforded by the law, of striking out the word 'bearer',
and writing 'order'. The effect of this was, as you are all no doubt
aware, to necessitate the endorsement of Mr Cook upon the back
of the cheque; but since Palmer did not intend that these proceeds
should find their way into Mr Cook's hands, he accordingly forged
the signature 'John Parsons Cook' on the back of that cheque. He
then paid the cheque into his banker's at Rugeley: the proceeds
were realized, paid by the bankers in London, and went to the
credit of Palmer. Mr Cook never received the money, and you
will see that at the time of his last illness this bill, which was a bill at

three months, in respect of these transactions of September 10th, would be due in the course of ten days; when it would appear that Palmer had forged Mr Cook's endorsement on this cheque and pocketed the proceeds.

Gentlemen, I wish that this were the only transaction in which Mr Cook had been mixed up with the prisoner Palmer; but there is another to which I must refer. In the September of 1855, Palmer's brother having died, but the profits of the insurance not having been realized, he induced a person by the name of Bate to insure his life. Palmer had succeeded in raising money on former insurances and, I have no doubt, pressed or induced Mr Cook to assist him in this transaction; his object was, by representing Bate as a man of wealth, and producing a policy on Bate's life, to get further advances upon this collateral security. I put it no higher, nor do I suppose Mr Cook would have been a party to any other transaction. It seems that, on the 5th of September, Mr Bate, the prisoner, and Mr Cook were together at Rugeley. Mr Bate was a hanger-on of Palmer's, a person who had before been better off in the world, but who had fallen in decay and was now compelled to accept employment from Palmer as a sort of superintendent of his stables. He had run through everything, and had nothing left; though he remained a healthy young man. Palmer proposed to insure his life, and handed him that common form of proposal with which we are all familiar. Mr Bate, however, said: 'No, I do not want to insure my life,' and declined the notion of such a thing. Palmer pressed him, and Mr Cook interposed with: 'You had better do it, Bate; it will be for your benefit; you are quite safe with Palmer.' They pressed him to sign the insurance proposal, which Cook attested and Palmer filled in, for no less a sum than twenty-five thousand pounds. In it Palmer was described as the medical attendant, and his assistant, Thirlby, as the referee and friend who would speak to Bate's habits; and these proposals were sent off, I think, to The Solicitors' and General Office. That office not being disposed to effect the insurance on Bate's life, they sent up another proposal for ten thousand pounds to The Midland Office, on the same life. In each case, further information was required as to Bate's position; but instead of it turning out that he was a gentleman of responsibility and means, it turned out that he was a mere labourer in Palmer's employ. The office was not satisfied, and the thing dropped.

> LORD CAMPBELL: Whatever you have stated so far bears on the question the jury are to try. I suppose that this will have the same tendency?
> THE ATTORNEY-GENERAL: If your Lordship trusts me, I will take care not to state anything that is not important.
> LORD CAMPBELL: By our law we cannot allow one crime to show the possibility of another, but whatever may bear on the charge to be tried is strictly admissible.
> THE ATTORNEY-GENERAL: I trust, your Lordship will give me credit for the greatest anxiety not to bring forward anything unimportant. This seems to me a matter which may have a most important bearing by and by.

Gentlemen, the prisoner's attempt failed; and no money could be obtained on the security of that policy. The affair may be important in more ways than one, but it is important in this respect: that it shows the desperate pecuniary straits to which he had by that time been reduced.

Now we go back for a moment to the insurance on the brother's life. I find by the correspondence between Palmer and Mr Pratt, which will be produced to you, that Mr Pratt, having applied to the office at which the insurance on Walter Palmer's life had been effected, experienced difficulty in getting the money, and thereupon began to press Palmer for immediate payment of his bills. These letters are here in my hand; and before reading them, I will state what I shall by and by prove—that Palmer had the Postmaster at Rugeley completely under his influence, and that the letters addressed by Pratt to his mother, Mrs Sarah Palmer, were intercepted in the Post Office and handed over to Palmer himself.

The learned Attorney-General then read extracts from certain letters that passed between Mr Pratt and Palmer in September and October, showing the manner in which Mr Pratt was pressing Palmer for the payment of various overdue bills and the interest upon them.

Gentlemen, on the 6th of November two writs were issued for four thousand pounds, one against Palmer, the other against his mother. Mr Pratt wrote on the same day, informing Palmer that he had sent these writs to Mr Crabb, but that they would not be served without further direction; he therefore strongly urged Palmer to raise the money, and also to visit him in London and make an arrangement regarding a bill for one thousand five hundred pounds, which would fall due in three days' time. On the 10th of November, the day to which Pratt had said he would delay the service of the writs, Palmer visited London and paid Mr Pratt a sum of three hundred pounds which, with two sums of two hundred and fifty pounds, already paid, made up a total of eight hundred pounds, Mr Pratt deducted two hundred pounds from this, for two months' discount, thus leaving six hundred pounds to the credit of the two-thousand-pound bill falling due on the 25th of October. On the 13th of November, which is a very important day, for it is the one on which Polestar won at Shrewsbury, Mr Pratt writes a letter referring to The Prince of Wales policy, and saying that steps will be taken to enforce its payment by the company.

That, gentlemen, was the state of things in which Palmer was placed on the 13th of November. You will find from this correspondence that Mr Pratt, the agent through whom this bill had been discounted, held at that time twelve thousand five hundred pounds of bills in his hands, minus the six hundred pounds which had been paid off on this, the whole of which bore the forged acceptances of Palmer's mother: acceptances either forged by him or by some one at his desire, and for which, in consequence, Palmer was criminally responsible. You will also find that since The Prince of Wales Office declined to pay the sum for which Walter Palmer's life had been insured, namely thirteen thousand pounds, Mr Pratt, who held that policy as a collateral security, would not have been justified in further renewing these bills. He had therefore issued writs against the mother, which were forthwith to be served in case Palmer could not, at all events, discharge part of his debt.

Now we come to the races at Shrewsbury. Mr Cook was the owner, as you are aware, of a mare called Polestar, which he had entered for the Shrewsbury Handicap. She was very advantageously weighted. The race was run on the 13th of November, the very day on which Mr Pratt's last letter was written, which would reach Palmer on the next day, the 14th. Polestar won the race. Cook was entitled in the first place to the stakes, which amounted to £424, subject to certain deductions, leaving a net sum of £381.19s. to Cook's credit. He had also betted large sums upon the race, partly for himself and, I am told, partly on commission. As a result, his betting-book showed a winning which amounted, together with the stakes, to two thousand and fifty pounds. Cook had also spent the previous week at the Worcester Races, and by the end of the

Shrewsbury Meeting had a sum of seven or eight hundred pounds in his pocket, mainly from bets paid there on the course. Other bets, which he was entitled to be paid at Tattersall's, on the ensuing Monday, amounted, as we shall afterwards find, to one thousand and twenty pounds. He would receive the stakes through Messrs Weatherby, the great racing agents in London, with whom he kept an account, as many betting men do.

Now, within a week of that time, Mr Cook died, and the important inquiry of today is how he met his death; whether by natural means, or whether by the hand of man; and, if the latter, by whose hand?

CHAPTER XV

DEATH AT THE TALBOT ARMS

The evidence elicited at the coroner's inquest on John Parsons Cook, who died at The Talbot Arms Hotel, Rugeley on November 20th, 1855, exactly a week after Polestar's capture of the Shrewsbury Handicap, has now been supplemented by further evidence elicited at Dr Palmer's trial for murder—some of it, however, plainly irreconcilable with the original depositions made by the same witnesses.

Dr Palmer, it appears, owned so little ready cash on the opening day of the Shrewsbury Meeting, that he borrowed twenty-five pounds for the trip from a Rugeley butcher. He later claimed to have put himself in funds by borrowing another hundred and fifty on the race-course and laying it on Polestar at seven to one; yet, in fact, he made no cash profit at all, only winning back two hundred and ten pounds from a Mr Butler to whom he had owed seven hundred since the Liverpool Meeting. As soon as the race had been run, Dr Palmer took train back to Rugeley, where he found two letters waiting for him at his house. There was the one from Pratt (mentioned by the Attorney-General), threatening legal proceedings against his mother, if he would not at once pay the fourteen hundred pounds now due and covered by her acceptance. The other came from a Stafford girl named Jane Bergen, whom he had got with child during Eliza Tharm's pregnancy, and for whom he had procured an abortion. She possessed thirty-four love letters written by him in most lascivious language, and threatened that she would show them to her father unless he paid fifty pounds for their return. At first, she had priced the collection at one hundred pounds—a sum which, he told her, far exceeded their worth.

Elated by Polestar's victory, Cook asked a few of his friends to celebrate it with him by dining at The Raven Hotel, Shrewsbury; where two or three bottles of champagne were consumed. This was Tuesday, November 13th. He retired to bed in good health and spirits, not having drunk much; and the next day rose cheerfully and visited the course again. There he found Dr Palmer come back from Rugeley and reproached him for not having attended the Polestar dinner. That night, Wednesday, November 14th, at about eleven o'clock, Mr Ishmael Fisher, a wine merchant of Victoria Street, Holborn—but also a betting-agent who usually collected Cook's winnings, or paid his losses, each settling day at Tattersall's—decided to call on him. Fisher was also lodging at The Raven. When he entered the sitting-room which Cook and Dr Palmer shared, he found the two of them seated at table over brandy and water, in the company of George Myatt and Samuel Cheshire.

Cook invited Fisher to join the party, and then turned to ask Dr Palmer: 'Will you take another glass?'

The Doctor replied: 'Not until you down yours. You must play fair, old cock—drink for drink, and no heel-taps.'

'Oh, that's soon done,' cried Cook, and seizing the tumbler, half full of strong brandy and water, which stood on the table before him, tossed it off at a gulp, leaving perhaps a teaspoonful at the bottom of the glass.

A minute later, he complained that the grog tasted queer, and looked accusingly at Dr Palmer.

The Doctor reached for Cook's tumbler, sipped the little liquor remaining, rolled it around his tongue, and exclaimed: 'Come, what's the game, Johnny? There's no taste but brandy here!'

Cook then made some remark, about how dreadfully his throat had been burned, which was interrupted by a second knock on the door. Another wine merchant, named Read, whose tavern near Farringdon Market is a favourite haunt of many sporting men, entered to congratulate Cook on his success. Dr Palmer, pushing the glass towards Read and Fisher, said: 'Cook fancies that there's something in this brandy and water. Taste it! I've just done so myself.'

Read laughed and answered: 'It's easy enough to say "Taste it!" but you've swigged the lot between you. Fetch me more of the same brew, and I'll give you my professional verdict.'

'Well, at least smell it,' the Doctor urged him. Read smelt Cook's glass, and could detect no odour but that of spirits. A new decanter of the same brandy was now sent for, and Cook mixed the grog with water poured from the same jug as before. All the guests rose to toast Polestar, a buzz of jovial talk ensued, and Cook's suspicions were forgotten.

Ten minutes later, Cook retired to his bedroom, and presently came back, looking very pale.

He told Fisher, who was sprawled on the sofa, that he wished to make a request of him.

Fisher led Cook to his own sitting-room. 'What ails you, friend Johnny?' he asked.

'I've been as sick as a cat,' Cook answered. 'I do believe that damned Palmer dosed my grog, for a lark. Fisher, pray take care of these bank notes, like a good fellow. I trust nobody but you in this Cave of Forty Thieves; and Billy Palmer least of the lot.' He handed over a bulky packet, tied with tape, and sealed. Then he muttered: 'Excuse me, my dear Sir, I must vomit again,' and stumbled off.

On his way along the corridor, he passed a law-stationer by

the name of Jones, also lodging at The Raven. Jones remarked to Fisher, who had followed Cook: 'He's got this sickness too, that's knocking people down like ninepins. They all act as though they were poisoned.'

'He thinks he *is* poisoned,' rejoined Fisher, 'and, what's more, he's drunk enough to accuse his friend Billy Palmer of the deed. I believe, by the bye, that Billy's treating him for the pox.'

Cook then lurched into Fisher's sitting-room. 'I swear that damned Billy Palmer has dosed me!' he repeated; but before he could substantiate the remark, out he had to run again.

Fisher and Jones followed him into his bedroom, where he was vomiting violently into a wash hand-basin. 'Let me send for a doctor,' offered Fisher.

'Pray do so at once,' Cook groaned.

A certain Dr Gibson arrived at half an hour past midnight. Cook complained of pains in his stomach and heat in his throat, repeating constantly: 'I think I have been poisoned.'

Dr Gibson recommended an emetic, but Cook said: 'No, there's no need of anything from a chemist's shop. I can make myself sick on warm water. I often do.'

A drowsy chambermaid brought a jugful of warm water. When Cook had drained it, Dr Gibson ordered: 'Now tickle the back of your throat with a feather from your pillow, Mr Cook, if you please!'

Cook replied: 'There's no need to open the pillow, either. The handle of my toothbrush will do as usual.'

He presently vomited up the water, having nothing else by now to offer the basin. Dr Gibson laid him on the bed, probed his abdomen, found him to be severely constipated, and thereupon prescribed compound rhubarb pills and calomel, to be followed by a black draught of senna and magnesia. With that, he turned on his heel and left the hotel.

Half an hour later, Fisher knocked up Dr Gibson again, telling him: 'Don't go fooling about, Sir; give my friend something to settle him for the night!' Dr Gibson aggrievedly prepared an anodyne draught and paregoric, which Fisher took back to The Raven, and by two o'clock in the morning Cook told his friends that he was somewhat improved. No longer feeling bound to wait up for Dr Palmer, who had some time before disappeared, they bade Cook good-night, and he thanked them heartily.

At nine o'clock Cook arose, shaky and feeble, but much relieved by an undisturbed sleep. He went across the corridor to call on Fisher, from whom he retrieved his packet of notes, still securely sealed. Dr Palmer now returned to The Raven, after an all-night absence. He found Fisher breakfasting, and said: 'Cook's recovered, I'm glad to see. But I wish the damned fool wouldn't publicly accuse me of dosing his drink! I've a good mind to sue him for slander.'

'Then what ailed him, Billy?' asked Fisher. 'We were up with him until the small hours.'

'He was beastly drunk, that's what he was,' cried the Doctor. 'And I keep telling him that drink is the worst thing possible for his old complaint.'

'Well, at least his stomach has got a long-delayed clean-out,' remarked Fisher, not wishing to argue the point. 'Dr Gibson told us that Johnny can't have been to the bogs for a week or more.'

There is a certain Mrs Anne Brooks of Manchester who, much against the wish and orders of her husband, a prominent Mancunian, frequents race-meetings, bets on commission, and has at her disposal a number of jockeys from whom she secures mounts. These jockeys, together with black-legs, tipsters and other members of her private intelligence service, form what the French call a *salon sportif* around this remarkable personage. Mrs Brooks had met Dr Palmer in the street on the Wednesday evening; and when asked what news there was of a horse called Lord Alfred, which the Earl of Derby had entered for the same race next day as Dr

Palmer's The Chicken, she gaily answered: 'Nay, Lord Alfred's said to be in champion form, lad.'

The Doctor answered: 'Good, ma'am! That means I'll get longer odds. I'm putting my whole sack on The Chicken.'

At about 10.30 P.M., Mrs Brooks sent a servant to Dr Palmer, requesting a private word with him. When he agreed, the servant showed her upstairs. She found him standing in the corridor, holding a tumbler, which seemed to contain a small quantity of water, close against the gas-light, and examining it. Though Dr Palmer heard her coming, he continued to hold the tumbler in the same position, now and then shaking it.

'Dirty weather tonight,' remarked Mrs Brooks.

'Yes, the running will be agreeably soft tomorrow,' he answered. 'It should suit The Chicken. He loves mud so much, I have a mind to rename him The Duckling. Excuse me, I'll be with you presently.'

He went into his bedroom and, emerging half a minute later, carried the same tumbler into the sitting-room where Cook, Myatt and Cheshire sat drinking convivially. Mrs Brooks waited outside until he fetched her a similar tumbler full of brandy and water, which she drank without any ill consequences. They discussed Lord Alfred's chances in low tones, and the Doctor told her: 'Do as I do, and remember me when you win! I'm still backing The Chicken.' The remainder of their conversation was private, and may well have been sentimental; which would account for Dr Palmer's disappearance from The Raven between midnight and nine-thirty.

According to Mrs Brooks's statement at the Old Bailey, many racing men whom she knew were seized by nausea that Wednesday, and vomited their dinners, and there was talk of a poisoned water supply. She added: 'I assumed Dr Palmer to be mixing a cooling drink when he stood in the corridor.' The Prosecution's case is that the liquid was water doctored with tartar emetic, which is a form of antimony; and that Dr Palmer poured this colourless poison into Cook's tumbler. The Defence contends that he held up to the light a glass of the city's drinking water, in the hope of detecting a cloudiness which might explain the general sickness. However, we accept neither theory, since Mrs Brooks has since privately told Will Saunders, the trainer: 'Billy Palmer was hinting in dumb-show that Lord Alfred would be made "safe" with a drug of his own concoction. I acted on this hint; but whether he deceived me, or whether Lord Derby's stablemen were too wide-awake, my people can't find out.' At any rate, Lord Alfred stayed un-nobbled, The Chicken displayed no liking for mud, and Dr Palmer lost several hundred pounds.

On the Thursday evening, the races over, Dr Palmer, Cook, Cheshire, and Myatt caught the Express train to Stafford, and thence went together by fly to Rugeley, where the Doctor engaged a room at The Talbot Arms Hotel for Cook. If we are to believe Mr Herring, the betting-agent, who had attended the Polestar dinner, Cook asked him on the Thursday morning: 'Don't you think Palmer drugged me last night?'

'I shouldn't like to venture an opinion,' Herring answered, 'but if you so mistrust him, why are you going to Rugeley with him tonight?'

Cook, Mr Herring declares, replied sadly: 'I really must go there; you don't know all.'

Mr Herring, *alias* Mr. Howard, is held in high esteem by his clients, and we should be prepared to accept his word; save that he told this story (which makes remarkably little sense) while smarting under a natural resentment. Dr Palmer had, by then, swindled him out of a large sum of money.

Perhaps the following light-hearted account of Mr Cook's illness at Shrewsbury, which appeared in a London newspaper on the last day of the meeting, may not be far from the truth:

After indulging freely in the foreign wines of Shrewsbury, the owner of Polestar called for brandy and water to restore his British stolidity. Tossing off his glass, he grumbled that there was something in it, and complained of a burned throat. Perhaps those who have drunk strong brandy and water with similar haste may recognize the sensation; perhaps also, like Mr Cook, they have vomited afterwards. Mr Cook bolted his brandy and water down at Dr Palmer's challenge and bolted it up again when it encountered the cold champagne. That night he was very drunk, and very sick, and very ill. His dinner he cast into a basin; his money he deposited with his friend Mr Ishmael Fisher, a sporting City wine merchant, expressing his belief at the same time that Dr Palmer had dosed him for the sake of his money. If such had been the Doctor's intention, would he not have followed his victim from the room, and kept close to him all night? But he never went near the ailing Mr Cook, a neglect that certainly shows how hollow was his friendship, yet proves his innocence; for a guilty man would have been much more officious. The next morning, Mr Cook looked very ill, as men are apt to do after excessive vinous vomiting, but his drunken suspicions of Dr Palmer had evaporated with the fumes of the brandy, and they were again friends and brother-sportsmen.

Arrived at Rugeley, Cook retired to his room at The Talbot Arms Hotel, where he lay in bed all night, and all the next morning. At one o'clock, he got up for a walk through the town; ate bread and cheese with Jeremiah Smith at The Shoulder of Mutton, and watched some lads playing an unseasonable game of cricket. Without revisiting The Talbot Arms, he then accompanied Smith

to dinner at Dr Palmer's house. At about 10 P.M., he went across
the street and back to bed. That was Friday, November 16th; and
early on Saturday morning, Dr Palmer came knocking at his bedroom door to announce breakfast. It had been agreed that Cook
should lodge at the hotel, but take his meals at the Doctor's.

Since the subsequent events are obscured by a conflict of evidence, we shall content ourselves with a summary of unchallenged
facts. That Saturday morning, Cook preferred to drink a cup of
coffee in bed rather than step over to Dr Palmer's and breakfast
on bacon and eggs. Coffee was accordingly brought up by Elizabeth Mills, the flirtatious young chambermaid, who placed it
in his hands; and the Doctor departed to his own breakfast. An
hour later, Cook was seized by the same nausea as had plagued
him at Shrewsbury, and vomited the coffee into a chamber pot.
By this time, Dr Palmer had gone off to Hednesford for a review
of his horses. Soon after he had returned, Mrs Ann Rowley, of
The Albion Inn, arrived with a saucepan of broth and put it by a
fire in the back kitchen to warm. 'Mr Jerry Smith's compliments,
and this is a gift for Mr Cook,' she told him. Dr Palmer presently
poured the broth into a 'sick-cup', a covered two-handled vessel
used by invalids, and sent it to The Talbot Arms with Smith's message. The cup, on arrival at the hotel, was taken up to Cook by a
hare-lipped waitress named Lavinia Barnes. Cook at first refused
the broth, complaining that he felt sure it would not stay on his
queasy stomach; but the Doctor, who then appeared, persuaded
him to try it. Cook proved to be in the right: for the broth followed the coffee into the chamber pot without a moment's delay.

At three o'clock, old Dr Bamford of Rugeley visited Cook, as
requested by Dr Palmer; but, not taking a serious view of the case,
merely prescribed rest and a diet of slops. Later, Cook was brought
barley-water and arrowroot from the hotel kitchen, which his
stomach seems to have retained. Dr Palmer was in and out of

Cook's bedroom all day, and that night Jeremiah Smith occupied the spare bed to keep him company.

At about noon on Sunday, November 18th, Dr Palmer's gardener brought over a second gift of broth, likewise made at The Albion Inn by Mrs Rowley. In The Talbot Arms kitchen, Elizabeth Mills sipped at the broth and said that it tasted very good—of turnips and celery. How much of the beverage Cook kept down is not recorded; at all events, he had only occasional short bouts of vomiting that afternoon, and appeared to be in high spirits. Nevertheless, Dr Palmer, remembering Cook's recent suspicions of him, wrote as follows to Dr William Henry Jones of Lutterworth, Cook's most intimate friend, who had taken part in the Polestar celebrations at The Raven Hotel, and was a surgeon of repute:

> *My Dear Sir,*
>
> Mr Cook was taken ill at Shrewsbury and obliged to call in a medical man. Since then he has been confined to his bed with a very severe bilious attack, combined with diarrhoea; and I think it advisable for you to come to see him as soon as possible.
>
> *Yours very truly,*
>
> WM PALMER

Nobody slept in Cook's room that night. The next morning he told Elizabeth Mills, when she inquired after his health: 'I'm tolerably well now, thank you kindly, but what I suffered! I was just mad for two minutes, a little before midnight.'

She asked: 'What do you mean, Sir?'

Cook explained that, when he awoke, he had been in an agony of terror—possibly alarmed by the noise of a street quarrel.

'Why didn't you ring the bell for me?' she asked winsomely.

'I feared you would all be asleep, and didn't want to disturb you,' Cook replied with a slight frown. 'At all events, the madness passed, thank Heaven, and I managed to drop off again without rousing the household.'

On Monday, November 19th, Dr Palmer travelled to London, where he had an appointment to meet Mr Herring, the commission agent. Arriving at Beaufort Buildings, off the Strand, soon after one o'clock, the Doctor apologized that Cook had been unable to accompany him. 'The poor fellow's still suffering from his Shrewsbury sickness. His physician has prescribed calomel, and told him to keep indoors, out of the damp,' he said. 'So he's entrusted me with a list of bets to be settled this afternoon at Tattersall's. He wants you to handle them this time; because (strictly between the two of us) he now regards Fisher as somewhat unreliable. It seems that there should have been more money left in a packet of bank notes which he entrusted to Fisher as soon as the puking fit began.'

When Mr Herring accepted the commission, Dr Palmer read out a list of the various sums due from the layers against Polestar, and instructed him to pay Cook's creditors with the proceeds—though these were, in reality, his own creditors: Pratt for four hundred and fifty pounds, Padwick for three hundred and fifty pounds, etc. He had, it seems, compiled the list of winnings from Cook's betting-book, temporarily abstracted from where it hung against the bedroom mirror. The three hundred and fifty pounds paid to Pratt—not in settlement, but merely on account, of larger debts—would stave off the threatened writ against old Mrs Palmer. Herring duly collected the money (all except three stakes, which had not yet come in) and made the payments without further question, afterwards writing to tell Cook what had been done. Why Dr Palmer engaged Herring rather than Fisher to collect Cook's debts can be simply explained. Not only did Cook owe Fisher two hundred pounds, which would have been deducted from the total, but Fisher knew that Dr Palmer had no right to any of Cook's winnings.

Meanwhile, Cook felt a deal better, though exceedingly weak. He got up once more, shaved, washed and dressed himself as if to go out. Mrs Bond, the housekeeper, sent him some arrowroot, which he managed to retain, and three visitors came calling: Will Saunders, the Hednesford trainer, and the two brothers Ashmole, both jockeys. When they left early in the afternoon, he went back to bed, and appeared happily relaxed. At about 8 P.M., Dr Bamford sent him a small box of morphine pills, which were placed on the bedside table. Dr Palmer left London by the Express train, reaching Stafford at 8.45 P.M., took a fly from thence to Rugeley—an hour's drive—and on arrival briefly visited Cook before obeying an angry summons from old Mrs Palmer at The Yard. That night, one of the maids noticed the betting-book hanging against the mirror.

At a quarter to twelve, Lavinia Barnes aroused Elizabeth Mills, who was already asleep, saying that Cook had been taken ill again and rung for assistance. Elizabeth Mills dressed hurriedly and, hearing screams, entered Cook's room. She found him seated upright in bed, madly threshing the coverlet with his hands. His pillow lay on the floor. When he demanded Dr Palmer, she said that Lavinia Barnes must have run across the road to summon him, and indeed the Doctor appeared two or three minutes later. He administered the pills left by Dr Bamford—these, however, stuck in Cook's throat—and made Elizabeth Mills give him a tablespoonful of toast-and-water to help them down. Next, he administered a dark, thick, heavy-looking draught which, when Cook vomited it up again, left an odour like opium hanging about the room. Dr Palmer asked Lavinia Barnes to hold a candle while he took a quill from his bag and with it searched for the pills in Cook's vomit. They did not appear to have been returned.

Cook now seemed better, but asked would Dr Palmer listen to his heart, how loud it was beating. The Doctor, having obligingly listened, reassured him that all was well. Presently the women went to bed, and Dr Palmer stayed with Cook until shortly before dawn.

Dr Jones of Lutterworth, a well-qualified and most experienced medical man, had been unable to visit Cook on the Monday, although Dr Palmer's request reached him by the first post. He was himself still suffering from the epidemic of nausea that, as we know, affected many other visitors to Shrewsbury Meeting. However, he arrived by train at three o'clock on the Tuesday, which was November 20th. Dr Jones found Cook's pulse steady and, learning that his bowels were now acting normally, and that he felt fairly comfortable, made no prescription; but saw him several times in the course of the afternoon.

That evening, Samuel Cheshire got a written message from Dr Palmer: 'Pray come to my place, Sammy, and bring a receipt stamp with you.' When Cheshire complied, Dr Palmer told him that it was imperative for an order to be sent by Cook to Mr Weatherby, Secretary of the Jockey Club, at Birmingham; but that Cook was too sick to sign anything. He therefore begged Cheshire to do him a great favour, namely copy an order, which he had drafted, and sign it in Cook's name. 'It concerns Cook's racing debts to me,' he said. 'I can't wait for his recovery, because if I don't get the money by Thursday, the bailiffs will seize the furniture of this house.' Cheshire obligingly copied out: 'Please pay Mr William Palmer the sum of £350,' and signed himself: 'J. P. Cook'. This order Dr Palmer posted to Mr Weatherby's office, with a covering note:

Gentlemen,

I shall thank you to send me a cheque to the amount of the enclosed order. Mr Cook has been confined here to his bed with a bilious attack which has prevented him from being in town.

Yours respectfully,

WM PALMER

When Dr Bamford called again at seven o'clock, he, Dr Jones and Dr Palmer held a consultation. Dr Palmer suggested that, although Cook objected to Dr Bamford's morphine pills which were administered on the Monday night, he should nevertheless be given a second dose.

That night, the spare bed in Cook's room was made up for Dr Jones. At about eleven o'clock, Dr Palmer brought the morphine pills in a box wrapped around with the paper of directions. 'What an excellent handwriting Dr Bamford has, for so old a man!' he remarked, and Dr Jones agreed. Though Cook at first refused to take the pills, on the ground that the others had made him so ill, he yielded after a while. The two doctors were soon searching for the pills in the toast-and-water which he had immediately vomited, but could not find them.

Cook, relieved by the vomiting, got up and sat in a chair by the fire, where he joked with Dr Jones of what sport he would have in the hunting field that winter. Dr Palmer had already said goodnight. Dr Jones went contentedly down to his supper, from which he returned at 11.45 P.M. Cook was now in bed, but still awake, and ready for another drowsy fox-hunting chat. All of a sudden, before Dr Jones had fallen asleep, Cook sang out: 'Doctor, Doctor, I'm going to be ill again! Ring the bell and send for Billy Palmer!'

He did so, and Dr Palmer was there within the space of two or three minutes, remarking: 'I never dressed so quickly in my life.' Meanwhile, Cook had asked Dr Jones to rub the nape of his neck. Dr Jones, who complied, found a certain stiffness of the neck muscles. Dr Palmer had brought two ammonia pills, which Cook swallowed but then uttered a cry of agony, and flung himself back on the bed.

There being only a single mould-candle in the room, Dr Jones could not get a clear view of Cook's face, which lay in the shadow of the chamber pot on the bedside table; yet his body was dreadfully convulsed and all the muscles were in spasm. Cook gasped: 'Raise me up, or I shall suffocate.' Though the two doctors tried to raise him into a sitting position, his head and spine were bent back like a bow, and they could do nothing. Dr Palmer hurried away to fetch spirits of ammonia from his surgery. On the stair, he met Elizabeth Mills and Lavinia Barnes, and when they asked after Cook, waved them away. 'Be off with you, my good girls!' he said, 'Cook's not so bad by a fiftieth part as he was last night.' Nevertheless, they were not to be got rid of and, as soon as he returned, followed him into the sickroom.

They heard Cook say: 'Turn me over on my side,' and when this was done, he lay quiet.

Dr Palmer prepared to administer the ammonia as a stimulant, but first felt Cook's pulse. Suddenly he turned to Dr Jones and the maids by the bedside and cried, aghast: 'Oh, my God! The poor devil has gone!' Dr Jones listened to the heart with a stethoscope—a curious instrument, somewhat like a sixpenny trumpet—and agreed that life was extinct. The convulsions had lasted for a quarter of an hour only.

The maids were sent off to summon Dr Bamford and, while Dr Jones took a glass of spirits at the bar with Masters, the landlord, Dr Palmer stayed by the corpse. Elizabeth Mills, returning to announce that Dr Bamford would soon come, found him going through Cook's pockets and feeling beneath his pillow and bolster. Later, he handed Dr Jones, as Cook's nearest friend, five pounds in sovereigns and half-sovereigns, five shillings in silver, and the dead man's gold watch and fob; but neither bank notes nor personal papers. In answer to Dr Jones's inquiries, Dr Palmer said: 'No, somehow I can't find the betting-book. Still, it's not a particle of use to anyone. Death, my good Sir, voids all gambling debts.' After a while, he added: 'I doubt if you are aware, Jones, what a very bad thing for me this is? Cook and I jointly owe betting debts of between three and four thousand pounds. Let us hope Cook's friends won't make me responsible for his share as well; because, unless they show me a little charity, every one of my horses will be seized.'

Layers-out were sent for, but it was not until one o'clock in the morning that a respectable widow named Mary Keeling arrived, with her sister-in-law, to undertake the task. Mrs Keeling had been delayed by the necessity of engaging a neighbour to look after her sick child while she was absent from home. The two women found the corpse lying so stiffly on the bed that they needed tape in securing the arms, which Elizabeth Mills had officiously crossed over the breast, to either side of the body; and in making the right foot, which was twisted outwards, lie flat against its fellow; they also experienced great difficulty in closing the eyes. However, attendants at a death-bed usually close the corpse's eyes, place its arms along the sides, and straighten its feet as soon as the last moment has come; the rigour was therefore less remarkable than the Prosecution has alleged. Indeed, Cook's body must have been perfectly lax at death, to let Elizabeth Mills cross the arms over his heart.

Dr Jones at first suspected tetanus but, since some of the symptoms seemed irreconcilable with this diagnosis, afterwards decided that Cook died of violent convulsions, due to over-excitement. Upon Dr Bamford's suggesting apoplexy, he replied that, though the case still puzzled him, the seizure, in his opinion, rather pointed to epilepsy.

CHAPTER XVI

STEP-FATHER TO
THE DECEASED

On Wednesday, November 21st, the morning of Cook's death, Palmer wrote to Pratt, the moneylender:

My dear Sir,

Ever since I saw you I have been fully engaged with Cook and not able to leave home. I am sorry to say that, after all, he died today. So you had better write to Saunders; but, mind you, I must have Polestar if it can be so arranged; and should anyone seek to know what money or moneys Cook ever had from you, don't answer questions until I have seen you.

I will send you the £75 tomorrow and, as soon as I have been to Manchester, you shall hear about other moneys. I sat up two full nights with Cook and am very much tired out.

Yours faithfully,

WILLIAM PALMER

Pratt replied by return of post:

My dear Sir,

I have your note and am greatly disappointed at the non-receipt of the money as promised, and the vague assurances as to any other payment. I can understand, 'tis true, that your being detained by the illness of your friend has been the cause of not sending up the larger amount, but the smaller sum you ought to have sent.

If anything unpleasant occurs, you must thank yourself. The death of Mr Cook will now compel you to look out as to the payment of the bill for £500 on the 2nd of December.

Yours faithfully,

THOS. PRATT

The seventy-five pounds which Dr Palmer intended for Pratt was to come from the three hundred and fifty pounds which Weatherby owed Cook; and the five hundred mentioned by Pratt was the loan made to the Doctor in September, supposedly on Cook's behalf, and supported by an assignment of Polestar and his stable mate Sirius. Dr Palmer, as has already been explained, had laid his hands on this money by forging Cook's receipt to Pratt's cheque, and placing it in his own account at the bank. He now also wanted Polestar, the value of which had risen to over seven hundred pounds. However, Weatherby did not send the three-hundred- and-fifty-pound cheque, being mistakenly informed by the Clerk of the Course at Shrewsbury that Cook had already received the value of the Handicap Stakes, and thereby exhausted his funds.

On November 26th, Dr Palmer wrote to Pratt again:

Strictly Private & Confidential!

My Dear Sir,

Should any of Cook's friends call upon you to know what money Cook ever had from you, pray don't answer that question or any other about money matters until I have seen you. And oblige

Yours faithfully,

WILLIAM PALMER

This anxiety about possible inquiries resulted from the suspicions of Dr Palmer which Cook's next-of-kin, Mr William Vernon Stevens, began to entertain. Mr Stevens, a retired City merchant, had married Cook's mother (now dead) eighteen years previously; and been made executor to the grandfather's will, under which Cook inherited twelve thousand pounds. He last saw Cook alive at Euston Square Station, a fortnight before he died. His greeting on that occasion was: 'My boy, you seem to be very well; you don't look anything of an invalid.' Cook, striking himself firmly on the chest, exclaimed: 'Indeed, I'm quite well now, Pater, and I'd be a happy man but for so many financial anxieties.'

Mr Stevens, not having heard of Cook's illness, was shocked when Dr Jones arrived on November 22nd to report his death, bringing with him the five guineas and the watch. The next day, accompanied by Dr Jones, he visited Lutterworth to search for Cook's will and any personal papers he might have left. They found the will, which appointed Mr Stevens sole executor, and took it to Rugeley that Friday, November 28th.

Meanwhile, Dr Palmer had gone up to London, where he paid Pratt one hundred pounds on account. He also paid some Rugeley drapers sixty pounds long owing them, plus the cost of a writ issued against him; and settled a debt of some forty-six pounds with Spillsbury, a local farmer who had supplied fodder to his mares. This money Dr Palmer cannot have drawn from the Market Square Bank, where his balance then stood at no more than £9.6s; and since the packet of notes which Fisher returned to Cook were missing from the money-belt, it looks as if the Doctor had purloined them.

Mr Stevens met Dr Palmer in a corridor at The Talbot Arms Hotel, and at once asked to be shown the body. It is important to observe that Dr Jones, who had been Mr Stevens's constant companion for the past two days, made no suggestion to him of foul play, but only mentioned the mysterious disappearance of the betting-book. Thus Mr Stevens was the first to suspect that the death had been caused by poison.

When informed of the arrival of Cook's step-father, the story goes, Dr Palmer exclaimed: 'Good God! But he has no relatives!' This, however, is a plain falsehood. Dr Palmer had met Mr Stevens, briefly, at Lutterworth in 1854, and told The Talbot Arms maids of his existence shortly before Cook died. He also knew that Cook had a sister and a half-brother living, and a maternal uncle who owed him money.

Mr Stevens went upstairs with Dr Palmer to view the body; and the door, locked on the morning of the death, was opened for him. The sole visitor since then had been Dr Palmer himself when he borrowed the key, on the excuse of retrieving a silver paper-knife which he had lent to Cook, and rummaged awhile in the chest of drawers and cupboard. Dr Palmer now removed the sheet from the corpse. The tightly drawn skin across the face surprised Mr Stevens, though a corpse's appearance sixty hours after death can be but a poor indication of how it looked at the time of death. He came down to one of the sitting-rooms, where he called for drinks, and presently addressed Dr Palmer: 'I hear from Jones that you know something of my step-son's affairs.'

'Indeed I do,' was the ready answer, 'and I'm sorry to say he had four thousand pounds' worth of bills out with moneylenders. The Devil is that they bear my name. Fortunately, however, Mr Cook signed a paper drawn up by our lawyer, which proves that I never received any money from him to cover this friendly accommodation.'

'Four thousand pounds!' exclaimed Mr Stevens. 'Impossible! How could he have incurred so large a debt?'

'By betting heavily and unwisely,' the Doctor replied.

'Well,' said Mr Stevens, 'I fear there won't be four thousand shillings to pay you from his bank account or mercantile investments. Moreover, his house is entailed and reverts to a sister. Tell me: has he no horses? And no sporting debts owing to him?'

'Why, yes, he has some horses,' Dr Palmer sighed, 'but they are mortgaged; and his sporting creditors outnumber the debtors. I do know of three hundred pounds owed him by an uncle, which may be recoverable; yet this is not a race-course debt, and I understand the uncle to be in poor health and circumstances.'

Mr Stevens said: 'Well, I suppose his creditors had better take his sporting effects. I want nothing to do with the business myself, having always set my face against the Turf and, so long ago as 1852, warned him that it would prove his undoing. But whether he has left money or not, John must be buried.'

'Oh, I'll bury him myself, if that's all,' cried Dr Palmer.

Mr Stevens protested: 'My dear Sir, I certainly couldn't think of your doing that, since you stand to lose so much by his death. I shall see to everything.'

Meanwhile, Cook's brother-in-law, Mr Bradford, had arrived and also expressed a wish to undertake this melancholy task, yet Mr Stevens, as executor, would not budge from his resolution. 'No,' he said, 'I shall arrange it, though the funeral cannot take place immediately, because he must go to London for burial in his mother's grave. I'm sorry to inconvenience the landlord by keeping the corpse here a little longer, but all arrangements will be made as soon as possible.'

Dr Palmer shrugged his shoulders, saying: 'Oh, that's of no consequence for a day or two.

Nevertheless, he surely ought to be fastened up at once? The poor beggar was diseased.'

Dr Palmer and Dr Jones then went away, leaving Mr Stevens in earnest talk with his son-in-law. Half an hour later, they returned, and Mr Stevens asked: 'Can you give me the name of a reputable undertaker in this town? I should like to order a coffin.'

Dr Palmer smiled amiably. 'Keeyes is the very man,' he said, 'and I have already been and done what you suggest. I ordered a shell and a strong oak coffin.'

'Humph!' ejaculated Mr Stevens, in surprise and displeasure. 'I gave you no authority for that. I must see Keeyes and instruct him myself.'

The Doctor had, in fact, gone to Keeyes and told him: 'My friend Mr Cook has died of a nasty disease, and needs a strong oak box. I advise you to screw him down quick.'

Mr Stevens, having already ordered dinner at The Talbot Arms for himself, his son-in-law, and Dr Jones, invited Dr Palmer to join them. Meanwhile, he went out and strolled through the town. They all dined together at three o'clock. Afterwards he asked Dr Jones to be so good as to get him Cook's betting-book and whatever other papers might be in the death-room. Dr Jones climbed upstairs, followed by Dr Palmer, and about ten minutes later both came down again. Dr Jones reported: 'I regret to say, Sir, that the betting-book is still missing, nor can we find any personal papers.'

'No betting-book!' exclaimed Mr Stevens. 'But he always carried one: a long, green- covered book with gilt edges, a clasp, and a pencil-holder.' Turning to Dr Palmer, he asked abruptly: 'How is this?'

The Doctor said: 'Why, Sir, the betting-book will be no manner of use even if you find it.' 'No use, Sir!' Mr Stevens expostulated. 'Pray don't try to gammon me. I am the best judge of its use, I believe. Dr Jones informs me that my step-son won a large sum of money at Shrewsbury, and calculated his winnings from the book in his presence. I ought to know something about that.'

The Doctor repeated: 'It is no manner of use, I assure you. When a man dies, his sporting bets die with him, and Mr Cook received the greater part of his money on the course at Shrewsbury.'

'Then where is it now?' asked Mr Stevens. 'He will have carried the notes in his money- belt.'

'I should hope, Sir, you're not accusing me,' Dr Palmer cried in menacing tones. 'Gentlemen, gentlemen, pray let us all be civil!' pleaded Dr Jones.

'I accuse nobody for the present,' said Mr Stevens. 'But the betting-book must be found.' Dr Palmer replied in a quieter voice: 'Oh, it will be found, no doubt.'

'Sir, it *shall* be found,' Mr Stevens insisted. He opened the door and calling to Mrs Bond, the housekeeper, who stood behind the bar, announced: 'Madam, it is my desire as the executor of the late John Parsons Cook that everything in the room where his corpse lies shall be locked up. No persons whatsoever must be admitted until I either return or send someone with authority to take possession. And before I catch the London Express, I shall view the corpse once more; for I'm by no means satisfied that my step-son met his end fairly.'

He went upstairs to the death-room where, at his instructions, Mr Keeyes the undertaker had measured the body for a coffin and, with the help of his assistant, already placed it inside a shell. Mr Stevens knelt down beside the corpse for a last farewell, taking one cold hand in his. He noticed that it was tightly clenched, and so also was the other hand. Then he descended, bade Dr Palmer a curt good-bye, adding: 'You shall hear from me again, Sir!' and strode briskly off to the Railway Station.

In London, he communicated with Cook's sick uncle, and with his own solicitors, who recommended that he should entrust his affairs to a respectable firm of Rugeley solicitors named Gardiner and Landor. The next day, Saturday, November 24th, on the platform of Euston Square Station, he ran into Dr Palmer, who greeted him effusively with: 'Why, good day, Mr Stevens! Are you by any chance travelling down to Rugeley?'

'I am,' he replied.

'Why not let us share a compartment?' suggested Dr Palmer. 'I have found a nearly empty one farther along the train.'

'Many thanks,' answered Mr Stevens, 'but the porter has already placed my bag on the rack in this carriage, where I have acquaintances.'

'No offence taken,' Dr Palmer said smiling. 'By the way, I was summoned to London by telegraph soon after you left Rugeley.'

'Where are my step-son's horses kept?' asked Mr Stevens presently.

'At Hednesford, some three miles out of Rugeley,' came the answer. 'I'll drive you there, if you please.'

'That would be civil of you,' Mr Stevens said, and bowed slightly. The guard then rang a bell, and they parted, each to his carriage.

Dr Palmer had just paid Pratt another four hundred pounds in notes, but it is unknown whom else he saw during his short visit to London. Possibly the nature of his other business there, though nefarious, would have proved him innocent of Cook's murder; this, however, is only a surmise.

Much as he disliked Dr Palmer, Mr Stevens thought fit to smother his feelings for the time being. When the train stopped at Wolverton, and they met in the refreshment room (among stale sandwiches and slices of pork-pie, grey with engine grit) he reopened the conversation. First apologizing for his heat in the matter of Cook's betting-book, he continued ingratiatingly: 'Doctor, this sudden death of my step-son is a very melancholy event and may, I fear, have impaired my usual good manners. His poor mother, you see, died young, and so did his father, at the age of a mere thirty-one. For the sake of his brother and sister, who are also delicate in health, I should like to know more about John's complaints, and therefore intend to have his body opened.'

'Why, that can easily be done,' assented Dr Palmer; but the interview was once more interrupted by the guard's bell, and they did not meet again until the train pulled up at Rugby. Mr Stevens then said: 'Since I live far from Staffordshire, and the horses at Hednesford are supposed to be valuable, I think of asking some solicitor in your district to manage my affairs.'

'Yes, that would certainly be prudent,' Dr Palmer agreed. 'Do you know any solicitors there personally?'

'None,' Mr Stevens answered, after a moment's hesitation. But the Rugby stop is short, and service at the refreshment room is slow. The bell rang imperatively, and Mr Stevens tipped his cupful of scalding tea into a saucer to cool; then drank from the saucer, spilling some down his waistcoat as he did so, and ran for his carriage. He found Dr Palmer very forwardly, as he thought, ensconced in the seat next to his.

'You were talking about Rugeley solicitors,' said the Doctor.

'No, Sir, you were,' Mr Stevens snapped at him.

'Pray allow me to dry your waistcoat with this handkerchief,' offered Dr Palmer; but Mr Stevens curtly declined, and resumed conversation with the lady and gentleman, sitting opposite, who shared his interest in German instrumental music. Dr Palmer did not venture to put in an oar.

On arrival at Rugeley, Mr Stevens gave his acquaintances a polite good-bye and alighted with Dr Palmer, who lowered his bag for him from the rack to the platform. As they waited for a luggage-porter, Dr Palmer said: 'If you will pardon my correction, Sir, there was certainly talk of a solicitor. Unless I misheard your remark, you know no Rugeley man personally?'

'My intention was,' explained Mr Stevens, 'to cut short a profitless discussion.'

'Well,' continued Dr Palmer unabashed, 'I know them all intimately, and can provide you with a most reliable one. Let me go home for a cup of coffee first; then I'll step across to The Talbot Arms and tell you about him.'

'Many thanks, but pray don't trouble yourself. With the help of Mr Masters, who seems to be knowledgeable and judicious, I'll soon engage the sort of agent I require.'

'At all events, Sir, you'll not find a solicitor tonight.' 'And why not, pray?'

'It's late, and some of the best go out of town at the week-end.'

'Upon my word,' said Mr Stevens, 'I never in my life experienced any difficulty in finding a solicitor when I needed one, whatever the hour.' Then suddenly altering his voice and manner, he asked: 'Sir, if I should engage a solicitor as my adviser, I suppose you would not mind answering any questions he might care to put?'

Though Mr Stevens claims that Dr Palmer's reply: 'Oh, no, certainly not,' was accompanied by a nervous spasm of the throat, the moonlight can hardly have been strong enough for this to be distinctly observed. They were now boarding the station omnibus, and no more was said.

The omnibus stopped outside The Talbot Arms. Dr Palmer entered his own house, and Mr Stevens, after leaving his bag in the care of Mrs Bond, went off at once to find Mr Gardiner, the solicitor—who was out of town, as it happened—and presently returned to supper at the hotel.

Later, Dr Palmer sought him out and said: 'I fear those bills I negotiated for Cook are going to affect me in a deucedly unpleasant way.'

Mr Stevens replied, somewhat menacingly: 'I think you should know, Sir, that, since last we saw each other, I have heard a rather different account of John's affairs.'

'Oh, indeed?' remarked the Doctor politely. 'Well, I hope that the matter will be settled amicably, at any rate.'

'It will be settled, Sir, only in the Court of Chancery,' was Mr Stevens's severe rejoinder. 'Oh, indeed?' repeated Dr Palmer, coolly and offhandedly.

They did not meet again until six o'clock the next evening (Sunday), by which time Mr Stevens had consulted with Mr Gardiner, and the Doctor had attended divine service at St Augustine's Church, where he laid a sovereign in the collection plate.

Mr Stevens was now seated at a table in the coffee-room, writing a letter, while the cook prepared his dinner. Dr Palmer entered with a paper in his hand. He offered it to Mr Stevens who, however, took no notice of him, but went on writing. After a while, Mr Stevens looked up and said: 'Ah! Good evening, Sir! Do you know a local man named Smith?'

Dr Palmer answered: 'Smith? Smith? Smith? It's a common enough name hereabouts. I can think of at least a dozen Smiths.'

'I am referring to a Mr Smith who sat up with my step-son one night,' explained Mr Stevens. 'Why, of course,' said the Doctor. 'That's Mr Jeremiah Smith, a very good fellow, a

solicitor, the very man whom I should have recommended to you, had you let me.'

'I raised the question because, since the betting-book has been lost, it is important for me to know who was with my step-son . . .' Then he paused and inquired: 'Did you attend him in a medical capacity?'

'Oh dear, no!' replied Dr Palmer, caught off his guard.

Mr Stevens said: 'I ask you because of my determination to have his body opened. If you attended him professionally at any time, doubtless the medical man I engage will think it proper for you to be present at the examination.'

'May I ask whom you have in mind?' Dr Palmer ventured.

'I shall not know myself until tomorrow,' Mr Stevens replied, 'but think it only proper to disclose my plans. Whether you are present or not is a matter of indifference to me.'

With a curt nod of dismissal, Mr Stevens returned to his writing and this lack of civility so nettled the Doctor that he snapped back: 'And equally a matter of indifference to me, Sir.'

Mr Stevens, his eyes still on the letter before him, observed: 'That is surprising. I thought that as a close friend of Mr Cook's, you would be interested to learn whether some other medical man may have accidentally given him a fatal dose.'

Then he re-read his letter, signed it with a flourish, and proceeded to address an envelope which he had already stamped.

Dr Palmer again offered the paper in his hand. Mr Stevens waved it away, saying: 'It looks like a financial document. You will excuse me: I never discuss finance on a Sunday.'

It was a sheet of yellow post-quarto written in Dr Palmer's handwriting, but signed 'J. P. Cook'. On the day after Cook's death, the Doctor had again summoned Samuel Cheshire to his house, poured him a glassful of brandy and pleaded: 'Sam, I count on you to save my life and fortune. When Cook and I drew up this document some days ago, we omitted to get it witnessed. It refers to a business in which I freely assisted him, without any hope of benefit for myself except his continued friendship. In point of fact, I raised four thousand pounds for him in loans on my own security to help him out of his difficulties, and here he acknowledges the various sums he had, together with the dates of receipt. Be a good fellow and witness it, predating your signature to last Saturday, the morning after Cook's arrival. It won't be legal otherwise, and my horses and furniture may be seized by the moneylending leeches.'

'Billy, old chum,' Cheshire answered, 'I very much regret that I can't oblige you. I have already broken the Postal Regulations in steaming open letters and allowing you to read their contents; but this would be going too far. Neither did Cook sign the document in my presence, nor would I recognize his signature. So I shouldn't fancy being summoned to give evidence on the matter at some future date—especially since this paper is supposed to have been witnessed at your house, on a Saturday morning, when the Post Office is at its busiest and many people saw me at work.'

'Oh, very well,' said Palmer. 'I'm disappointed in you, Sam! But it doesn't signify much; perhaps Cook's executors won't object to its not being attested—for at least he signed over a receipt stamp as the Law requires.'

Mr Stevens had taken care that Dr Palmer should steal a glance at the letter on the coffee-room table. It was addressed to Mr William Webb Ward, the Stafford Coroner, and demanded an inquest on Cook's body. He had already written asking Dr Harland of Stafford whether he would kindly conduct the *post-mortem* examination.

Next morning, in the hope of forestalling trouble, Dr Palmer caught old Dr Bamford just before he went out on his rounds, and requested him to sign Cook's death certificate. Dr Bamford did so, but on entering the cause of death as 'an apoplectic seizure' said: 'Properly, my boy, you should do this yourself. He was your patient, not mine.'

CHAPTER XVII

THE INQUEST ON JOHN PARSONS COOK

Dr Harland had been in practice since the year of Waterloo, and won a medical degree at Edinburgh only a few years later. He was a negligent and easy-going man of whom people said: 'If his patients recover, they pay him well; if they die, their heirs don't dispute the fees.' He used few drugs, reposing great faith in the power of Nature to effect cures if left to herself. Rhubarb, magnesia, calomel, and sulphur were, in general, the limit of his prescriptions: he chiefly favoured rest, and a diet of slops. It was Dr Harland who had obligingly passed Walter Palmer as a good life, and been rewarded by Dr Palmer for this kindness with a dozen of 1834 port. Yet he could by no means be called ignorant of his profession.

On reaching Rugeley from Stafford, the morning of Monday, November 26th, Dr Harland went to visit Dr Bamford and, as he passed The Talbot Arms, was greeted by Dr Palmer who emerged from the back of his house. 'Why, good morning, Harland,' said Dr Palmer, 'I'm glad that Mr Stevens has chosen you for this *post-mortem* job. Someone might have come with whom I'm unacquainted.'

Dr Harland shook hands, and asked: 'What *is* this case? I understand there's a suspicion of poisoning?'

'Oh, no,' replied Dr Palmer. 'I don't think so. But it seems that a meddlesome London merchant named Stevens accuses Dr Bamford of treating the case wrong. I have the highest respect for the venerable doctor, and not merely because he brought me and my brothers into this delightful world. He's a wise, kind-hearted old man, and I couldn't bear to have doubt cast on his medical ability. So, as I say, I'm glad you're here. There'll be no prejudice.'

'I feel ashamed to tell you, Sir,' Dr Harland confessed, 'that I carelessly left my instrument case behind at Stafford.'

'Then by all means use mine,' cried Dr Palmer, 'and get the business done with quick. To be frank, I believe that this queer fellow also suspects me. I can't guess what he's at, or what he wants. He's making a loud hue and cry about a lost betting-book. Not only is it of no use to anyone, but at least fifteen people were in the room while Johnny Cook lay ill'—here he began ticking them off on his fingers—'two servants, a couple of jockeys, the housekeeper, the landlord, a trainer, a barber, our Postmaster, not to mention two qualified doctors beside myself—so why he has picked on me, God alone knows. I feel justly aggrieved.'

Dr Harland nodded in sympathy. 'Yes,' he said, 'families are apt to turn very nasty on these occasions, as I know to my cost. Death from natural causes don't satisfy them. They nurse a grudge against Heaven, and try to work it off on those who have busied themselves most heartily in attendance on the deceased.'

After parting with Dr Palmer, he proceeded to the house of another Rugeley surgeon named Freer, from whom it had been arranged that he should receive a stoneware jar to contain parts of the dead body intended for analysis. There he met Charles Devonshire, a medical student at the London University. Mr Devonshire, while apologizing that Dr Monckton, his employer, was unable to open the body as agreed, showed a readiness to do so himself. He had considerable experience in dissection and *post-mortem* anal-

ysis during his five years at King's College, and with the help of
Charles Newton would do what was required of him under the
supervision of Drs Harland and Bamford.

'And who is this Newton?' asked Dr Harland.

'He assists Dr Salt,' explained Devonshire, 'and, though he can
show no diploma of any sort, calls himself a medical man. This will
be his first *post-mortem*.'

'Rugeley seems to be particularly rich in medical men,' commented Harland.

'Oh, that's not the half of it,' laughed Devonshire. 'Some of us
are very juvenile, and some very ancient, with few indeed mid-
dle-aged, except Dr Palmer; but he prefers horses to humans.'

The *post-mortem* examination was held at The Talbot Arms, next
to the room where Cook had died. There were present, besides
Drs Bamford and Harland, and their two young assistants: Mr
Tom Masters, Jeremiah Smith, Samuel Cheshire, Ben Thirlby, and
the minister of a Dissenting Chapel; also Drs Salt, Jones, Richard
Freer, Junior, and Palmer.

Dr Palmer and Newton stood alone together, for a few minutes, at the entrance to the Assembly Hall, awaiting the return
of Dr Harland, who had gone to buy a pencil and note-book.
Dr Palmer gave a little shudder, and said: 'This will be a dirty job,
Charles. Let's go to my house and have a brandy!'

They walked across the road, and the Doctor offered him half
a tumblerful of neat brandy. 'You'll find that poor fellow suffering
from a diseased throat,' he said, sipping at his own drink. 'He had
syphilis and took a good deal of mercury in consequence. Come,
let me refill your tumbler!'

On their return to the Assembly Hall, the examination began.
Mr Devonshire, under Dr Harland's surveillance, applied himself to the dissection. Dr Monckton, his employer, had lent him
instruments, but neither scales nor measuring glasses; this being

a casual, country affair, where one measures bulk and quality by the eye alone. The bowels, stomach, heart, brain, lungs, throat, and private parts were examined, with about half an inch of spinal cord. All appeared to be healthy, except for evidence of former syphilis, also a slight affliction of the throat, some whitish pustules beneath the tongue, and an undue quantity of dark fluid in the lungs, which Devonshire diagnosed as a morbid symptom. The heart was found empty and spasmodically contracted.

Only one incident disturbed the quiet course of proceedings. Devonshire had removed a yard of intestines for insertion in the jar; but as he opened the stomach with a pair of scissors, according to his instructions, Newton lurched against him. Dr Harland cried: 'Stop that!' because Dr Palmer was standing close enough to have given Newton a push. Devonshire then called attention to certain yellowish-white spots about the size of a mustard seed at the end of the stomach. As a result of Newton's push, the stomach, which contained two or three fluid ounces of a brownish liquid, had been punctured and a spoonful splashed on a chair. Dr Harland tied up the puncture with a piece of string but, while he and Devonshire examined the lining membrane, Newton suddenly turned the stomach inside-out. Another half-teaspoonful of liquid fell on the floor as he placed it in the jar, which Dr Harland then sealed with two pigs' bladders, saying: 'So that is that! Little seems to be amiss here. I don't even subscribe to Devonshire's view that the lungs are unhealthy.'

Dr Palmer clapped Dr Bamford on the shoulder and exclaimed in a stage whisper: 'Well, they won't hang us yet.'

'Hey, speak up, my boy,' piped Dr Bamford, who is very deaf.

'I said that they won't hang us yet,' he reiterated in loud tones, grinning about him. While Dr Harland was jotting down his notes and Devonshire collecting his instruments, Dr Palmer carried the jar towards the doorway, where he set it on the floor.

Dr Harland looked up and called: 'Where's the jar?'

Dr Palmer replied: 'It's here. I thought it would be more convenient by the door, to take away.'

'Pray bring it back!' said Dr Harland, vexed at such officiousness. He rose to meet Dr Palmer, who was already returning the jar, and then noticed that both bladders had been pierced with a clean cut an inch long.

Looking around the room, Dr Harland inquired: 'Who made this cut?' 'I didn't,' said Dr Palmer. 'I haven't even a knife on me.'

'Nor I,' said Devonshire.

'And you, Mr Newton?' Dr Harland asked. Newton mutely shook his head.

The mystery was never solved, but no harm had been done. Dr Harland untied the bladders, replaced them so that the cut came below the neck of the jar, tied them up again, and secured the knot with sealing wax. Then he wrapped the jar in stiff brown paper, which he also sealed.

'Where is it going?' Dr Palmer wished to know. 'To Freer's,' Dr Harland answered.

'I would rather you took it to Stafford and kept it under your eye,' Dr Palmer complained. 'No, Mr Stevens wants it left at Freer's,' said Dr Harland. 'It's to be analyzed by the celebrated Professor Taylor of Guy's Hospital.' He then carried the jar to Dr Freer's surgery, whence it was taken to London by one Boycott, Messrs Gardiner & Landor's chief clerk.

Newton sought out Boycott at Rugeley Railway Station. 'Let me come up with you, Boycott,' he pleaded, 'I must speak to Mr Gardiner.'

'I'll give him a message, if you like,' said Boycott.

'No,' cried Newton in agitation, 'I'd rather address him personally.'

When pressed, he explained: 'I'm in a pretty dangerous position, Boycott. You see, on the night of Monday, I did what I shouldn't have done. Dr Palmer stopped at Salt's surgery where I'm employed, and wished me to sell him three grains of strychnine. I told him I couldn't sell it, for that's not Dr Salt's way; besides, he and Salt are on bad terms. Yet, I gave it him, wrapped in a paper. You see, Ben Thirlby's working for Palmer and, as you perhaps know, I'm his natural son; that's why I obliged him. But if these spasms of Cook's were due to strychnine poisoning, I'm afraid of being hanged as an accomplice or, at the best, transported.'

Boycott asked him: 'Why don't you tell the Coroner?'

'I daren't,' said Newton. 'I made no entry in the Poison Book, as I should have done.

However, I'll tell Mr Gardiner on oath, just to clear myself, if there's trouble.'

Meanwhile Jim, the ostler at The Talbot Arms, had been told to drive Mr Stevens in the hotel fly to Stafford, after having taken tea at home. Dr Palmer presently met Jim coming back from his tea, and said: 'Good evening, Jim. Boots has the fly waiting for you, I see. Are you going over to Stafford?'

'Those are my orders,' Jim answered.

'It's a humbugging concern!' cried the Doctor. 'This meddlesome fool arranges a *post-mortem*, and sends Cook's stomach up to London in a jar for analysis! Gardiner's clerk is taking it by train. Hark'ee, Jim, if you'll upset old Stevens into a ditch of stinking mud, it'll be worth ten pounds to you.'

Dr Palmer was laughing as he spoke, but Jim replied with mock gravity: 'I don't think as I could do it for ten pound, Doctor; why, I might end in jail, or the Infirmary, which would be worse!'

Dr Palmer then offered Jim a drink, which he declined, being already two minutes late. At nightfall, Dr Palmer caused a stir in Rugeley by reeling through the streets, drunk and muttering to himself. He had never been seen in such a condition before.

Professor Taylor, the toxicological expert at Guy's Hospital, and his assistant Dr Rees, received the jar. Professor Taylor made some harsh remarks about it, saying that the contents had been so jolted and shaken on the train journey that the feculent matter from the intestines and the liquid contents of the stomach were all mixed together. He judged these remains inadequate for the close investigation demanded by Mr Stevens, and telegraphed at once for further organs. This time Dr Monckton and Dr Freer, who took charge of the examination, sent him up, in another sealed jar, the kidneys, part of the liver, the spleen, what remained of the dissected heart and brain, and three teaspoonfuls of blood from the lungs.

The Stafford Coroner summoned a jury for Thursday, November 29th, at The Talbot Arms Hotel; but all they did that day was to view the body, the-inquest being then adjourned until December 5th.

Here, while observing that Dr Palmer showed no fear of strychnine being found, we may express the opinion that it was Newton who pushed Devonshire; Newton who punctured the jar with a lancet; Newton who, when he emptied the stomach, unasked, into the jar, deliberately spilled some of the contents; and Newton who vigorously shook this jar, while Boycott left the carriage at Rugby for refreshment. His motive throughout is clear: to make the strychnia, which he believed Dr Palmer to have administered, less easily discoverable.

Cook was buried on November 30th, not in the family vault near London, but in Rugeley churchyard. Dr Palmer attended the funeral service with Jeremiah Smith. Among the other mourners were Mr Stevens, his son-in-law Mr Bradford, and George Herring, the commission agent, who grew very angry indeed when he learned from Mr Stevens that Cook had never received the money entrusted to Dr Palmer, and that the betting-book was missing. Yet because the Doctor walked weeping miserably behind the bier, Herring did not have the heart to speak his mind until the funeral was well over—but then found that he had slipped away. Afterwards, Dr Palmer frequented The Talbot Arms bar and stood treat to all the assembled riff-raff, who voted him a jolly good fellow. Of his former friends only Myatt, the saddler, Jeremiah Smith, the solicitor, Ben Thirlby, the chemist, and Samuel Cheshire, the Postmaster, remained loyal. When Dr Palmer complained of being almost universally called a poisoner, Cheshire asked what he could do to clear him of so cruel a suspicion.

'God bless you!' said the Doctor. 'Just keep your eyes and ears open, like a dear fellow!'

On the Sunday evening, December 2nd, Dr Palmer visited Cheshire's house in a pitiable state of anxiety and inquired, in his wife's presence, whether he had heard or seen anything fresh. Cheshire led him into another room and said: 'Billy, if you are tempting me to show you the contents of a sealed letter, that I dare not do.'

'Oh, no,' the Doctor cried, 'you mustn't injure yourself on my account! But I can't sleep of nights for worrying what Professor Taylor will report to Mr Gardiner about that damnable analysis. Though it's true that I've done nothing wrong, what if Mr Stevens should have manufactured evidence against me? He's quite capable of bribing Gardiner's clerk to put poison in Cook's remains and so getting me hanged. No, Sammy! All I ask, all I beg of you on my knees, is that you'll steam open Professor Taylor's letter, and if he says he's found poison, tip me the wink, and I'll give them the slip. I'll ride off to Liverpool and board a vessel for America. You know I could never kill a man, don't you, Sammy?'

Cheshire weakly consented; and on December 5th, three days later, intercepted and read Professor Taylor's letter to Mr Gardiner, afterwards reporting its gist to the Doctor, whom he found in bed, seriously ill of a liver complaint brought on by his excessive consumption of brandy.

The letter ran:

Guy's Hospital,
Tuesday, Dec. 4th, 1855.

My dear Sir,

Dr Rees and I have compared the analysis today. We have sketched a report, which will be ready tomorrow or the next day. As I am going to Durham on the part of the Crown in the case of *Regina v. Wooler,* the report will be in the hands of Dr Rees, No. 26, Albemarle St. It will be most desirable that Mr Stevens should call on Dr Rees, read the report with him, and put such questions as may occur. In reply to your letter received here this morning, I beg to say that we wish a statement of all the medicines prescribed for the deceased until his death to be drawn up and sent to Dr Rees. We did not find Strychnia, nor Prussic Acid, nor any trace of Opium. From the contents having been drained away, it is now impossible to say whether any Strychnine had or had not been given just before death. But it is quite possible for tartar emetic to destroy life if given in repeated doses; and, so far as we can at present form an opinion, in the absence of any natural cause of death, the deceased must have died from the effects of antimony in this or some other form.

I am, Sir, Yours very truly,

ALFRED S. TAYLOR

Dr Palmer gleefully told Cheshire: 'Of course, they found no poison! And of course, almost every man's stomach has some traces of antimony in it. I'm as innocent as a babe.'

The news afforded him great relief because, in addition to those three grains of strychnine given him by Newton at about eleven o'clock on the Monday night, he had bought six more grains from

Messrs Hawkins, another Rugeley chemist, between eleven and twelve on Tuesday morning—also two drachms of Batley's solution of opium, and two drachms of prussic acid. He knew that Mr Stevens had obtained evidence of his purchases from Hawkins' Poison Book. All these drugs, by the way, were found in the Doctor's surgery after his arrest—all, that is, except the strychnine.

While visiting London on December 1st, Dr Palmer had taken the precaution of sending a gift-hamper to Mr William Webb Ward, the Stafford Coroner. This contained a twenty-pound turkey, a brace of pheasants, a fine cod, and a barrel of oysters, and was sent by railway to Mr Ward's private residence at Stoke-on-Trent, without a sender's name. It is understood that Dr Palmer wrote to Mr Ward by the post, but that Mr Ward destroyed the letter in disgust and very correctly sent the hamper to the Stafford Infirmary for the benefit of pauper patients. Whether the patients, rather than the medical staff, enjoyed them is, however, highly doubtful.

Dr Palmer could never leave well alone. The news of Professor Taylor's findings so elated him that, the next morning, he sent two letters to Stafford by the hand of George Bate. The first was sealed, and addressed to Mr Webb Ward; the second, an open note, ordered Mr France, the poulterer, 'to supply the bearer with some nice pheasants and a good hare.'

Bate found a boy who for threepence would take the hamper of game to Mr Ward's house, and delivered tie letter to Mr Ward himself at The Dolphin Inn, as he played billiards in the smoking-room. This letter, which Mr Ward at once handed to Captain Hatton, the Chief Constable of Police, bore no date, but ran as follows:

My dear Sir,
    I am sorry to tell you that I am still confined to bed. I do not think it was mentioned at the inquest yesterday that Cook was taken ill on Sunday and Monday night in

the same way as he was on the Tuesday when he died. The chambermaid at The Crown—Master's hotel—can prove this. I also believe that a man by the name of Fisher is coming down to prove that he received some money from Cook at Shrewsbury. Now, here Cook could only pay Jeremiah Smith £10 out of the £41 he owed him. Had you not better call Smith to prove this?

And again, whatever Professor Taylor may say tomorrow, he wrote from London last Tuesday night to Gardiner, to say: 'We have this day finished our analysis and find no traces of either strychnine, prussic acid, or opium.'

What can beat this from a man like Professor Taylor, if he says tomorrow what he has already said—and Dr Harland's evidence? Mind you, I know, and saw it in black and white, what Professor Taylor said to Gardiner, but this is strictly private and confidential; but it is true. As regards the betting-book, I know nothing of it and it is of no good to anyone.

I hope the verdict tomorrow will be that Cook died of natural causes, and thus end it.

Ever yours,

WM PALMER

The inquest did not, in the event, take place on the next day, being postponed for another week. Since neither of the hampers was returned to him, Dr Palmer concluded that he now had the Coroner 'in his breeches' pocket', as the cant saying is, and therefore on Thursday, December 13th, wrote him another letter. This should have gone in a sealed envelope with a present of money; but finding that he had only a fifty-pound note in his possession, he asked Bate to borrow a 'pony' from Ben Thirlby. Bate went off and presently returned with a five-pound note.

At this moment, what he had been dreading so long at last happened. A knock sounded at the door; Eliza Tharm opened it, and in came two Sheriff's officers to arrest the Doctor for forgery. Bate was ordered from the room while they performed their duty, but as soon as both had retired downstairs, Dr Palmer summoned him again, put the bank note in the envelope, and said: 'George, take this to the Coroner at once. Let nobody see you!'

Bate protested: 'Nay, Mister, can't you send someone else? I don't like this hole-and-corner game, indeed I don't, not with the Police in the house.'

'Why, George,' Dr Palmer answered, 'as to this poor fellow Cook, they'll find no poison in him. He was the best pal I ever had in my life—why should I have poisoned him? I'm as innocent as you are, George.'

Bate therefore took the missive which, an hour later, catching Mr Ward on the road between Stafford Railway Station and The Junction Hotel, he handed to him with a knowing wink. Mr Ward angrily crumpled and thrust it into his pocket. The envelope, when opened, contained no letter, but only the five-pound note, and a message scribbled on a piece of newspaper: 'I understand that France, the poulterer, was one pheasant short of my order. This I sincerely regret. W.P.'

The inquest was finally held on the next day, Friday, December 14th. Elizabeth Mills, Lavinia Barnes, Dr Jones, Dr Bamford, who were the principal witnesses, testified that Cook had suffered first from vomiting, and then from tetanic convulsions. Professor Taylor, however, argued that these convulsions were produced by strychnia, even though he and Dr Rees had been unable to find traces of such a drug in the organs sent them for analysis.

'With a nicely calculated dose,' Professor Taylor wrote, 'this was not to be expected, since strychnia is a poison rapidly absorbed into the blood.'

Roberts, assistant to Messrs Hawkins, the chemists, then testified that he had sold Dr Palmer six grains of strychnine on the Tuesday morning. Newton kept quiet about his gift to the Doctor of the earlier three grains; and the eye-witnesses' account of Cook's illness was strictly as we have recorded it in the foregoing chapter.

The Coroner invited Dr Palmer to give evidence, but he sent word that illness prevented him from attending. It has been said, by the way, that the Sheriff's officers prompted this plea, not wanting him to escape.

On the following day the jury retired. Some minutes later, disregarding a plain conflict of testimony; misdirected by the Coroner, who perhaps wished to assure the Police that the proffered bribes had not warped his judgement; and, finally, stirred up by their foreman, Mr Tunnicliffe, Newton's father-in-law, they returned a verdict of 'Wilful Murder' against Dr Palmer.

Captain Hatton, to whom the Coroner had forwarded the incriminating letters, made the arrest. Ben Thirlby was sitting by Dr Palmer's bedside at the time, and felt so convinced of his innocence that he leaped at the Captain and tried to seize him by the throat. 'The charge is wicked and diabolical!' he cried. But the police officers gave Thirlby a rough handling for his pains. Dr Palmer then summoned Jeremiah Smith, who delayed half an hour before he dared comply, first fortifying himself at The Albion public bar. 'This news makes me feel sick,' said he.

Smith, it should be explained, had fallen in disgrace with old Mrs Palmer on the Monday night—the night on which Newton handed Dr Palmer the three grains of strychnine. After bidding Cook good-night, he and Dr Palmer had gone together to The Yard, where the old lady gave them both a terrible brushing down. Having been informed by her son George, the solicitor, that a moneylender wanted him to certify her signature on an acceptance of a bill for two thousand pounds, which he had refused to do, she now charged Smith with drafting this document for her Billy.

'I know well,' she cried, 'that Billy here would never have expected me to pay. This was just his way of tiding himself over a bad situation—but that you aided and abetted him and said never a word to me, I cannot forgive! Be off now, Mr Smith, I don't want to see your treacherous face ever again. It's not even as if you'd been faithful to my bed.'

When Smith at last entered the bedroom, he saw Dr Palmer surrounded by police officers. Pointing to them, he gasped: 'William, oh, William, how is this?'

The Doctor could not answer, but tears trickled down his cheeks.

He was judged unfit to be moved until the next day, when the Police, after examining his house from attic to cellar, and taking close precautions against his attempted escape or suicide, conveyed him in a covered van to Stafford Gaol. He had bidden an affecting good-bye to Eliza Tharm, throwing his arms around her neck, and requited her love with the gift of his last fifty-pound note. Their illegitimate child, by the bye, had died at five weeks old, not long before this: it was sent out to a poor nursing mother near the Canal Bridge at Armitage, three miles from Rugeley, but she neglected her charge.

Samuel Cheshire was presently arrested on a charge of tampering with the Royal Mails. Dr Palmer's letter to Mr Webb Ward provided the Postal Authorities with the necessary evidence, and he earned a severe prison sentence.

CHAPTER XVIII

STAFFORD GAOL

While describing Stafford, in an earlier chapter, we purposely reserved our account of the 'County Gaol and House of Correction' until this story should reach the point where Dr Palmer entered it as an inmate. It has very much the appearance of a solid, squat brick castle, because of the round towers placed at its four corners, and the steep outer walls which connect them. The pile gives off a glare like the embers of a coal furnace. The principal entrance, however, is built of stone, and we found it quite refreshing to approach its cool shade.

Facing the porter's lodge stands the Governor's house, with a little bit of garden stretched before it; but the grass seems to know that it is prison grass and therefore denied all such luxuries as manure or prepared soil. The beds grow no flowers worthy of notice, and are rich only in flints. A pathway leads thence to the debtors' airing court, a sizeable gravelled square surrounded by white painted wooden railings; and next to this rises the prison bake-house from which proceeds a hum of machinery and a grinding noise. The power that turns the mill stones is that of a tread-wheel, worked by thirty-two felons, in prison-grey, trudging for an hour at a time up the endless stairs which turn away beneath their feet. Prison officers armed with cudgels discourage the rebellious or the laggardly from a neglect of their task. The result is both a sensation of health produced by wholesome exercise, which many of the felons are taking for the first time in their disorderly lives, and a large quantity of flour—not perhaps of the highest quality, yet passed as fit for human consumption. Through the bake-house windows may be seen great stacks of bread, baked into slabs three inches thick, which are then sawn into yard lengths and piled together in orderly fashion, like planks of rare timber at a cabinet- maker's shop. Square loaves, such as free men eat, are suspect as serving to conceal such forbidden objects as bottles of spirits, rope-ladders, and weapons of destruction, smuggled in with the grain.

When Dr Palmer reached the Gaol, he still felt ill; and, immediately donning nightcap and nightshirt, went to bed again. Major Fulford, the Governor, took advantage of this removal of his clothes to remove them even farther, fearing that poison might be concealed in them. He ordered another suit to be made for Dr Palmer, not of prison-grey, since he was not yet a convict, but of a sober broadcloth. However, he declined to wear these new clothes, insisting that the Governor had no right to force them on him, and that they were badly cut. His wilfulness convinced the prison officers that poison must surely lurk in the seams or corners of coat, waistcoat or trousers; two or three grains of prussic acid or strychnine would, of course, suffice to end his life. When, a fortnight later, his own clothes were at last returned, every garment had been searched with a fine comb and beaten hard to dislodge any powder. All the seams had also been opened; the buttons examined lest one of them should serve as a miniature poison-box; the heels unfastened from his boots, lest these too should serve as receptacles for poison, and put back after careful scrutiny.

Much as Dr Palmer hated sleeping alone, almost more he hated being cut off from the racing news; but the Governor had strong views on the subject of horse-racing and gambling and let him read no newspaper which contained any talk of 'form' and 'odds'. In his despondency, Dr Palmer determined on self-destruction. No easy means offered, however, since he might use neither knife nor fork for his meals, ate off a tin plate and drank from a tin mug. He therefore resolved on starvation, simply sipping a little water from time to time, and lying motionless in bed, his face turned towards the wall. The Governor, on his usual morning visit, became alarmed by this behaviour, and tried to argue him into eating. Dr Palmer replied courteously that he was not hungry, and wanted nothing. Since, by the seventh day of this obstinate abstention from food, his prisoner had lost a stone of weight and seemed in danger of making good his resolve, the Governor had a savoury bowl of soup prepared, and sent for a spoon and a stomach pump.

He told Dr Palmer that, according to the prison doctor, his pulse was regular, his looks those of a healthy man, and there seemed no reason why he should not partake of this succulent soup.

'It's only that I have no appetite for coarse food,' Dr Palmer murmured faintly.

'Then, Sir,' cried the Governor, 'you shall choose between this spoon and that other instrument! I don't care a fig (let me be frank) whether you live or die, except in so far as my own appointment is concerned. But if I pander to your desire for self-extinction, my superiors will punish me severely; which I do not intend to happen. You have five minutes to decide whether you will drain your bowl, or oblige me to take compulsory measures. In the latter case, I shall summon a force of officers, of whom I have fifty at my orders, wedge open your jaws, drop the tube of this pump down the gullet, and pretty soon soup will be warming your stomach. It is by no means the pleasantest way of eating, but what other recourse have I?'

Dr Palmer said: 'I had not considered, Sir, that my loss of appetite might endanger your appointment here. And though I don't welcome your poor opinion of me—which I find unbecoming when I'm not yet pronounced guilty, and won't be, neither—nevertheless, if you insist, I'll consent to drink the damned beverage with your greasy spoon.'

He gave no further trouble in this respect, beyond asking one day that meals might be sent to him from his own kitchen. The Governor refused, for fear poison might be conveyed in the dishes, but told him that he was at liberty to order what victuals he pleased, within reason, for cooking in the debtors' kitchen. 'Ah, but it's not the same,' sighed Dr Palmer. 'Your prison cooks murder good food.'

'I trust at least that they do not poison it,' tardy retorted the Governor.

Meanwhile, numerous bills fell due which Dr Palmer could not, and old Mrs Palmer would not, meet. One morning Mr Wright, a solicitor from Birmingham, arrived at Dr Palmer's house and demanded admittance in virtue of a bill of sale to the amount of £10,400 given by Palmer some six months before for his horses, furniture, and all other movable property.

Mr Bergen, the Rural Superintendent of Police, who was charged with safeguarding the papers, drugs, and other contents of the house, refused to admit Mr Wright; however, one of Mr Wright's men presently gained an entry by breaking a pane of glass in the scullery window and unlatching it. Once inside the house, the Law protected Mr Wright, and arrangements were soon made for selling off the Doctor's effects by public auction.

We gather from Mrs Bennett, a next-door neighbour whose husband is a shoemaker, that if it had been Prince Albert's own sale there couldn't have been more folks about. They flocked in from Birmingham and all around, coming only to gaze, not to buy. The sale, according to the catalogue, should have occupied three days, but was got over in ten hours.

'The business was altogether too hurried,' Mrs Bennett told us. 'If the things had been brought out into the open air they would have fetched more; but the auctioneer didn't allow the bidders' time. It was along of the crowds that tramped through the house and prevented dealers from examining the articles at leisure. Nobody could see what was what, and the auctioneer wanted to get done quickly; even so, a mort of small things got stolen as souvenirs. The books, most of them new and up to date, were almost given away. And the furniture was beautiful!'

Mr Fawcus, a cabinet-maker, who stood waiting for Mr Bennett to finish cobbling a pair of boots, agreed with Mrs Bennett. 'Yes, Sir, the furniture was very good indeed, and not merely the pieces that I made at his orders according to Sheraton's models. I know he paid forty guineas for a sideboard—that's large money—and sixteen for a chiffonier. He had excellent taste in furniture.'

Mrs Bennett fetches us the catalogue: *Contents of drawing-room: one fine-toned semi-grand pianoforte in rosewood by a celebrated London maker.* 'Poor Mrs Palmer used to accompany herself on that, while singing Thomas Moore's Irish Songs,' Mrs Bennett said. 'She had a sweet voice. But the pianoforte went for a song—no joke intended.'

Rosewood couch with spring seat, squab and pillow in blue damask, and six elegant rosewood chairs in suite. 'My work,' said Mr Fawcus. 'Bought at the sale by Mr Bergen, the Rural Superintendent of Police, whose daughter took a fancy to them. He'd have bidden up to the original price, he would, but there was no competition—there isn't likely to be when Mr Bergen bids—so he got them cheap, and afterwards told me: "Fawcus, these people here, they don't know good stuff when they see it." He's a very knowing gentleman.'

Handsome mahogany book case, six foot by nine foot long, with plate glass and sliding shelves. 'That went at a better price to the Hon. Mr Curzon's steward.' *Pair of handsome chimney glasses.* 'Those were in the same lot,' remarked Mr Fawcus, 'big as chimney pots, and real cut crystal.'

Contents of best bedroom: handsome German bedstead with pan-elled foot-board, carved cornice and fringe, and figured damask hangings. 'Ah,' said Mrs Bennett, 'that's where poor Mrs Palmer bore her unfortunate children, and where she died, and where the Doctor was lying when arrested.'

'It's a good deal too heavy and fanciful for my taste,' confessed Mr Fawcus, 'but then I'm English, you see. It was old Mrs Palmer's wedding gift to the Doctor, and she bought it back. I think she wished to show that she hasn't lost faith in her son, despite all the ugly rumours.'

'Which I don't believe, neither,' cried Mrs Bennett, 'whatever the Coroner may say, and the judge, and the jury, and Captain Hatton, and Mr Bergen and all! It made my ears burn to hear some of the comments, dropped by those ill-mannered Birmingham folks as they roamed the house. They'd whisper: "That's where the wicked devil used to sleep with his mistresses." And when they came to the surgery, the remarks they passed about the bottles there was perfectly sinful!'

Contents of dining-room: eight fine Elizabethan carved oak chairs with seats upholstered in purple plush velvet. Also two valuable oil paintings: 'Charles Marlow, the Jockey, with Nettle' and 'Goldfinder, Winner of the Queen's Plate at Shrewsbury.' Twenty-five shillings a chair, just imagine!' exclaimed Mr Fawcus, 'originally purchased by the Doctor for four guineas, and a bargain at that! And the pictures went for five shillings, the frames alone being worth a guinea.'

'All that I bought,' said Mrs Bennett, 'was a nice deal box con-taining fishing tackle and pills. The Police didn't seem to mind the pills being sold and, of course, I burned them in the grate to keep them out of the children's clutches. "A box of fishing tackle is a funny place to put pills in," the auctioneer told us. But the tackle was a bargain at a shilling. My husband enjoys his bit of fishing of a Sunday afternoon, and the box was handy for garden tools.'

'The only fair prices were paid for the Doctor's cellar,' chimed in Mr Fawcus. 'He had 222 gallons of home-brewed ale, according to the catalogue, 67 dozen of port, and 43 gallons of spirit. A very fine cellar for so abstemious a man. It never occurred to the inn-keepers who bid for them that every bottle might contain rank poison; they were a deal less suspicious than the officers at Stafford Gaol.'

We strolled round to the back of the house, where the garden stretches—half an acre of land 'in very good fettle,' as Mr Fawcus called it. The low hedge dividing the courtyard from the garden has been carefully clipped, and the small garden in front of the house, with a little pile of imitation rock to spruce it up, is thoroughly well tended. Though we noticed at least six beds of leeks and spring onions, a patch about the size of his drawing-room carpet was all the space Dr Palmer devoted to flowers. The beds, cut out of the turf in curious shapes, such as stars and lozenges, contained only a few pinks and wall flowers.

We came across a well-built stable and coach-house with a pear-tree trained against the brick wall facing the noon sun, and a horseshoe nailed to the door. The large tank is of slate and clean rainwater flows into it for horses' drinking—soft water improves their health. In one corner, next a pig sty, a manure tank is sunk, into which the slush of the stable and piggery formerly drained; there being a pump to raise the liquid as it was required for the cultivation of vegetables. All these improvements to the property had been added by Dr Palmer.

Following the kitchen-garden path, where clothes poles and the cord along them formed a kind of telegraph, we found a fine rhubarb bed, behind which grew forty gooseberry and currant bushes, all neatly pruned. And beyond these, we suddenly came on a gentleman in check coat and trousers sitting on an upturned oyster barrel. He rose and addressed us in a hoarse Manchester accent, pressing upon us a tradesman's card which we reproduce here:

For a Fortnight
Photographic Portraits
C. *ALLEN*
Respectfully informs the Ladies, Gentry & Inhabitants
of Rugeley and elsewhere that he can produce

A Very Superior Photographic Portrait
in gilt and other frames
FROM ONE SHILLING TO ONE GUINEA
and invites their patronage at the rear of
PREMISES LATELY OCCUPIED BY W. PALMER
Specimens may be seen at Mr James's, Bookseller

Commencing at 10 o'clock Mornings until 6 in the
Evening. Rugeley, June 2nd, 1856

We thanked Mr Allen, but informed him that another day would suit us better. 'Oh, that's all right, bless you, Sir,' he said, 'I don't want for custom. The number of fashionably dressed folks who journey over here from the surrounding districts for a sight of Dr Palmer's house, barred and empty as it is, still astounds me. It's early yet for the rush, which don't commence much before noon. I do very well indeed from them, and take their portraits standing against the stable door, with one hand on the pear-tree to steady 'em. Yes, Sir, 'tis a superb place for my trade.'

Dr Palmer's creditors had all gathered together like a flock of vultures, and on January 21st, 1856, his brood-mares, horses in training and yearlings came up for auction. We were present to witness that interesting occasion.

At Hyde Park Corner, close to where carriages and horsemen enter the park, and where the mob stands roaring and screaming to see Her Majesty the Queen drive by in her landau—not far, in fact, from Decimus Burton's Arch topped by that formidable equestrian statue of the late Field-Marshal the Duke of Wellington, you will find Tattersall's Ring, the *sanctum sanctorum* of Turfites. It is a haunt as familiar to the young Yorkshire tyke as to the finest swell in London: a name as suggestive of good faith, honour, prompt payments, splendid horseflesh and noble company as it is of swindling, robbery, *non ests*, defaulting, levanting, screws and blackguards.

There's a sporting air about 'The Corner', from the red-jacketed touts who hang around its entrance to the shrewd cast of the auctioneer's countenance. We went down the yard, already filling at the news that Palmer's nags would come under the hammer, and hundreds who had no intention whatever of bidding, were assembled there through curiosity. Here they stood: gentle and simple, young and elderly, peers of the Realm, gentry, tradesmen and legs. That lanky old man with the fine aristocratic face, and neck swathed in the thick white choker, is a clergyman, and as thorough a sportsman as ever stepped; nor are his sermons any the worse for that. The dirty little man in the brown coat is a Viscount, exceedingly rich but so mean that he is said to go through the refuse bins outside his former club, from which he has been ejected, searching avidly for remnants of lobster and crayfish, which he grudges to buy for himself. Yonder goes the 'Leviathan' of the Ring, Bill Davies, tall and thin, dressed entirely in black, with a blue speckled handkerchief about his throat. He started life as a carpenter, and his word is now good for fifty thousand pounds; beside him walks young Frank Swindell, another commission agent, wearing a bunch of early violets in his buttonhole. Both of them have made an odd discovery, that, in the long run, straight dealing pays even in the betting ring. Since they scorn 'daylight robbery', which is to encourage betters to lay money on dead'uns—horses that will never run—engineers of dirty work no longer trouble to approach them.

Tattersall's stables are the acme of neatness and cleanliness. Here to the right is the Subscription Room, into which we might not go; instead we visited a public house mainly frequented by little grooms and jockeys, and listened to their gossip. 'The Rugeley Poisonings' were all the talk, and feeling ran high, the sporting fraternity being about equally divided between pro's and con's. Some swore that Billy Palmer was a bold sportsman, a good loser, and a generous friend; others that he was Ananias, Cain and Judas Iscariot rolled into one.

'He's lower than an animal, and worth a deal less,' cries a ferret-faced stable-boy to young Ashmole the jockey, 'and I'll undertake to prove it—at even money in half-sovereigns!'

'Done,' young Ashmole answers, 'let the landlord hold the stakes and be umpire.'

'Well,' says Ferret Face, 'Palmer was denied entrance to Tattersall's, now wasn't he? And a horse is an animal, isn't it? Well, there's seventeen of his horses admitted today where he wasn't, and a couple of 'em will sell for well over five hundred guineas, and none for lower than fifty. Well, what's Palmer worth? There's bills for fifteen thousand pounds out against him, and ten thousand of 'em won't be met. And as for his life, I wouldn't back his chances to live the year out, not at a hundred to one.'

Young Ashmole, defeated by this crude logic, which satisfied the landlord and raised loud cheers at the bar, paid up sulkily; but, having done so, he soused Ferret Face with a mug of beer full in his grinning phiz.

Bidding at the auction was spirited, and high prices were realized. Prince Albert's name has already appeared in our account of the other auction, if only as a metaphor; here we heard it used in a direct and practical manner. For Major Grove, Her Majesty's Commissioner from the Royal Paddocks, bought Trickstress, an eight-year-old mare, for 230 guineas on Prince Albert's behalf. Strange to relate, though the Major appeared anxious to secure Nettle, a decidedly superior animal, in the end he let her go to Mr F. L. Popham for 430 guineas. (Nettle, it will be recalled, was favourite for the Oaks last year, and her tumble over the chains sealed Dr Palmer's financial doom.) The Chicken went for 800 guineas to Mr Harlock, who has since changed her name to 'Vengeance'. In the aggregate, the sale amounted to £3906, which included the high price of 590 guineas for a three-year-old filly, by Melbourne out of Seaweed, which fell to Mr Sargent.

While Dr Palmer was attempting suicide by starvation, the bodies of his wife and brother were exhumed, and coroner's inquests held on them. In the first case, Annie Palmer's, the gaseous exudations of the corpse had, since the fifteen months of burial, escaped through the fibre of the oaken coffin and left the corpse comparatively dry. Dr Monckton made the *post-mortem* examination, and again the organs were sent to Professor Taylor, who reported antimony in the stomach, liver and kidneys and judged that death was due to this antimony administered in the form of tartar emetic, and to no other cause. The jury found Dr Palmer guilty of wilful murder.

Exceptionally distressing was the *post-mortem* done on Walter Palmer's body. He had been buried in a lead coffin and, the wooden shell being removed, a hole was bored through the lid. At once a most noxious effluvia permeated the entire Talbot Inn. Fifteen of the persons present, including seven of the jury, were seized with nausea, and some of them remained seriously indisposed for the next two or three days. The lid being opened, the corpse wore a terrible aspect, being a mass of corruption, dropsy and gangrene. Professor Taylor inclined to think that death was caused by prussic acid, though he could find no trace of the poison in the organs sent him for analysis; and though Dr Day, who had signed the death certificate, testified that he had not smelt the tell-tale fumes of prussic acid on the dying man's breath., but only those of brandy! Dr Day stood firmly by his original opinion that death was due to apoplexy, consequent on excessive drinking. Since Drs Monckton, Harland, Campbell, Hughes and Waddell supported Dr Day, Professor Taylor felt it wise not to press his view.

Nevertheless, when the case came before the Coroner, the jury, instigated by Mr Hawkins, the chemist, who had been chaffed a good deal for having supplied Dr Palmer with enough poison to destroy the whole parish, brought in yet another verdict of wilful murder. Walter's widow, Mrs Agnes Palmer, had attended the Court, but so broken by grief that the Coroner led her to a private room where he took her evidence in the presence of the Foreman and the Clerk. Among others who appeared were George Palmer, the solicitor, who told the Court: 'Mr Hawkins feels rancour towards my brother, and will, I am sure, find him guilty of murder whatever the evidence. At my brother's sale, Mr Hawkins bought a medical book to use against him when he comes to be tried on the equally false charge of poisoning his friend, the late Mr Cook.'

Pratt, the moneylender, was also called, because he held Walter Palmer's life-insurance policy as collateral security for Dr Palmer's debts to him, and because he had approached the insurance companies on the Doctor's behalf; which led him to be suspected of complicity in the supposed murder. The Coroner and jury asked him searching questions; denounced his rate of interest—sixty per cent a year—as usurious; and treated him so roughly that at last he screamed in falsetto, tears of rage streaming down his plump face: 'How can you ask such questions of a family man with three young children and a dear wife, who will probably be ruined by this affair? I lost over four thousand pounds through Palmer!'

The Court burst into loud laughter.

This, however, was not yet the end of the matter, for George Palmer appealed. The case was duly carried before the Grand Jury at Stafford Assizes, who threw out the bill against Dr Palmer for wilful murder of his brother Walter, finding the evidence insufficient.

Now, if it is asked why Professor Taylor had been so ready to name prussic acid as the cause of death, the answer is clear. A detective, employed by Mr Stevens to make inquiries at Wolverhampton, discovered that on the Monday before Walter's death, while the race meeting was in progress there, the Doctor had visited a chemist's shop and bought a quantity of prussic acid and jalap from the assistant. Mr Stevens acquainted Professor Taylor with this news, and the evidence which the assistant gave at the inquest, supporting Professor Taylor's seemingly unaided diagnosis, prompted the verdict of wilful murder. But George Palmer prudently took the precaution of checking the Poison Book and found no entry, on the date concerned, referring to prussic acid. He then threatened to indict the assistant for perjury—a crime which carries the statutory punishment of transportation—if he would not publicly withdraw his statement. This the young man hastened to do, though transportation has, of course, been suspended since 1846, when the authorities of Van Diemen's Land, overwhelmed by a horde of idle and depraved convicts, far outnumbering the free settlers, begged the Government to send no more. The probability is that the assistant had made Dr Palmer a present of the prussic acid, just as Newton did; and that the Doctor intended to use it on other owners' horses—for it can at least be said that he always ran his own to win.

While held in Stafford Gaol, Dr Palmer was only once allowed outside the building. On January 21st, policemen escorted him to Westminster where he appeared as a witness at a trial in which Padwick, the moneylender, was plaintiff, and old Mrs Palmer defendant. (This, it will be recalled, was the day artfully chosen by the managers of Tattersall's to put the 'all-yellow' horses under the hammer; the coincidence excited high bidding.) Padwick was trying to recover a two-thousand-pound loan, in the form of a bill which apparently bore old Mrs Palmer's acceptance. She denied the handwriting, and was supported in this by three of her children: Mr George Palmer, the Revd John Palmer, and Miss Sarah Palmer. The dramatic appearance of Dr Palmer, who had presented the bill to Padwick, caused quite a stir. The door of the judge's private room was thrown open and he entered, cool and collected, in the custody of a large and muscular police officer. From the witness box he leisurely surveyed the crowded audience, to some of whom he gave a familiar nod, before fixing his attention on a person located between him and the learned counsel who conducted Mrs Palmer's case. This was a young red-haired woman, believed to have been the same Jane Widnall, or Smirke, lately returned a widow from Australia, who had first seduced him from the narrow path of virtue. She afterwards applied for a seat at the murder trial, but the demand being too great, failed of her expectation.

Dr Palmer was then sworn and answered the following questions in a low, yet firm and distinct voice, without betraying the least hesitation or nervousness.

> MR EDWIN JAMES (*handing him the bill of exchange*): Is the signature 'William Palmer' as the drawer of this bill in your handwriting?
> DR PALMER: Yes.
> MR JAMES: And you applied to Padwick to advance you money on it?
> DR PALMER: I did.
> MR JAMES: Who wrote Mrs Sarah Palmer's acceptance on it?
> DR PALMER: Ann Palmer.
> MR JAMES: Who is she?
> DR PALMER: She is now dead.
> MR JAMES: Do you mean your wife?
> DR PALMER: Yes.
> MR JAMES: Did you see her write it?
> DR PALMER: Yes.

A shudder went through the audience. That a man should accuse his dead wife of a crime which he had himself forced upon her seemed a heartless proceeding; yet, she being dead and past caring, his chief concern was to preserve his mother's esteem. She had assured Jeremiah Smith that 'my Billy would never seek to rob me,' nor was she disappointed; his honest confession of fraud now saved her two thousand pounds, for Mr Padwick's Counsel saw no course open to him but retirement from the case. The jury found in favour of old Mrs Palmer, and the prisoner was hurried back to Euston Square Station.

It is an ironical circumstance that Mr Padwick, half an hour earlier, had purchased two of the Doctor's horses: a bay yearling colt, by Touchstone out of the Duchess of Kent, at 230 guineas; and a brown yearling filly, by Touchstone out of Maid o' Lyme, at 250 guineas. He swore that had he known how the verdict would go, he'd never have 'bought hoof or hair of that twister's blood-stock.'

CHAPTER XIX

UNRELIABLE WITNESSES

Dr Palmer's brothers, George the solicitor, and Thomas the Anglican clergyman, had cooled off considerably towards him of late years; yet kept the peace to please old Mrs Palmer. Since she never disguised her fondness for 'my roguish Billy', they did not vex her by evincing their repugnance for him; in part, no doubt, because she was worth some seventy thousand pounds, but principally because she was their mother. When the Police arrested the Doctor on a charge of murder, they at once rallied to his defence. Neither of them, from their long experience of him, could bring himself to believe in the charge; nor, being respectable citizens, would they consent to be known as the brothers of a murderer, without doing everything that might lie in their power to wipe out this stigma. Old Mrs Palmer, though repudiating the debts which Dr Palmer had incurred in her name, promised to engage the best lawyers available.

George secured Mr John Smith of Birmingham—the famous 'Honest John Smith of Brum'—as solicitor for the Defence, and consulted with him as to what leading Counsel should be retained. John Smith swore that the most suitable man in all England would be Mr Serjeant Wilkins, Q.C., who had enjoyed a medical education until taking to the Law, and could therefore confidently handle the abstruse evidence expected. Serjeant Wilkins agreed to act; and appeared for them in January when, in the suit brought by Padwick, Dr Palmer admitted having forged his mother's acceptances to the bills—but, three weeks before the trial, he threw up his brief, pleading ill-health. In point of fact, we understand, the duns were after him and it was with difficulty that he escaped by fishing-smack to Dieppe. This came as a great disappointment to John Smith. Having failed to secure the services of Sir Frederick Thesiger, who had been Attorney-General during the Peel administration, he fell back on an Irishman, Mr Serjeant Shee, Q.C., M.P. for Kilkenny. Serjeant Shee, though an able barrister is, however, a devout Roman Catholic.

More than a quarter of a century has elapsed since the disabilities from which Romanists suffered in Britain were removed by Act of Parliament, but a strong prejudice against them still undeniably pervades public life. Mr Smith dared not hope that the jury would remain ignorant of Serjeant Shee's faith (this anti-Catholic sentiment being particularly rife among London trades-people of the Roundhead tradition), if only because he had been prominent as an advocate of Emancipation, and had of late spoken very forcibly in Parliament on the subject of the late potato famine in Ireland and the absentee Protestant landlords. Yet this prejudice seemed unlikely to affect the Bench. True, Lord Chief Justice Campbell, a Scottish 'son of the manse', had read Divinity, rather than Law, at St Andrews University, and might well regard all Roman Catholics as eternally damned. But Mr Baron Alderson was known as a humane judge, anxious to restrict capital punishment, and Mr Smith counted on him and Mr Justice Cresswell to restrain the Lord Chief Justice if he showed undue animus towards either Serjeant Shee or the prisoner.

Nevertheless, the Usher of the Central Criminal Court assured us on the first day of the trial: 'Sir, Dr Palmer will swing, you may be bound.'

Upon our questioning him, we were told familiarly: 'I know Jack Campbell's hanging face well, and his hanging manner.' 'What is that?' we asked.

'His hanging face, Sir, is bland and benignant, and his hanging manner unctuous. As soon as the prisoner entered the dock and Lord Campbell invited him to be seated, I would have offered long odds against his chances of life.'

'But it takes twelve good and true men to hang a criminal,' we insisted, 'and there are a couple of other judges on the bench beside the Lord Chief Justice.'

He shook his head sagely. 'Sir Cresswell Cresswell is a humane and honest man,' he pronounced, 'but Alderson would as lief hang Shee as he would Palmer. Those two legal gentlemen have always been at loggerheads, I can't say why—it may be a political dis-agreement, it may be a personal one. Moreover, Attorney-General Cockburn is a beloved compatriot of Jack Campbell's, and he's out to destroy Palmer. Even if the pair of them weren't as thick as thieves, it would take a mighty firm Lord Chief Justice to handle a determined Attorney-General. Cocky, you know, is due for his judgeship any day now and wishes to make this a memorable fare-well to the Bar—a savages' feast with fireworks, drums, bloody sacrifices and all. So that's three of them teamed together—Jack Campbell, Alderson and Cocky! They can do what they list, for the Under-Sheriffs have a hand-picked jury ready to serve them. Will you dare lay against Palmer's conviction?'

'I'm not a betting man,' was our cautious answer.

The twelve-day trial, which opened on May 14th, 1856, was mem-orable not only for brilliant forensic displays by the prosecuting and defending Counsel, but also, as we shall not hesitate to point out, for a singular conflict of evidence and surprising irregularities in judicial procedure.

On the opening day, the Attorney-General promised to show that Dr Palmer was financially interested in murdering John Parsons Cook, and that, having weakened his system with tartar emetic both at Shrewsbury and at Rugeley, he purchased strychnia at the latter town and administered it in the form of pills, substituting these for the rhubarb, calomel and morphia pills which Dr Bamford had prescribed. No strychnia had been found in Cook's body, yet the Attorney-General insisted (with leave from Professor Taylor) that strychnia, being rapidly absorbed into the system, evades detection in the tissues of its victim, and that Cook's symptoms were consistent with strychnine poisoning.

The first witness called was Mr Ishmael Fisher, the sporting wine merchant, whom we can hardly describe as unprejudiced, since Dr Palmer had defrauded him of two hundred pounds. He testified forcibly to Cook's suspicion of having been poisoned at The Raven Hotel; and was followed by other members of his sporting party, none of whom, since reading about the verdicts at the inquests on Annie and Walter Palmer, and on Cook, wished to be known as the prisoner's friends or supporters.

Next appeared Elizabeth Mills, formerly chambermaid at The Talbot Arms Hotel, Rugeley, a sharp-featured young woman, wearing a fashionable bonnet. Her account of events varied to a great extent from the depositions she had made before the Coroner. She now reported fresh and striking symptoms, hitherto undisclosed; and it came back to her that she had tasted Cook's bowl of broth and found herself severely poisoned by it. The Prosecution sought to prove that these vital matters must also have appeared in her depositions, had the Coroner's Inquest been properly conducted.

Serjeant Shee's cross-examination of this flighty miss on the second day proves, to our satisfaction at least, how successfully Mr Stevens had contrived to suborn her. She was, it seems, shown an account of the recent atrocity at Leeds (where a Mr Dove poisoned his wife with strychnine), and then asked to remember the same medical particulars in Cook's case.

The following is a somewhat abbreviated record of Elizabeth Mills's disingenuous answers to Serjeant Shee's questions:

> SERJEANT SHEE: How long did you stay at The Talbot Arms Hotel after Cook's death?
> MILLS: Till the day after Christmas-day. Then I went home.
> SERJEANT SHEE: Where is 'home'?
> MILLS: Shelton, in the Potteries.
> SERJEANT SHEE: Have you been in service since?
> MILLS: Yes, as chambermaid at Dolly's Hotel, Paternoster Row.
> SERJEANT SHEE: Are you in service there now?
> MILLS: No. I stayed only six weeks; until February.
> SERJEANT SHEE: After you came to London, did you see Mr Stevens?
> MILLS: Yes.
> SERJEANT SHEE: Where and when did you see him?
> MILLS: At Dolly's, about a week later.
> SERJEANT SHEE: How many times?
> MILLS: Perhaps four or five.
> SERJEANT SHEE: Will you swear it was not ten times?
> MILLS: It might be six or seven; that was about the outside. I cannot exactly keep account . . .
> SERJEANT SHEE: Where at Dolly's did you see him?
> MILLS: Sometimes he would speak to me while Mrs

Dewhurst, the landlady, was there, in one of her sitting- rooms.

SERJEANT SHEE: But sometimes you went into a sitting-room and spoke to him alone?

MILLS: Perhaps twice or three times.

SERJEANT SHEE: Was it always about Mr Cook's death that he spoke to you?

MILLS: No, it was not. He would call to see how I liked London, and whether I was well in health, and all that.

SERJEANT SHEE: Mr Stevens is a gentleman, not in your station. Do you mean to say he called so often to inquire after your health?

MILLS: That, and to see whether I liked the place.

SERJEANT SHEE: He called six or seven times on you to see whether you liked the place: do you mean to tell that to the jury on your oath?

MILLS: I am not going to take my oath: but when he called on me he always asked how I liked London.

SERJEANT SHEE: Then what did he call about?

MILLS: Sometimes one thing, sometimes another. SERJEANT SHEE: What else besides Mr Cook's death? MILLS: Nothing besides that.

SERJEANT SHEE: Had you conversed with him much at The Talbot Arms while he was lodging there just before the funeral?

MILLS: Some little.

SERJEANT SHEE: Had you never been in a room with him alone at The Talbot Arms?

MILLS: No.

SERJEANT SHEE: At Dolly's Hotel he spoke to you

about Mr Cook's death, and your health, and your
liking for London, but nothing else; is that so? On
your oath, did he speak to you about anything else?

MILLS: Yes, many more things.

SERJEANT SHEE: What else?

MILLS: I cannot remember.

SERJEANT SHEE: Tell me a single thing of importance that he spoke to you about except Mr
Cook's death?

MILLS: I do not keep such things in my head for
weeks or months together.

SERJEANT SHEE: Did you not say to him after he
had been calling two or three times: 'Why, Mr
Stevens, you have been here often enough; I have
told you all I know'?

MILLS: No, I did not.

SERJEANT SHEE: Did he give you money during
the time you were there?

MILLS: Never a farthing.

SERJEANT SHEE: Has he promised to get you a
place?

MILLS: Not at all.

SERJEANT SHEE: When did you talk to him last?

MILLS: On Tuesday at Dolly's Hotel.

SERJEANT SHEE: Was Mr Cook's death still the
subject of his talk?

MILLS: He merely said 'How do you do?' and asked
me how I was; plenty more were present.

SERJEANT SHEE: Does he live at Dolly's?

MILLS: He may do, for aught I know.

SERJEANT SHEE: Where was it at Dolly's you saw
him last Tuesday?

MILLS: In a sitting-room.

SERJEANT SHEE: Were you alone with him?

MILLS: No.

SERJEANT SHEE: Who else was there?

MILLS: Lavinia Barnes, of The Talbot Arms. SER-
JEANT SHEE: Did she have a place at Dolly's
too? MILLS: She is working there now.

SERJEANT SHEE: So Mr Stevens had an interview
with you and Lavinia Barnes?

THE ATTORNEY-GENERAL: I beg your pardon,
the witness has not said so; do not put an ambig-
uous phrase into her mouth.

LORD CAMPBELL: If you repeat what she says,
you must repeat it correctly.

SERJEANT SHEE: What am I to call it, my Lord,
but an interview? Was there a meeting between
him and you and Lavinia Barnes in the same
room?

MILLS: There were two other gentlemen in the
room besides us three.

SERJEANT SHEE: Who?

MILLS: Captain Hatton and Mr Gardiner.

SERJEANT SHEE: On this occasion, was all the
talk about Mr Cook's death?

MILLS: I cannot remember; it might be mentioned.
I don't pretend to keep in my head what the conversation was.

SERJEANT SHEE: Will you undertake to say there
was no single subject of conversation mooted
between you and

Lavinia Barnes and those gentlemen except the subject of Cook's death?

MILLS: There were many more things talked about.

SERJEANT SHEE: What?

MILLS: That I do not wish to mention.

SERJEANT SHEE: You must mention what was the subject of conversation.

MILLS: I cannot remember. They were not talking with me alone, but among themselves; I paid no attention to what they were talking about. Perhaps my thoughts were occupied about something else.

SERJEANT SHEE: They did talk about Mr Cook's death?

MILLS: They might, but I cannot remember.

SERJEANT SHEE: Did they talk about the evidence that you were to give at this trial?

MILLS: No; not that I heard.

SERJEANT SHEE: Did they read your depositions over to you, those taken before the Coroner?

MILLS: No, they did not.

SERJEANT SHEE: Was anything read to you from a newspaper?

MILLS: No.

SERJEANT SHEE: Did Mr Stevens then, or at any previous time, talk to you about the symptoms which Mr Cook exhibited shortly before his death?

MILLS: He did not.

SERJEANT SHEE: Was that the first time since Mr Cook's death that you had seen Captain Hatton?

MILLS: No, I had seen him once before. He was dining at Dolly's. SERJEANT SHEE: Did he speak at all about Mr Cook's death to you? MILLS: He might, but I cannot remember.

SERJEANT SHEE: Do not tell me you cannot remember: what did he speak to you about? Did he, upon your oath, speak to you about Mr Cook's death?

MILLS: I cannot remember. He might do.

SERJEANT SHEE: Do you recollect anything else he said?

MILLS: He asked me how I was, I remember.

SERJEANT SHEE: Had you seen Mr Gardiner before, since Mr Cook's death?

MILLS: Yes. Three or four times.

SERJEANT SHEE: Where?

MILLS: I have met him in the street.

SERJEANT SHEE: Spoken to him?

MILLS: Merely said 'How do you do?' or 'Good morning'. SERJEANT SHEE: You have not been to any attorney's office with him? MILLS: No.

SERJEANT SHEE: You left Dolly's in February. Where are you living now?

MILLS: At Rugeley, with my mother.

SERJEANT SHEE: Where were you living before that?

MILLS: Among my friends.

SERJEANT SHEE: Was that at Hitchingley? MILLS: Yes. I have some friends there. SERJEANT SHEE: Who are they?

MILLS: Friends are friends, I suppose.

SERJEANT SHEE: I do not mean to ask you any rude questions, but that is hardly a proper answer. Do you know a man of the name of Dutton?

MILLS: I do. He is a friend of mine.

SERJEANT SHEE: Was it with him you were living?

MILLS: I stayed at his cottage a short time.

SERJEANT SHEE: What is Mr Dutton?

MILLS: A friend of mine: a labouring man of some thirty perhaps. I have known him about two years.

SERJEANT SHEE: Is there a Mrs Dutton?

MILLS: Yes, his mother. She lives in the cottage.

SERJEANT SHEE: How many rooms?

MILLS: Two down and two up.

SERJEANT SHEE: His mother slept in one of the upstairs rooms?

MILLS: Yes.

SERJEANT SHEE: Where did you sleep?

MILLS: In the bed with her.

SERJEANT SHEE: Will you swear that you always slept in that bed?

MILLS: Yes.

SERJEANT SHEE: Why did you leave Dolly's?

MILLS: I did not like the place; it was of my own accord.

SERJEANT SHEE: You can read newspapers, I suppose?

MILLS: Yes.

SERJEANT SHEE: Have you read the case of a Mrs Dove?

MILLS: I do not remember; I may have done so.

SERJEANT SHEE: It is a case that lately occurred at Leeds, of a lady who was said to have been poisoned by her husband.

MILLS: No, I did not read it; I heard it spoken of.

SERJEANT SHEE: By whom?

MILLS: By many. I cannot mention one more than another.

SERJEANT SHEE: By Mr Stevens, or Mr Gardiner, or Captain Hatton?

MILLS: No, by no one belonging to this trial.

SERJEANT SHEE: Were you told what the symptoms of Mrs Dove were?

MILLS: I think not; I merely heard it was another strychnine case.

SERJEANT SHEE: Were the symptoms of strychnia ever mentioned to you by anyone?

MILLS: No, never.

SERJEANT SHEE: When and to whom did you first use the expression 'twitching', which, with 'jerking', occurred so repeatedly in your evidence yesterday?

MILLS: To the Coroner, I did. Or, if I did not mention 'twitching', I mentioned something to the same effect.

SERJEANT SHEE: It is fair to tell you, as I have the deposition before me, that you did not. THE ATTORNEY-GENERAL: If you do so, I shall show how these depositions were taken. SERJEANT SHEE: I intend to put them in.

When did you first use the word 'twitching', which you used so frequently yesterday?

MILLS: I cannot remember when first I used the word, but I believe it was in Mother's house before I came to London.

SERJEANT SHEE: Will you swear to that?

MILLS: Yes; and I described the symptoms the young man died under.

SERJEANT SHEE: Will you swear you used the word 'twitching'?

MILLS: Yes; at Mother's.

SERJEANT SHEE: Is your mother here?

MILLS: No, she is not.

SERJEANT SHEE: Have you ever been asked by anybody if there were not 'twitchings'?

MILLS: I cannot remember.

SERJEANT SHEE: You stated yesterday on oath that on the Saturday between twelve and one o'clock some broth was brought to The Talbot Arms Hotel in a breakfast-cup; that you took it up into Cook's bedroom; that you tasted it, and drank about two tablespoons; that you were sick; that you were sick the whole afternoon, and vomited at least twenty times?

MILLS: I do not remember that I used the words 'twenty times'.

SERJEANT SHEE: Had you said one word about this sickness in your depositions before the Coroner?

MILLS: It never occurred to me then; it occurred to me three days afterwards.

SERJEANT SHEE: Did you state this before the Coroner: 'I tasted the broth on the Sunday before Cook's death; it was not made in this house; I thought the broth very good after I had tasted it; I believe some broth had been sent over on the Saturday; nothing peculiar was in the taste of the broth'?

MILLS: No, I could not taste anything peculiar.

SERJEANT SHEE: If you tasted it, and if it made you sick, and if you vomited frequently in the course of the afternoon, why did you not mention that to the Coroner?

MILLS: It never occurred to me; I did not think it was the broth at the time.

SERJEANT SHEE: You stated yesterday you saw a pill-box in the hotel on the Monday night, which was sent over there about eight o'clock, wrapped up in paper?

MILLS: Yes.

SERJEANT SHEE: And that you placed it on the dressing-table of Cook's bedroom?

MILLS: Yes.

SERJEANT SHEE: And that on that same evening you saw Palmer in Cook's room between nine and ten o'clock?

MILLS: Yes.

SERJEANT SHEE: Did you say a word about that before the Coroner?

MILLS: I might do.

SERJEANT SHEE: Don't you remember that you made no such statement before the Coroner?

MILLS: Perhaps I was not asked the question; I did not say anything, only when I was asked.

SERJEANT SHEE: Will you now swear he was there between nine and ten o'clock?

MILLS: Yes; he brought a jar of jelly and opened it.

SERJEANT SHEE: About how long after nine will you swear to his presence there?

MILLS: I cannot remember; I should fancy it was nearer to ten than nine.

SERJEANT SHEE: You say it was half-past ten when you left Cook, but you cannot recollect whether Palmer was still there?

MILLS: I cannot.

SERJEANT SHEE: Then you have no certain recollection of seeing him after that time?

MILLS: Not until he was fetched over about midnight. SERJEANT SHEE: Do you know when Cook took the pills? MILLS: I do not.

SERJEANT SHEE: You stated yesterday that you asked him on the Tuesday morning what he thought the cause of his illness was. Did he reply: 'The pills which Palmer gave me at half-past ten'?

MILLS: Yes.

SERJEANT SHEE: Did you tell the Coroner that?

MILLS: No.

SERJEANT SHEE: Since Mr Cook's death, have you been questioned by anyone respecting what you said about these pills before the Coroner?

MILLS: Yes, by a Dr Collier. He came to see me at Hitchingley.

SERJEANT SHEE: Did you tell Dr Collier that the gentlemen in London had altered your evidence on that point, and that it was now to be: 'Cook said the pills which Palmer gave him at half-past ten made him ill'?

MILLS: I did not tell him that the gentlemen had altered my evidence.

SERJEANT SHEE: Did you say that the evidence had since been altered by anybody?

MILLS: It had been altered by myself since; because Mr Cook's words had occurred to me.

SERJEANT SHEE: Did you say to what gentleman you had given this information?

MILLS: No, because I did not remember, except that I met him at Dolly's.

SERJEANT SHEE: So an unknown gentleman
came to you at Dolly's! Did he tell you from
whom he came?

MILLS: No, he asked: 'Will you answer a few questions?' I said: 'Certainly.' He did not tell me his
name, neither did I ask it.

SERJEANT SHEE: Did he ask you many questions?

MILLS: Not very many.

SERJEANT SHEE: Did he write down your answers?

MILLS: Yes.

SERJEANT SHEE: But he did not tell you who he
was, or whom he come from, or for what your
answers were wanted?

MILLS: No.

SERJEANT SHEE: Did he mention Mr Stevens's
name?

MILLS: Yes.

SERJEANT SHEE: What did he say about Mr
Stevens?

MILLS: Mr Stevens was with him in the sitting-room; he called Mr Stevens by name.

SERJEANT SHEE: Why did you not tell us that
before?

MILLS: I was not asked. [*Laughter in Court.*]

We have heard of judges warning juries to place no reliance
on witnesses whose conduct and demeanour were in every way
superior to those of Elizabeth Mills; yet the Lord Chief Justice
supported her with romantic fervour and characterized Serjeant
Shee's suggestion that Mr Stevens paid her money as 'a most foul
charge'. The Dr Collier mentioned by Elizabeth Mills had gone,

at John Smith's request, to Hitchingley, where he took down her statements. When informed that he was now in Court, Baron Alderson exclaimed angrily: 'Dr Collier should be absent, if he is to be examined for facts. He is here under the false pretence of being a doctor!' Baron Alderson forgot that three doctors called by the Prosecution to be examined for facts were also in Court.

Further evidence that day came from Lavinia Barnes, who docilely supported Mills's new story of having been poisoned after tasting the broth, but otherwise added nothing to the stock of common knowledge; from Dr Jones, Cook's oldest friend, and the only medical eye-witness of his death, who kept to his view that Cook had died of natural causes; from Dr Savage, the London physician, who gave evidence that Cook was in reasonably good health, save for a weakness of the lung, up to a fortnight before his death; and finally by Charles Newton, Dr Salt's assistant.

Newton now testified to having given Dr Palmer three grains of strychnine crystals at nine o'clock on Monday night, November 19th. He also told a most improbable tale about a meeting on Sunday, November 25th, the eve of the *post-mortem* examination.

Cross-examined by Mr James, Q.C., for the Prosecution:

> JAMES: Do you remember Sunday, the 25th of
> November?
> NEWTON: I do.
> JAMES: Where were you at about seven o'clock that
> evening?
> NEWTON: At Dr Palmer's house.
> JAMBS: What was the cause of your going there?
> NEWTON: I was sent for.
> JAMES: Where did you find Palmer when you went,
> and what was he doing?

NEWTON: He was alone, sitting by the kitchen
    fire, reading.
JAMES: What did he say to you?
NEWTON: He asked me how I was, and would I
    take a little brandy?
JAMES: Did he say anything else to you?
NEWTON: He asked me: 'What dose of strychnia
    would be required to kill a dog?' I told him, 'A
    grain.' He then asked me whether it would be
    found in the stomach after death.
JAMES: What did you say?
NEWTON: I told him there would be no inflam-
    mation, and that I did not think it would be
    found.
JAMES: Did he make any remark upon that?
NEWTON: I think he said: 'It is all right,' as if
    speaking to himself. Then he did that (*snapping
    his fingers*).

Newton's evidence was greeted by a loud clapping of hands in
Court, as though he had delivered a telling dramatic speech at
Drury Lane. Lord Chief Justice Campbell made no attempt to
quell the applause.

Cross-examined by Mr Grove for the Defence:

GROVE: You were examined at the inquest, I think
    you have stated; did you then say anything either
    about your conversation with respect to the dog,
    or about the three grains of strychnia?
NEWTON: No, I did not.
GROVE: Did you say anything about the conversation
    of Cook's suffering from diseased throat—syphilis?

NEWTON: Yes, I did.

JAMES: At the inquest?

NEWTON: I was not questioned there about the *post-mortem* at all . . .

Re-examined by Mr Attorney-General Cockburn:

THE ATTORNEY-GENERAL: You have said that you gave information to the Crown on Tuesday about this fact of the three grains of strychnia. How was it you did not give that information before?

NEWTON: On account that Dr Palmer had not been friends with Dr Salt; they never speak to each other.

THE ATTORNEY-GENERAL: What had that to do with it?

NEWTON: I thought Dr Salt would be displeased at my letting Dr Palmer have anything.

THE ATTORNEY-GENERAL: You say they did not speak?

NEWTON: No; Mr Thirlby lived with Dr Salt for nineteen years . . .

THE ATTORNEY-GENERAL: Was it in consequence of Mr Thirlby going to Dr Palmer's that this difference took place between Dr Palmer and Dr Salt?

NEWTON: Yes; Dr Salt did not speak to Dr Palmer, or Mr Thirlby either.

THE ATTORNEY-GENERAL: Was there any other reason besides that for your keeping it back?

NEWTON: That was my only reason.

SERJEANT SHEE: Will your Lordship ask this witness whether he has not given another reason:

the reason being that he was afraid he should be
indicted for perjury?

NEWTON: No, I did not give that as a reason,
though I mentioned it to the gentleman sitting
there [Mr Greenwood]. I stated that I had heard
about a young man from Wolverhampton whom
Mr George Palmer had indicted for perjury because this young man could not produce a book
to show that he had sold Dr Palmer some prussic
acid.

THE ATTORNEY-GENERAL: In what case was
that?

NEWTON: The inquest upon Walter Palmer.

The Defence did not challenge Newton's reliability as a witness,
but it has since been revealed that he was Ben Thirlby's illegitimate son by one Dorothy Newton of Bell's Yard, Long Row,
Nottingham. His half-brother John was sentenced to four years'
penal servitude for picking pockets at Lincoln Races; and he himself, as a boy, had been caught breaking up a stolen silver spoon
belonging to his employer Mr Crossland, a wine merchant, and
thereupon spent three days in the Nottingham House of Correction. The records show that his mother, a charwoman, begged
him off from the magistrates who examined the case, promising
to make good Mr Grassland's losses. A second offence has been
mentioned, but we lack details. Newton later, after attendance
at the National School, assisted a Nottingham surgeon; and was
then cunningly insinuated by Thirlby into Dr Salt's employment.
Dr Salt did not know of the blood-relationship between these two.

When the trial was over, the same obliging Newton, prompted
perhaps by certain insurance- company officials, called on the
Attorney-General. He said that if Sir George Grey considered

granting a reprieve (on the ground that Dr Palmer did not have time to make up the strychnine pills in his own surgery, and then administer them at the hour stated by the Prosecution) he would willingly swear to having given Dr Palmer the strychnine in the form of pills already made up—a fact he had hitherto forgotten! The Attorney-General undertook to bring this new evidence before his fellow-Minister, should Dr Palmer's lawyer sue for a reprieve.

CHAPTER XX

ABSENT WITNESSES

Serjeant Shee's main ground of defence was that Dr Palmer did not stand to gain financially by John Parsons Cook's death, since it made him liable to repay debts which they jointly incurred, in an amount far exceeding such small sums as the Prosecution accused him of robbing. He had, indeed, bought six grains of strychnine on the Tuesday morning from Hawkins's shop, openly and for a legitimate reason; Serjeant Shee, however, preferred to deny his having procured any from Newton on the Monday evening. Therefore, the convulsions reported by Elizabeth Mills that night were not, he argued, attributable to strychnine poisoning, but rather to tetanus or epilepsy, or some other ailment, as were also those of the Tuesday night which carried Cook off early the following morning. Furthermore, had Dr Palmer planned to murder Cook, he would never have sent for his friend, Dr Jones of Lutterworth, an experienced physician, to sleep in the same bedroom and witness his death agonies. Nor would he have dared to rob Cook of the Shrewsbury winnings when Dr Jones was aware of their exact value and when Cook, being perfectly conscious, would have complained to him if Dr Palmer had stolen his hoard.

Upon Newton's testifying that the Doctor asked him one day to describe the effect of strychnine on a dog and say whether its presence in the stomach could afterwards be detected—though having himself, as the Prosecution showed, a precise knowledge of poisons, whereas Newton was young and ignorant—Serjeant Shee, who should have rejected this as an improbable fiction, made the mistake of accepting it in support of his case. The Prosecution had called George Bate (despite Serjeant Shee's protests against the irrelevance of the matter) to give evidence about Dr Palmer's attempted insurance of his life for twenty-five thousand pounds. With this witness in the box, Serjeant Shee now contended that the strychnia was bought at Hawkins's shop to poison certain dogs which, as Bate knew very well, had been worrying the Doctor's brood-mares. However Bate (or so Inspector Field privately assured us) bore a grudge against Dr Palmer for having plotted his death; and, though forced to admit that The Duchess of Kent had slipped her foal, pretended ignorance that the same thing had also happened to Goldfinder in the previous week. He would give only artful and evasive answers to any of the questions put by Serjeant Shee, though he had been in charge of the Doctor's stables at the time of these mischances. Here is a sample of the cross-examination:

> SERJEANT SHEE: Can you give me any notion of these mares' value?
> BATE: I don't pretend to tell the value of the stock.
> SERJEANT SHEE: Do you know that one of them sold for eight hundred guineas?
> BATE: I have heard so.
> SERJEANT SHEE: Were any of them in foal shortly before or at the beginning of November?
> BATE: I cannot say. I should suppose there were some in foal.

A witness who behaved in this sullen way would have been sternly rebuked by most judges and ordered to give fair and proper answers. But the Lord Chief Justice was seen to smile; and his smile widened as Bate adroitly parried Serjeant Shee's subsequent questions.

> SERJEANT SHEE: Had any complaint been made about the dogs going into the paddock?
> BATE: I think I once said to Harry Cockayne: 'The turf seems a good deal cut up here; how is it?'
> SERJEANT SHEE: What did you see on the turf that induced you to make that observation?
> BATE: I saw it cut up, which I supposed to be the horses' feet, for they couldn't cut it up without they galloped.
> SERJEANT SHEE: Did you attribute that to anything?
> BATE: Why, yes, I attributed it to the mares' galloping about. [*Laughter.*]
> SERJEANT SHEE: Had you any reason to think they had been run by dogs?
> BATE: I never saw any dog run them.

This was no answer to the question, but it much amused the Lord Chief Justice. The exchange continued:

> SERJEANT SHEE: Did Harry Cockayne keep a gun in the stable?
> BATE: I have seen one there.
> SERJEANT SHEE: Did he keep a gun, which belonged to his master, for any purpose?
> BATE: I have seen a gun at the paddock.

SERJEANT SHEE: Did it belong to the master?

BATE: I cannot say.

SERJEANT SHEE: Did you ever see it used?

BATE: No.

SERJEANT SHEE: Was it in a condition to be
used?

BATE: I never had it in my hands to examine it.

In the end, Bate stood down without admitting that Dr Palmer
had complained about the hounds, or threatened to poison them,
or ordered Harry Cockayne to use the gun. According to Harry's belief, Bate had himself revengefully introduced hounds into
the paddock; and Harry, if called, could at least have testified to
the hounds and the gun. His sworn deposition concerning them,
made at the inquest, lay before both the Lord Chief Justice and
the Attorney-General. But though Serjeant Shee counted on
cross-examining Harry, whom the Prosecution had subpoenaed
as a witness, he found himself checkmated. The Crown lawyers
kept Harry under their thumb, yet never put him in the witness
box; and, as soon as the case for the Prosecution was over, smuggled him out of Court and away to Staffordshire, where Captain
Hatton told him to lie low if he knew what was for his advantage.

Serjeant Shee lost two other important witnesses—one of them
being Will Saunders, the trainer from Hednesford. When the
Grand Jury held the inquest at Stafford, Saunders had deposed on
oath that Cook sent for him, on the Monday afternoon, thirty-six
hours before his death, gave him ten pounds on account of a £41.6s.
debt, and excused himself for not paying the remainder—because
of having handed Dr Palmer all his cash to settle urgent business
affairs in London. This evidence, collusive though it may well have
been, would have decidedly weakened the Crown's case that the
Doctor had stolen Cook's money. The Crown lawyers, therefore,

engaged Saunders to give evidence on their behalf, refrained from calling him, and then packed him off out of Serjeant Shee's reach.

The third important witness was a man by the name of All-spice, who drove Dr Palmer in a fly from Stafford to Rugeley on the critical Monday evening—the evening when Newton stated that, about nine o'clock, he had freely presented Dr Palmer with three grains of strychnine. Allspice would have been ready to swear that the train reached Stafford at eight forty-five; that the Doctor engaged him at The Junction Hotel for the drive to Rugeley; that, on arrival there, at ten minutes past ten, Dr Palmer had gone straight to The Talbot Arms, where Jeremiah Smith was anxiously awaiting him; and had then, after a brief visit to the hotel, returned, paid the fare, and walked away with Smith in the direction of The Yard. Had this been proved, the Crown must needs have abandoned the charge that Dr Palmer was given the strychnia at nine o'clock; took it to his surgery, made it up into pills and, at about half-past ten, administered these to Cook in place of Dr Bamford's prescription.

Two letters on this point are extant, written by Dr Palmer from Newgate Gaol where he was being kept during the trial, to Jeremiah Smith. We copy them here verbatim:

Dear Jerry,

No man in the world ever committed a grosser case of Perjury than that vile wretch Newton—he positively swore last Friday 16 May, that he let me have 3 grs. of Strychnine the Monday before Cook's death and that I went to Mr Salt's surgery for it, and got it from him at 9 o'clock.

It is a base lie, for I left London on that very night at 5 o'clock by Express and arrived at Stafford at 10 minutes to 9, brought a Fly from the Junction and arrived at Rugeley at Masters' door about 10 o'clock.

Now, as there is a God in Heaven (I am sure you can't have forgotten it) you know that you were waiting for my coming and when I got out of the Fly you told me that my Mother wanted to see me particularly, and after bidding Cook good-night we walked together down to The Yard and got a good brushing from the Old Lady about a writ of Brown's that Arminshaw had sent for; that Arminshaw told to George, and George to my Mother—and if you recollect she was very cross.

We then walked back to my house and you said: 'Well, let me have a glass of spirit.' I went to the cupboard and there was none—you said: 'Never mind,' and bid me good-night. This must have been after 11 o'clock—now I should like to know how I could get to Mr Salt's shop at 9 o'clock on that night? You can also prove this truth, that Cook dined with me (and you) at my house on the Friday before his death and that we had a quantity of wine. Cook then went with you and had a glass of Brandy and Water—and that he was then the worse for liquor. You can further prove that Cook handed me some money on this day, for he told you so in my presence when he gave you the £10. He told you at the same time I had won over £1000 on his mare at Shrewsbury, and lastly you can prove that he and I betted for each other, that we owned 'Pyrrhine' jointly, and that we had had bill transactions together. These are solemn truths and I am fully persuaded that they cannot have escaped your memory.

Therefore let it be your most bounden duty to come forward and place yourself in the witness box and on your oath speak these great truths. Then rest assured you will lie down on a downy pillow and get to sleep happy.

Bear in mind I only want the truth. I ask for no more.

Yours faithfully,

WM PALMER

P.S. Newton no doubt calculated upon my coming by the
luggage train, but this had been discontinued more than a
month—thus my reason for going to Stafford.

Dear Jerry,

Do, for God's sake, tell the Truth—if you will only consider I am sure you will recollect meeting me at Masters'
steps that night, Monday the 19th of Nov. I returned from
London and you told me my Mother wanted to see me. I
replied: 'Have you seen Cook? And how is he?' You said:
'No.' I then said: 'Let us go upstairs and see him.' We did
do so. When upstairs Cook said: 'Doctor, you are late! Mr
Bamford has sent me two pills which I have taken.' And he
said to you: 'Damn you, Jerry, how is it you have never been
to see me?' You replied that you had been busy all the day
settling Mr Ingram's affairs and we then wished him good-
night and went to my Mother's.

Yours ever faithfully,

WM PALMER

Jeremiah Smith did, indeed, vouch for these facts under oath
when called by the Defence.

The Crown lawyers played much the same trick with Allspice
as with Cockayne and Saunders, though they did not subpoena
him. They merely arranged for his temporary dismissal from The
Junction Hotel, and his employment by Mr Bergen of the Rural
Constabulary in a remote situation. Serjeant Shee dared not accuse
the Attorney-General of sharp practice in spiriting away his witnesses, because to do so and thus, by inference, reproach the Lord
Chief Justice of condoning a felonious act, would have ruined him
professionally. Shee was aiming at a judgeship, and had perforce to
swallow his discomfiture. As it was, the Lord Chief Justice rebuked

him pretty sharply for a delay of ten minutes in producing another of his witnesses and, we may be certain, would not have waited until Saunders, Cockayne, and Allspice had been routed out and, despite all the efforts made by the Stafford Constabulary to detain them, brought up to London from the Midlands.

Now, if anyone asks us: 'Do you really believe that Mr Stevens, a retired merchant of modest fortune, was powerful enough to force these extraordinary and disgraceful tactics on Messrs Chubb, Dean & Chubb, the Crown lawyers?' we shall unhesitatingly answer 'No, Sir!' But to the next question: 'Whom, then, do you suspect?' we shall reply with all possible circumspection, as follows: 'The jurymen were warned before the trial began that, if any of them happened to be shareholders of certain powerful insurance companies, they must retire as interested parties. But what of the Crown lawyers? Has anyone dared inquire into their impartiality? If Dr Palmer had been found innocent of poisoning Cook (as the Stafford Grand Jury found him innocent of poisoning his brother Walter), would not the companies have been liable in consequence to pay the Doctor the thirteen thousand pounds of Walter's life insurance? And what of the Stafford Police? Are none of them venal?'

We will, however, say no more, for fear of libel, but simply invite our questioner to decide whether it is impossible that representatives of the insurance companies privately acquainted Messrs Chubb, Dean & Chubb, and Captain Hatton, with their strong interest in the prisoner's condemnation.

It is perhaps a not very remarkable circumstance that the judges, the Lord Mayor, the Sheriffs, the aldermen and (we are told) the jury, the majority of them, were united in a fond love of the Turf. We believe that most loyal Turfites would feel a hundred times less aggrieved with a man who garotted a fellow-criminal, an unwanted child, or an ailing relative, than with one who poisoned race-horses—as Dr Palmer was suspected of doing. The Doctor's reputation at Tattersall's was bad enough to condemn him for any crime charged against him: from petty larceny to high treason; and if Serjeant Shoe had pleaded that his client bought the strychnia from Messrs Hawkins for the purpose of poisoning one of the Earl of M——'s, or the Duke of D——'s swiftest and noblest horses, such a plea would necessarily have been construed as an invitation: 'Pray hang this villain!' Be that as it may, a tacit agreement was reached over the nightly turtle-soup and pineapples consumed at the Guildhall during the trial, that no person of honour could dare support Dr Palmer, even in the name of abstract justice; for surely a man capable of doctoring a gallant thoroughbred would not hesitate an instant before murdering a score of plebeian bipeds? To poison foxhounds was an equally grave crime; and this explains why Serjeant Shee respected the feelings of all good foxhunters in Court by referring to 'the dogs' in his cross-examination of George Bate, as though they were not foxhounds, and therefore sacrosanct, but common and savage mongrels!

Alderman Sidney was hardly to be envied: as the sole Rugeley man present in that distinguished gathering, and one whose father had opposed the Lord Chief Justice, then Mr John Campbell, when he stood for Parliament as member for Stafford in 1830. Being suspected of partisanship, the alderman must needs dissociate himself absolutely from Dr Palmer—the son of his former patron, old Joseph Palmer, the sawyer—as the vilest of vile men, wholly untypical of Rugeley; and whimper more excitedly on his trail than the Attorney-General himself. This prejudice against the prisoner supplied seats in Court, by order of Lord Campbell, to all the medical witnesses whom the Crown called; whereas those called for the Defence, however highly they might rank professionally, must stand meekly in the crowded aisles, day after day, during the eight or nine hours of the hearing!

Here we may mention that the book bought by Hawkins at Dr Palmer's sale, and produced at the trial, was a work entitled *Manual for Students Preparing for Examination at Apothecaries' Hall.* It contained a pencilled note, evidently written in his student days: 'Strychnine kills by causing a tetanic fixing of the respiratory muscles.' The Attorney-General insisted that he attached no great value to this note; but did so in an apologetic manner which left a directly opposite impression on the minds of the jurymen.

It came as a general surprise that two further witnesses for the Defence were missing: namely Eliza Tharm, who could have sworn that Dr Palmer did not make up the pills on that Monday evening in the surgery between nine and ten-thirty; and old Mrs Palmer, whom he had visited in Jeremiah Smith's company at about ten-fifteen. We have already shown why Mrs Palmer's tongue was tied: the Prosecution would have put in the shamelessly lascivious letters she had written to Cornelius Duffy, and represented her as a woman of bad character.

Let Eliza Tharm tell in her own words, as she told us, why her tongue was likewise tied.

ELIZA THARM

When dear Mrs Annie Palmer died, the Doctor was so broken in spirit that I felt exceedingly sorry. Indeed, I loved him with all my heart, and gave him all I had to give. He used to call me his 'little missus', and treated me very sweetly, though he said he was not as yet in a position to make me his wife. Race-going took him away a deal; and that he slept with other girls I knew—for example, one Jenny Mumford, whom he got with child and had to buy off. But that he loved me best, I knew also; and he gave me his solemn promise not to go with any that had a nasty disease.

Well, among his friends was a Miss Bergen, supposed to be a respectable girl, who had written some very randy letters, inviting him into her bed. Says I: 'Doctor, don't mind me! When you're over at Stafford with Mr Walter and can't get back home to my arms, well, I know how you hate sleeping alone . . .'

So he kissed me and called me an angel, for he knew what I meant.

'But mind,' I told him, 'I don't want to hear about what you and she do together! It might make me jealous.'

The Doctor comes to me one day in a great pother. 'Lizzie, my duck,' he says, 'I'm in trouble with that Stafford girl. She's in pod and wants for to make me her husband. But I promised you that I wouldn't marry anyone save your little self; so here you'll have to advise me.'

'It's no business of mine, Doctor,' says I. 'Do as you think fit.'

Well, he wrote to Miss Bergen, giving the name of an abortionist who would be as silent as the grave; and the baby was turned away, with nobody none the wiser. But when she wrote that her 'stomach ache', as she called it, had got better, the cold tones of his answer warned her she had no hope of becoming Mrs Palmer. So Miss Bergen threatened to show her father the letters he had written. Now, that was serious, because he was none other than Mr Daniel Scully Bergen, Chief Superintendent of the Stafford Rural Constabulary! First she demanded a hundred pounds for their return, and then fifty; but in the end she settled for forty, and he gave her the halves of four ten-pound notes, undertaking to send the others when all the letters were safe in his hands. The money he paid her was part of the sum that he had from Mr Cook to settle bills owing in London. Well, when Captain Hatton made the arrest, Dr Palmer called me and said privately: 'Lizzie, pray do me a service. Take this packet to Miss Bergen. In it are the other halves of those four ten-pound notes. They're no good to me, and I'd rather keep my word even to a bad woman.'

So I went, and right glad I am that I did, as it turned out.

You may know that when they took him away, he gave me a fif-. ty-pound note, all the money he had, bless his kind soul! Captain Hatton tried to take it from me, but I wouldn't give it up. He says: 'Mr Stevens has a list of the numbers of all the ten-pound and fifty-pound notes paid to Mr Cook at Shrewsbury, and this will be one of them. It's wanted as evidence.'

The Doctor turns very coolly to Captain Hatton and says: 'I think you'll be wise to leave Miss Eliza in possession of the note.'

'And why, may I ask?' the Captain wants to know.

'I'll tell you why,' Dr Palmer answers. 'The money was entrusted to me by Mr Cook, not stolen from him and, with his consent, I sent four of the ten-pound notes to pay off a young lady who has been blackmailing me because of some foolish letters I wrote her.'

'That's no concern of mine,' says the Captain.

'By your leave, Sir, it should be,' retorts the Doctor. 'The young lady is the daughter of a colleague of yours; and the letters show that she wanted the money to pay for an illegal operation.'

At this point I break into the conversation: 'Yes, Captain Hatton,' I says, 'it's true. I brought her the other halves of the notes—for the Doctor had sent only half-notes to make sure she'd play fair—and watched while she gummed them together and went to change them at the bank. The bank clerks, they'll have taken the numbers, I've no doubt, and the notes can be traced to her.'

This piece of news seemed to dismay the Captain, so I went on: 'Come, Sir, your hand on the bargain! You leave me with this fifty-pound note, which I'll change at the same bank, and trust me to keep silent.'

'Nobody would believe a word of what you say, you common slut,' Captain Hatton shouts. 'Now, just for that,' says I, quiet but very vexed, 'I've a good mind to do what I first thought of doing, which is to sell the young lady's blackmailing letters to *The Illustrated Times*. I could get another fifty pounds for them quite easy.'

'Where are they?' the Captain asks threateningly.

'Ah, wouldn't you like to know?' I answers, laughing in his face, I was so emboldened by rage.

The Captain grins back at me and says: 'You're a smart lass.' Then we shake hands on our bargain. But he turns to the Doctor and growls: 'This smart trick of yours isn't going to help you, Palmer!'

The Doctor answers, most polite: 'I trust that you'll do nothing dishonourable, Captain Hatton. The Stafford Constabulary have a high reputation for fair dealing, you know.'

CHAPTER XXI

IF DOCTORS DISAGREE

We refer our readers to *The Times's* verbatim report for details of the plentiful and complicated medical evidence offered. Dr Bamford, suffering (curiously enough) from English cholera, the very disease to which he had attributed the late Annie Palmer's death, was unable to attend the trial, but made a sworn statement to the effect that the antimony which Professor Alfred Taylor found in Cook's organs had not been prescribed by himself in the form of tartar emetic.

So far, so good; then the egregious Professor Taylor mounted into the witness box. He had at first diagnosed antimony as the cause of death, though discovering only half a grain, which is no more than most of us healthy modern men carry about in our vitals, without trouble or hazard. He conveyed this opinion to Mr Gardiner in the letter which Cheshire, the Rugeley Postmaster, intercepted and opened at Dr Palmer's request; but hearing then that Cook had been overcome by a convulsion shortly before he died, and that Dr Palmer had bought the strychnia from Messrs Hawkins's shop, the Professor changed his mind. Death, he now decided, must have resulted from strychnine poisoning, because the human body can absorb up to sixty grains of antimony and suffer no fatal consequences. To us this seems a *non sequitur*. As a wag has put it:

> In antimony, great though his faith, The quantity found
>   being small,
> Taylor's faith in strychnine was yet greater, For of that
>   he found nothing at all.

When Professor Taylor laid stress on this negative evidence, the Lord Chief Justice remarked, with a challenging look at Serjeant Shee: 'Of course, upon this the whole defence rests.' Since it had yet to be proved that Cook did not die of natural causes, the absence of strychnia in the organs examined struck many judicious persons as a most feasible defence! But Professor Taylor led the hanging-party with the contention: 'Though no strychnia was found, it would be very improper to believe that none had been administered.' 'Then why trouble to analyze for strychnia?' some asked, 'if its presence and its absence may alike point to its having caused death?' Others remembered the Professor's strange message, unwarrantably presuming murder, which he addressed to a daily newspaper some weeks before the trial: 'Society demands a victim in this case!' They commented: 'We may legitimately doubt whether Dr Palmer fell a victim to the demands of society in general, rather than to those of the race-horse owners whom he had dishonoured, and the insurance-company shareholders whom he had defrauded. But certain it is that British Justice has likewise fallen a victim.'

The Professor's admission on his *volte-face* deserves particular scrutiny. A plain question was put to him: 'Can you say upon your oath that, from the *traces* of antimony found in Cook's body, you were justified in concluding death to have been caused by this poison?' He answered: 'Yes, perfectly and distinctly.' We fail to see what sophistical process can divest so direct, so positive, and so unqualified a statement of its simple meaning. Professor Taylor *did* believe that Cook died from the effects of antimony;

and he arrived at that belief not merely from finding slight traces of the poison in Cook's remains, but from the reports given him of Cook's vomitings and convulsions. Then, when a new light shone within, and the claims of strychnia made him a renegade, his rational powers were severely taxed to satisfy the needs of this sudden change. He knew well that the healthiness of Cook's brain was quite inconsistent with strychnine poisoning; and that so was the length of time—one and a half hours—between the alleged administration of the strychnine pills and the tetanic paroxysms. Yet, for the jury, his total conversion from antimony to strychnia seemed a proof that here was an honest man who cheerfully admitted former error.

Let us now briefly summarize and compare some of the theories and views held by the medical witnesses.

Dr Monckton's *post-mortem* examination of Cook's spinal cord revealed the presence of certain granules, which he read as indicating organic disease. Dr Devonshire and Dr Harland, it appears, had discounted them during the preliminary examination; and at the trial several shades of opinion marked the medical evidence on 'this head. For instance, Dr Todd, physician at King's College Hospital, asserted that such granules would be unlikely to produce tetanus; while Professor Partridge, who lectures on anatomy at the same College, quoted cases where they had heralded fatal attacks of tetanus. Professor Nunnely of the Leeds School of Medicine, Dr Macdonald of the Royal College of Surgeons at Edinburgh, and Dr Robinson of the Newcastle-on-Tyne Fever Hospital, confidently supported Professor Partridge. Other doctors, however, saw in the granules no sufficient cause to produce either tetanus or death.

Dr Todd held that the state of a person suffering from tetanus is identical with that induced by strychnine poisoning—an opinion roundly rejected by all other witnesses for the Crown. Dr Harland remarked that, though he found the spinal cord softened, this condition would not cause tetanus; and, so far as he knew, no disease of the spinal cord could do so. Then young, plain-speaking Mr Devonshire declared that tetanic convulsions *do* result from derangements of the spinal cord; but was dismissed by Mr Baron Alderson as an ignoramus. Sir Benjamin Brodie, no less skilled a physician than he is cautious of his opinions, would not commit himself here; and Professor Alfred Taylor, though holding that strychnia acts on the spinal cord, also seemed to be in the dark on this subject.

Nor was there agreement about muscular rigidity after death. Dr Monckton stated that Cook's muscles were not more rigid than is usual; Dr Francis Taylor of Romsey, that distortion from rigidity *generally* continues when death has supervened; Professor Taylor, that it *sometimes* does. Professor Nunnely related that, in two cases of strychnine poisoning which had come to his attention, there was no such rigidity.

That epileptic convulsions *occasionally* assume tetanic features was a doctrine held by Dr Jones of Lutterworth and others; Dr Macdonald, Dr Robinson, and Dr Richardson (a London physician) concurred in saying that this is *invariably* the case.

Cook had suffered from locked-jaw, according to Elizabeth Mills's new evidence; but locked-jaw, as a primary symptom of tetanus, was another dogma that invited dispute. Nearly all cases commence with locked-jaw, said Dr Curling, Surgeon to the London Hospital; and Dr Todd agreed that it is an early symptom; but Dr Macdonald contradicted all his colleagues by testifying that locked-jaw is generally a *late* symptom.

Cook had suffered from an ulcerated throat, and that ulcerations cause tetanus was yet another theory productive of no little discord. Dr Curling quoted two such cases from the records of the London Hospital; Sir Benjamin Brodie, however, had never heard of tetanus proceeding from ulcers or sores.

Opinion was also divided on the question of Cook's heart, which had contained no blood. Dr Todd observed that the heart is rarely full after death by strychnine poisoning. Sir Benjamin Brodie could not say whether it would be full or not. Dr Morley asserted that it is generally very full.

Cook had shrieked on the Sunday night. Shrieking, as a special symptom accompanying attacks of convulsions, found no greater identity of views.

Cook had remained conscious to the end. Dr Solly, of St Thomas's Hospital, stated that epileptic convulsions are not always attended with want of consciousness; Professor Nunnely agreed with him. Dr Robinson and others, on the contrary, asserted that consciousness is lost in almost every instance.

What do we learn from *The Times* report on the subject of paroxysms and the several causes that stimulate them? Dr Corbett, the Glasgow physician, denies that touching produces paroxysms in cases of strychnine poisoning. Dr Morley of Leeds asserts that they *are* so induced. Professors Taylor and Letheby, opposed on so many points, agree that the very slightest touch or exertion induces paroxysms, and that the symptoms of strychnine poisoning are: irritability, aversion to touch, noise, light, or currents of cool air; also dilated pupils, with continuous twitchings and jerkings. But the intolerance to touch, they say, is the truly diagnostic, the leading symptom, and touch invariably produces paroxysms. Yet Cook had rung the bell, and suffered no paroxysm in consequence. He had, moreover, invited Dr Jones to rub his neck; and Dr Bamford deposed to having gently applied his hand to Cook's abdomen without occasioning the least discomfort or paroxysm.

'Asphyxia,' Dr Curling rules, 'does not produce death in these cases.' Professor Taylor states exactly the opposite. Dr Todd here differs from Professor Taylor, and supports Dr Curling. Professor

Christison of Edinburgh University thinks that death *may* arise from asphyxia, but leaves the question open.

Cook's attacks, which in each case occurred at midnight, after a day comfortably spent, were attributed by some doctors to tetanus. Drs Todd and Watson hold that the symptoms of tetanus are intermittent; Professor Christison and Sir Benjamin Brodie insist that they are continuous.

On the question of what immediately caused death, we find a grand *melée* of disputants. Their arguments and counterarguments fog every uninitiated mind, and damp all hope of reaching a just verdict. We are left with one consolation only—that we never ourselves won a professorship in a science offering facilities for such profound discord!

That Cook died of strychnine poisoning is affirmed by Professors Taylor, Brodie, Rees, and Christison; and Drs Todd, Daniel and Solly. Here are seven eminences on one side. That Cook died of some other cause is affirmed by Professors Rodgers (of the St George's School of Medicine), Partridge, Letheby, Herapath, and Nunnely; also by Drs Macdonald, Robinson, Bamford, Jones, Bainbridge of St Martin's Work House, and Richardson of, we believe, Stepney. Thus eleven eminences range themselves in opposition. Eleven more venture no opinion at all.

The jury perhaps drew inspiration from the modern proverb 'The minority are always in the right', for to make any choice based on a clear perception that the seven strychnine-minded doctors had incontestably proved their case, leaving the eleven champions of natural causes to wander in the illusive moonshine of gratuitous speculation, was as far beyond the power of this stolid jury as it was to raise John Parsons Cook from the dead. Yet somehow the Lord Chief Justice expected the atmosphere of science, murky from the vapours of twenty-nine discursive intellects, to be irradiated and resolved into a pure sky of truth by the miraculous intervention of twelve respectable traders!

In what way were the opinions of the Crown's medical witnesses to be judged sounder than those held by the opposite side? Not one of the seven had ever seen a single case of strychnine poisoning in the human subject—some had never even witnessed an experiment on animal life—and several confessed to but very limited experience of simple tetanus. Yet no less than three of the medical witnesses called by the Defence had been present at numerous *post-mortem* examinations, where death had been admittedly due to strychnia. Professor Nunnely, the target of so much of the Attorney-General's abuse and the victim of the Lord Chief Justice's privileged, courteous insults, had made *post-mortem* examinations of two persons carried off by this poison; had experimented with strychnine on forty animals; and with other poisons on two thousand more; thus claiming a body of experimental research one hundredfold greater than that possessed by all the other doctors and professors together. Nevertheless, his evidence was spoken of by the Prosecution in terms well calculated to excite contempt.

Professors Taylor and Rees, called for the Crown, pronounced that the fiftieth part of a grain of strychnia cannot be detected. Yet Professor Herapath of the Bristol Medical School, and Professor Letheby, Medical Officer of Health to the City of London, stated for the Defence that the fifty-thousandth part can!

Professor Taylor's testimony was, without doubt, the mainspring acting so powerfully on the minds of the jury. Some twenty-three years ago, he had experimented with strychnia on twelve wild rabbits—'which is the only personal knowledge that I have of strychnia, as it affects animal life'—but had never seen any human being exposed to its influence. And 'though I met a case of tetanus in the human subject years ago, I have not had much experience in such matters.' He constantly failed to detect the presence of strychnia after poisoning animals, even when the dose was as much as a grain and a half; and had never thought to conduct experiments on dogs or cats, though they resemble man far more closely in that they vomit, whereas rabbits do not. Professor Taylor has published *The Principles and Practice of Medical Jurisprudence*—in part a treatise on poisons—and there one may find listed experimental facts and the reports of several deaths by strychnia. But none of this is the product of his own research—the Professor's light shines with borrowed rays, like the deceptive Moon.

Of Sir Benjamin Brodie little need or can be said. Though he had considerable experience of tetanus, he also excelled in tact and avoided any positive statement that could contradict other people's opinions, qualifying his evidence with such phrases as 'according to my knowledge', 'so far as I have seen', 'at least so it has been in my experience', 'I believe I remember cases'—and so forth. He took the safe course of a man who, being himself benighted, will not pretend to set a neighbour's foot on the right path. But Professor Taylor's forthright evidence was even at variance with itself. In reply to the question: 'Were the symptoms and appearances in Cook's case the same as those you have observed in the animals which you poisoned with strychnia?' he declared: 'They were.' Yet he had repeatedly laid down that no prognosis of the symptoms likely to ensue from the human consumption of strychnia can rest on those observed in lower animals similarly poisoned; so that even his youthful experiments with rabbits were irrelevant here.

To quote a tithe of the evidence on the above subjects would protract our comment far beyond convenient limits. Indeed, we find so much that is criticizable in the evidence, the addresses of Counsel, and the charge to the jury, that our own patience as well as that of our readers would soon suffer exhaustion. However, a letter written to *The Times* by F. Crage Calvert, Esq., F.C.C., a Cheshire chemist, about his discovery of strychnia in the bodies of several wilfully poisoned hounds—at least three weeks after death—convinces us that Professor Taylor's theory of 'perfect absorption' is quite fallacious. So does another written to the same newspaper by Professor Herapath, the greatest analytic chemist now alive among us, whom the Attorney-General browbeat and flustered during the trial. He once found strychnia in a fox dead for over two months.

How Professor Herapath came to be subpoenaed by the Prosecution is a curious story. According to an anonymous letter received by the Crown lawyers from Keynsham in Somersetshire, the Professor had publicly declared: 'I have no doubt that there was strychnia in Cook's body, but Professor Taylor could not find it.' Professor Herapath was known to be at loggerheads with Professor Taylor, whom he looked upon as an ignorant theorist, and seems to have incautiously made some such remark to Mr Twining, the Mayor of Bristol, and a party of his friends. It was, however, based on partial newspaper accounts of the case, including a most inaccurate one printed by *The Illustrated Times*. This anonymous letter also reported him as saying: 'A word from me would hang that man!'—yet the remark was, in effect, made by Mr Twining. The Attorney-General eagerly seized on Professor Herapath's observation which he had read as meaning that strychnine might evade the analysis of even the most experienced analyst; whereas, in truth, the Professor had merely referred to Professor Taylor's incompetence. At the trial, the Attorney-General realized his mistake, and was skilful enough to repair it with Pharisaic ingenuity by entangling Professor Herapath in his talk.

If we may give our studied opinion for what it is worth, founding it upon that of Mr John Robinson, the well-known lecturer on Medical Jurisprudence, and others, equally distinguished, we will say that the sore on Cook's body—where, according to the evidence, excoriation of a syphilitic scar had been rubbed off—was well capable of inducing tetanus, especially in one who frequented stables; for stables breed the disease. To this we will, however, add that the nightly recurrence of Cook's attacks rather suggests an obscure nervous disorder—'epileptic convulsions with tetanic symptoms', as Dr Bamford called it—which, in his weakened state, Cook could not resist. Dr Palmer, in all probability; had assisted this weakness, for a felonious object, possibly by introducing tartar emetic into Cook's toast- and-water; but never, we are convinced, did he foresee or desire that it should have a fatal ending.

It may be objected that epilepsy seldom makes its first appearance in mature persons and that, if Cook had previously experienced epileptic seizures, this fact would surely have come out in the trial. But such epileptic seizures as occur only late at night, when the patient is suffering from gastric disturbances, or has worked himself up to an anxious frame of mind, often escape general remark; and if Dr Jones, a capable physician and Cook's country neighbour, diagnosed epilepsy, he must have suspected a proneness to this unusual disorder. The suggestion that Dr Palmer procured three grains, and then another six grains of strychnia— in his own home town, too—for the purpose of murdering his friend, afterwards adjusting the dose so nicely as to leave no vestige of the crime—this seems to us one of the most far-fetched that we have ever heard.

CHAPTER XXII

THE VERDICT

Many incidents in this trial, we confess, surprised us unpleasantly. Mr Baron Alderson, who shared Lord Chief Justice Campbell's partiality for the Prosecution, made even less attempt to conceal it, and frequently amused himself by suggesting questions to Mr James, Q.C., the Counsel for the Crown. He would raise his hands in feigned astonishment if evidence favourable to Dr Palmer was elicited by cross-examination; stare at the jury with a look of incredulity and contempt if Serjeant Shee called attention to such evidence; and assist the Lord Chief Justice in over-ruling almost every legal objection raised by the Defence. Once, when Serjeant Shee asked a medical witness: 'Where are the pathionic glands?' Mr Baron Alderson started angrily from his seat and exclaimed in loud tones: 'Humbug!' To another similar question he answered for the witness: 'You will find that in any Encyclopaedia.'

By contrast, Mr Justice Cresswell Cresswell, who had been educated, like Mr Baron Alderson, at the Charterhouse and Cambridge, comported himself with dignity and strict impartiality. It was clear that, but for his intervention at many important points, the Lord Chief Justice would have admitted illegal evidence against Dr Palmer, or excluded evidence operating in his favour. When, on one occasion, Mr Justice Cresswell respectfully addressed Serjeant

Shee as 'Brother Shee', Mr Baron Alderson's impatient ejaculation: 'O, bother Shee!' was heard by everyone present.

The Lord Chief Justice first showed his prejudice by allowing the Attorney-General to acquaint the jury with the story of Bate's life insurance, while omitting circumstances which Samuel Cheshire, or Jeremiah Smith, or Dr Palmer himself—who, by a quirk of British legal procedure, must keep silent throughout the trial, whatever falsehoods might be told—could have supplied in extenuation. Dr Palmer, let it be observed, had never been granted the privilege of stating his case from any witness box, or before any public authorities whatsoever. Serjeant Shee strongly objected to this evidence about the insurance as irrelevant, and it was excluded, but too late for the true facts to appear. Thus the black impression remained fixed in the minds of the jurymen: 'Dr Palmer attempted to take George Bate's life; as he had already taken those of his own wife and, perhaps, his brother.'

Again, it is a first principle of our Law that nothing which has been said while a prisoner was absent may be quoted in evidence against him. Yet the Lord Chief Justice allowed the Prosecution to prove a talk between Mr Cook and Fisher, held in Dr Palmer's absence when the latter had no means of contradicting Cook's drunken suspicions of the brandy. It seems that Mr Justice Cresswell noted the impropriety, because he later interposed at this point in the Lord Chief Justice's summing up and prevented him from reading to the jury evidence which should never have been given. Yet the passage had produced a decisive influence on their minds, and blinded them to the fact that Cook later went to Rugeley with Dr Palmer, dined at his house, constantly sent for him, made no mention of any 'dosing' to Dr Jones, his closest friend and his physician, and kept an affectionate faith in Dr Palmer until death carried him off.

Serjeant Shee objected time after time to Mr James's illegal questions, but the Lord Chief Justice over-ruled him so constantly that at last he told Mr John Smith, Dr Palmer's solicitor: 'I dare not object further.'

John Smith replied: 'This, Sir, is an organized conspiracy to hang our client; and so I suspected from our correspondence with the Crown solicitors. You will remember how we failed to extract a report from them as to Professor Taylor's analytic methods. They refused my demand, and were supported by Sir George Grey at the Home Office, who stated that it was an unprecedented one, and that these matters would doubtless appear in cross- examination. I answered that the case was equally unprecedented, this being the first in which strychnia had been cited as a means of murder; and respectfully denied that Professor Taylor's analyses could form a proper subject of cross-examination, unless they were duly recorded in writing and the depositions read to the judges and the jury. Nevertheless, Sir George brushed me off. Yes, Sir, Mr James's questions are inadmissible, as every member of the Bar knows well; but what remedy have we?'

Mrs Brooks's testimony that she had seen Dr Palmer holding up a tumbler of water against the gas-light at The Raven Hotel was not unfavourable to the Doctor; for she had also deposed that many other people in Shrewsbury, whom Dr Palmer could not possibly have dosed, suffered from the same sickness as Cook. Yet in his summing up the Lord Chief Justice failed to remind the jury of this important fact.

When Herring, the commission agent, known on the Turf as 'Mr Howard', was examined, and the Prosecution wished him to reveal the contents of Cook's betting-book, Serjeant Shee objected: 'We cannot have this given in evidence, my Lord, since the book is lost.'

The Lord Chief Justice, gazing sternly at Serjeant Shee, said: 'According to the last account we heard, it was in the prisoner's possession.'

Serjeant Shee replied with a reproachful cough: 'My Lord, I don't think there is any proof of his ever having touched it.'

Here the Attorney-General interrupted: 'We will show that it lay in the dead man's room on the Tuesday night before his death, and that the prisoner was afterwards observed looking about . . .'

Yet nobody at The Talbot Arms Hotel claimed to have seen the book later than the Monday night, when Elizabeth Mills noticed it hanging from the mirror.

Nor did the Lord Chief Justice point out the patent discrepancy between a statement promised from Elizabeth Mills by the Attorney-General; namely, that she handed Cook's cup of coffee, ordered on the Monday morning, to Dr Palmer (who therefore had an opportunity of doctoring it); and the statement which she actually made, namely that she gave it directly to Cook. He also withheld comment on the even graver discrepancy pointed out by Serjeant Shee between her statements at the inquest and at the trial. Whereas she had told the Coroner that the broth tasted very good, and mentioned no harmful after-effect, her new story was that she had been seized by violent vomiting which incapacitated her for five hours. Moreover, her original deposition contained no reference to the twitchings and jerkings which she now described with much pantomimic by-play.

It was noted, too, that the Lord Chief Justice eulogized all the medical witnesses called for the Crown and allotted seats in Court; while seeming to regard all witnesses for the Defence as ignoble or inferior beings since, by his own orders, they were condemned to stand. Some of these he offered undeserved disrespect, and applauded only one, Dr Wrightson of Birmingham, whose evidence lent some slight support to Professor Taylor's theories. His recommendation of Sir Benjamin Brodie went: 'The jury will take into consideration the solemn opinion of this distinguished medical man: that he never knew a case in which the symptoms he has heard described arose from any disease. He has witnessed the various diseases that afflict the human frame in all their multiplicity, and he knows of no natural disease such as will answer the symptoms which he has heard described in the case of Cook; and, if death did not arise from natural disease, then the inference is that it arose from other causes.'

The alleged cause was, of course, strychnine poisoning. Now, Sir Benjamin Brodie based his solemn opinion on two irreconcilable statements: the first made by Elizabeth Mills—who was proved to have greatly enlarged and embroidered on the evidence she gave at the inquest—and the other by Dr Jones of Lutterworth, whose evidence had remained unchanged. If what Elizabeth Mills swore was all true, and if Sir Benjamin was omniscient, then the Lord Chief Justice might have been justified in saying that Cook's symptoms accorded with no known disease, and that strychnine might therefore be suspected—except that neither did some of the symptoms reported coincide with those expected from strychnine poisoning. On the other hand, if Elizabeth Mills lied, then the description of Cook's death as given by Dr Jones, a trained medical practitioner, became perfectly consistent with natural disease. This is to say: if Mr Stevens and Mr Gardiner had influenced Miss Mills by culling a number of symptoms from the recent case of Mrs Dove, who had died from strychnine, and suggesting that she had noticed them in Cook; and if she perjured herself in swearing to these; and if her evidence must be given equal value with Dr Jones's—why, then Sir Benjamin Brodie could hardly make any other reply than he did when asked the question. How could he assign the cause of Cook's death to any known disease, when most of the symptoms were fictitious and irreconcilable with the genuine ones?

Serjeant Shee made great efforts to bring out this point in cross-examining Sir Benjamin:

SERJEANT SHEE: Would you think that the description of a chambermaid, and of a provincial medical man who had seen only one case of tetanus, could be relied on to state what sort of disease Cook's was?

THE LORD CHIEF JUSTICE (*nodding wisely to the jury*): He is asked, on the assumption that *both* witnesses are

speaking the truth.

SIR BENJAMIN BRODIE (*uncomfortably*): I must say, I thought that the description was clearly given.

SERJEANT SHEE: On which of the two would you rely, supposing that they differed—the chambermaid or the medical man?

THE LORD CHIEF JUSTICE (*in injured tones*): This is hardly a proper question.

MR BARON ALDERSON: It is a proper observation for *you* to make, *Brother* Shee!

The question was, of course, disallowed. Surely it had been most properly put? If Sir Benjamin had answered that he relied on Elizabeth Mills's untrained observations, then the jury would have set the fact against their memories of certain most disingenuous answers given by this witness when questioned about her meetings with Messrs Stevens and Gardiner. If, however, Sir Benjamin had answered that he preferred Dr Jones's testimony, the inference would have been that Cook died from natural causes.

We believe that this ruling by the Lord Chief Justice did more to hang Dr Palmer than any other. Yet it is an axiom of the Law, dear to all Englishmen, that in any criminal trial, the presiding judge is 'prime counsel for the prisoner'.

Serjeant Shee's speech for the Defence was eloquent enough. He could show that Dr Palmer and Cook owned a race-horse in common; had contracted certain debts jointly; and trusted each other to lay money on horses. The brotherliness of their relations was suggested by a letter, produced in evidence, which Cook wrote Dr Palmer from Lutterworth, on January 4th, 1855.

> *My dear Sir,*
> I went up to London on Tuesday to back St Hubert for £50, and my commission has returned 10/1d. I have there-fore booked £250 to £25 against him, to gain money. There is a small balance of £10 due to you, which I forgot to give you the other day. Tell Will Saunders to debit me with it on account of your share in training Pyrrhine. I will also write asking him to do so, and there will be a balance due to him from me.
> *Yours faithfully,*
>
> J. PARSONS COOK

But Serjeant Shee attempted too much. Cheshire's and Pad-wick's testimony proved conclusively that Dr Palmer had forged Cook's signature to a paper and got for himself the money Cook won at Shrewsbury. Granted, Cook's murder could have benefited him neither in the long run nor in the short, since liabilities to the amount of twelve thousand pounds were outstanding; yet the evidence of fraud was plain. A plea that Dr Palmer had taken advantage of Cook's natural sickness to rob him would have been a safer one. Dr Palmer would, it is true, have received a very severe prison sentence in consequence; but the crime of forgery, which he had admitted on oath, already made him liable to that.

Serjeant Shee surprised the Court with a most remarkable state-ment. 'I believe,' he said, 'that truer words were never pronounced than those uttered by the prisoner when pleading "Not Guilty" to this charge. I will prove to you the sincerity with which I declare my personal conviction of his innocence—when I meet the case foot by foot.'

The Attorney-General replied: 'You have heard from my learned friend the unusual and, I may add, the unprecedented assurance of his personal faith in his client's innocence. When he made it—and I know no man in whom the spirit of truth is more keenly alive—he gave expression to what he sincerely believed. But what would he think of me if, imitating his example, I at this moment revealed to you upon my word and honour, as he did, what is my personal conviction from a meticulous review of the whole case?'

The Attorney-General could not, it seems, forget his private conversation with Frank Swindell, who had accused Dr Palmer of 'doctoring him for death' at the Wolverhampton Races.

Among the witnesses, other than medical, called for the Defence and present in Court, where George Myatt, the Rugeley saddler; John Sergeant, a racing man; and, finally, Jeremiah Smith. Myatt testified that he had been at The Raven Hotel on the night when Cook complained of the brandy, and that nobody could have doctored Cook's brandy and water without his knowledge. He also testified that a great many people fell sick at Shrewsbury Meeting, and that Dr Palmer himself had vomited violently out of the carriage window on his return to Rugeley by the six-o'clock Express. Cook, Dr Palmer, and himself had then discussed the prevalence of these symptoms and thought that the Shrewsbury water supply must have been tainted. Myatt swore that Cook had been very drunk, even before he took the brandy and water; and that Cook's words were not: 'It burns my throat dreadfully,' but: 'There's something in it.'

Sergeant testified that at the Liverpool Races, a week previously, Cook had asked him to look at his ulcered throat, and that he had made the same request on several other occasions. 'He also went to Dr Palmer,' Sergeant continued, 'and in my hearing applied for a mercurial lotion called "black wash".' From Sergeant's further evidence it seems probable that Cook's remark, 'It burns my throat dreadfully', did not refer to the brandy, but was a retrospective complaint about an injury done him at Liverpool Railway Station. Gingerbread nuts were sold on the course—some innocuous, others containing cayenne pepper—and when the races had ended Dr Palmer humorously gave Cook one of the latter sort. At The Raven, Cook drunkenly suspected Dr Palmer of dosing the brandy too—the peppered ginger-nut being still active in his memory.

Jeremiah Smith testified to Cook's not possessing enough money, after the Shrewsbury Races, to pay him more than five pounds of the £41.10s. debt due, and saying: 'I can't let you have the remainder, Jerry, because I've given most of my winnings to Palmer, but you shall be paid when I've been to Tattersall's on Monday.' Smith also testified that he had waited for Dr Palmer's return to Rugeley on the fateful Monday night, and met him at ten minutes past ten outside The Talbot Arms Hotel. Cook, whom they then visited briefly, in his bedroom, complained: 'You're late tonight, Doctor. I didn't expect you to look in. So I took Dr Bamford's pills'—the inference being that he would not have taken them, had Dr Palmer come earlier. When Cook told them both: 'I was up this afternoon talking with Saunders and Ashmole,' Dr Palmer answered: 'You oughtn't to have done that.'

Afterwards, so Jeremiah Smith testified, Dr Palmer and himself walked to The Yard, a few hundred paces away, and spent half an hour in the company of old Mrs Palmer, who had important business to discuss. He then left Dr Palmer at The Yard, and went home. As for the allegedly poisoned broth, he had sent it as a gift to Cook, who was not well enough to accept an invitation to dine; this broth being the liquor in which his own leg of mutton had been boiled at The Albion Inn. That Mrs Rowley, the cook, should take it along the street in a saucepan, to be warmed up at Dr Palmer's and there poured into the invalid-cup, was very natural, considering the distance and the state of the weather. Jeremiah Smith also testified to having once watched Ben Thirlby, Dr Palmer's assistant, dress Cook's ulcered throat with caustic.

Nevertheless, the good impression thus made on the jury was entirely swept away by the Attorney-General's cross-examination of Jeremiah Smith, on matters irrelevant to the trial. Serjeant Shee knew that any objections to these he might lodge would be vain. Indeed, Smith gave such a lamentable exhibition of cowardice that the spirit of tragedy which had for days brooded over the Old Bailey gave place, at times, to farce.

> THE ATTORNEY-GENERAL: Have you known Palmer long?
>
> SMITH: I have known him long and very intimately, and have been employed a good deal as an attorney by Palmer and his family.
>
> THE ATTORNEY-GENERAL: In December, 1854, did he apply to you, asking you to attest his brother Walter
>
> Palmer's proposal for £13,000 in The Solicitors' and General Insurance Office?
>
> SMITH: I cannot recollect; if you will let me see the document I will tell you.
>
> THE ATTORNEY-GENERAL: Will you swear that you were not applied to?
>
> SMITH: I will not swear either that I was not applied to for that purpose, or that I was. If you will let me see the document I shall recognize my writing at once.

THE ATTORNEY-GENERAL: In January, 1855, were you applied to by Palmer to attest his brother's proposal for £13,000 in The Prince of Wales Office?

SMITH: I don't recollect.

THE ATTORNEY-GENERAL: Don't recollect? Why, £13,000 was a large sum for a man like Walter Palmer, wasn't it, who hadn't a shilling in the world? Didn't you know that he was an uncertified bankrupt?

SMITH: I knew that he had been a bankrupt some years before, but not that he was an uncertified bankrupt. I knew that he had an allowance from his mother, and I believe that his brother William [the prisoner] gave him money at different times.

THE ATTORNEY-GENERAL: During 1854 and 1855, where in Rugeley did you live?

SMITH: In 1854, I think, I resided partly with William Palmer, and sometimes at his mother's.

THE ATTORNEY-GENERAL: Did you sometimes sleep at his mother's?

SMITH: Yes.

THE ATTORNEY-GENERAL: Did you sleep in his mother's room—on your oath, were you not intimate with her?—you know well enough what I mean.

SMITH: I had no other intimacy, Mr Attorney, than a proper intimacy.

THE ATTORNEY-GENERAL: How often did you sleep at her house, though having an establishment of your own close by?

SMITH: Frequently. Two or three times a week.

[*Here one of the jurymen sniggered, and slowly a laugh spread through the Court.*]

THE ATTORNEY-GENERAL: Explain how that happened.

SMITH: Sometimes her son Joseph or other members of her family were on a visit there, and I went to see them. We used to play a game of cards, and have a glass of gin and water, and smoke a pipe perhaps; and then they would say: 'It is late—you had better stop all night.' And I did.

THE ATTORNEY-GENERAL: Did that continue for three or four years?

SMITH: Yes; and I sometimes used to stop there when nobody was at home—when they were all away, the mother and everybody.

THE ATTORNEY-GENERAL: And you have slept at the house when the sons were not there and the mother was?

SMITH: Yes. Two or three times a week. [*More laughter.*]

THE ATTORNEY-GENERAL: But since there was no one to smoke and drink with, you might have gone home. Will you say on your oath that there was nothing but a proper intimacy between you and Mrs Palmer?

SMITH: I do.

THE ATTORNEY-GENERAL: Now, I shall turn to another subject. Were you called upon to attest a further proposal for £13,000 by Walter Palmer, in The Universal Assurance Office?

SMITH: I cannot say; if you will let me see the proposal I shall know.

THE ATTORNEY-GENERAL: Answer me, Sir, as an attorney and a man of business: did William Palmer ask you to attest a proposal for a £13,000 assurance on the life of his brother Walter?

SMITH: If I could see any document on the subject I daresay I should recollect.

THE ATTORNEY-GENERAL: Do you remember getting a five-pound note for attesting an assignment of such a policy by Walter Palmer to his brother?

SMITH: I don't recollect positively.

THE ATTORNEY-GENERAL (*handing a document to witness*): Is that your signature?

SMITH (*after considerable hesitation*): It is very like my signature, but I have some doubt about it.

THE ATTORNEY-GENERAL: Read the document and tell me, on your solemn oath, whether it is your signature.

SMITH: I have some doubt whether it is mine.

THE ATTORNEY-GENERAL: I will have an answer from you on your oath, one way or another. Isn't that your handwriting?

SMITH: I believe that it is not my handwriting, but a very clever imitation of it.

THE ATTORNEY-GENERAL: Will you swear that it is not?

SMITH: I will.

MR BARON ALDERSON: Did you ever make such an attestation?

SMITH: I don't recollect, my Lord.

THE ATTORNEY-GENERAL: Look at the other signature there, 'Walter Palmer'; is that his signature?

SMITH: I believe so.

THE ATTORNEY-GENERAL: Look at the attestation and the words 'signed, sealed and delivered'; are they in Mr Pratt's handwriting?

SMITH: They are.

THE ATTORNEY-GENERAL: Did you receive that from Mr Pratt?

SMITH: I can't swear that I did. It might have been sent to William Palmer.

THE ATTORNEY-GENERAL: Did you receive it from William Palmer?

SMITH: I don't know; very likely I did.

THE ATTORNEY-GENERAL: If that be the document he gave you, and if those are the signatures of Walter Palmer and of Pratt, is not the other signature yours?

SMITH: I'll tell you, Mr Attorney . . .

THE ATTORNEY-GENERAL: Don't 'Mr Attorney' me, Sir! Answer my question! Will you swear that it isn't your handwriting?

SMITH: I believe it is not.

THE ATTORNEY-GENERAL: Did you apply to The Midland Counties Insurance Office in October, 1855, to be appointed their agent at Rugeley?

SMITH: I think I did.

THE ATTORNEY-GENERAL: Did you yourself send them a proposal on the life of Bate for £10,000?

SMITH: I did.

THE ATTORNEY-GENERAL: Did William Palmer ask you to send that proposal?

SMITH: Bate and Palmer came together to my office

with a prospectus, and asked me if I would write and get appointed agent for that company in Rugeley, because Bate wanted to raise some money.

THE ATTORNEY-GENERAL: And you did so?

SMITH: I did.

THE ATTORNEY-GENERAL: Was Bate at that time superintending William Palmer's stud and stables at a salary of one pound a week?

SMITH: I can't tell his salary.

THE ATTORNEY-GENERAL: After that, did you try to make the widow of Walter Palmer give up her claim on her husband's policy?

SMITH: I did.

THE ATTORNEY-GENERAL: Did you receive a document from Pratt to lay before her at Liverpool?

SMITH: William Palmer gave me one which had been directed to him.

THE ATTORNEY-GENERAL: Did the widow refuse to sign the document?

SMITH: She said she would like her solicitor to see it. So I said: 'By all means,' and brought it back because I had no instructions to leave it.

THE ATTORNEY-GENERAL: Didn't she say: 'I understood from my husband that the insurance was for £1000?'—or words to that effect?

Serjeant Shee objected to the question. What passed between Walter Palmer's widow and the witness could be no evidence against the prisoner. The Attorney-General explained that the question was intended to affect the witness's credit, and was most important in that respect. The Court ruled that it could not be put.

THE ATTORNEY-GENERAL: Don't you know
that Walter Palmer obtained nothing for making
that assignment?

SMITH: I believe that he ultimately did get something for it.

THE ATTORNEY-GENERAL: Don't you know
that what he got was a bill for £200?

SMITH: Yes; and had a house furnished for him.

THE ATTORNEY-GENERAL: Don't you know
that the bill was never paid?

SMITH: No, I do not.

THE ATTORNEY-GENERAL: Now, I'll refresh
your memory a little with regard to those proposals (*handing witness a document*). Look at that,
and tell me whether it is in your handwriting.

SMITH: It is.

THE ATTORNEY-GENERAL: Now, I ask you, were
you not applied to by William Palmer in December, 1854, to attest a proposal on the life of his
brother Walter for £13,000 in The Solicitors' and
General Insurance Office?

SMITH: I might have been.

THE ATTORNEY-GENERAL: Were you, or were
you not, Sir? Look at that document, and say
have you any doubt upon the subject?

SMITH: I have no doubt that I might have been
applied to.

THE ATTORNEY-GENERAL: Do not trifle, Sir,
with the Court, and with the jury, and myself!
Have you any doubt whatever that in January,
1855, you were called on by William Palmer to
attest a further proposal for £13,000 on his broth-

er's life in another office? Look at the document and tell me.

SMITH: I see the paper, but I don't recall the circumstances.

THE ATTORNEY-GENERAL: That piece of paper seems to burn your fingers?

SMITH: No, upon my honour, it does not. I might have signed it in blank.

THE ATTORNEY-GENERAL: Do you usually sign attestations of this nature in blank?

SMITH: I have some doubt whether I did not sign several blanks.

THE ATTORNEY-GENERAL: On your oath, looking at that document, don't you know that William Palmer asked you to attest that proposal upon his brother's life for £13,000?

SMITH: He did apply to me to attest proposals in some office.

THE ATTORNEY-GENERAL: Were they for large amounts?

SMITH: One was for £13,000.

THE ATTORNEY-GENERAL: Now the truth is coming out! Were you asked to attest another proposal for a like sum in The Universal Assurance Office?

SMITH: I might have been.

THE ATTORNEY-GENERAL: They were made much about the same time, were they not? You did not wait for the answers to the first application before you made the second?

SMITH: I don't know that any answers came back at all.

> THE ATTORNEY-GENERAL: Will you swear that
> you were not present when Walter Palmer execut-
> ed the deed assigning the policy upon his life to
> the prisoner, William Palmer? Now, be careful,
> Mr Smith, because, depend upon it, you shall
> hear of this again if you are not!
> SMITH: I will not swear that I was; I think I was
> not. I am not quite positive.

The Attorney-General's questioning of Jeremiah Smith's relations with old Mrs Palmer, and his previous questioning of George
Myatt, the saddler, as to whether he ever slept in the same hotel
bed as Dr Palmer, were both by way of revenge. Serjeant Shee,
to throw discredit on Elizabeth Mills's testimony, had suggested
that she was a woman of loose morals. Elizabeth Mills, however,
answered with jaunty and mocking defiance, whereas Jeremiah
Smith vacillated—torn between the fear of losing his character if
he owned to being the bed-fellow of a rich woman over twenty
years his senior, and fear of offending her if he denied the imputation too indignantly. Very few of his answers were given without
hesitance and a decided embarrassment, which left its imprint on
the jury's mind.

Serjeant Shee tried to make good the damage when he re-examined Smith.

> SERJEANT SHEE: How long have you known Mrs
> Palmer?
> SMITH: For twenty years. [*In answer to further ques-
> tions*:] I should think she must now be about sixty
> years of age. William Palmer is not her eldest son.
> Joseph, the eldest, resides at Liverpool, and is a
> timber merchant. He must be forty-five or forty-six

years of age. George, the next eldest son, resides at
Rugeley and was frequently at his mother's house.
John, the youngest, a clergyman of the Church of
England, lived there until two years ago, except
when he was away at college. There is also a
daughter, who lives constantly with her mother;
and three servants are kept. The house is a large
one, and contains many spare bedrooms. I slept in
the room nearest the old church.

SERJEANT SHEE: Is there any pretence for saying
that you have ever been accused of improper
intimacy with Mrs Palmer?

SMITH: I hope not.

SERJEANT SHEE: I repeat: is there any pretence
for saying so?

SMITH: There ought not to be.

SERJEANT SHEE: Pray answer me directly! Is there
any truth in the suggestion?

SMITH: People may have made it, but they had no
reason for doing so.

SERJEANT SHEE: But was there any truth in such
a statement if made?

SMITH: I should say not. There ought not to be any
pretence for anything of the kind. [*Laughter.*]

MR BARON ALDERSON: No, Brother Shee.
It was only two or three times a week he slept
there! [*Loud laughter.*]

The Attorney-General then made a telling speech for the
Crown, secure in the knowledge that he had the last word, and
need fear no rebuttal—though why the Prosecution always
should have the last word in murder trials, we have been unable

to fathom. Serjeant Shee nevertheless contended that since the Attorney-General had raised the new matter of Walter Palmer's life insurance, and the proposals for it made to various offices, the Defence was entitled to reply. But the Lord Chief Justice ruled: 'We are of opinion that you have no right to reply,' and Mr Baron Alderson supported him in this.

Dr Palmer, while in the dock, wrote a facetious note to his Counsel:

I wish there was two and a half grains of strychnia in old Campbell's acidulated draught—solely because I think he acts unfairly.

The Lord Chief Justice summed up in a sense which left the jury no choice but to find a verdict of 'Guilty'; yet Serjeant Shee courageously ventured on a final protest:

> SERJEANT SHEE: The question which your Lord-
> ship has submitted to the jury is whether Cook's
> symptoms were consistent with death by strych-
> nia. I beg leave . . .
> THE LORD CHIEF JUSTICE (*in a tone of vex-
> ation*): That is not *the* question which I have
> submitted to the jury; it
> is *a* question! I have told them that unless they consid-
> er the symptoms consistent with death by strych-
> nia they ought to acquit the prisoner.
> SERJEANT SHEE: It is my duty not to be deterred
> by any expression of displeasure; I stand before a
> much higher tribunal than even your Lordships',
> and must therefore submit what I believe to be the
> proper question. I submit to your Lordships that
> the question whether Cook's symptoms are consis-
> tent with death by strychnia is a wrong question,

unless followed by the phrase: '. . . and inconsistent
with death from other and natural causes'. I submit
that the question should be whether the medical
evidence has established, beyond all reasonable
doubt, that Cook died by strychnia. It is my duty
to make this submission, as it is your Lordships', if
I am wrong, to over-rule it.

MR BARON ALDERSON: It is done already. You
did so in your speech.

THE LORD CHIEF JUSTICE (*addressing the
jury*): Gentlemen, I did not submit to you that
the question upon which alone your verdict
should turn is whether the symptoms of Cook
were those of strychnia. I said that this is a
most material question, and I desired you to
consider it. I said: if you think that he died
from natural disease—and not from poisoning
by strychnia—you should acquit the prisoner. Then I went on to say that if you believed
that the symptoms were consistent with death
from strychnia, you should consider the other
evidence given in the case to see whether
strychnia had been administered to Cook and,
if so, whether it had been administered by the
prisoner at the bar. These are the questions
which I now again put to you. You must not
find a verdict of 'Guilty' unless you believe that
strychnia was administered to the deceased by
the prisoner at the bar; but, if you do believe
that, it is your duty towards God and man to
find the prisoner guilty.

At the conclusion of this address the jury retired from the Court, at eighteen minutes past two o'clock. They filed back into their box at twenty-five minutes to four, after an absence of one hour and seventeen minutes. The prisoner, who had meanwhile been removed, was simultaneously placed in the dock.

A buzz of excitement which ran round the Court on the re-appearance of the jury was instantly hushed by the Clerk of the Arraigns' question: 'Gentlemen of the Jury, are you all unanimous in your verdict?'

The Foreman replied with a downright: 'We are.'

Whereupon the Clerk of the Arraigns asked: 'How say you, gentlemen? Do you find the prisoner at the bar guilty, or not guilty?'

The Foreman rose and announced in distinct and firm tones: 'We find the prisoner guilty.'

Dr Palmer, who exhibited some slight pallor and the least possible shade of anxiety upon the return of the jury to the box, almost instantly won back his self-possession and his demeanour of comparative indifference. He maintained his perfect calm; and when sentence was being passed, he looked an interested, although utterly unmoved, spectator. We may truly say that during the whole of this protracted trial his nerve and calmness have never for a moment forsaken him.

The Clerk of the Arraigns then turned to him with: 'Prisoner at the bar, you stand convicted of murder; what have you to say why the Court should not give you judgement to die according to the law?' This question is of a formal nature; and the prisoner neither made, nor was expected to make, any answer.

Thereupon the judges assumed the black cap, and Lord Chief Justice Campbell pronounced sentence in the following terms:

'William Palmer, after a long and impartial trial you have been convicted of the crime of wilful murder. In that verdict my two learned brothers, who have so anxiously watched this trial, and myself, entirely concur. The case is attended with such circumstances of aggravation that I will not dare to touch upon them. Whether this be the first and only offence of the sort which you have committed is certainly known only to God and your own conscience. It is seldom that such a familiarity with the means of death can be achieved without long experience; but for this offence, of which you have been found guilty, your life is forfeited. You must prepare to die; and I trust that, as you can expect no mercy in this world, you will, by a repentance of your crimes, seek to obtain mercy from Almighty God. The Act of Parliament under which, at your own request, you have been brought here for trial, allows us to direct that the sentence shall be executed either within the jurisdiction of the Central Criminal Court, or in the county where the offence was committed. We think that the sentence ought to be executed in the county of Stafford, and we hope that this terrible example will deter others from committing such atrocious crimes: for it will be seen that, whatever art, or caution, or experience may accomplish, yet such an offence will surely be found out and punished.

'However destructive poison may be, it is ordained by Providence, for the safety of its creatures, that there are means of detecting and punishing those who administer it. I again implore you to repent, and to prepare for the awful change which awaits you. I will not seek to harrow up your feelings by enumerating the circumstances of this foul murder; but content myself now by passing upon you the sentence of the law.

'Which is: that you be taken from hence to the gaol of Newgate, and be thence removed to the gaol of the county of Stafford—the county in which the offence for which you stand convicted was committed—that you be taken thence to the place of execution, and there hanged by the neck until you be dead, and that your body be afterwards buried within the precincts of the prison; and may the Lord of Heaven have mercy on your soul!

'Amen.'

Dr Palmer's notorious comment on the verdict—the sporting phrase: 'It was the riding that did it', which he wrote on another scrap of paper and tossed to his solicitor—has been read as an unwilling tribute to the Attorney-General's masterly conduct of the Prosecution. But we have it from his solicitor, John Smith, that it referred solely to the Lord Chief Justice's discreditable jockey-ship on the Bench.

CHAPTER XXIII

A CHANGE IN PUBLIC OPINION

Back in his cell at Newgate Gaol, Dr Palmer complained to the Under-Sheriff that he had not received anything like a fair trial. The Under-Sheriff replied: 'You can have no reason for complaint, my man. Why, the Attorney-General laid his cards face upwards on the table, saying that, since so much prejudice had been excited in this case, all the evidence against you would first be communicated to Counsel for the Defence, and not sprung upon him.'

'I saw in that only the hypocrisy of a Scot,' Dr Palmer retorted. 'There were several cards missing from the pack, including the high trumps.'

'Moreover,' went on the Under-Sheriff, 'no less than three judges agreed with the jury's finding.'

'Well, Sir, but that don't satisfy me,' said the Doctor. He then stated that Lord Chief Justice Campbell had failed to consult his fellow-judges before announcing their unanimous agreement with the verdict; and that it should properly have fallen to Mr Justice Cresswell, as junior judge, to pass sentence.

Later, Dr Palmer admitted: 'Despite old Campbell's unfair speech at the close, I had hoped to get off; but when the jury returned to Court, and I saw the cocked-up nose of that perky little Foreman, I knew it was a gooser with me.'

He appeared greatly mortified when given a grey suit of convict clothes and curtly told to change into them. Having done so, he was hand-cuffed and fettered. 'You are bound for Stafford tonight,' said the Under-Sheriff.

A Black Maria stood waiting in the courtyard, where the crowd had gathered thick for a sight of the prisoner; but Mr Weatherhead, the Governor of Newgate Gaol, smuggled him out by cab to Euston Square Station. Though met there with angry and derisive shouts, he was safely assisted to the eight-o'clock train and thrust into the middle compartment of a first-class carriage; the blinds being at once drawn. He had pleaded to travel by the Great Western Railway, over a less direct route, on the ground that if he went by the London & North Western, he would be recognized all along the line. This favour was denied him.

When he arrived, rather fagged, at Stafford Station late that night—only to be greeted with prolonged boos and cat-calls— Mr Wollaston, Superintendent of the Stafford Police, took one of his arms, and Mr Weatherhead the other. The Police having dispersed the crowd, Dr Palmer picked his way carefully through the puddles, saying: 'Dear me, it's very wet! Have you had much rain down here?'

'We have,' Mr Wollaston answered shortly.

No further word was spoken for some time, but after about five minutes Dr Palmer sighed and said: 'I've had a wearying trial of it: twelve long days!' Then he stumbled in the dark and cried: 'Bother these chains! I wish they were off. I can't walk properly.'

The Doctor's brothers, George and Thomas, had leave to visit his cell a day or two later. When they begged him to declare whether he were guilty or not guilty, he forcibly replied: 'I have nothing to say, and nothing shall I say!'

Within half a week of returning to Stafford he overcame his fatigue, and was allowed several more visits from them; also from the Rev. Mr Atkinson, the Vicar of Rugeley, who had baptized, confirmed, married, and never ceased to feel affection for him; from Mr Wright, the philanthropist of Manchester; and from the Rev. Mr Sneyd of Ripstone. All these urged on him the necessity of confessing, but he kept a polite silence. Serjeant Shee sent Dr Palmer a Bible, carrying a sympathetic note on the fly-leaf; and he passed much of his time reading this, and other religious books, lent him by the prison chaplain, the Rev. H. J. Goodacre. At his request, old Mrs Palmer spared herself the pain of a farewell, and took sole charge of little William, his son.

For a while, he was generally assumed to be guilty beyond dispute, and the crowds at Newgate would have cheerfully torn him to pieces, had the Police permitted them. Yet among medical men in Edinburgh, London, and Dublin, the prevalent view now seems to be: 'Hang Palmer for the insurance offices, or for the Jockey Club, or for the greater glory of the Attorney-General. Hang him as a rogue, if you will, but it must be on circumstantial evidence alone, not on the medical evidence; because that has broken down, horse, foot and guns!'

Yesterday, the President of the College of Surgeons, lecturing to a packed audience on the subjects of tetanus and strychnine, referred pointedly to Dr Palmer's trial: 'I have heard of grand jurors and petty jurors, special jurors, and common jurors, but these were twelve most uncommon jurors—very respectable confectioners and grocers into the bargain, I have no doubt—who boldly cut the Gordian knot, and settled the most difficult problem in the world, which is the anatomy of the brain!' He added that ninety-nine parts in a hundred of the surgical evidence at the trial were irrelevant to the case, since Cook had doubtless died of no surgical disease, but of a medical one—namely, a convulsion.

Guy's Hospital is in a ferment. One of Professor Taylor's colleagues has represented the speech of the Attorney-General as one of the greatest examples of medical extravagance and folly ever proffered to the public. Another pre-eminent surgeon calls it 'a piece of cold-blooded cruelty, disgraceful to the nineteenth century.' Professor Taylor himself receives cold looks from his own associates and pupils. At King's College Hospital, where Professor Partridge lectures, the pupils are indignant at the Attorney-General's attack on Mr Devonshire, who performed the first *post-mortem*, and is regarded as one of the most promising young surgeons in that institution.

A considerable change of opinion has therefore been observed among the educated public.

We reprint the following fro m *The Daily Chronicle:*

A public meeting, organized neither by Dr Palmer's family, nor by the Defence, but spontaneously by a number of disinterested citizens, took place today in St Martin's Hall, Longacre, to consider the propriety of staying Wm Palmer's execution on the ground of doubtful and conflicting testimony given at the trial. Most persons present were working men, with a considerable representation of the middle classes, and here and there a few women.

When the doors opened, the hall soon filled, and hundreds who could not find standing room remained outside during the proceedings. A petition praying that the hanging might be postponed, to allow time for a medical inquiry into the facts at issue, lay in a lobby at the entrance throughout the evening, and a stream of people appended their names to it. The feeling manifested by the greater part of the audience was in favour of a respite, though a few score vociferously asserted an opposite view at all stages of the proceedings. So high, indeed, did feeling run at one time that a well-dressed, portly man named Bridd jumped upon the platform and, defying the remonstrances of the chairman, Mr P. Edwards, began addressing the meeting while another speaker held the chair. Bridd was brought to reason amid a scene of indescribable confusion only by the appearance of police constables.

Mr P. Edwards announced that he and his fellows on the platform had not the least personal sympathy with William Palmer, knew nothing of him, and had never seen or conversed either with him or with any member of his family. Nor did they feel a morbid sympathy with criminals, and if the verdict had satisfied public opinion as correctly given, he for one should never have considered arresting the progress of the Law, which was always a thing to be respected. (*Cheers.*) But, since public opinion found much cause to doubt Palmer's guilt, and since a number of first-class medical men, such as Professor Herapath of Bristol, Dr Letheby, and others, stated that, given more time, they could throw additional light on this subject, the meeting had been convened to ask for more time. (*Cheers.*)

He, and those who acted with him on this occasion, demanded neither a reprieve, nor the Royal clemency; they demanded simple justice. If his listeners considered the evidence submitted at the trial to have been doubtful, he hoped that they would endeavour, with him, to procure a re-investigation of the case, so that there might afterwards be no cause for resentment at a judicial scandal. He had not met with a single man who ventured to assert that Palmer's guilt was proved. (*Cheers and uproar.*) Despite the show of a fair trial, most people thought that Palmer had too many counsel against him, and that Lord Campbell himself might be included in their number. (*Renewed uproar.*) He thought Lord Campbell to stand high above all interested and petty motives, yet all judges are fallible human beings, and he might well have erred in his direction of the trial.

Though Mr Edwards admitted that he himself believed in Palmer's guilt, belief (he insisted) was one thing and certainty another. Surely a man was not to be hanged on mere belief?

Mr Baxter Langley now moved the resolution: 'That, there being grave doubts as to whether or not John Parsons Cook died from strychnine, and it being essential to the interests of society, the progress of science, and the safety of individual life, that such doubts should be removed, this Meeting is of opinion that the execution of William Palmer should be delayed till an opportunity has been afforded of proving whether or not strychnine can be found in all cases where it has caused death.'

Mr Langley, too, denied that he had any sympathy with the convict Palmer, or with his pursuits. He stood there to vindicate the majesty of the Law, which was dear to all Englishmen as a protective, and not as a destructive, principle; and he wished the public mind to rest satisfied, before the sentence was executed, that no link was wanting in the chain of evidence against the prisoner. He did not affirm Palmer's innocence, but he asked the Meeting for their own sakes and for the sake of the Law, to give Palmer the benefit of the doubt which still hung over his guilt.

He went on to say that Lord Campbell, when summing up, had assumed the prisoner was a murderer, and then laid before the jury facts to prove his own hypothesis. ('*No, no!*' *and counter-cheers.*) The summing up of Lord Campbell was unfair, because he did not put the question to the jury whether strychnine had, or had not, been administered to the deceased—but whether his death was consistent with poisoning by strychnine—thus assuming that death had occurred from strychnine, which was not found in Cook's body. He himself believed that if Palmer were executed, he would be executed to satisfy an unproved scientific hypothesis. (*'No, no!' and uproar.*)

Mr R. Hart, who seconded the resolution, contended that if capital punishment must take place, it should take place only in cases admitting no doubt of guilt. If a man has been haled to the scaffold and hanged, and if proof of innocence be afterwards established, what compensation for the wrong does this bring his relatives, and what alleviation for the remorse of those who hanged him? (*Cheers.*) They were not there to consider whether Palmer was a gambler, a black-leg, or a forger. The question was: had the crime of poisoning been legally proved against him? (*'No, no!' and uproar.*) He could hardly do Lord Campbell the injustice of supposing that he was a willing accessory to legal murder. Yet the evidence was wholly circumstantial, not only as to Palmer's guilt, but as to the fact of any crime having been committed; for though the doctors had contradicted one another, and advanced opposite theories throughout the trial, most of them held that Cook died a natural death. The whole operation of the old English Law observed on trials for murder had, in this case, met with a reversal: first, when, before proceeding to prove a murder, they proceeded to prove a murderer; and second, when, instead of inferring the criminal from the crime, they inferred the crime from the criminal.

The motion, which the Rev. Mr Thomas also supported, was put and carried by a considerable majority.

Mr H. Harris, a surgeon, then moved the appointment of a deputation, consisting of the chairman and several other gentlemen on the platform, to wait upon Sir George Grey, the Secretary of the Home Department, and lay the resolution on his table.

An amendment moved by Mr Bridd, and seconded by the Rev. Mr Pope, to the effect that the verdict of the jury was perfectly correct according to the evidence given at the trial, was lost on a show of hands, and the original motion re-affirmed by a large majority. The Meeting then dispersed.

'Honest John Smith', Dr Palmer's solicitor, had meanwhile pressed for a further *post-mortem* examination of Cook's mangled remains, and their analysis by chemists who claimed that, in cases of strychnine poisoning, they could detect the ten-thousandth part of a grain. He was supported in his demand by Professor J. E. D. Rodgers, Lecturer in Chymistry at the St George's School of Medicine. Professor Rodgers wrote to *The Times*:

To the Editor:
Sir,

I cannot conceive an opinion more dangerous to promulgate than that a fatal dose of poison can be so nicely adjusted as to escape detection after death. Yet such has been the tendency of many letters published in the Press for some time past. It was with feelings of deep regret that I noticed in your edition of today a communication from a former colleague of mine, Mr Ancell, who, I am sure, would never have sent it, had he been aware of the nature and results of numerous experiments lately made by myself independently, and in conjunction with Mr Girdwood, Assistant-Surgeon, Grenadier Guards. I have asserted, and do still assert, that strychnia cannot evade discovery if proper processes be employed for its separation.

In this view I am supported by the highest chemical authorities of the day; and now request a space in your valuable columns to give the world a process which will form the conclusion of my letter. It has enabled myself and Mr Girdwood to detect that fearful poison in the blood, liver, tissues, and stomachs of animals poisoned by doses such as those Professor Taylor administered in experiments mentioned at the late trial. It has even enabled us to separate the strychnia from the tissues and organs of a dog after its body had been interred twelve months. The results of these experiments, though not a description of the process employed, were forwarded by myself and Mr Girdwood for the scrutiny of Sir George Grey. We hold that if John Parsons Cook was poisoned by strychnia, no matter how small the fatal dose, its presence could even now be clearly demonstrated should the victim's tissues be subjected to the same analytic process: for of all known poisons, there is not one more readily detected.

The process is as follows:—

The tissues are rubbed with distilled water in a mortar to a pulp, and then digested, after the addition of a little hydrochloric acid, in an evaporating basin. They are then strained, and evaporated to dryness over a water bath. The residue is digested again in a spirit filter, and once more evaporated to dryness. We next treat it with distilled water, acidulated with a few drops of hydrochloric acid, and filter it. We thereupon add excess of ammonia, and agitate in a tube with chloroform; the strychnia in an impure condition being thereby entirely separated with the chloroform.

This chloroform is to be carefully separated by a pipette, poured into a small dish and evaporated to dryness; the residue being moistened with concentrated sulphuric acid, and heated over a water bath for half an hour. We then add distilled water and excess of ammonia—again agitated with chloroform—and the strychnia will have thus been again separated by the chloroform now in a state of sufficient purity for testing. The test is made by evaporating a few drops on a piece of white porcelain, adding a drop of strong sulphuric acid and a minute crystal of bichromate of potash.

> J. E. D. RODGERS,
> *Lecturer in Chymistry, at the*
> *St George's School of Medicine.*

John Smith wrote from London to Sir George Grey at the Home Office, two days before the execution:

To The Right Hon. Sir G. Grey,
Sir,

Notwithstanding the unabated anxiety which exists in the public mind relative to the fate of William Palmer, I have hitherto postponed addressing you on this subject. Long since his relations and friends would have rushed, in the intensity of their grief, to the Home Office; but as I have been charged with this matter of life and death, the arduous duty of making an appeal falls upon me. Let me, then, claim your largest indulgence. I have now, when the sand of William Palmer's life has run until the eleventh hour—when only a few days stand between him and the grave, unless your clemency be exercised on his behalf—to address you as the head of that department which is recognized as the

last sanctuary of injured justice. Although since the period of your administration the records of mercy adorn it
more than at any other time—notwithstanding murder in
its blackest form was committed, its perpetrators, under
your merciful and wide dispensation, have been allowed to
make atonement in exile or in solitude—still I shall not
appeal to your sense of mercy.

I shall merely ask that a respite should take place in the
execution of William Palmer until the serious doubts, medical and circumstantial, connected with this case, are laid at
rest. No matter how popular passion may have been excited
to its late state of madness against my client, your spirit of
justice must examine into the obscurities that do exist. Sir,
I trust you will not reverse one of the first principles of our
criminal code, but allow my client the full benefit of doubt,
if doubt be well founded.

I therefore ground this application for my client's respite—

First: Upon the character of Charles Newton, the principal witness for the Crown; as also upon the character of
Elizabeth Mills; both of whose antecedents were unfortunately hidden from me at the time of the trial.

Secondly: Upon the absence of two witnesses who
could, as I believe, have given satisfactory proofs as to the
disposal of the poisons purchased by the prisoner, as well
as to the disposal of Cook's money.

Thirdly: Upon the discrepancy of the medical evidence
as to the finding of strychnia.

Lastly: Upon the judge's charge to the jury.

The importance as to Charles Newton's testimony in
procuring a conviction for the Crown cannot be over-rat-
ed. Newton said he sold strychnia to the prisoner on the

Monday night before Cook's death; and upon that night Cook was first seized with symptoms of illness. The medical evidence for the Crown pronounced this illness to have been connected with the administration of strychnia; but there was sufficient in Charles Newton's evidence to render him a witness un-worthy of belief. The hour which he fixed for the delivery of the poison was incompatible with the hour when the prisoner was seen at Stafford on the same night. The suppression of this incident (if it took place) before the Coroner; the consultation relative to the effects of strychnia, which he said had occurred between Palmer and himself; and the unfeigned joy with which he represented Palmer to have been seized when he lent him his boyish knowledge of the powers of strychnia—all these circumstances and incidents rendered his evidence at the trial such that even the consummate ability of the Attorney-General could not deal with it as he wished. Yet the jury gave implicit faith to this witness.

I have now, Sir, to tell you that the same Charles Newton has been twice in custody for theft at Nottingham; and that some of his more recent acts are under investigation by the Police. Ought this man then to be relied upon in a case of life and death, under the circumstances I have narrated?

As to the witness Mills, she swore on the trial that she slept with Mrs Dutton, when lodging at the house of Mrs Dutton's son. I assert, upon most unimpeachable testimony, that Mrs Dutton lives four miles from her son's residence, and has not been in his house for over nine months. It may be said that perjury by a witness to conceal the offence of fornication is venal, and that the rest of the testimony of such a witness can be perfectly relied upon. My belief is that any person who departs from the paths of virtue, and then perjures herself to cover her shame, may also commit perjury for motives not more honest. Again, let me ask whether life should be sacrificed on such evidence?

I now, Sir, approach a most important part of the case—which is medical and chemical testimony. So much has been written, spoken, and laid before the world on this head, that it requires but a few words from me. Sir, the point upon which so much doubt exists has created a universal and wide-spread feeling relative to the justice of the verdict. No man ought ever to ascend a scaffold with a doubt attached to his guilt. Let not that ill-fated man, William Palmer, whom prejudice has long since consigned to the gallows, do so!

Dr Letheby and Professor Herapath, two of the most eminent toxicologists of this day, declared upon their solemn oaths that they could discover the fifty-thousandth part of a grain of strychnia in the body of a dead man; and that, if Cook died from that poison, they could now find it. Their opinions were confirmed by almost equally distinguished members of the schools of London, Leeds, Edinburgh, and Dublin. Yet the body of Cook did not yield to the manipulations of Drs Taylor and Rees the smallest particle of strychnia. Since the unfortunate end of the trial, my table has been laden with letters from scientific men in support of Dr Letheby and his party. If you honour me by your commands, I shall be proud to place these letters before you. Yet I hope that the new light thrown on the characters of Newton and Mills alone justify me in the strong assurance that a respite, for the object of further inquiry, and for the consequent elucidation of truth, will be granted. Upon the last point which I am calling to your attention, I must, to a certain extent, be mute—I mean the Lord

Chief Justice's charge to the jury. As an officer of his Court, I owe him every respect and duty, so that nothing but the dearer interests of my client would induce me to criticize his conduct of the trial. I cannot, however, refrain from saying that if a similar rule existed in the criminal law as in civil law, my Lord Chief Justice's charge would be open to the complaint of misdirection. The voice of the public has unanimously condemned it as one-sided and mistaken. Upon this point I pray your earnest thought.

I sincerely trust that I have given sufficient reasons to postpone the hour of death, and that the 14th inst.—a day which will witness the nation's common celebration of joy with our brave allies, the French, in the baptism of the future Napoleon IV[*]—may not bathe in tears of bitterness, sorrow, and resentment all the numerous relatives and friends of the unfortunate William Palmer.

May I seek as early an answer as is compatible with the consideration of this sincere plea?

I am, Sir, your most obedient servant,

JOHN SMITH

John Smith had his answer on the next evening:

Sir,
Whitehall, June 12, 1856

Secretary Sir George Grey has received and considered your letters of the 10th and 11th inst., in behalf of William Palmer. He directs me to inform you that he can see nothing in any of the points that you have pressed upon his atten-

---

[*] The Prince Imperial. Killed by the Zulus in 1879, while serving with the British cavalry.

tion which would justify him in interfering with the due course of law in this case.

I am, Sir, your obedient servant,

H. WADDINGTON

By the same post he received a letter from Dr Palmer himself:

Stafford, June 11th, 1856

My dear John,

The governor has been kind enough to allow me to write to you, as I am anxious to see you, and shall be glad if you will come as soon as you can. Thank God, I am very well in health and spirits. Write to me immediately.

I am, my dear John, yours ever, here and hereafter,

WILLIAM PALMER

CHAPTER XXIV

THE EXECUTION

Mr John Smith could not catch the Express that evening, but took train to Wolverhampton, and went thence by fly, reaching Stafford Gaol at about eleven o'clock. Dr Palmer had just parted from his brothers, among them Joseph (now somewhat paralytic), and his sister Sarah, in an affecting farewell. When Mr Smith told him that Sir George Grey had refused a last-minute stay of execution, his face suddenly paled, his mouth twitched, and he did not recover his usual florid looks for some little while.

Major Fulford, the Governor, was present at this interview. Since Dr Palmer had waited up to a late hour until Smith came, the prison officers supposed he had something important to tell him; but when the Governor informed the Doctor that whatever private disclosure he might make, on family matters, to Mr Smith would be kept secret, he simply thanked Mr Smith for his great exertions and the prison officers for their kindness—and re-affirmed that Cook had not died from strychnine.

The Governor then expressed a hope that Dr Palmer was not quibbling with the question, and urged him to say plainly whether or not he had committed murder.

Dr Palmer answered: 'Lord Campbell summed up for poisoning by strychnine, and I never gave Cook any of that.'

'How the deed was done,' retorted the Governor, 'is of scant importance. Pray give me a plain yes or no to my question!'

'I have nothing more to add,' said he. 'I am quite easy in my conscience, and happy in my mind.'

Immediately after leaving the Gaol, Smith wrote to a friend as follows:

> My interview ended in Palmer's making me pledge myself that Cook's body should be exhumed, and asserting that he was never poisoned by strychnine. Palmer—God help him!—remained as cool as though any ordinary question had been discussed. Then he presented me with a book, inscribed in a fair hand: 'The gift of Wm Palmer, June 13, 1856.' It is titled *The Sinner's Friend*, and the prelude, underscored by him, runs thus:
>
> > '*Oh! where for refuge should I flee,*
> > *If Jesus had not died for me?*'

Early in the morning of Saturday, June 14th, Dr Palmer retired to rest, and slept two hours and a half, when he was visited again by the Rev. Mr Goodacre, the prison Chaplain. Between five and six o'clock he took his breakfast, a plain cup of tea, and made his gallows toilet with unwavering serenity. Breakfast over, the Chaplain entered the cell, to offer Dr Palmer the ultimate consolations of religion, and found him still calm and resigned. Shortly afterwards, the Sheriff and other officials appeared. When about to leave his cell for ever, Dr Palmer said in reply to the High Sheriff that he denied the justice of his sentence, and that he was a murdered man. These were almost the last words he uttered.

The doomed prisoner walked, in the company of the Sheriff, to the press-room, where he met Smith, the hangman, and submitted to the final preparations no less quietly than if he had been under the hands of a valet dressing for a dinner party. At about seven o'clock, a turn-key brought him another cup of tea, which he drank with enjoyment, and when asked: 'How do you feel?' replied: 'Thank you, I am quite comfortable.' Among the foolish stories current is one that at ten minutes to eight he was offered a glass of champagne, to prepare him for his ordeal, and that when it was brought he blew off the bubbles, remarking: 'They always give me indigestion a few hours later, if I drink in a hurry.'

The intense interest in the hanging had been manifested a day beforehand by the numbers pouring into Stafford from every direction. The town assumed more the appearance of some antici-pated festivity than of the fearful spectacle so soon to take place. The streets, despite torrents of rain which fell during nearly the whole of Friday, were thronged. The public houses did a roaring trade, and in many of them jocund songs and merry dances were kept up all night with untiring energy by holiday-makers who had travelled far to feast their eyes on Dr Palmer's death-strug-gles. One favourite resort was the house where the hangman had located himself, everyone being anxious to catch a glimpse of the man who was to be Dr Palmer's executioner.

In the immediate vicinity of the Gaol, raised platforms were erected on every available spot which afforded a sight of the gal-lows. Twenty-three of them crowded the Gaol and County Road; and the charge of admission to some of the front seats was as high as a guinea for each person. Half-a-guinea seemed to be the ordi-nary rate, but places at the back were obtainable for less money. In the County Road, the roof of one house had been boarded over to afford a vantage point from which the execution could be wit-nessed. In other instances, householders let the produce of their well-kept gardens be trodden under foot, for the price of standing room. As early as ten o'clock on Friday night, scores of people had taken up positions on the platforms, expressing a resolve to stay there until they saw Palmer hanged; drenching rain, however, soon compelled them to seek shelter in adjoining inns. During the night, the streets were tolerably empty, except for visitors arriving by the midnight mail trains, north and south; but as soon as the grey dawn scattered the darkness, all Stafford burst into renewed life and activity. The public houses gradually disgorged their occupants, and a continuous stream of vehicles, from the four-in-hand to the overladen pony-cart, poured into the town—a traffic augmented by droves of pedestrians. Long before five o'clock, every street leading to the Gaol was choked. By eight o'clock, it was estimated that some twenty thousand strangers had arrived in Stafford. Bands of colliers from the neighbouring pits formed in the midst of the crowd and seemed so bent on forcing their way nearer to the scaffold that the great preparations which the magistrates and Police made to preserve order and avoid accidents, were fully justified.

Barriers had been erected at intervals in the streets to lessen the pressure of the crowd, and detachments of the County Constabulary, to the number of 160, under the command of Captain Hatton, the Chief Constable, were stationed at all salient points. One hundred and fifty specially sworn constables assisted them.

Since scarcely one half of the assembly could get a view of the scaffold, the rest struggled with all their might to improve their positions. The setting up of the scaffold, at about four o'clock in the morning, was taken as a proof that the execution would not be deferred; which further encouraged those who were unfavourably placed to press close and, if possible, hear the dying speech which it was hoped Dr Palmer would deliver.

As the hour of eight approached, the excitement of the mob grew more intense, yet there was no disturbance that warranted police interference.

About eighty thousand tracts suitable to the occasion, and a number of Bibles, were distributed by Mr Radcliffe, a religious gentleman from Liverpool, and his helpers, among the immense crowd. In several dissenting chapels continuous services on behalf of the unhappy culprit had been held all night, and numberless preachers exercised their calling from the platforms when daylight appeared.

Contrary to the usual custom in small country towns, the scaffold, a huge affair, somewhat resembling an agricultural machine and hung with black cloth, was not built upon the top of the prison, but brought out in front, so as to bar the road. Smith, the man selected to execute the sentence of the law, was once a nailer—a great, coarse fellow, standing five feet ten inches—but left his original vocation soon after he became hangman in the year 1840, and now pursues the precarious trade of a higgler. Smith hanged Moore for the murder of the Ash Flats, four years ago; and once ran a race against time, almost naked, through Wednesbury town, being sent to gaol immediately on accomplishing this feat. The rope destined for Dr Palmer's neck was twisted by a ropemaker named Coates, who is also a porter at the Stafford Railway Station. All the Railwaymen lent a hand in this task, and Coates, having an eye to the main chance, made thirty yards, cut the surplus length up into small pieces of two or three inches, and hawked them through the streets of Stafford, at a shilling the inch.

When Mr Wright, the philanthropist, visited Dr Palmer a few days before, the rumour went around that he had elicited a confession. But a warder whom we questioned at the time shook his head: 'Well, Sir, I haven't much to wager, but I'll bet every stick and stump I possess that Dr Palmer doesn't confess after all. Why, he ate half-a-pound of steak last night for his tea, and complained of the milk not being good! I shall never forget the scowl he gave us when we took away his brush and tortoise-shell pocket comb.

We thought, you know, he might hurt himself with the comb. He went into such a passion! "Send for the barber," he said, "send for the damned barber! I'll have every bit of my hair cut off." And he did, too. He looks so different, you can't imagine—sharp, like. He's given away locks to all his family, for what good those may do them . . . Yes, Mr Wright may be a very pious man, but I cannot believe that Dr Palmer said so much as he is supposed to have done. You mark my words, Sir—and I've seen a deal of him—he'll die hardened, and a coward.'

In the event, the warder's prediction proved to be wrong. Dr Palmer's bearing in this supreme ordeal amazed all who witnessed it. Just before eight o'clock, when the prison bell tolled and the procession was formed which conducted him from his cell to the scaffold, he tripped jauntily along between his guards. Though, contrary to usage, he wore prison dress, this was not meant as an indignity; it happened that the clothes in which he was tried were left behind in London, and no others had been since supplied. Despite the considerable distance he must traverse, Dr Palmer maintained his bold front to the last, stepped lightly up the stairs leading to the gallows, took his place on the drop, and cast a single look at the vast multitude below, not without emotion, but without anything like bravado.

A deafening roar greeted him: of curses, shouts, hootings, shrieks, groans, and execrations from nearly thirty thousand throats. The miners and colliers, maddened by drink and enthusiasm, clamoured: 'Murderer!' 'Poisoner!' He joined in a brief prayer with the Chaplain, then turned and, while the crowd suddenly stood silent, awaiting the speech which, in fact, he did not make, had the rope put round his neck and the long cap drawn over his face. Finally he shook hands with the hangman and said in a low voice: 'God bless you!' As he spoke, the bolt was shot, the drop fell; and after a slight convulsion of his limbs, Dr Palmer hung lifeless from the gallows. The disappointed colliers roared again: 'Cheat!' 'Twister!'—not having had their money's worth.

Presently the corpse was cut down and carried inside the Gaol, where Mr Bridges, the phrenologist of Liverpool, took a cast of the head which is, in his opinion, decidedly a criminal one. Then, according to the sentence, Dr Palmer's body was buried naked in quick-lime within the prison precincts.

Rugeley had earned so infamous a reputation because of Dr Palmer, not only in these islands, but on the Continent, that there was serious talk at the Town Hall of changing its name. The Mayor even approached the Prime Minister, through Mr Alderman Sidney, M.P., and demanded an Act of Parliament to this end. The Prime Minister, having recently come to power at a time of immense national anxiety, felt the request to be frivolous; yet he replied obligingly enough: 'By all means, gentlemen; so long as you name your town after me.' They were out of the room before they realized what a joke he had played on them. It would hardly have suited their book to re-name Rugeley '*Palmers*-ton'. So 'Rugeley' it remains.

Here let us conclude our history with an interesting anecdote. An artist of our acquaintance, employed by Messrs Ward & Lock, Publishers, to make sketches of Rugeley for a *Life of Wm Palmer*, was busily at work the other day on the canal bank beside The Yard, when he became aware of a spirited elderly lady, dressed in the fashion, bearing down on him, a gay parasol held over her French bonnet. In politeness he asked her to inspect his sketch.

'That's well done,' she said, 'I can see you're no slouch of an artist. By the bye, I'm Dr Palmer's mother, and not ashamed of it, neither. Yes, they hanged my saintly Billy! He was a bit of a scamp right enough, but a good son to me; the best of the brood, except

Sarah, and no murderer. Yonder merry child riding on the swing is his son, my little grandson Willie, and I shall see he doesn't lack for money, poor creature! When the time comes, I'll send him abroad with Sarah, and have his name changed. Sarah promised Billy that; she always loved Billy.*–Yes, the pretty nursemaid in charge of Willie is Eliza Tharm all right; she's a brave, good-natured girl, and I shan't forget her in my will.'

Our artist had the hardiness to ask Mrs Palmer whether she knew what her son had meant when he said: 'I did not poison him by strychnine.'

'Why, that's plain,' she answered. 'It would have gone against his conscience to say "I didn't poison Cook"; he had got his own back on Cook, do you see? for that ill-natured lark of George Bate's insurance, by giving the joker a drug to make him feel sick and sorry. It was tartar emetic, which contains antimony. Billy told Shee of it, which was why Shee believed his innocence. He didn't make it a fatal dose, of course; but the devil of it was, Professor Taylor had pronounced, at first, that Cook died of antimony. That turned tartar emetic into a poison, which it never was reckoned before; so Billy couldn't own up to his lark. He thought himself safe when Taylor changed his mind and spoke of strychnine; but he had disposed of what he bought from Hawkins's to that mis-shaped dwarf Dyke in London, for his nobbling business, and it was not to be got back. Worse still, Cook must go and die of some unknown disease, like a fool! The trouble is, I understand, that if one accidentally causes the death of a man while engaged in a felony—and so Billy was—the Law reckons it as murder. Billy feared the tartar emetic might have caused the convulsions. That's what was on his mind, my poor, dear rascal!

---

* Old Mrs Palmer survived for another five years, outliving Jeremiah Smith by three. I cannot discover what happened to Sarah Palmer, who is not buried in the family vault at Rugeley. Little Willie inherited the Brookes curse from his mother: he committed suicide in 1925.

Will Saunders, who's a fine fellow, would have sworn that Billy intended to use the strychnine on those hounds which were running his mares; but Captain Hatton—damn his eyes!—made Will "safe", as they say.

'I've had a great many unkind letters from all and sundry. For the most part, they speak of my affair with that cowardly rogue Jerry Smith. But I've finished it, once and for all. He can sink or swim as he pleases.

'There's been kind letters, too, and some strange ones, and the strangest of all came from a lady who signs herself "Jane Smirke"—Jane Widnall, as was. She knew my Billy at Liverpool and Haywood, and feels guilty for leading him astray. He was a very good boy, she says, and now if she can be of any service to me in my affliction, etc. . . .

'But that letter I could not answer; my heart was too full; besides, she gave me no address . . .'

One of English literature's fiercest practitioners, **ROBERT GRAVES** (1895–1985) was a preeminent poet, novelist, memoirist, critic, translator, children's book author, and scholar of classical mythology. He served and was injured as an infantry officer in France during World War I—an experience recounted in his 1929 autobiography, *Good-Bye to All That*—and later became the first professor of English literature at the University of Cairo. Graves is best remembered today for *I, Claudius* and other acclaimed historical novels, *The Reader Over Your Shoulder* with Alan Hodge (which popular grammarian Patricia T. O'Conner has called "the best book on writing ever published"), and his works of classical mythology for adults and children, including *The White Goddess*, *The Siege and Fall of Troy*, and *Greek Gods and Heroes*. Others among his many acclaimed works of poetry, fiction, and nonfiction include *Collected Poems*, *Homer's Daughter*, *Wife to Mr. Milton*, *They Hanged My Saintly Billy*, and *The Golden Fleece*; and for children: *Ann at Highwood Hall* and *The Hebrew Myths*.

CATHERINE PELONERO is the author of the *New York Times* best seller *Kitty Genovese: A True Account of a Public Murder and Its Private Consequences*. As a true crime author and commentator, Pelonero also appears on national TV news broadcasts and crime shows. Her latest book is *Absolute Madness: A True Story of a Serial Killer, Race, and a City Divided*. She lives in Los Angeles.

THE
ROBERT GRAVES
PROJECT

In an unprecedented publishing initiative, Seven Stories pays homage to Robert Graves, one of the English language's greatest practitioners as poet, memoirist, classicist, novelist, and children's book writer. Working in close partnership with Graves's estate, the press is bringing back fourteen major, previously out-of-print titles that express the full range of Graves's restless creativity, most with new introductions by noted authors:

ANN AT HIGHWOOD HALL
POEMS FOR CHILDREN
illustrated by Edward Ardizzone

COUNT BELISARIUS

THE GOLDEN FLEECE
with a new introduction by Dan-el Padilla Peralta

HEBREW MYTHS

HOMER'S DAUGHTER
with a new introduction by Michael Wood

THE ISLES OF UNWISDOM

LAWRENCE AND THE ARABS
with a new introduction by Dale Maharidge

MYTHS OF ANCIENT GREECE RETOLD FOR THE YOUNG

PROCEED SERGEANT LAMB

SERGEANT LAMB OF THE NINTH

THE READER OVER YOUR SHOULDER
with a new introduction by Patricia T. O'Conner

THE SIEGE AND FALL OF TROY
with a new introduction by Dan-el Padilla Peralta

THEY HANGED MY SAINTLY BILLY
with a new introduction by Catherine Pelonero

WIFE TO MR. MILTON